Praise for

Resenting the Hero

"This incredible romantic fantasy will appeal equally to fans of both genres. The sexual tension between the two protagonists is so strong that readers will feel sparks fly off the pages."
—*The Best Reviews*

"An enchanting fantasy that introduces two interesting and complex protagonists and a fascinating world . . . The tale has everything—magic, mayhem, a hint of romance, and a thread of wry humor."
—*Romance Reviews Today*

"[A] fast-paced plot . . . The various threads come together in a satisfying way."
—*SFRevu*

"A wry twist on classic fantasy . . . *Resenting the Hero* is a funny book with occasional dramatic spans . . . a good choice for a rainy afternoon."
—*Infinity Plus*

"An entertaining read . . . sure to be a hit with romance as well as fantasy readers."
—*Fresh Fiction*

Ace titles by Moira J. Moore

RESENTING THE HERO
THE HERO STRIKES BACK
HEROES ADRIFT

Heroes
Adrift

Moira J. Moore

ACE BOOKS, NEW YORK

THE BERKLEY PUBLISHING GROUP
Published by the Penguin Group
Penguin Group (USA) Inc.
375 Hudson Street, New York, New York 10014, USA
Penguin Group (Canada), 90 Eglinton Avenue East, Suite 700, Toronto, Ontario M4P 2Y3, Canada
(a division of Pearson Penguin Canada Inc.)
Penguin Books Ltd., 80 Strand, London WC2R 0RL, England
Penguin Group Ireland, 25 St. Stephen's Green, Dublin 2, Ireland (a division of Penguin Books Ltd.)
Penguin Group (Australia), 250 Camberwell Road, Camberwell, Victoria 3124, Australia
(a division of Pearson Australia Group Pty. Ltd.)
Penguin Books India Pvt. Ltd., 11 Community Centre, Panchsheel Park, New Delhi—110 017, India
Penguin Group (NZ), 67 Apollo Drive, Rosedale, North Shore 0632, New Zealand
(a division of Pearson New Zealand Ltd.)
Penguin Books (South Africa) (Pty.) Ltd., 24 Sturdee Avenue, Rosebank, Johannesburg 2196,
South Africa

Penguin Books Ltd., Registered Offices: 80 Strand, London WC2R 0RL, England

This is a work of fiction. Names, characters, places, and incidents either are the product of the author's imagination or are used fictitiously, and any resemblance to actual persons, living or dead, business establishments, events, or locales is entirely coincidental. The publisher does not have any control over and does not assume any responsibility for author or third-party websites or their content.

HEROES ADRIFT

An Ace Book / published by arrangement with the author

PRINTING HISTORY
Ace mass-market edition / March 2008

ISBN: 978-0-441-01598-6

ACE
Ace Books are published by The Berkley Publishing Group,
a division of Penguin Group (USA) Inc.,
375 Hudson Street, New York, New York 10014.
ACE and the "A" design are trademarks belonging to Penguin Group (USA) Inc.

PRINTED IN THE UNITED STATES OF AMERICA

10 9 8 7 6 5 4 3 2 1

*To Marilyn's Bookclub
and The Bookstore Commandos*

Chapter One

Sometimes, when I was feeling particularly stupid, I thought if I hadn't been born Shield Dunleavy Mallorough, I would have liked to earn coin by bench dancing. It was a ridiculous idea, because, aye, I was a Shield, which meant working as a Shield was the only thing I could do. And if I hadn't been born a Shield, I would have been steered into the family business, trained to do whatever merchant- and traderlike things my sister and brothers did. Which meant I wouldn't have gotten the daily practice in bench dancing that I received at the Shield Academy, so I wouldn't have been nearly as good at it as I was.

Plus, I was just too short to be among the best. Damn it.

But at least I could join the odd competition, just for the fun of it, without worrying that someone might try stoning me. Just for the fun of it.

It had taken a while, but I was once more welcome at the bench dancing competitions. I could add my name to the list without half the competitors withdrawing. I could dance, leaping from bench to bench and over the moving bars, without worrying about the stalkers—the four people moving the bars—deliberately crushing my ankles. I could win a round without being booed.

The residents of High Scape had taken a long time to forgive the Pairs for our failure in regulating the weather that had virtually destroyed everyone's livelihoods over the past summer. And from some of the comments I had heard, some of them still thought we could have done something, but hadn't. Which didn't make sense. If we'd been able to control the blizzards in summer, the drastic changes from torrential rain to torturous droughts, why wouldn't we? What would we have gained from our refusal?

Sources and Shields could calm the earthquakes, the tornadoes, the volcanoes, all of the other natural disasters that frequently threatened our cities. Sources channeled the forces that created these events, Shields made sure those forces didn't curl back and destroy the Sources as they worked. We couldn't do anything about the weather, like rain or snow. Well, nothing reliable. We'd suffered from the same food shortages, the same uncomfortable temperatures, the same danger of getting lost in sudden blizzards. If we could have fixed it all, we would have.

Whether the regulars, those who were not Sources and Shields, believed us or not, they seemed to have forgiven us. We no longer had to worry about being assaulted in the streets, or given clothing deliberately designed to be ill fitting. I still didn't want to eat in taverns, unsure of what unregulated ingredients might have been added to the meal, but I'd finally felt brave enough to join the dancing lists. I'd missed dancing.

Bench dancing wasn't actually dancing, and at times I wondered how it had come to be so named. It was a feat of athletics, two people facing each other on either end of two long wooden benches, laid side by side in sand, each bench about a foot high and a hand-span wide. Two people knelt at each end and handled four bars, slightly longer than the benches, raising them and clashing them together in time to the drums. The dancers were to leap over the bars as they moved without ever standing on both benches at the same time and without falling to the sand.

Shields learned how to dance the benches in childhood. It was an excellent way to force us to pay attention to our immediate environment, something our nature caused us to neglect. And I'd fallen in love with it upon first introduction. It was such a glorious exercise of every muscle and sense. I just wished I were better at it.

That day, I made it to the quarter finals before being beaten, and I felt nice and loose and sweaty. I happily shook hands with my beaming opponent and sat down on one of the dressing benches to catch my breath.

"Much as I esteem you," a pleasant baritone spoke into my ear, "I am happy enough I didn't wager on you this day. I don't have the coins to spare."

I looked up at the young man with the charming smile and an unintimidatingly pleasing countenance. A land-poor, coin-poor younger son of a less-than-wealthy lord, Doran Laidley was, dare I say it, my suitor, and I couldn't be more pleased with him. He made me laugh, he had no dark corners, and he had so far demonstrated no controlling nor obsessive behaviors.

"Off the bench, lordling," I told Doran. "It's only for contestants."

"Then why are you sitting on it? You've lost."

I stuck my tongue out at him and stood up, bending over at the waist to stretch out my legs. "I thought you weren't going to be here today." I'd been counting on it. There was no way to look good while you were bench dancing. The sport required loose-fitting clothing. My hair had bounced out of its ties and grown to resemble a bird's nest, never a good look on a redhead. And I didn't shine, I didn't glow, I sweat. I looked a proper treat, I did.

Not that I ever looked particularly good or sharp without hours of planning and execution. Still, there were certain depths to which I could sink for which I would prefer there were no witnesses.

"Sweet Ride came through for me on the second. I decided to count my blessings—and my coins—and move on before I lost my luck."

With my heel digging into the ground, I pressed the ball of my foot against the leg of the bench and stretched my calf. "From what I understand, it's unusual for a gambler to know when to quit."

"What can I say? I am unique among men."

"Uh-huh." I smiled. Sometimes Doran demonstrated these trumped up flashes of arrogance that I found just too cute. There were a lot of things about him that were just too cute. "What is that?" I gestured at a piece of jewelry he was wearing on the left side of his chest. Doran wasn't the type to wear jewelry—he didn't even wear rings—and this was an unusual piece. A sort of brooch, I supposed, made of gold, with the body of it suspended from the pin by a short slender chain.

"It's a harmony bob," he said. "For luck."

I stared at him, shocked. "For luck? What do you mean?"

"The act of wearing it is supposed to bring me luck," he said slowly.

I'd known what he meant. That hadn't been my point. "You don't actually believe in luck, do you?" How horribly disappointing.

"No," he said, then added, "not really. But I like the idea of them, and the look of them."

"And what do you wish luck for?"

"Oh." He smiled. "Just life in general."

Some would say he'd already been granted luck in life in general. "I must head home and clean up."

"Before you rush off, I want to ask you something."

Uh-oh. Build up to a question was never a good sign.

Doran opened his purse and pulled out a small cream-colored envelope. "My mother is holding a dinner party next week." He held out the envelope. "I know it's very short notice, but she would like you to attend. So would I."

If I were as good a Shield as I liked to think I was, I wouldn't have said "Your mother?" with quite that tone.

"I think it's time you met her, don't you?"

Time? Why? "I'm not good with mothers."

His eyebrows flew up at that. "You don't kill them, do you?"

"Not yet." Though Karish's mother had brought me pretty close. So, at times, had mine.

"Mine's a decent sort, or I wouldn't inflict her on you. And I've talked about you so much that she's ordered me to bring you in the flesh, so she might meet the paragon."

Paragon? "What in Zaire's name did you tell her?"

"That you were beautiful beyond compare, with an intelligence to rival the Empress, and divine humor to keep you from being annoying."

I stared at him. "So no pressure, then."

He laughed, and I was pleased that I could make him laugh. "Don't worry. I let her know you were human. She likes human people."

What was that supposed to mean? "Was it your intention to flog me into a panic?"

"That's something I'd like to see," he said. "You in a panic. May I walk you home?"

"No you may not," I told him tartly. "And shame on you. Of course I don't feel comfortable being in your company when I'm this much of a mess."

He rolled his eyes. "I've grown up with sisters, you know. I grew up with Lydia. I happen to know women are actual people who get dirty sometimes."

"And with all that female influence one would think you've learned we don't like to be seen when we're dirty." Of course, I'd been seen by everyone at the match, and I would be seen by everyone I passed on the street as I walked home, but this was different. I flicked a hand at Doran. "Be a good lad and run away."

He bowed with sardonic humor. "As my lady wishes."

"Oh, shut up."

"Do let me know when you consider yourself present-able."

"You'll be the first."

I smiled to myself as I walked away from him, congratulating myself on my good sense. He was a thoroughly decent man. He was handsome but not alarmingly so, polite but not rigidly so, witty and calm. And calm was important. I liked calm. Calm was easy and soothing. I was happier when those around me were calm.

Most unique of all, he liked Karish, my Source. And Karish seemed to have no real objection to him. Or so I assumed. Karish called Doran by his personal name and pronounced it properly, which was always a good sign. He never said anything snide about him, and hadn't yet asked if "this one" was showing any homicidal tendencies. There was a certain reserve in his manner when he spoke of Doran, and a kind of blankness would come over his face, which was not his wont with people he admired, but there were no signs of hostility. So I supposed that meant Karish approved of him, even if he didn't actually like him.

There should have been no problem.

But there was something missing. I didn't know what. I just knew that when I thought of possibly remaining with him for the rest of my life, there was something in me that cringed away from the idea. I wasn't sure why. Not that we had to spend the rest of our lives together. Neither of us had ever said anything to imply that was the plan.

Except now Doran was expecting me to meet his mother. That meant something, didn't it?

I raised the envelope to my nose. It smelled nice. Of quality paper, the perfume of the writer, and subtle scents of a home.

I looked at the address on the envelope. Doran's mother lived in the Upper Western Quadrant of High Scape. The city was divided into six sections by the trade routes, and each section was like its own miniature city, with its own hospitals, markets, and Runner headquarters. The city, as a whole, housed approximately twenty thousand people, but the population was not equally distributed among the quadrants. The North Quadrant, where the wealthiest lived, had the fewest residents, most of which lived in large houses with even larger lawns. The South Quadrant, the home of the poorest residents, had the most.

I lived in the Upper Eastern Quadrant, where the mid level merchants and minor politicians lived. It was nice enough to have cobblestone streets that ran relatively straight, but not nice enough to avoid hideously skinny buildings that were up to ten stories high. Carriages rattled about, carrying those with business in other quadrants. I walked everywhere, as I rarely left the Upper Eastern Quadrant except to go to the Observation Post, located just outside the city limits, where a Pair, comprised of a bonded Source and Shield, stood watch against destructive events.

I reached the Triple S boarding house. The only person there was Ben Veritas, the middle-aged regular paid by the Triple S to keep our residence in order and cook and clean for us. He took one look at me, clucked in disapproval, and sent me upstairs to get out of my clothes while he drew a bath for me in the antechamber of my suite. I felt pampered beyond measure when I entered my private bathing room and found the iron tub filled with steaming oiled water, fluffy towels warming by the fire, a jug of white wine on a table within easy reach. "Ah, Ben, you spoil me."

"It is only what is due to someone as fortunate as you. You should appreciate it."

It was, I thought, an odd thing to say, especially as I had already expressed my appreciation. Or so I'd thought. Perhaps I hadn't been clear. "Thank you for all of your effort."

"My pleasure, Shield Mallorough," he said, bobbing his head before backing out of the room.

What an odd little man.

I sank into the tub with a sigh of delight. Simple pleasures really were the best. What could be better after a match well danced than soaking in a large tub of warm, scented water, feeling dirt scrubbed away and muscles easing while sipping sweet white wine?

The last couple of months had been wonderful. While the sharp decline in natural disasters had made watches at the Observation Post, more sarcastically called the paranoia stall, a little less interesting, it also made me feel things were finally back to normal. No madmen using their Source abilities to try to shake High Scape to the ground. No Reanists sacrificing aristocrats and infecting the general population with their craziness. Just routine. Go to the Stall and sit seven hours either channeling events or beating Karish at cards. Sometimes both. Then, going out with friends, usually just for drinks, but that was fun enough. Bench dancing, when I could.

There were art galleries I wanted to take a look at. And maybe I'd learn to paint. That seemed like an activity with a lot of potential rewards.

After the water and the wine had both gone tepid, I stepped out of the tub and dried off with the warm towels. I brushed out my hair and put on one of my favorite dresses, old and shapeless from frequent washing, soft against my skin and so loose it left my limbs completely unrestrained. I curled up on my settee and immersed myself in the new history text one of my favorite professors at the Shield Academy had given me, sipping at my wine when I turned a page.

I had lit two candles to combat the thickening darkness and had sunk back into the text when a light knock broke into my comfortable little world. "Come in," I called, closing the book over my finger.

Source Shintaro Karish opened the door and stepped into the room, looking uncharacteristically grim and . . . guilty? He was, as usual, beautifully dressed, solid colors and simple lines showing off his slim form. An emerald stud in one ear was hidden by the black hair he'd left untied, which meant he'd been running his hands through it.

Karish was too good-looking. Perfect for a character in

a play, simply ridiculous in real life. The slanted black eyes, the slightly curling black hair, the perfect cheekbones and jaw. His skin was slightly golden, his teeth straight and white. He was slim with slender hands and beautifully held shoulders. When he smiled, the unfortunate recipient lost all ability for independent thought. It was just too stupid.

He didn't kiss my cheek in greeting as he usually did. He wouldn't even look at me, and he was rubbing his hands together in an annoyingly fidgety manner. "I have some bad news," he announced.

"How bad?" I asked. He didn't answer me immediately. I slipped my finger out of my book and set it aside. "Have a seat."

He didn't sit. A chill tapped across the back of my shoulders. "I'm really sorry, Lee," he said.

Just making me feel worse, here. "Don't try to soften the blow, Taro."

He chose to take me at my word. "We have to go back to Erstwhile. The Empress is summoning us back."

"Summoning *us*?"

Karish pulled a piece of paper from beneath his belt and held it out to me. After I took it from him he started pacing.

I unfolded the letter with reluctance.

It was addressed to Taro and was filled with warm greetings and enthusiastic declarations of missing him. He really had made a favorable impression on the Empress.

It was a sizable letter. The relevant paragraph at the end was this:

I need you to perform a delicate service for me, Taro. I have informed the Triple S council that you are to be removed from your duties for the time being. I expect you to attend me in Erstwhile immediately. Bring your Shield with you that you might be made more comfortable.

There were those who dreamed of travel. I wasn't one of them. Weeks of riding and saddle sores and bad food.

Making do with rinsing the face and hands instead of bathing. No roof, no floor, no bed. Not comfortable at all. "Why does she want me there? And why did she put it like that? So that you might be made more comfortable."

He grabbed my glass of wine and finished it, wincing at the taste. "This is why I'm saying sorry."

I waited.

"Back when I was visiting with the Empress, she didn't want me to leave."

"That's hardly surprising."

He shot me a look of impatience. All right, no humor allowed.

"Whatever you might believe, I didn't want to be there. Court life is boring. All the stupid politics and the backstabbing and the games. There was nothing for me to do there. I didn't know anything about law or politics or social policy. I didn't care who was sleeping with who and what the implications of that would be for the building of the Stanwick drains or the passing of the paper coin bill. It was all just—" He threw up his hands as though finding words to describe it all simply wasn't worth the effort. "And I couldn't go anywhere alone. No matter where I went, there was some court dweller tagging along behind me. And if I so much as hinted that their company wasn't welcome, all of a sudden I was some arrogant parasitic cicisbeo who needed to be sliced down a peg. It was *not* a good time. So after a while, when it looked like the Empress wasn't going to dismiss me any time soon, I asked Her Majesty if I could go home. She was"—he hesitated briefly—"displeased."

So was I. Why wouldn't he want to go home? Had she planned on keeping him there forever?

"She wanted to know why I wanted to leave. I told her I had a duty to perform. She told me no duty could be higher than one's duty to the Empress."

Selfish wench. Duty to do what? Provide decoration? She was really willing to take a badly needed Source out of service so she could have something pretty to look at? Why didn't she just have a portrait done of him and hang it in her bedroom?

"I told her I missed my home. She told me a mere few months spent in a city couldn't make it one's home."

I had to agree with her there.

"I told her I was missing my friends and my life. She said that was impossible, that Erstwhile was filled with cultural resources and entertainments and the most fascinating people. There was nothing to miss." He started swearing then. "I hate talking to royalty. You have to choose your words so carefully. They are never wrong and they are ridiculously easy to offend. It makes my head hurt just thinking about it."

I could sympathize with that. I hated dealing with them, too. It was like they thought they weren't just people like the rest of us, and that they could bend reality into whatever shape they liked. Of course, royalty weren't the only ones guilty of that little delusion.

"I didn't know what to do. I couldn't think of what to say. And I was afraid to ask anyone else for advice, in case it got back to the Empress. So eventually I came up with an idea that was, well, pretty stupid." And he looked at me almost fearfully.

I felt my eyes narrow. "What did you say to her, Karish?"

"Well, I didn't say this at first," he told me quickly. "It was only after weeks of trying to hint about being dismissed, and making all those excuses, that I decided to bend the truth a little."

"Bend which truth how?"

"Well, you know that there are those rumors about Sources and Shields and Pairs."

"Yes-s-s-s-s." All sorts of rumors. Regulars seemed to find the very notion of Sources and Shields and bonding exotic and romantic, and believed all sorts of bizarre things about us. So he needed to narrow it down a little.

"Well, someone asked me a question that I thought might be useful."

"Stop saying well, Karish."

"Stop calling me Karish, Lee," he snapped back. Then he pulled in a deep breath. "I was asked if, once bonded, I experienced any difficulty being separated from my Shield for any length of time."

My eyebrows shot up in surprise. I hadn't heard that one before.

"I, being an honest lad, was about to tell him the truth, when an evil impulse, no doubt acquired from you, overtook me."

A horrible thought came to me. "Please tell me you didn't."

"I confided to him with great trepidation that yes, for certain Pairs it was very difficult to be separated once bonded, and you and I just happened to be one such Pair."

"All those misconceptions about Pairs out there, and you decided you had to add one more?"

"What would you have done to get away?" he challenged me.

I had no idea. Such a thing would never happen to me. I wasn't Shintaro Karish, ex-lord and the Stallion of the Triple S.

"And of course, the secret I had divulged in confidence was spread throughout the entire court in about two days. Many of them found it quite romantic."

"Romantic?" I echoed weakly.

"Romantic," he confirmed. He was no longer apologetic. Rather accusatory, actually. "How could it be anything else? The dashing Shintaro Karish, surrounded by some of the most powerful and beautiful members of society, pining for his Shield back in High Scape. One clever fellow even composed a ballad about it."

I poured another glass of wine and took a large swallow, hoping it would stop the sinking sensation in my stomach. I wanted to curl up in a hole somewhere. Everyone in Erstwhile thought I was in love with Karish. It was so humiliating.

"The Empress heard of it, of course. And thought it was

most amusing. This brightly colored peacock in love with a—" He cut himself off, his lips pinched with disapproval. I knew what the Empress had said, or I had a general idea. A wren maybe. Or a crow. "She said I appeared to be bearing up well, and there was much in the city to mend a young man's heart, and I realized I had to use more drastic measures."

More drastic than telling the whole city he was in love with me? What was more drastic than that?

"So I stopped eating," he said. "Some greens to make sure I didn't keel over, but that was it. And I slept as little as possible. Drank a lot of coffee." He grimaced with disgust. He didn't like coffee. "I went to every party I was invited to, went on every outing I could think of, to make sure I didn't get much sleep. I looked a wreck in about two weeks."

"Good lord, Taro." He starved himself? What was the matter with him? There had to have been a better option. "You can't do things the easy way, can you?"

"I didn't know what else to do, Lee. Tell me what I should have done."

I didn't know. Karish really couldn't afford to displease the Empress. She also knew something strange had gone on in Middle Reach. And wasn't she a mean-spirited bitch, to hold it over him like that? But to abuse himself in that way . . . "That's why you looked so terrible when you came back."

He smiled bitterly. "You accused me of going to too many parties," he reminded me. "You were right, of course."

Thank you, Karish. Make me feel like a worm. I really needed that.

"Eventually, the Empress believed that I was in some amount of danger and she dismissed me. But she's firmly convinced that we have some deep, mystical love and we can't bear to be separated. So this time she wants you to come with me."

I sighed and rubbed my face and tried to think. "Damn it, Taro," I said with not much vigor. I suddenly felt weary.

"I'm sorry, Lee," he snapped. He wasn't sorry. Not any-more. And why should he apologize, really? He hadn't planned any of it. It was the Empress's fault.

How could she do that? Just snap her fingers and re-arrange our lives? We had jobs to do, damn it. "So we're going to Erstwhile."

"I'm sorry," Karish said, and this time he seemed to mean it. "I know you were really enjoying things being calm."

Yes, I was. I should have known better than to think it would last. I'd obviously jinxed it.

But hey, at least I had an excellent reason not to go to Doran's mother's dinner party. Always a silver lining.

Chapter Two

Risa Demaris was a regular and a Runner, a professional thief catcher, who had looked for Karish when he'd been abducted by Creol. I liked Risa. Like Karish, she wore her emotions on her skin, and while that could be wearing, I couldn't help but feel a certain admiration for people who could do that. And she was a rough and ready look into the world outside the Triple S, a harsh jolt of reality when I forgot, as I frequently did, that the life I had was quite different from that which most others experienced.

And she was fun.

I went to her flat first because she would be the easiest to say good-bye to. She lived in one of the rougher quads of town, where the streets were narrow and lacking in cobbles, as Runners didn't make a lot of money. There were times when I felt that if Risa would stop spending money on high-priced liquor and other unnecessary things she couldn't afford, she could live in a nicer area. On the other hand, Risa was a good Runner, and as able to take care of herself as anyone I knew. Maybe where she lived didn't matter much to her. And it wasn't any of my business.

It was the evening before Karish and I were leaving, and I hadn't been invited to go tavern crawling, so that meant Risa was probably home. If not, I would have to track her down. Not only would it be plain mean-spirited to leave High Scape without saying farewell, after all Risa had done for me, but she would likely roast me over a spit when we saw each other again.

If we ever saw each other again. I had no idea where this thing with the Empress would take me.

I knocked on Risa's door. I heard no answer. I knocked again, imitating the heavy and distinctive rap I'd heard Runners using, hoping Risa, if she were there, would be less inclined to ignore it. One more knock, and I would leave.

Instead, I heard, "Keep your britches on!" from deep inside the flat, and something rattled. The door was yanked open, and Risa stood there, tying on her black Runner's cloak. In the solid black of the Runner's uniform, Risa was an imposing figure. She stood taller than Karish, with long lean muscles and beautiful brown skin. Her hair was red, brighter than mine and shocking against the darkness of the rest of her person.

At the sight of me, Risa let her hands and her cloak fall. "What are you doing, knocking like that?" she demanded. "I thought you were from Headquarters."

"I apologize for alarming you, but I need to speak with you."

"It'll have to wait until tomorrow, Dunleavy," she said impatiently. "I've got company."

"Karish and I are leaving early tomorrow," I said quickly, before she could shut the door. "I don't know when we'll be back."

"What do you mean, you're leaving?" Risa scowled. "You've only been here, what, two years? Posts last longer than that."

"We've been taken off the roster."

Risa stood aside, inviting me in with a gesture of her head. She did have company, a man lolling in her bedroom.

She had been prepared to let him lie there when she thought she was going to answer a call of duty, but she was now insisting that he leave. Over my protests, though I thought I was more embarrassed than the irritated man hopping along as he yanked on his boots on the way to the door.

"I really wish you hadn't done that," I muttered once the door had closed behind him.

"Sit," Risa ordered.

"Yes, ma'am." I sat on the settee.

Risa, having returned to her bedroom for a few moments, came back out without her black boots and tool belt and with a wine bottle. She fetched two mugs from the kitchen and sat in a chair opposite from me, filling the mugs with a golden fluid. She clinked her mug against mine. "Hardy health," she said.

I tasted the liquid. Not quite wine, it was a little heavier and sweeter than wine. It went down very nicely. "I like this."

"You should. It cost a press."

I refrained from commenting on price.

"So, out with it."

I sighed, hating to be reminded. "There's really not much I can say." Although we had received no orders on the subject, Karish and I had decided not to tell anyone where we were going, or why. We didn't know what the Empress wanted us to do yet. "We've been taken off the roster and called from High Scape."

"Reassigned?"

"Possibly. I'm not sure."

"Can they do that to you people? Just ship you around and not tell you what's going on?"

She was assuming the Triple S was behind the move. I wasn't going to correct her. "Aye."

"Doesn't seem right to me," she muttered. "That they can control you like that."

I was surprised. Risa was a wonderful, generous person, but sometimes, I thought, a little resentful of me, and other members of the Triple S. She worked hard, and from what

I could determine, gained little from her labor. She thought Shields and Sources were given too much and did too little for it. I didn't think she blamed us as individuals. It was more like she held it against all of society, that we lived lives she thought so easy.

Now, she was seeing a negative aspect to our lives. Perhaps for the first time. And I couldn't correct her. "It's one of our responsibilities, to go where we're sent. Our lives can't be made only of benefits. It wouldn't be fair."

Risa snorted. "Life's not fair."

Feeling depressed, I took another sip of the golden fluid.

"Going to miss you, girl," Risa said.

I couldn't help feeling pleased. "Really?"

Risa laughed. "Why are you so surprised?"

I shrugged. I'd found it hard to make friends since leaving the Academy. Regulars had strange expectations that I didn't know how to meet. "I'll miss you, too."

After I'd finished the mug of liquor, Risa offered me another, and despite the temptation, I had to turn her down. There was someone else I had to visit.

I had never been to Doran's rooms before. He believed it was inappropriate, as a lady, for me to visit him. Asking around, I learned that such was a rule followed by many aristocrats, though not by the classes that had any real sense. I was a Shield, so I didn't belong to any class, but I couldn't make Doran believe that. One of his annoying quirks.

Doran, like Risa, had company. In the room he used as a sitting room, four men sat around a small, round table, playing cards. Two of them I had seen before, though I had never met them. They were brothers, I knew, dark haired and dark eyed, stocky and stolid looking, and I had seen them in the street with Doran, at times when I noticed him, but he didn't notice me. A third man was significantly older than the others, his hair silver and thinning, his softer frame ruining the close lines of his vest. The final man, a lanky blond, had managed to sprawl in a stiff, upright chair, and he was smirking at me.

Doran didn't look pleased to see me there, which irked me. He dropped in at the Triple S house often enough. "Is something wrong?" he asked.

"I apologize for disturbing you at home," I said formally. "Karish and I have been ordered away from High Scape. We leave tomorrow morning." Maybe I should have just sent a note.

My announcement knocked the irritation out of him. "For how long?"

"I don't know."

"Right, you lot," Doran said to his friends. "Out."

"Don't make them leave." I really didn't want privacy. Saying farewell would be easier with an audience.

"Never mind, love," the older player drawled, picking coins out of the pot in the middle of the table. "I had a lousy hand, anyway." The others picked out their wagers as well, and all of them squeezed past us to the door. The blond smirker was very tall, and he winked at me as he passed.

"Please be seated," Doran said, swiping the cards off the table with one hand while moving the table into a corner with the other. "Would you like some wine?"

"No, thank you. I can't stay long. We just got the orders today, and there's still a lot I have to do."

Doran poured himself a glass from a decanter and sat in the chair across from mine. "What's going on?"

"I can't tell you any more than I already have."

"Well, where are you going?"

"I can't tell you that, either."

"I could go with you."

I tried not to stare at him. "You don't know where we're going."

"That doesn't matter."

Gods. I couldn't believe what I was hearing. Why would he offer something like that? "I can't tell you what hearing you say that means to me." Shock, and a bit of panic. Did he even understand what he was suggesting? "But we aren't permitted to have regulars traveling with us. Not in these circumstances."

"Triple S business," he said grimly.

No, but it was an excuse I'd used often enough that I felt safe using it then. Doran was one of those people who felt they had no real right to understand how the Triple S worked. It was an attitude I'd never hold, if I were in his place, but it was convenient. "Aye."

Then we had one of those oh-so-awkward silences, where neither of us knew what to say. I, for some reason, wanted to apologize. Which was stupid. It wasn't my fault we were being called from High Scape.

"So," I said finally, rising to my feet. "I just wanted to thank you, for all your kindness." I wanted to wince at that, how stiff and clumsy I sounded. A Shield was supposed to be diplomatic. Hell, we'd gotten classes on how to be diplomatic. But those classes, their purpose had been to enable me to placate regulars who might be offended by the weird uncomprehensible stuff my future Source would say. Which was a joke. Because while Karish had the Source trait of phrasing his thoughts in bizarre ways, and he often baffled people, he never caused offense.

I did that.

And while my manners were all right, Karish had charm. Real charm, not the smarmy, greasy kind. If he were bidding Doran farewell, it would end with Doran feeling disappointed but valued and cherished.

I reached toward the door. Doran moved quicker, standing against it. "So that's it?" he asked.

"I'm sorry." I couldn't prevent that from slipping out. I was fouling up this conversation beautifully. "It has to be. I have to go." I reached for the latch again, but his hand was already there. I shot him a look, and he quickly opened the door. "Farewell."

I did wince as I left, as no one could see me. That had been so spectacularly bad, clumsy, ham-handed, just stupid stupid stupid. Much as I would miss Doran, I was almost glad that I was leaving the next day so I wouldn't have to face him again after making such an idiot of myself.

When I got back to the Triple S house, I helped Karish write notes to all the people he had to inform that he was leaving. He simply didn't have the time to meet all of them personally. He didn't like letting me help; he thought it was arrogant. But it was that or have him up all night writing. And if the Sources and Shields of the six other Pairs found the sight of the two of us writing dozens of letters to all of Karish's followers ridiculous and worthy of laughter, well, at least they had a pleasant last memory of us.

Chapter Three

Erstwhile. The city of politics. Where the aristocrats who considered themselves serious about power established their careers, if they could, serviced by the merchants who attempted to acquire similar power through familiarity and osmosis. The other class, the peasants, couldn't live there. Licensing for building was strictly regulated, with standards so high no one could afford to build the kind of housing people with low or moderate incomes could afford to live in, and the only people who weren't rich were the servants who were employed by the people who were. Beggars were ruthlessly prosecuted. Property taxes were so high that even those of fading glory, who had once been able to buy the grand houses gracing every street but had since suffered a decline in fortune, were ultimately driven out.

Erstwhile didn't need Pairs. It had been a completely cold site for centuries. There were jokes about it, about royalty and sitting positions and frigid temperatures. The royalty themselves, one suspected, preferred to think their inherent superiority awed the elements into remaining stable.

This complacency was contagious and had been caught

by the architects. They had forgotten or discarded the commonsense rules for construction. Homes, shops, government buildings, all stretched wide and high in grand arcs of white rock. No give at all in case of a natural event. Expensive to replace, and while being replaced no one had anywhere to work or do business. It was a beautiful city, white and clean with wide curving streets, but it made me uneasy. The grand residents of the city would do well to hope the site didn't decide to go hot all of a sudden.

Despite the lack of need, there was always a Pair stationed at Erstwhile. Prerogative of the Empress, and she, not the Triple S, chose the Pair that received that particular honor. I wasn't sure what criteria she used in her selection. From her past choices, I knew they weren't necessarily the best among their peers, or the most diplomatic, or the most worthy in any sense that I could determine.

Because I didn't know the criteria, I worried about why she wanted us there. It wasn't impossible that she might be calling us to be the new Pair. She was enamored of Karish, after all, and that was all the reason she needed. And while some might have considered it an accomplishment to be called to serve the Empress, among Shields and Sources who took their responsibilities seriously, it was a joke. Called to Erstwhile to be a decoration, an amusement, or a symbol of prestige for the Empress, with no chance to use my skills—that wasn't why I'd gone to the Academy.

After an argument, which Karish won, we rode to the Imperial, the most expensive boarding house in Erstwhile. There were boarding houses called the Imperial in all of the larger cities, and they all cost too much for anyone who wasn't among the wealthiest of the aristocrats. I felt uncomfortable staying in such places, given that Sources and Shields didn't pay for their accommodation. Karish saw no reason why we shouldn't take advantage of the opportunity. And he was more persuasive than I.

Knowing the guards who let us in the city gates would have taken news of our arrival to the palace, I enjoyed the

bathing facilities offered by the boarding house and talked
to the landlord about things I could do while waiting to be
summoned by Her Imperial Majesty. And started another
argument with Karish, because he assumed we'd be spending all our time together while we were in Erstwhile, and
he had no interest in visiting museums and libraries.

To my surprise, when I woke up the next morning there
was a summons from the Empress waiting for me. I'd
heard of some people waiting for months before actually
being able to see the Empress. While I hadn't expected the
Empress to make her favorite wait so long, neither had I
expected her to summon us the day after we arrived.

Just as well, though. Perhaps I'd be able to convince the
Empress that Karish and I weren't actually joined at the
hip. He could do whatever she wanted done, and I could go
back to High Scape. And everything else would just blow
over. I was sure of it.

Really.

A small dark carriage, lacking in any identifying orna-
mentation, picked us up at the Imperial and dropped us off
at a small gate in the wall far behind the palace. We showed
our summons to the guards lurking at the gate, a tight iron-
door almost obscured by the vines crawling up the wall.
They let us in and then one of them led us down a path.

Our escort handed us off to another guard, who took us
not to the sprawling palace, as I'd expected, but to the almost
equally sprawling stables. We passed row after row of spacious square stalls, as clean smelling as constant mucking
could achieve. And then, solid doors were slid aside to allow
us into the indoor arena. Two more guards were standing in
the middle of the arena holding the reins of three horses.

"If you could, sir, madam." Our current escort gestured
at the horses.

I was not dressed for riding. My thin-soled shoes, chosen for the purpose of visiting the Empress in one of her
receiving rooms, picked up uncomfortable clumps of dirt
from the arena floor. The fabric of my gown was too thin.

And the horse waiting for me had a sidesaddle. I'd ridden sidesaddle once, when I was thirteen, for the Academy's instructor had thought it important to expose us to that humiliation at least once, in case we ever had to do it again. At least he'd been evenhanded about it. He'd made the boys ride sidesaddle, too.

If there was a way to get into a sidesaddle unassisted, no one had ever taught it to me. That was one of the reasons I hated it. I stepped up to the left side of the horse and waited, resigned to having the guard toss me up on the horse like a sack of potatoes.

Instead, Karish moved in, as I should have expected, putting long hands around my waist. There was no feeling of being tossed as I was carefully raised off my feet and placed on the saddle, and I wondered anew where Karish got his strength from. I could think of no physical activity in which he engaged on a regular basis.

Well, except for one.

We followed one of the new guards out of the arena into a paddock, far from the main part of the grounds. "Are you comfortable on horses?" the guard asked us.

I thought she should have asked us that before we got on them. "Aye."

"A canter is acceptable?"

In this dress? Must I? "Perfectly." My calves and thighs would punish me that night, but she didn't need to know that.

So once we cleared the paddock we were cantering, over the small field, along the paths through the dense collection of trees and into the wider expanse of plains on the other side. There, in a small open carriage she was driving herself, waited the Empress.

"If you'll excuse me, sir, madam," said the guard, before galloping off back through the trees.

Karish and I exchanged a look. He shrugged. We walked our horses toward the Empress.

I had heard she was ill. Seriously ill, the sort of illness that led to a long, slow but irreversible decline toward death.

She was definitely thinner than I remembered, and her face carried more lines. Yet there she was, ramrod straight on her seat, confident and alert.

Karish and I stopped our horses a respectable distance from the Empress, dismounted and bowed. We waited to be acknowledged.

There was no one else with her. No attendants, no guards, no servants of any kind. Just the Empress, the horses, and us. I was pretty sure that wasn't the way things were supposed to be done.

"Good morning, Source Karish," the Empress greeted him, her voice quiet and level. Not resonating, though it could be when she was making a speech. Not arch or haughty or regal. Just an average, everyday sort of voice. "You seem much heartier than you were when you left last summer. I hope your recovery was not unduly long."

"Not at all, Your Majesty. Thank you for inquiring."

And then the Empress looked at me. I hated it when she did that. "Shield Mallorough, my deepest apologies for the injury caused to you. Had I known separating you could cause such damage, I would not have dismissed you before your Source."

So she would have kept us both hanging and useless in Erstwhile all those months? We never would have gotten back on the roster. "It is of no moment, Your Majesty. It is a rare condition"—nonexistent, rare, kind of meant the same thing—"and not one we cared to make public."

The Empress chuckled dryly. "Too late, my dear. It has already become old news among my court."

"Aye, Your Majesty. So I was given to understand." I could still kill Karish for that. So what if his death would carry me along? I'd sacrifice a lot to avoid embarrassment.

"I hope your travels were uneventful."

Small talk. Zaire. Something was up. Let's get to the point, why don't we?

But we all had to be polite, and talk about traveling and the weather and the least significant of politics. We wasted a good half hour in this manner, to my ever-increasing concern. Did the fact that she was prepared to chat mean whatever she called us to Erstwhile for wasn't that serious? And if it wasn't, could I then get irritated with her?

Karish didn't flirt at all. It took me a few moments to notice, because I always assumed he was going to flirt. Because he always did. Age and status had no impact, except perhaps on the subtlety and style of the flirting. He had flirted with the Empress in the past. Yet right then, he was perfectly polite, his smile cool and distant, with no hint of a double entendre in any of his words.

I noticed the Empress noticing. A small frown line appeared between her eyebrows.

"I require your assistance, Source Karish," she announced.

He bowed. "How may I serve you, Your Majesty?"

Careful, Karish. She isn't about to ask you to pick a daisy for her.

"I was most impressed by your handling of my son over the summer," Her Majesty said.

Really? How was that possible? We'd infuriated him. Yes, I'd heard all manner of stories about the estrangement between the Empress and the Crown Prince, but it disturbed me to learn it had gotten to the point that the Empress would congratulate strangers for irritating our future ruler.

"It is my understanding that he somehow came under the impression that you wished to have your title after abjuring it."

"His mother was a little confused, Your Majesty," I jumped in. Not usually my manner, but I wanted it known by all, from the very beginning, that it was the Dowager Duchess of Westsea who had been seeking the title for Karish, never Karish himself. "And she was naturally disappointed to learn her son wasn't taking the title."

"It appears that both of us have family members who are willing to violate the law," the Empress said to Karish.

"I have heard my son was prepared to hand the title over to you, were you willing to accept it."

Karish avoided answering that question by saying, "My cousin had already taken title before there was any discussion of it with the Prince, Your Majesty."

"Due to your actions, correct?"

Karish raised his eyebrows in an attempt to look innocent. "Your Majesty?"

"The new Duchess of Westsea has informed me that it was you who acquired the code from the Dowager Duchess and promptly delivered it to the new Duchess, so that she might prove herself before your solicitor. Is this not true?"

Lie, Karish. Lie.

Karish said nothing, merely clenched his teeth. He had told his cousin to keep quiet about the whole event. His lack of a verbal answer, however, told the Empress what she wanted to know.

"You cannot be swayed, then, by the promise of wealth, power and prestige?" she asked.

That question seemed to come out of nowhere. This conversation was getting more frightening by the moment.

"I am not so noble, Your Majesty. But having never lacked money, I have developed no need to acquire it. And, as you know, a Source can have anything he wants, any nature of home or accessory, merely by asking for it."

"Not quite, Source Karish. You cannot have a palace like that of the Westsea family. No servants to make your life comfortable, especially in your old age. No claim to the crest. No ability to build something new, as a monument to your life and name. You can never own land, and can leave no legacy to your children. There are those who would find the loss of such possibilities an embittering experience."

"Perhaps, Your Majesty. However, I am very happy with my life as it is, and in order to acquire these assets that you mention, I would have to give up everything that I have now. It would not be to me a profitable trade."

"I see."

That was the wrong answer. For some reason, I knew that was the wrong answer. There would be unfortunate consequences to that answer.

"I noticed, Source Karish, that during your last stay in Erstwhile, you were scrupulous in maintaining your distance from the political maneuvering of my courtiers."

"I must confess to little interest or talent for politics, Your Majesty."

"You have no interest in becoming a courtier yourself? As the Duke of Westsea, you would wield immeasurable influence."

"And have immeasurable responsibility along with it. I am far better suited to being a Source."

As if there were no great responsibility in being a Source.

"What if I were to tell you that I am prepared to create for you from the Imperial treasury an estate equal to that of Westsea, yours to name and rule?"

What the *hell* was she doing?

"There would be no hint of a violation of the law. You would not be encroaching on the rights of the Duchess of Westsea. You would be the duke of your own lands, the beginning of a whole new line. With the funds to build your own property. And to staff it. Free to live life as a regular should you wish. Free to create your own traditions and procedures, with no interference from anyone else. What say you to that?"

Oh hell. Not again. I didn't want to go through that again. And this was worse. If he accepted this offer—was it a real offer? would she really do this?—he would still remain free of his mother. And the rest of the family he had insulted in previous conversations. He could decide what responsibilities he would have, without the weight of former titleholders and the expectations of others hampering his movements. It was all the advantages of having a wealthy title, with many of the liabilities sliced away.

Damn damn damn.

I couldn't look at him. I couldn't watch. I knew, from peripheral vision, that he looked at me, but I wouldn't look back. He knew what I felt about such an idea; he had to. But I wasn't going to do or say anything else about it. I wasn't going to try to influence him. I had no right to. It had nothing to do with me.

"Your Majesty's generosity overwhelms me, but in order to assume such responsibilities, I would have to withdraw from the Triple S. I cannot do that. I have no experience or talent for ruling. I have both for being a Source."

Thank the gods. Thank Zaire. Thank everything.

Maybe I could hug him now.

But why was she asking? What was this all about?

"What do you think of the quota, Source Karish?"

"The quota?"

"The movement to have members of the merchant class"—she flicked a look at me—"in the council."

"Your Majesty." Karish appeared a bit flustered. "I have to admit I have no real opinion on the matter."

"And you really don't care?"

Karish was a shade away from squirming.

"And what do you think of the idea of dividing our lands into stricter jurisdictions?" she asked.

"Your Majesty?"

"It has been suggested by some that small collections of cities should be amalgamated, somewhat, so that all the cities would have a central form of government between them, such government then answering to me. What do you think?"

"Uh," and here Karish was obviously caught completely off guard. "I'm afraid this is the first I've heard of such an idea, Your Majesty."

The Empress looked surprised. "Shield Mallorough, have you heard of this scheme?"

I glanced at Karish.

"Come come, Shield Mallorough, everyone already

knows that Shields are more aware of such things than Sources. Surely Source Karish will not be offended if you admit to knowing something he does not."

True, he wasn't the sort to get in a temper over such things. Still, I didn't like doing anything that might embarrass him in front of strangers. "Yes, I have heard a little about it, Your Majesty."

"And what do you think of the idea?"

Hm. Panic. That's what it feels like.

The Empress smiled. "You don't know which side I favor," she teased gently.

That was, indeed, the problem.

"Speak, Shield. What do you think?"

Hell. "While centralization of services can eliminate duplication of expenses, it seems to create more problems than it solves. By necessity, a site must be chosen for the government offices to exist, and people hired to work in them. That site and those people will know all about the problems and issues of their own cities, but have little experience with or feeling for other cities. Each city has its own difficulties, its own culture and priorities, and as much as possible their government institutions and services should reflect that." Actually, I could go on about that for a good hour, because I thought it was a stupid idea, but for one thing, one did not lecture the Empress, and for another, she might be all for centralization. Offending royalty was bad.

"And what do you plan to do to advance your opinion, to attempt to have it received by those with the power to do something about it?"

"Nothing, Your Majesty."

"Why not?"

"I don't pay taxes, Your Majesty." Did she know that? Did I just say too much? Wouldn't it be brilliant if Triple S members started getting taxed because of something I'd said? "And I know I'll be spending much of my life traveling from city to city. I'll probably never get any sort of fellow feeling for the people I live with. So I suppose I feel it isn't my place to interfere with politics. And I don't know much about it, really."

The Empress snickered. "Lack of knowledge doesn't seem to interfere with anyone else's plans."

Perhaps not, but I was a highly superior individual.

"It was you, Source Karish, who discovered who was behind the unusual attacks on High Scape last year, was it not?"

"I think that particular phrasing might be giving me too much credit, Your Majesty."

"And the disappearances last summer?"

"Oh no, Your Majesty. That was entirely the Runners."

"You were there, and I know you were involved in the investigation."

"Not at all, Your Majesty."

Her Majesty looked impatient. "I have read certain reports, Source Karish, in which it is admitted that your Shield was instrumental in the making of certain connections that led to the arrest of the Reanists."

Karish looked at me. I looked back in some alarm, and shrugged. I had asked Erin Demaris some questions, who had then asked Risa, his sister, the Runner, and perhaps that had started someone thinking along certain lines that may have contributed to the ultimate arrest of the Reanists. But my influence, such as it was, would have been so minor it wouldn't deserve mention. And I hoped to find everyone who'd written reports that claimed the contrary so I could smack them up the back of the head.

"You cannot deny, Source Karish, that you certainly seem to be around whenever these mysteries are revealed."

"I do seem to enjoy a certain amount of bad luck, Your Majesty."

Please, let this not be an example of that bad luck.

Send us home, Your Majesty.

"Have either of you seen anything like this?" The Empress pulled down the glove on her left hand, revealing her wrist.

We leaned in closer to have a look. It was a tattoo, thin lines of light blue, outlining what looked like the shape of a flower, only no flower I had ever seen. It looked like only three petals, one leaning to either side and one above them, on a vertical line.

"No, Your Majesty," said Karish, and I echoed him.

"Good," she said. "Only those born to the royal line have them. Our intimates see them, of course, but no one but those born to the royal blood have them, and those so born must have them. It is like our own little code, in addition to the words that must be spoken to our solicitor."

Well, as conversations went, this was certainly tangential.

"I have it, as does the Crown Prince and his children. So do certain of my aunts and uncles, and my cousins. It is a means of recognizing each other, even when we haven't heard of each other previously."

She was fiddling with her glove. She suddenly looked nervous. What could she be nervous about?

The Empress appeared to draw in a fortifying breath. "I am about to tell you a family secret," she said. "The label itself is misleading, as I am in fact the only one who knows this secret. I am required to speak of it to you. Should you accept this secret, you will give me your oath that you shall never reveal it to anyone. If I find that you have—and I will learn of any such indiscretions—I will have you both executed. Is that understood?"

Perfectly. So, did this mean I could choose not to accept the secret? Because I had enough of my own, thanks.

"Will you accept this burden?"

No.

Like we actually had a choice.

"Yes, Your Majesty," said Karish, ever tactful, ever stupid.

The Empress looked at me, because she wasn't stupid, and she knew I needed prodding to take on this responsibility with Karish. "Aye, Your Majesty."

She nodded. Then she hesitated a moment, possibly

trying to determine how to broach whatever awful subject she was about to introduce to us. "I had a sister, born little more than a year after me," she said. "Her name was Ara, and when she was herself less than a year old, it was said that she had died. But she had not."

Strange. I had never read of an Ara in the royal family. Even one who had allegedly died.

"She was not my father's child, and when I was young, to have a child outside of marriage was nearly a criminal act among royalty, a violation of the promises made between the two families to have what was considered only pure children within the household. My mother then had been cursed with an unruly court, greedy and ambitious and striving to grow beyond the roles set down for them. It was feared that a sexual indiscretion might be just the thing to tip balance from my mother's favor, especially if she lost the support of her husband's family, who were very powerful in their own right.

"It became obvious very early that the child was not my father's issue. Her hair, eyes and skin were all too dark. My father, you may recall, was very fair. Having little interest in infants, my father had not yet noticed the differences, but he would. And so the logical thing to do would have been to have the child killed, poisoned perhaps, and tell my father and the world that she had died."

The logical thing. Very logical. Cold. Poisoning a child. I hoped my Shield training was holding firm. It wouldn't do for the Empress to see that I was disgusted with her.

"My mother, however, couldn't bear the idea of killing her daughter. And so, instead, the child was sent away with a single companion. She was sent to one of the Southern Islands, off the south continent. Flatwell, it was called. And she was fostered with a farming family called the Bryants. Prosperous but not prominent. Ara was to be raised as a daughter of the house."

It had always irritated me, how often children were the ones to pay for the stupidity of their parents.

"She was not to be told of her parentage, but she had been given the tattoo at birth, and the companion, a woman by the name of Laura Secord, was to be sure that any children of Ara's were similarly tattooed. Just in case it would suit us to have another royal line."

Having your cake and eating it, too. I was not impressed.

"My mother maintained a certain level of correspondence with Secord for a while, but the correspondence suddenly halted when Ara would have been a young girl. My mother didn't feel able to investigate into the halt. She feared showing too much interest in the girl."

Uh-huh. Sounded a little weak to me.

"When I was old enough, my mother told this secret to me, and impressed upon me its importance. Before today, I have never spoken of it." The Empress paused, a faraway look in her eyes. "I wish to know what has happened with Ara and her descendants. You will go to Flatwell and bring her descendants to me. You will not leave Flatwell until you have found them or, if there are none, until you have learned what happened to Ara."

Karish looked stunned. "Me, Your Majesty?"

"And your Shield, of course. I wouldn't want you to experience any discomfort during your travels."

Was she . . . was she serious? She couldn't be serious. What the hell kind of assignment was that to send a Pair on?

She didn't want us as decoration. She didn't want us as Erstwhile's Pair. She wanted us to head out into the middle of nowhere and do some nasty, secret little job for her.

She had no right to make us do anything of the sort. We belonged to the Triple S, not the royal family. Other than the choice of her own Pair, an exception for the sake of courtesy, the Empress was to have absolutely no authority over Triple S members. Certainly, she didn't have the right to pull us off the roster and send us off for something that had nothing to do with our legitimate duties.

On the other hand, we had already been pulled off the roster. Our position with the Empress was precarious, to say the least. She knew something had gone on in Middle Reach, something we hadn't told anyone.

Zaire, what a mess.

"But Your Majesty," Karish sputtered on, brave lad. "For that kind of work, that kind of expertise, you want a Runner."

"Reveal my personal business to a Runner? I hardly think so."

Why not? Couldn't she threaten his life, too?

"Then a member of your own guard."

"None of them are trained to do this sort of work."

"Neither are we," Karish said rather desperately.

"But you have done it before, haven't you? With Creol and that mad Lord Yellows."

"That wasn't due to any kind of skill on our part. Just a sort of luck."

"Fortunately, this time, you won't have to rely on luck." The Empress removed from the seat beside her a small package. "Maps of Flatwell, marked with the last known location of the Bryants. And orders granting anyone who travels with you passage back to the mainland." She held the package out to me. "You are not to tell them who they are. I will do that."

We were supposed to convince strangers to travel to another part of the world, without telling them why? Was she drunk? I pulled in a quick fortifying breath. "With all due respect, Your Majesty, this is highly inappropriate. There is no good reason to send Karish on a task such as this, and dozens of reasons not to."

The Empress narrowed her eyes at me. "Were you not paying attention, Shield Mallorough? I am sending you to look for descendants of my royal sister. These descendants are contenders to the throne. Who should I send? Runners who could be bought? Imperial guards who report more faithfully to their own superiors than they do to me? Or someone who has already demonstrated skill in this area, who has proven himself resistant to the lures of wealth and power?"

Just wonderful. That's what came, I supposed, of Karish letting people know he wasn't a spineless weasel. Maybe his act as an empty-headed peacock had been the best way to go after all.

"Take the package, Shield," the Empress ordered. "And be at the docks at first light tomorrow morning. You'll be sailing on the Wind Dancer."

I took the package automatically, my mind suddenly a little frozen.

I looked to Karish, waiting for him to bedazzle her with his stunning smile and talk her into agreeing that yes, sending us on this kind of task was the depth of stupidity. And he was smiling. But it was a soft curve of the lips, reflective rather than alluring, and he said nothing.

"You may go now," the Empress said, slapping her reins. The horse jolted into a trot.

What? Wait! No! She couldn't just dump that kind of information—that kind of job—on us and then dismiss us. I mean—what? Go to the Southern Islands? Hunt down exiled members of the royal family? What the hell was this?

"She's the Empress," Karish said.

"Huh?" I knew that.

"That's who the hell she thinks she is."

He was so cocky. I hadn't even gotten that far in my mental ranting yet.

"This is stupid. This is so incredibly stupid. Sending a Source out to do the work of a Runner."

"We've done it before." He pulled on his horse to get us moving back toward the stables.

"By accident!" I pulled my horse around to follow him. "And no we haven't! You were kidnapped by Creol and I was led to him by Kelly. And we just happened to be there when the Yellows thing exploded. You said that yourself."

"Of course I said it to her. I didn't want her knowing what really happened."

"That's exactly what happened!"

"We can do this, Lee. We go to the last known location of the Bryants and start asking around."

"As simple as that, eh?"

"Aye."

"Nothing's ever as simple as that."

"Stop scowling, Lee. This is a good thing."

I looked at him. And yes, he was excited, the smile still playing about his lips, his eyes glowing. He had clearly lost his mind. "How do you figure that?"

"We get to go to the Southern Islands!" he announced gleefully, as though I hadn't been right there hearing the conversation.

And why was this a good thing? "Yay," I said flatly.

"Are you serious, Lee? You have your choice between standing around among the Empress's court, being polite to arrogant parasites while you're slowly being driven insane with boredom, or exploring an area of the world that few Northerners have ever seen. Which sounds better to you?"

"I'm not sure. Remind me which one doesn't involve being on a boat."

He frowned. "What's wrong with being on a boat?"

"Besides the tendency to capsize and kill everyone on board? Nothing, I'm sure." Plus there was something about the thought of all that open air and water that made me want to shiver.

"You're afraid of boats?" As soon as the words were out of his mouth, he pressed his lips together, as though wishing he could snatch back the question by the act of shutting his mouth.

But that was what it came down to, an irrational fear based on no experience with an activity others had no difficulty with. "Apparently so."

"You never told me that."

He appeared to be accusing me of something. "I didn't know until just now, did I?"

"Don't worry about it, Lee. It'll be fine."

I gritted my teeth. "Oh, I'm sure it'll be a treat until the boat sinks."

"Actually, I think they prefer to have it called a ship."

"Don't even start with me."

He laughed. "It will be fine, Lee, you know it will. After all, why do ships sink?"

Icebergs? "They capsize."

"Why do they capsize?"

I really didn't want to be thinking about it in any great detail. "Waves. Wind."

"Bad weather."

"Well, aye."

"You'll be able to handle that."

"What have you been drinking?"

"What did we spend all that time experimenting last summer for if it wasn't for you to learn how to manipulate the weather?"

"For you to learn to manipulate the weather." Only it hadn't worked out that way. He'd been unable to see the details, the fine elements in the forces that allowed a person to nudge the weather this way or that. I'd been the one to see it. I'd been the one to do the nudging. With nasty results. "I never became competent at it."

"Maybe you lacked sufficient motivation."

I couldn't help it. Years of training went down the drain. I slapped him up the back of the head. Lacked sufficient motivation, indeed. Last summer had been a nightmare.

"You are upset, aren't you?" He rubbed the back of his head, as though I had really hurt him. "Most people who travel by ship survive the trip, Lee."

"Aye, most people," I grumbled. "But knowing my luck—"

"Your luck?" He raised an eyebrow at me. "Do you consider yourself unlucky, Lee?"

I had to think about that. And be embarrassed by my

behavior. Because yes, I was acting like a child. "No, I suppose not." But I was still scared, and it was humiliating.

"It will be fine, Lee, I promise."

It always irked me when people made promises about things over which they had no control.

Chapter Four

We did not see the Empress again. Which was just as well, because I would have been tempted to try to show her the error of her thinking. Sending us out to do a task like that was just stupid. And an insult. We already had a task to perform, an essential one. We should have been left to perform it.

We spent most of our single day in Erstwhile attempting to learn what we could of Flatwell and finding appropriate gear. Only no one really knew anything about the Southern Islands—except that they were hot. I managed to get my hands on some light trousers that fit well enough, a couple of pairs of boots, and a couple of bags in which to carry them. Durable travel clothes. I would pick up something more suitable once I was there. Anyone wishing me in something more fancy could go hang.

To describe the sea voyage, well, there was a mixture of good and bad. Or fascinating and awful. I found, to my surprise, that I liked being on a ship. The subtle rocking of the boat, the feeling of the wind against my skin. All the gadgetry with the names that didn't make sense, and the ranks of the sailors that I couldn't keep straight.

The food was damn awful. The sleeping accommodations were uncomfortable. The sailors took issue with Karish and I being a Pair. Not because it meant we didn't pay for our journey, but because they found the nature of our work almost immoral, and a lure to bad luck. They threatened to toss us overboard if we interfered, as they put it, with any storms we might face during the voyage.

What they didn't know wouldn't hurt them. I wasn't going to let their superstition sink us.

Karish was seasick the whole time, poor fellow. He couldn't find his balance on the boat, he claimed the constant wind was driving him crazy, and he couldn't keep down anything more substantial than water and light broth.

The captain claimed she'd seen other passengers react just as badly, and to her knowledge none of them had died of it. It wasn't terribly reassuring to hear. She appeared to feel that the death of people so fragile that they couldn't handle a sea voyage was no great loss.

Karish was a terrible patient, and I was no nursemaid. We spent most of the trip bickering. Not that that was so very different from how we usually spent our time.

I did get bored in time. I'd brought nothing to read, and there was no useful place for anything like bench dancing. The ship, large as it was, was just too confining. I was beginning to long for the ability to walk with a healthy stride without having to continually turn corners or ease by ropes or other people. The ship's sailors were too busy to talk during the day, and at night they either gambled or played music to which it wasn't safe for me to listen.

That was the one irksome thing about being a Shield. The sensitivity to music. Depending on the music, and the Shield, the effects could be like alcohol or worse, driving us to behaviors in which we normally wouldn't engage. Mournful music could send us to tears. Martial music could make us violent. The music the sailors most often liked to play, I could only call raucous. There was no telling what I'd do at the sound of it, and Karish was in no shape to keep me under control.

I missed Doran. I couldn't tell anyone I missed him. I didn't feel comfortable talking about him.

So I was happy, for a variety of reasons, when Flatwell came into sight. It didn't take long to pack up all of our gear, which was carried to a small rowboat.

Karish was surly as he made his way out of his cabin, clutching the walls. I didn't say a word, and I didn't touch him. I walked a couple of steps behind him, close enough to catch him if he fell but not close enough to crowd him.

He really did look gaunt, with dark circles under his eyes. Rather as he had looked after being captured by Creol. Also how he'd looked when he first returned from Erstwhile the previous summer. I didn't like how easy it was to put him in poor health. I never would have considered Shintaro Karish at all delicate, but after this, I feared there was some inherent weakness in his blood. Maybe it was inbreeding.

We got into the dinghy, already loaded with our gear, and two crew members rowed us to shore. The ship itself wasn't stopping at the island, merely dropping us off on the way somewhere farther south.

I had never seen water so brilliantly blue, or such glaringly white sand. The air smelled strange, salty and heavy. Just beyond the beach there was dark, dense greenery. There were no buildings in sight, though I could see a road, nothing more than a beaten path really.

"You remember which way to go?" one of the men asked me.

"Aye, Captain Vo told me." The proper harbor was on the other side of the island, and the captain didn't want to spend the time to get there and allow us to disembark. She promised me she had set other passengers down at this location, and they never experienced any difficulty finding their way. And she had given me directions which indicated to me she knew her way around.

Then again, if such previous passengers had gotten lost and were never found, she wasn't likely to hear about it, was she?

One of the crew leapt out of the boat and pulled it farther up onto the shore. Once we were on dry land I grabbed up my two bags and stepped onto solid earth. I waited until Karish had likewise disembarked. Then we watched the two sailors shove off back into the water and row back toward the ship.

The beach was soft and white and very narrow. Only a few steps would place us within the thickest greenery I'd ever seen. Odd trees with thin trunks and huge leaves completely blocked any distance of viewing. I could smell the forest, too, dense and a little bitter.

"Zaire, it's hot," Karish muttered, stripping off his cloak and shoving it into his pack.

It was warm. And there was a moist heaviness in the air that wasn't pleasant.

"I knew it was hot in the South, but I didn't think it would be this bad this late in the year." He tugged on the thin cotton of his shirt, a light sheen rising to his skin.

"I think I might have mispacked." I hadn't expected it to be so warm either. I had defined warm as what we experienced in High Scape during the summer. This was different. "The sooner we reach civilization, the sooner we can get some more appropriate clothes."

We had been told by Captain Vo that there was a village called Pink Shell only a few miles from the shore, where we could pick up some proper clothes and some food. Or we could find a place to stay, if we had to, though from the sounds of it the accommodations would be fairly rustic.

The footpath was disturbing in its obvious state of impermanence. It was nothing more than a tiny little break twisting through what felt like solid walls of dark vegetation. Strange chirping sounds and rustles, and the feeling that I couldn't see anything more than a few feet in front of me, combined with the almost total lack of sunlight, and it was suffocating.

Although it was only half a mile until the first sign of life, neither of us was in the kind of shape we had been in before the voyage, and it took us much longer than it should have to get there. Even I was starting to feel uncomfortable in the heat. I was looking forward to sitting somewhere dark and drinking something cool.

I was set for disappointment, however. The first building we saw was not, as far as I could see, part of a larger establishment. It appeared to be something of a shack, made of strange round strips of something like wood, solitary and sad looking. A withered old woman was sitting on the porch, her dark skin deeply lined and her iron gray hair cropped short. She was drawing on a pipe with a long, curved stem. I had never seen the likes of the shirt she was wearing, sleeveless and collarless and cropped short under the breasts. She wore a dangerously short skirt. Dark writhing lines were tattooed from her ankles up to her knees, and from her wrists up to her elbows.

I looked beyond her, to the windows of the shack, hoping to see someone else. She appeared to be alone.

"Excuse me, ma'am," I said, approaching the porch. "Are we anywhere near Pink Shell?"

She looked me over, gaze raking me from head to toe. After a long moment she pulled the pipe from her mouth. "I'm the road keeper."

I know I stared at her far longer than was polite. It took me that long to decipher what she had said. She had the thickest accent I had ever heard, speaking about three sounds for every vowel in each word, and slurring the consonants together. Once I was able to figure it out, I said, "Oh." Was that an answer to my question?

"Road tax," she announced.

"Road tax," I parroted with no comprehension.

She rolled her eyes. "You got ta pay the road tax."

"I have ta—" Was she serious? "You expect us to *pay* a road tax?"

"Everyone pays the road tax."

"I'm a Shield." See the white braid? "He's a Source."

She looked at me blankly. "So."

So? *So?* "We don't pay taxes." Or anything else.

Her eyes narrowed. "Neither do thieves. 'Til they hang."

"Hang?"

"Nice shirt" were the next words out of her mouth. "Like the braid."

"What?"

With a sigh of impatience she spoke again, slowly and carefully, like I was an imbecile. "I like your shirt."

What did that have to do with anything?

And how could she possibly? Even I knew it was drab and shapeless.

"Give her your shirt, Lee," Karish hissed at me.

"What?" Yes, I did feel like an idiot echoing the same word over and over again, but under the circumstances it was warranted. Everyone had gone insane.

"That's the road tax. Give her the shirt."

"That's theft! I'm not giving her my shirt."

"Coin'll do, too," she said.

"I'm sure it would, but that's not the point. We're a Pair. Pairs don't pay taxes. We don't pay for anything. That's one of the benefits of being a Pair."

"We don't need Pairs," she said.

"That's not the point."

"You pay or you don't pass."

I raised an eyebrow at her. I pointedly looked down one side of the road, then the other. Just empty long stretches with no one but her and the two of us in sight.

"Dunleavy Mallorough!" Karish gasped with shock, apparently able to read my mind.

"She's the one violating the law, Taro."

"This is a new place for us, Lee. Let's not start things on the wrong foot, all right? If she is so lacking in taste that she finds that rag appealing, count yourself lucky. She might have wanted something valuable." Prat. "We can get this straightened out in Pink Shell, and get you another shirt. There's no harm in giving her that one for now."

All right, all right. A proper bed and a bath were powerful motivators. Still, "I wonder if you would be so sanguine about this if it were your shirt she were demanding." I yanked another shirt out of my sack. "I assume I may change in this structure?" I asked the highway robber, without pausing to wait for an answer. I swiftly changed and strode back out, ripping the white braid out of the garment as I did so. "You don't keep this," I told her, indicating the braid as I dropped the shirt on her lap. "And this isn't the end of things."

Karish whistled as I returned to him. "What's the matter with you?"

"Nothing," I snapped.

"It's a sad state when I'm the voice of reason."

"She just stole from me. Forgive me if that annoys me." And I couldn't stand that I hadn't been able to do anything about it. I was never able to talk people around when they tried to pull that kind of stunt on me. And I shouldn't have to. Why couldn't people just do what they were supposed to do?

All right. Calm down. It was only a shirt. And I would come back for it, I would. Until then, it was to be put out of my mind.

It was a couple of hours before we found another sign of human life. The road flattened and widened and hardened. The green undergrowth and vinery pulled back from the road. We heard a collection of feet hitting the dirt, and light voices shouting.

It was a pack of kids running down the road. We had warning of their approach, but they had none of ours. Two of the group—boys or girls or both I couldn't tell, as they all wore the same colorful loin cloths, earrings and bangles, with hair the same length, bare breasted and barefooted—stopped and stared at us while the others just giggled and parted to go around us. "Kiyo!" they all cried out, more or less in unison. The other two became unfrozen and ran after.

"Kiyo?" Karish asked.

I shrugged.

"They do speak like we do, don't they?"

"Did you not hear that wizened thief down the road?"

"That's just accent. They're the same words, though."

"I've never heard that Southerners were incomprehensible or anything." Hell, I'd never even thought of the possibility of them using different words than us. And why should I have? Everyone used the same words. I had read in history books that there had been different languages when we had first Landed, but the trials of survival and the loss of so many caused a merging of the languages. As far as I knew, that had never changed. "There hasn't been much contact with them, but they haven't been completely isolated. And we did understand the road keeper." The morally bankrupt old bat.

"Could you imagine the hassles if they all use different words?"

"I'd rather not, thanks."

"Aye, well, a bit of a rocky start, but we're here. And I'm dying for a bath. Damn it's hot."

"I'm just looking forward to sleeping in a bed that doesn't rock."

I knew, the moment those words came out of my mouth, that I shouldn't have said them, for Karish looked at me with the most evil glint in his eyes. "I'll have to see what I can do to change that, won't I?"

Just what I needed. Karish degenerating into using innuendo on me. I thought he'd lost that habit.

"How long are you thinking we should stay around here?"

I shrugged. "A few days, maybe. Gather some supplies and more suitable clothes. Find out what we can about their laws and whatnot." So I could storm back to that highway hag and get my shirt back. "And try to figure out where to start looking for the line."

"The line?"

"It would perhaps be wise to get used to not referring to certain people or using proper names."

Karish rolled his eyes. "Who's listening to us?" He indicated the empty space around us with a sweep of his arm.

"Might as well get into the habit now. We need some better maps, too. The ones I have are decades old and don't have the kind of detail I'd like."

Karish wasn't listening. He was pulling the laces out of his shirt.

"You're not taking that off," I said in my best stern voice.

He smirked. "Just what are you worried about, Lee, my love?"

"That you'll burn that lovely hide of yours to a crispy red that'll have you miserable with pain by tonight."

That wiped off the smirk. "Really?"

"Gods, Taro, do you never read anything?"

"Racing results," he answered promptly. "Otherwise, of course not. I have a life."

"Fine. Then you'll have a sunburn. And we need hats. I should have thought of that before."

"Yes. Shame on you for not thinking of everything all the time. How do you live with yourself?"

I heard the jingling of bells from farther up the road. A cymbal crashed, and voices chattered. "Something's going on. Something unusual."

"Of course. When is there not when we come into town?"

We started passing buildings. Flimsy looking structures, made out of light wood of a pale yellow color. The fronts of these buildings were completely open, revealing work being done within but also, to my untrained eye, personal living quarters. Plenty of people housed their businesses in their homes, but it was my understanding that the two areas were usually rigidly separated. It didn't seem to be the case here.

Unless they were such hard workers that they had to catch sleep when they could, taking naps at the work place. Which was, to me, a horrible idea.

The people in the buildings stopped and stared at us. Just stared. No subtlety about it at all, no air of self-consciousness. Like there was nothing wrong or impolite about the way they were pinning their gazes on us. How rude.

The jingling was joined by drums, of course. There were always drums. But they were farther away, and while the dull thudding caused my heart rate to increase a little, my head stayed clear. So that was something.

We came across a small crowd, men and women and children, standing around a woman with a table. Most of the children were dressed identically to those who had passed us earlier. Older children, those at the stage of adolescence or beyond, apparently assumed the garb of adults, but again both genders were similarly dressed. Short skirts riding low on the hips and slit up one side. Sleeveless shirts cut high above the midriff. Variation came from the color and the intricate stitching coiling over the material. Both genders wore their black hair braided, though the number of braids and the ribbons or flowers tied into the hair varied. The tattoos, worn only by the adults, were all black, but they, too, varied wildly in pattern.

As a group, they were beautiful.

The woman at the table wore even less than anyone else, a loin cloth that barely preserved her modesty, an opaque scarf wrapped over her breasts, one ear pierced with a multitude of silver earrings, and a crownlike piece woven into her cornrow braids. Her lips and eyelids were blackened with powder, and her tattoos were highlighted with a sprinkling of silver dust.

I noticed right away that her skin was much paler than that of those around her, a light creamy brown. She seemed to be of a slightly more voluptuous build. Her eyes were gray, and against the dark contrast of the eye makeup, looked almost silvery.

As she smiled and flirted with every member of her audience, her delicate hands moved three identical half shells over the surface of the table, dropping and picking them up again with smooth sweeps, a steady stream of indiscernible patter falling from her painted lips. A young man stepped up to her table, dropping some coins upon it, and chose one of the shells with a tap of his finger. The woman lifted the shell, revealing nothing underneath. She pouted at him sympathetically, and scooped up his money.

Some things, it seemed, were universal.

I couldn't understand the next words out of her mouth—raising Karish's fear of a different vocabulary once more—but the gesture was an unmistakable invitation for someone else to step up.

No one did, though, for they'd found something else to hold their attention. That something else being us. They let us know this by freezing in place and starring at us. A few whispers reached our ears.

I was not impressed. They'd seen Northerners before. I knew trades people, at least, had been down there. What was there to gawk at?

Other than Karish. He had that effect on people, sometimes.

The woman at the table was not well pleased. "Eh!" she called to us. The rest of what she said was unintelligible to me.

There's no polite way to tell someone you didn't have a clue what they'd just said.

But she ascertained that all on her own, clever girl. "Go or play," she ordered with more clarity.

I nodded and stepped away.

But my choice, it appeared, didn't please her either. "Challenge!" she said. She gestured at the shells imperiously.

"We have no coins."

I jerked back from the old woman next to me who appeared to be trying to touch my hair.

The woman at the table tugged on her earlobe.

Karish removed the gold hoop from his ear. "You do it, Lee. You'll catch it."

"I don't play these kinds of games." Didn't gamble at all, really, unless you included playing cards with Karish. And as I always won, that wasn't really gambling.

"If you don't do it, they'll either think we're cowards or that we think too highly of ourselves to participate. Either way, not a good first impression to be making." He made his way through the small crowd and placed his earring on the table. "Besides, we can use the money to buy your shirt back, if you're so keen on it. Come on. Do your thing."

I wouldn't need money to get my shirt back, but I saw no harm in complying. Karish loved to wager on things. And I wouldn't lose. Not that it would matter if I did. He had other earrings and could get more easily enough.

I stepped through the crowd, trying not to invade other people's space, a waste of effort as they had no compunctions about invading mine. I felt strange hands stroking my hair and brushing my skin. It was a most disquieting experience.

When I reached the table, I nodded at the woman to let her know she could begin. She did so, smoothly shifting the shells about while reeling off a practiced patter of words. I found that I could understand the odd word, perhaps one in five, and it was no doubt a matter of accent rather than language that was causing my lack of comprehension.

The woman stopped her shuffling and indicated that I could choose.

I did, lifting the shell myself and revealing the small brown ball underneath.

There was delighted laughter and applause behind me. With a triumphant chuckle, Karish scooped up his earring and slid it back into his ear.

The gamester was not impressed, of course. Her smile dropped off and she glared at me as she dropped a trio of coins on the table. "Again," she announced.

I shouldn't do it again. I had an advantage she was perhaps not aware of. It was hard to fool a Shield—a good Shield—with sleight of hand. It was part of our role to be particularly aware of what the object of our attention was doing. This was her livelihood, and the lack of sleeves on her person suggested she might be honest in pursuing it. It wasn't fair to meddle with that.

The woman raised her eyebrows in mockery. "Afraid?"

Good Zaire, she was trying to provoke me. How ludicrous. "Certainly not."

"Then play again."

I could decipher those words easily enough. And if she wanted it that badly . . . "All right, then."

This time there was no pretty verbal patter as she manipulated the shells. She was faster. Instead of keeping the three shells in a single straight line she moved and placed them all over the small table top, and I noticed her hands flowing in a different pattern. That didn't mean that when I chose my shell and picked it up, the brown ball wasn't under it.

More applause from the spectators. Karish curled an arm around my waist and kissed my temple like it was the most amazing thing he had ever seen me do. The woman dug into a sack lying by her feet on the ground and pulled out three more shells, identical to the ones already on the table. She then pulled out more coins, six of them, and looked at me.

"This is getting ridiculous," I muttered. "What am I supposed to do with all of these?"

"Give them to me," Karish said.

"What do you need them for?"

"To buy my way into a card game."

"You don't know that they play cards here."

"Everyone plays cards everywhere."

Well, all right, then. I nodded at the gamester. She nodded back.

Her hands moved incredibly swiftly, and with the additional shells it was much more difficult to follow the ball. Had the gamester been the sort to cheat she probably would have beaten me. But she didn't cheat and difficult didn't mean impossible. When I chose my shell I was awarded with another nice little pile of coins, and I was a hero among the spectators.

"You've bested me," the gamester said. She took the extra shells from the table and put them back into her bag.

I guessed the challenge was over. I took the coins and Karish's hand, depositing the former into the latter. "Gamble them away in good health."

He looked offended. "Hardly away," he objected. "I don't lose."

"Except to me," I reminded him with a smirk.

"Aye, no point in breaking a trend."

I frowned, trying to decipher that.

"Hey!" The gamester waved both hands at us. "Go, go, go! I—"

I couldn't clearly understand the rest of what she said, but hey, I could catch a hint with the best of them.

We moved on. Unfortunately, for both the gamester and us, nearly half the crowd moved on with us. I ended up with a lot of people touching my hair. And yes, it was red, a freakish color even at home, but couldn't they just look at it?

We soon came across a contortionist. In a costume more

paint than cloth, the young woman stood—sort of—on her hands. A fixed smile on her face, her back was bent nearly in half to allow her feet and shins to dangle over her shoulders. Looking at her made my spine hurt.

"Can you do that?" Karish asked.

I looked at him with disbelief. "Can you?"

As before, however, the performer lost a good part of her audience once they became aware of us. And again with the hair touching. Here was this woman turning herself inside out for their entertainment and they would rather stare at me. Didn't I feel like a freak? "Let's move on." I didn't want to detract from the profits of the performers.

So we moved on. To the jugglers. Gorgeous young men dressed in mere strips of red cloth hurling long shiny knives at each other. Drummers and tumblers. Tightrope walking and trapeze artists, a snake charmer and some kind of fortune-teller.

At each location, the spectators seemed more interested in us than in the performances. I was used to a certain amount of attention due to being a Shield. This was different, more invasive. It was definitely time to get off the street.

I had to ask to be pointed to a boarding house. Which, I discovered, was called a bunker. At least I was getting used to the accent, and if I listened carefully enough, I could understand what was being said.

The bunker was only two stories high, which was as high as any building I had seen so far. Two vertical flaps of cloth, pretty but insubstantial, served as a door. We ducked under and were yelled at before we'd moved more than a few feet past the door.

"Please," a man cried quickly, shuffling out from another room. "Kindly remove your, er, sandals."

We looked at our feet, and then at the neat collection of sandals piled on the step just inside the door. "We're very sorry," I said. We hastily pulled off our boots and added them to the collection. They looked out of place, not to mention ugly, next to the dainty beaded sandals.

"Thank you, madam, sir. You need a room?"

It was difficult to see whether this was a place in which we'd want to stay. I could see nothing but walls, bare walls of dull yellow wood, the foyer nothing but the small square in which Karish and I stood, a narrow hall crossing before us. It smelled clean, though, and it was quiet.

"Do you have two rooms available?"

He nodded. "Three grays for each room. That includes nightly bath and morning fruit."

"Ah." They really must have had next to no exposure to Sources and Shields. It made sense, as they didn't seem to produce any. "I am Shield Mallorough. This is Source Karish." I stressed the titles and waited for him to realize his mistake.

He nodded and beamed a smile. "Please call me Vikor. May your sun rise high."

Did that mean he'd understood? "You are aware that Sources and Shields do not pay for goods and services?"

His smile didn't dim a jot as he said, "Everyone pays."

"Uh, actually, no, Sources and Shields don't pay. It's the law."

He frowned then, but in puzzlement, not irritation. "There is no such law."

"It is the Empress's law."

The response was a blank stare.

"Empress Constia." That apparently didn't ring any bells for him. "In Erstwhile."

"Ah," he said. "The Northern Empress."

"The only empress. Her laws are valid here, too."

He tsked, but sympathetically. As if he pitied me. "She makes no roads here."

"I'm sorry?"

"She makes no roads. No schools. No tribunals. She sends no Runners here, no teachers or healers or surveyors. Or even"—a gesture in our direction—"your sort. She digs no ditches, builds no canals. So"—he smiled—"she makes no laws."

I stared at him, a horrible suspicion forming in my mind. "What?" was my most articulate interrogation.

"We have our speakers and our members and our own laws. And by our laws, everyone pays."

And here was panic, making another visit. "So Sources and Shields are expected to . . . to pay for accommodation and food and clothing and everything?"

"Why should you not?" And he looked honestly bemused, as though my expectations truly were bizarre.

Breathe. In. Out. "Because we risk our lives protecting people and their property from natural disasters and don't get paid for it." That sounded good. Firm. In control. Completely nonhysterical.

"Not here," he responded. Pleasantly, as he had throughout this upsetting little episode. So calm and reasonable I just wanted to reach out and smack him.

Was this how I made Karish feel?

"All right. Is there another bunker in this area?"

"No. But if there were, you would have to pay there, too."

"No one feels the need to follow the law here?" I asked coolly.

"That is the law here. Everyone pays."

"This can't be." It couldn't be. Surely, surely everyone didn't expect us to pay for things. That was just ridiculous. And the Empress, she wouldn't have sent us here if we were expected to pay our way.

Sources and Shields did not pay for goods and services. That was the law.

And a hell of a lot of good that would do us if no one cared to obey it, and there was no one there to enforce it. I hadn't seen anyone that looked like a Runner yet.

What were we going to do?

It wasn't like that all over the island, was it? It couldn't be.

I looked up at Karish, who was looking a little panicked himself. He dug out the coins I had given him earlier. What had appeared so numerous before now seemed pathetic and thin.

Oh gods. Oh Zaire. Oh hell. Stuck in this foreign place that expected us to pay for things, and we had no money. And no means of making any. And no way of getting back home. And, oh god, we were so nailed.

Breathe breathe breathe.

"Relax," the hatefully pleasant Vikor assured us. "It can't be too hard for two healthy young people like yourselves to find work."

"Work?" Karish demanded incredulously.

Vikor chuckled. Chuckled! "Kai. Work. What, are you feeble?"

No. Just useless.

"We are members of the Triple S!" Karish hissed. "We don't work!"

"Then I'm afraid you're going to starve." There was just a touch of sharpness to his voice, then, as though he were losing patience with us.

That was always a sign it was time to leave. "Thank you for your assistance," I said, trying not to sound as terrified as I felt. "We have to talk about this. We might be back."

He didn't appear to be relieved to be getting rid of us. I had to give him a lot of points for that. His gesture was half nod, half bow, and he wished us luck.

With no hope at all, we walked the curving stone streets of the village. After making a few inquiries we learned that there were, indeed, no other boarding houses. And that people expected us to pay for things. We went to merchant after merchant, and all of them, with varying degrees of patience and amusement, pointed out that they didn't care who or what we were, everyone paid.

We were in so much trouble.

I couldn't believe it. How could this happen? How could

we end up in a place where our skills were worthless? Why did no one warn us?

Maybe that was why the Empress had sent us, of all people, on this ridiculous mission of hers. Cheap labor. She wouldn't have to pay us, or pay our way. Only that had blown up in our faces. Mine and Karish's. Her Imperial Majesty was safe and comfortable and well fed in her palace in Erstwhile. Probably had a new pretty boy to decorate her court. Probably had forgotten all about us. Damn damn damn, what were we going to do?

We found a place to sit on the ground away from any of the performances sprinkled throughout the village. We didn't want an audience while we panicked.

And I was panicking. I had that roiling in my stomach, that sour taste in my mouth. My breath was coming short and sharp. Hell.

"We don't have nearly enough, Lee," Karish was telling me, flipping the coins over in his palm. "These coins are different from the ones back home, but I'm not sure we've got enough even for one night at that bunker."

Nightmare. A total nightmare.

"I've got a few earrings on me," he said. "I wish I'd kept my ring." When I'd first met Karish, he'd worn a family ring. He'd removed it after abjuring his family's title, in order to continue working as a Source.

I wished he'd kept it, too. I wished I'd cultivated the habit of wearing jewelry myself. I had nothing of value. Except, apparently, my shirts, and I had only a couple more of them on me.

What were we going to do?

That stupid, ignorant, careless bitch. How dare she do this to us? When we got back, if we got back, I was going to throw a tantrum worthy of Her Imperial Majesty Empress Constia herself.

All right. Breathe.

"Damn, it's hot," Karish muttered, pulling his collar from his skin.

There was nothing for it. We'd just have to find work of some kind. Lie to get a job and learn the skills after, if necessary. I didn't like that idea, and it might jerk back to smack us in the face, but I didn't know what else to do. We needed a place to sleep and food to eat. And really, it couldn't be impossible to find work. Thousands of people found work without having any real skills. Surely, we could as well.

Chapter Five

It so happened that we did have enough currency to spend a single night at Vikor's bunker, provided we shared one room. We even had a couple of coins left over, but we were too afraid to spend them. I was starving. Karish wasn't hungry, due to his difficult voyage, but he should have eaten something. We didn't have the money for a meal.

We had spent a terrifying and futile evening looking for work. It was obvious to everyone that we didn't have the first clue how to go about it. When asked what I could do, I listed my pitiful collection of non–Triple S related skills. People were shaking their heads before the words were half out of my mouth. Later, when asked what I could do, I asked what they needed doing. No one liked that response.

Everyone was very kind, of course. All very sympathetic and pleasant as they told me they had no use for me. Some of them referred me to their neighbors, naming names, and I wondered if the so named went back to the namees and visited upon them some physical retribution. But in the end, as the sun slid out of the sky, I met up with

Karish and had any faint hopes destroyed when he said
he'd had no more luck than I.

How could that be? Look at him. Who wouldn't pay to
have him stand in a room and beautify their home?

We went back to Vikor. Karish held out his hand with all
the money we had in the world in his palm, and Vikor told
us that while we didn't have enough currency for two
rooms, we could afford one. I didn't know whether this was
true or whether we were the recipients of pity. At that point
I didn't care. I was too scared to care about anything but
being scared.

We were shown to a small room with a huge window
and no furniture aside from a mattress and a lantern. It
smelled like dried grass.

Karish insisted on sleeping on the floor. It didn't matter
much. The mattress serving as a bed was no thicker than
the length of my thumb, and was laid directly onto the woven matting on the floor. We took advantage of the water
sent up to wash off the grime of the day. Separately, one
standing outside the room while the other bathed. And despite the early hour we blew out our candle and stretched
out to sleep.

Only I couldn't sleep. How could I? We were deserted
in a strange place with no means of support. What were we
going to do?

My breathing kept speeding up. Whenever I noticed
this, I worked to smooth it out and slow it down, but as
soon as I resumed thinking about our circumstances my
breathing once more became fast and short. I couldn't get
comfortable; my muscles were clenched too tightly. After
rolling over a few times I realized I was moving merely for
the sake of moving, and I forced myself to lie still. While I
didn't feel the heat nearly as badly as Karish seemed to, it
was too warm to be tossing about.

Karish reached over and stroked my temple with his
thumb. "We'll be all right, Lee."

"I know," I lied.

I saw him smile. "Of the two of us, I actually mean what I say."

He would. But he was insane.

"Honestly, Lee. It'll turn out in the end."

"How?" I challenged him.

"I don't know." He shrugged. "But it always does."

"Optimist."

"You say that like it's a bad thing." He continued to stroke my temple. The muscles along my back loosened despite themselves, worry swamped under fatigue.

I fell asleep.

I thought Vikor was generous with the amount of fruit and bread he sent up to us the next morning. It was more than needed to satisfy one person, which was all we had paid for. It was fruit like nothing I'd had before, bright and juicy and sweet. We freshened up with what was left of the water, and were almost—kind of—ready to face the day.

Except for the lack of coffee. I *wanted* coffee.

And, of course, the lack of money and of any hope of acquiring some.

I couldn't believe I was worrying about money. I was a Shield. I wasn't supposed to have to do that.

The performers were out again. So were the crowds, far thicker than they had been the day before. Perhaps the day before had been a work day for the villagers, while the current day was a rest day. To me it just meant more people to maneuver around, more people gawking at me, more people trying to paw at my hair.

"I wonder," Karish muttered, watching the contortionist.

"What?"

"Why don't we ask them if they need any laborers?"

"The contortionist?"

"The troupe. Or circus. Whatever they are."

I raised an eyebrow. "Do you not remember our dismal

performance at the Hallin Festival?" Because I sure did. It was way up there as one of the most embarrassing events of my life.

"Not as performers."

"Then what?"

"I don't know," he snapped with impatience. "But there's no harm in asking."

True enough. And it wasn't as though I had any ideas of my own. So we waited and watched the contortionist go through her routine, and I tried to be polite as I fended off the soft touches to my skin and hair.

The contortionist, in time, stood upright for a moment, and we took that as a sign that she was done for a bit. The spectators tossed coins at her feet. Some of them moved on but many lingered, watching us. Apparently, the prospect of us speaking was a form of entertainment all its own.

"Excuse me, my lady," said Karish, flashing his brightest smile and dropping his voice about half an octave. "May I beg a moment of your time?"

She looked at him with an amused smirk, lithe brown hand propped on her extremely bony hip. "First you take my speccies," she said in the same thick, syrupy drawl of the roadkeeper, "and now you want my time?"

Speccies? What the heck were those?

Ah. Spectators.

"Two such poor creatures as ourselves could never distract anyone from such a vision of beauty."

The woman, young and lovely, was entertained, but not, to my surprise, bowled over. There were some people immune to Karish's charm. They were usually older, cynical, or jealous. This girl didn't seem to fit the profile. She snickered. "Kai, charmer. What's fly?"

"I am," he said after hesitating just a hair of a moment, "Taro Karish. This is Lee Mallorough. We're strangers here." She snickered again because, aye, obvious. "We are looking for work. Who do we speak to about such things?"

"We travel, eh?" she said. "We're here just a few days."

"That actually suits us."

The smile dropped off and her eyes narrowed. "Why?" she demanded, suddenly cold.

Karish was surprised by the abrupt change in demeanor, but he rallied. "Because we need to get to another part of the island but lack the means to get there. If we can travel as we earn, it will be a benefit to us. Unless, of course, you're traveling in the wrong direction."

The woman relaxed. She looked us over. Karish, she scanned fairly quickly, but her gaze lingered on me for a disturbing length of time. What, had I put my shirt on backward? She nodded. "Follow that road north," she said, pointing. "Go left at the gray post. All the tents are there. Stop the first person you see and ask for Atara. Tell them Rinis sent you."

Karish gave her his biggest brightest grin, and she didn't melt at all. Was she blind? "Thank you for your assistance, Rinis."

"Kai, kai." She rolled her eyes. "Go, will you? You're disturbing the speccies."

We thanked her again and moved away. Too many people moved with us. Were we really that strange to look at?

Karish didn't seem to notice, or didn't seem to care. He took my hand and walked with a buoyant step. "She wouldn't have sent us to this Atara if there were no hope of us finding work."

"Unless she finds pleasure in sending ignorant strangers to get their heads taken off by her irascible employer."

"Pessimist."

"You say that like it's a bad thing."

We followed Rinis's directions, which were simple and correct. They led us, as she had said, to a huge collection of tents. No tents like I'd ever seen. Brilliant colors, every one of them, various sizes but all of them with large flaps suspended far beyond the entrance of the tent. They all shaded what I supposed were chairs, low to the ground and comprised of thick poles of wood, held together by thick sections of cloth that served as the seat and the back, so people could sit outside yet remain shielded from the sun. Ribbons hung from the flaps, tokens I couldn't identify tied to the ends. People sat in these chairs and watched us, a little wary but not overtly hostile.

A group of children ran by us with a chorus of "Kiyo!" I recognized them as the group who had run past us the day before. That explained why they hadn't been watching the performers with the rest of the villagers. It was all old news to them.

Slightly older children were practicing the stunts I'd seen their elders performing. Wires and trapezes were lowered, the items juggled were neither sharp nor on fire, but the activities still seemed too dangerous for children to me. Especially as adult supervision was pretty lax.

"Excuse me," I said to a youth who appeared to be standing around doing nothing. "This is Shintaro Karish. I am Dunleavy Mallorough. A woman named Rinis suggested we talk to Atara."

He looked me up and down and grinned. Karish, he barely glanced at. What was with these people? The youth started walking and, assuming he was taking us where we wanted to go, we followed.

The tent he took us to didn't look significantly different from the others, but then I couldn't find any tent in my sight that suggested a person of authority lived within. As soon as the youth was under the tent's flap he was toeing off his sandals. "Ma!" he nearly shouted. "Got seekers here!"

There was no response that I could hear, but that didn't keep the boy from ducking into the tent. A moment or so later his head popped back out. "Come now," he said to us with a trace of impatience.

We quickly divested ourselves of our boots and followed him in.

And damn that place was hot. I heard Karish gasp beside me. Over a dozen candles and lamps increased the temperature, and I felt the moisture accumulating on my face and under my arms. In the brutal light I was well able to see the colorful carpets stretched over the ground, hangings suspended from ceiling to floor in a bid to create rooms in the tent, and the occupant herself.

She was scary looking. That was the first, juvenile word to pop into my head. And I wasn't sure why, because she was also beautiful. She was tall and lean, with that hard, chiseled beauty middle age brought to some women. Her skin was a darker brown than the others I had seen, almost black. The weight of her black gaze when she glanced at me seemed to hit me like a blow to my stomach. Her stance and her movements and her very aura rang with intimidating confidence.

Her skirt and her shirt, as scanty as everyone else's, were brilliant red, each ear was filled with earrings, and a gaudy collection of chains and torques graced her throat and both wrists and ankles. She wore rings on every finger and—and this made me cringe with imagined discomfort—every toe.

I was surprised to see such a blatantly strong woman wearing such an excessive amount of decoration. I was also surprised to realize that I had previously assumed competence and extravagant frippery were mutually exclusive concepts. Always fun to learn new things about oneself.

She was standing by a small table. Most of the candles were arranged in a large square on its surface. Within the square was what looked like a map. It appeared to be a map of the island, though its shape was slightly different from mine and it had far more detail. The woman held a length of silver, laced through the bored center of a small white stone, suspended over the map. She was slowly moving the stone above the map, up and down, side to side. "Ah, she

said, cocking her head to one side as she slowed her movements, shifting the stone at a slower and slower pace. Then
she stopped. The stone rested in stillness for a moment.
The next moment, the stone started spinning.

Frowning, I looked up the length of silver to her fingers.
They were utterly still. There was nothing about the
woman to suggest how the stone might be spinning.

The woman grinned, a glorious wide smile that filled
me with sudden envy. A smile like that could halt conversations. "Harvest Moon," she announced, grabbing the
stone into her palm. "Tell Fin, will you, Ori?"

"Yes, Ma," and with another curious look at us the
youth ducked out of the tent.

The woman straightened, raking over first Karish and
then me with those relentless eyes. "I am Atara," she said,
and I realized her accent, although there, was fainter than
any I'd heard yet. "You are seeking work?"

Ah. Seekers. Seeking work. Got it. There were some
real interesting language ticks at play. "Yes, ma'am." I introduced us, then added, "We are from High Scape. Have
you heard of it?"

"I have." The woman pulled a small bag from a dresser
by one of the "walls," dropping the chain and stone into it.
"The place is popular with the dark spirits."

"The . . . dark spirits?" Oh no.

"It is a place of turmoil, is it not?"

"I suppose one could say that." Though not so much, recently.

"So, dark spirits linger there. Obviously."

Obviously. If you're the sort of nut to believe in dark
spirits. I looked to her bared temples but saw no sun-
shaped tattoos. I supposed, though, that one didn't have to
be a Reanist to be superstitious.

I was hoping none of those thoughts were showing up on
my face. The woman's personal beliefs, provided they didn't
include plans to sacrifice my Source, were no business of

mine. "We're looking for family in Golden Fields." That was the location of the Bryants, according to the information the Empress had given me.

"Ah," the woman said with satisfaction. "That explains it."

Cryptic babble. I hated cryptic babble. "Your pardon?"

"I have been calling for direction for nearly an hour." A languid hand waved over the map. "Never has it so long taken me. You enter my tent, and krechek, direction comes to me. It leads me to Harvest Moon, which lies in the direction of Golden Fields."

Coincidences. Had to love them. Those so inclined could make so much of them. On a positive note, they were heading in the right direction. That was something.

"Have you tents?" the woman asked us.

"I'm afraid not." I hesitated to call her by her name. It seemed inappropriate to address a person of authority in so familiar a manner. But I didn't know her proper title. "All we have is what you see." Well, except for our boots, which were hopefully still waiting for us outside the tent.

"Hm. I'm sure I can find someone willing to share."

"Excuse me?" Had I missed something? "Are you hiring us?" It couldn't possibly be that simple.

"When the spirits send me a good omen, I don't send it away." She rolled up the map with quick, efficient hands. "What can you do?"

"Uh—" While I could admit to myself that I could do nothing, I preferred not having to say it out loud.

She was looking me over again. I wondered if this was how a horse felt. "You will perform. You have beauty." While I was trying not to swallow my tongue over that pronouncement, she turned her critical eye on Karish. "You are plain. I will find handwork for you."

Karish's initial response to that was nothing more than the widening of the eyes.

Plain? Karish? Was plain? Was the woman *blind*? Yes,

Karish wasn't at his best. But it was obvious once he was back in full health he would be stunning. Any fool could see that.

The woman's face softened from the clinical scrutiny she had been employing. "Your forgiveness, please." She dipped her head a little. "Your shoulders are square. I thought straight speaking would not dim you."

It wasn't the straight speaking so much as the wrongness of the straight speaking. Look at him. Do you not have eyes? And who in the world thought I was beautiful, when they were sober?

"No offense is taken, ma'am," Karish said faintly. He was *blushing*. And suddenly I found myself wondering what the Stallion of the Triple S, toasted for his beauty, felt upon hearing that someone thought him plain. Not even his most jealous detractors could deny he was beautiful. "It is only that such a comment is not common where I come from. It surprised me."

I'd wager it did.

"And I would be happy to perform any handwork you can find for me."

The woman nodded, momentary awkwardness forgotten. "You have no gear and, what, no training?" We had to nod at that. "No decent clothes?"

That all depended on one's definition of decent, didn't it? "We have no clothes like we've seen on people here," I said.

"They're all like those?" She gestured at us and curled her lip at what she saw.

Hey, one of my shirts paid our road tax, woman. "Yes, ma'am."

"They are ugly." More straight speaking. "And looking at you makes me feel hot. You cannot wear them."

"We'd rather not, but . . ." How to say this without annoying our new desperately needed employer. "I couldn't comfortably wear the clothes you all wear here." The short short skirts, the clinging tops. I'd feel naked. And ridiculous.

She waved that thought away. "You'll learn." She bit on a red-colored fingernail, looking me up and down as she circled me. I did not like that.

"Can you sing?"

"Not really."

"Dance?"

"No."

"Well—" said Karish.

Atara looked at him. "Yes?"

"She can dance the benches."

Well, aye, but that wasn't what she meant.

Or perhaps it was, for her eyes lit up. "You dance benches? Are you professional?"

"No." And the light disappeared. "But I'm a Shield. We dance the benches a lot."

"And she's good," Karish added eagerly. "She's beaten professionals."

"Our circuits here are poor compared to the North lands," Atara mused. "Real skill will impress. With that hair—" I almost touched my hair at that. What was so great about my hair? It was red. "And a decent costume." She snapped her fingers. "Music. Not the regular drums. Change the music. Some sand singers. You dance at night. Under the pull of the moon. We'll put silver and copper bobs in your hair and they will reflect the torchlight. Make it less of a sport. But, oh! We can offer a challenge—if you really are that good—after they've seen you dance they can pay to dance against you."

It was a bit alarming to hear all those ideas coming out of her mouth. The pull of the moon? Bobs in my hair? What? "What do they win if they beat me?"

She shrugged. "The pleasure of knowing they beat you. All they are paying for is the right to dance with an exotic beauty of the night."

I didn't like that. It sounded perverted.

Atara moved some of the candles, placing three of them in the center of the table. From a basket on the floor, she retrieved something wrapped in dark cloth. It turned out to be a small loaf of bread, thinner and darker than what I was used to.

Atara held the loaf over the candles, close enough to the flames that I had to wonder if it stung a little. She broke off a chunk and looked at me. I took the chunk from her. She broke off a second chunk, which was given to Karish. Breaking off a third chunk, she took a bite, so we did, too. The bread was dense and almost sweet.

"Welcome to our cause," she said. Then she looked at me, obviously expecting a response.

When in doubt, go with "Thank you."

"We are honored," Karish added when Atara looked at him.

"Excellent," said Atara, and she put the remainder of her bread on the table. So we did the same.

"Come, we will see how good you are."

"Now?" Swallow down panic. "Really, ma'am, I am so far from my best right now. I didn't dance during our voyage here——"

"People are never at their best." Atara grabbed my wrist, and I was too shocked to resist when she pulled me out of the tent. "People are always tired or ill or angry or grieving. You still must be able to perform." She hesitated only long enough to pull on her footwear and allow Karish and I to do the same.

Hell. I was tired. I'd obviously come from a great distance. She expected me to work tonight? Maybe this was a bad idea after all.

"Ashti!" Atara called, and a young girl, about eight years old, came running up. "Fetch Fin, Panol, Setter and the drummers. Tell them to meet us on the practice grounds. Tell Panol to bring the dancing bars with him."

"Yes, Ma." The girl ran off with a ridiculous amount of energy.

Atara headed off in the direction of where I'd seen the

children practicing earlier. "We will gather together what supplies we can for you, but that will mean that you are in our debt."

I didn't like the sound of that. I didn't want to end up being indentured to these people. This was the only positive response we'd gotten, so maybe we had no choice. Still, not good.

"I don't pay you any coin. What you get from the speccies is what you get. A tenth of every taking comes to me, and if the tenth doesn't equal at least five grays for each performance, we leave you."

I guessed good omens got only so much leeway.

"Excuse me, Atara," Karish said. "Is there someone I can speak to about finding what kind of work I can do?"

What? He wanted to desert me? At this time?

"Fin. He'll be with us."

"Oh." Karish frowned.

What was the problem? Or maybe he just didn't want to witness the horrific performance I was going to be putting on. Must be awful knowing someone else's efforts were going to determine something so important. Then again, I'd trade places with him in a heartbeat. Why was I always the one who had to make a fool of herself?

I was out of condition. I was wearing the wrong clothes. And while I wasn't suffering from the heat to the same extent Karish was, it was unnaturally warm. And then, when a small group of men arrived, apparently the chaps the child had been sent to fetch, they had dancing bars, but no benches.

"We have no benches," Atara told me when I asked her about it. "We have the bars because sometimes Rinis uses them for her performances, but we've never had benches."

"I need the benches to stand on."

"The ground will suffice."

Spoken like someone who has never danced the benches. I hadn't danced from the ground since I was a child, first learning to dance. Dancing from the ground was awful. Uneven and broken and more punishing on the feet. Plus it was supposed to be part of the challenge, making sure you landed back on the benches well enough to leap again.

I pulled off my boots—no chalk to be seen—and retied my hair so it would survive the bouncing. I did a few warm-up jumps and stretched.

This was going to be bad. Bad bad bad bad bad.

And then a gorgeous mountain of a man—I was told his name was Leverett—began rattling rolls off his tall, narrow drum, and my breath hitched. The vibrations rolled down my back, loosening each notch, before shimmering low in my spine. That helped.

Panol, who turned out to be Atara's son, and Setter assured me they had seen enough bench dances to know how to handle the bars. Wasn't that heartening? I didn't point out that they were using only two stalkers for handling only two bars, when there were supposed to be four of each. I didn't want to come out of this with a shattered ankle. That would really be inconvenient. Two bars were safer.

As Leverett fiddled with his drum I tried to focus on the beats he produced and pull them into me.

I loved music. Whoever had invented it should be worshipped as a god.

People were wandering close to watch. Wasn't that just lovely?

Then Atara raised her eyebrows at me. That let me know she was impatient for me to get started. I walked over to where the men crouched with two rather beaten and cracked bars and assumed the start stance, standing as though I had two benches beneath my feet.

The men looked at Leverett rather than me for the cue to start. Which would have been normal in a competition but worried me right then. Fortunately, they started with the bars low and they moved them tentatively. They were afraid of hurting their hands as they smacked the bars together.

Lifting my feet out of danger was easy enough, but predicting the movement of the bars was impossible.

"You need to move to a beat, gentlemen," I reminded them. If I couldn't predict where the bars were going to be, I couldn't dance.

They improved immediately, moving with the music. Which wasn't exactly how it was supposed to work, but I wasn't going to complain about having both the aural and visual cues.

It was nice to stretch out and work the muscles. Leverett was a good drummer, and the movement of the bars was so slow and low I could close my eyes for brief snatches and just feel the gorgeous rolls against the surface of drum.

It would be too easy to let things continue at this easy pace. It wouldn't impress Atara. "Could we speed things up, gentlemen?" I called out. "Raise the bars just a little higher."

Leverett obligingly segued into a gorgeous allegro. The other men raised the bars, but not by much, and moved them with the music.

That was better. Muscles moved into well-remembered patterns. The drumming, unfamiliar to me but effective nonetheless, coiled through my blood. Very good. Strength I had forgotten in the course of our journey jolted through me and I found myself grinning with the pleasure of it.

All I lacked was an opponent.

And then it stopped. It took me a few steps to realize the bars had been dropped. I glanced at the handlers, and then the drummer, who had also ceased. Everyone looked all right, so what was going on?

I looked to Karish. It appeared he hadn't been watching, his gaze directed off to one side and his back angled a little toward me.

"That will work," said Atara, rubbing her hands together. "That will do."

"But I can do better." And I'd just been getting into it.

"I am looking for pretty, not athletic. Though a little of

that is good, too." She was looking me up and down again. "No silver. Just copper. Maybe we can find some gold. Yes, everything orange, yellow, gold. The Flame Dancer."

The Flame Dancer? Was she serious? I didn't dare look at Karish, who was no doubt snickering and would start me off.

"Dunleavy is no good."

I'd be sure to tell my parents they'd chosen an inadequate name.

"Leavy. Leavy the Flame Dancer."

Oh my good gods. How could I possibly face anyone carrying a name like that? "I fear such a title would be more appropriate for someone more flamboyant."

"You can learn to be flamboyant."

Oh aye. As simple as that, was it? "I'm a Shield, ma'am. It's the nature of a Shield to be sedate."

"By inclination or training?"

"A little of both."

"Inclination can be overcome. And if you can be trained to be sedate, you can be trained to be flamboyant. Everyone!" She clapped her hands twice, and I realized there were even more people watching than I remembered. "This is Leavy and Shintaro. They will be joining us for a while. They are good omens, and a guide for our next path." The fact that no one found this announcement startling disturbed me. "They have nothing. I think they will bring us much. We will provide them with what they need. We're leaving tomorrow."

Not much of a speech maker.

Everyone started moving. Some leaving, some disassembling the practice gear and carting it away.

An older woman picked her way to me, easily avoiding the flow. She was dressed in the same manner as the younger women, and I had to admire her bravery and self-confidence. "I am Corla," she said. "I read the future." Zaire save me. "I can share my tent with you and your husband."

"Oh, we're not married," I said.

"No matter. Many don't bother. That does not impair the invitation."

Before I could explain that wasn't exactly what I meant, Fin—a broad middle-aged man who still managed to carry off the scanty garb—approached. "We have enough spare fabric to fashion a sort of tent for you," he rumbled in the deepest voice I had ever, ever heard. "It might scar the eyes, but it will keep the sun off."

"Thank you. That is so kind."

Karish was then spirited away by Fin. I spent the rest of the day introducing myself to people, those who weren't out performing. They were, as a whole, a talkative bunch, and uncomfortably inquisitive. They wanted to know all about why we were there. I stuck with the same story I'd used in front of Karish—searching for long-lost family— with no embellishment, certain that they were questioning him as well. When they pressed me for details, I praised the beauty of their tattoos or asked them what they did for the show.

I learned that there were thirty people in all, adults and children, performers and handworkers. The troupe had belonged to Atara since her mother, who had owned it before her, had died, and they spent all their time traveling from settlement to settlement, performing for coins. As the island was rather small, it seemed to me that the show would end up visiting the same settlement twice in a year, perhaps more. The solution to that was variety. All performers were pushed to constantly change their acts. And the performers themselves were not constant. A couple of rope walkers had left the troupe a few stops back. This was one of the reasons Atara, whom everyone called Ma, was so quick to take us on. We were new, and as Northerners we would draw an audience by our mere presence.

Day slid into evening, and Karish found me sitting under the ovcas—what they called the extra flap suspended beyond the entrance of the tent—with a young girl named

Glynis. His hair was ringed with sweat and there were streaks of dirt across his face and his bare torso, not to mention caked under his nails. And yet he still managed to look good. Regular freak of nature, he was.

Of course, it might also have had something to do with the gleam in his eye and the odd glow about him. I was immediately suspicious.

"What have you been doing all day?" he asked.

"Uh, nothing," I admitted, immediately afflicted with that most useless of emotions, guilt, because it was obvious he had been working like a dog.

He grinned. "Nothing?"

I nodded, wondering why he thought that was something to smile about.

He chuckled. "Come along, then."

I took my leave from Glynis, who apparently found my manner amusing and giggled in response. I followed Karish through the camp, where most of the performers had returned and were showing signs of packing up. He led me to the edge of the camp, to a tent that was even more eye sticking than the others, each side a different color and pattern, the roof a faded, distasteful green. It was smaller than the other tents, and it had no ovcas.

"This is our tent," he announced with palpable pride.

I smiled at him. "You put it up."

"I did." Hence the glow. "I mean, Fin showed me how and helped me, but I did most of it."

The jokes that sprang into my brain, all about the likelihood of this effort collapsing or being blown away, were strangled into silence for being inappropriate under the circumstances. "I'm impressed."

"Really?"

"I couldn't do it."

Karish grabbed my elbow. "Look inside." He pulled me forward and opened the tent flap, latching it up against the nearest wall.

I was arrested by all the stuff littered on the floor of the tent. Bundles of clothes. Sandals of all colors. Pots and pans. Mats and sheets and small hard pillows destined to give me migraines. And things I didn't recognize. All filling the small front space of the tent.

"Atara showed me a list of everything that was here." Karish unwrapped one bundle of clothing, revealing a flashy golden length of cloth that filled me with dread. "And what the expenses of traveling are. And an estimation of how long it would take us to pay everything back."

I didn't bother asking for the numbers. They wouldn't mean anything to me. "Did it seem fair to you?"

He shrugged. "I really don't know, Lee. Different places put different values on things, having different wage rates and different standards for prices. It didn't seem outrageous to me, but"—he shrugged again—"I'm no expert."

"So how long will we be in debt to these people?"

"It depends on how much you bring in as a dancer. But she gave me an estimate for that as well." He pulled in a deep breath. Oh, no. "Something over two years."

My mouth dropped open, so I covered it with my hand. Two years? *Two years?* Were they insane? "Taro—"

"I know."

"We're not even going to be here two years!"

"I know. But, Lee, what else can we do? We have nothing here. No suitable clothing or gear." He looked at the cloth in his hand and shoved it back into the bundle. "No useful skills."

I sank to my knees on the mat that served as the floor. "Hey, you can erect a tent." I unwrapped a small leafy bundle and discovered a cool hard ball of cooked rice. "It's just . . . two years."

"The way I see it, we travel with them, find . . . the line . . . then sneak away—"

"Taro!"

"Let me finish. We sneak off when we can, and when we

get back to Erstwhile, we have the Empress send them back whatever money we still owe."

"They'll think we're thieves when we leave. And it's a poor way to repay them for taking a chance with us."

"We'll leave them a note. And aye, they probably won't believe it. But they will when they get the money."

I didn't like it. I didn't like any of it, being beholden to these people, belonging to them for two years, making a fool of myself for money and sneaking off once we didn't need them anymore. Reeked of dishonor. But Karish was right. I didn't see an option. And I was furious with the Empress for putting us in this position.

"So what will you be doing?" I asked to sort of change the subject.

The glow, which had dimmed when he revealed our financial situation, disappeared completely. "Fetching and carrying, because I don't know how to do anything. Useless aristocrat, indeed, eh?"

He was not useless. In any sense of the word. He had a rare, valuable, dangerous ability that the people on this damned island lacked the brains to appreciate. "You can raise a tent," I reminded him. "You can learn. So can I."

He hissed. "You don't have to, do you? You have something they want."

I looked at him, tucked a lock of his hair behind his ear. "Are you jealous?"

"Yes." His tone was bitter. "I'm here on sufferance. Because you can do something that appeals to them and they figure they can't have you unless they take me, too."

"Actually, we were both taken on because Atara thinks we're good omens. She obviously isn't guided by reason. And you're the one who knows how to handle money."

"No, I don't, Lee. Not really. Stop it."

Damn it. He was sliding into one of his moods. Damn all these people, anyway. "Ah, I know what the real problem is. You're just all bent because Atara doesn't think you're gorgeous."

Outraged was better than downcast. "That has nothing to do with anything!" he snapped angrily.

"Oh aye. After a lifetime of getting everything you wanted just by batting those eyes and flashing that simpering smile."

"I neither bat nor simper!"

"Please. You expect to be able to work your way around anyone."

"I do not manipulate people."

This was getting ugly. That hadn't been the plan. "That's not what I'm suggesting."

"Isn't it?"

I sighed. "Taro, we are in a strange place, with different rules. We both have to learn. And if you think I'm happy to take a sport I love and tart it up for the entertainment of ignorant—" I halted. The only words ready to leap off my tongue were derogatory, and they didn't deserve that. "Well, I'm not happy about it."

"Nice try, Lee. So you have to wear some flash and dance at something less than your standard. Doesn't change the fact that you can contribute something that these people want, and I can't."

I didn't comment. He wasn't believing anything I was saying, anyway.

We had a solemn, quiet dinner, and I didn't know what to do about Karish's mood. After years of being near worshipped for being a Source, it had to be a blow to have one's principal skill dismissed as useless. And no matter what he said, it had to be hard to be told he was plain. He wasn't used to being seen that way. I would have been annoyed if someone had said that right to my face, and they would have been telling the truth.

The remainder of the tent had been separated into two tiny bedrooms, little larger than the mats we were sleeping on. Lying on the mat, I realized the tents provided no protection from noise. I heard others moving around, talking, shouting. I heard things I really didn't need to hear. Very embarrassing.

And, unable to sleep for thinking of the bizarre mess we'd found for ourselves, I heard evidence of the return of Karish's emotional equilibrium. He started chuckling. "Leavy the Flame Dancer," he snickered.

So I glared at the cloth hanging between us, temporarily resenting its presence. Then I reached under it and slapped him on the shoulder. Four times.

Chapter Six

The camp was rolled up early the next day, and we started walking toward the next location. The path we traveled was a narrow one, barely wide enough to accommodate the troupe's one wagon, pulled by two mules and itself narrower than what I was used to seeing at home. The air was thick and seemed to settle on my skin like an extra layer of weighty discomfort. It was hard to breathe, and the dense foliage that surrounded us blocked the sky and trapped the heat. It felt like the inside of a damp, dark, hellishly hot box. During the worst of the day's heat, we stopped to eat and rest, but I was exhausted, my shins stinging with the unaccustomed activity.

"Just watching you is making me sweat," a low voice purred beside me, dragging my eyes up from the wheels of the covered wagon I was following. "One of us must have given you something deccy."

I wasn't sure what deccy meant. I looked at the shell gamester bouncing along beside me. Her clothing was far more subdued than it had been the first day I'd seen her, her skirt of thicker material and falling nearly to her knees, a shirt covering most of her torso, though leaving her arms bare. She had sturdier sandals, and most—though by no means all—of her jewelry was absent.

"People were most generous," I said. Though could it be called generosity when we were expected to pay for it? "But I don't know what 'deccy' means."

"Ah. Good. To wear."

"I'm not used to the sort of clothing your people wear."

"You will faint from the heat," she warned me.

"It's not likely. Shields don't feel temperatures as much as other people."

"Shields?"

I was starting to get over the shock of hearing people who didn't know what Shields were. A little. I explained what Shields were, and why that meant I felt physical sensations a little less acutely than most people.

"Oh," she said. "Fin told me they were tricksters."

"Tricksters." That was always a fun one.

"Claiming magic that isn't there. Halting storms that never were."

That again. "I can promise you," I said through gritted teeth, "that is not the case." Obnoxious brat. "And it's not magic."

She shrugged. "We have no such people here."

I noticed. But there was no point in beating the point into the ground. "Our skin isn't used to the sun. We can't wear your clothes yet." Karish being a case in point. His skin had gone a deep painful red from the waist up over the night, and he was stretched out and suffering in the wagon in front of me. He couldn't bear to be touched and he was, of course, highly irritable. He had ordered me off the wagon, telling me to leave him alone. I did, without comment.

"So you are not linking?"

I dragged my eyes up from the wheels once more. "I don't understand."

"You and the plain one aren't lovers?"

I stared at her. What the . . . ? Who was she to ask such

a question? And what in the world did that have to do with
what kind of clothing we wore?

"Fin told me the plain one refused double mats for sin-
gles."

"Fin should keep his mouth shut," I snapped. "And stop
calling Karish plain. You're all blind."

She laughed. "Everyone knows everyone's goings here.
Might as well get to it first stride."

Ugh. I'd forgotten about that sort of thing. One of the
reasons I'd been happy to leave the Academy. Everyone
into everyone's business. It exasperated me. Really, who
cared about the fights, who had been caught cheating on a
test, who had stolen the grammar teacher's hairpiece, who
was sleeping with who? In people trained to be discreet,
objective and mature, gossip was a disappointing vice.

Not that I'd never done it. And not that I hadn't enjoyed
the odd tidbit of information about people beyond our
walls, including one Lord (former) Shintaro Karish. It had
been a part of the package of news we received about the
outside world. But I never cared to engage in that sort of
thing about people I saw every day. There was something
more sinister and underhanded about it then.

I wasn't looking forward to diving back into that kind of
environment.

"And your man is plain," she insisted. "He is too pale."

"Then I must be hideous, because I am far more pale
than he."

Her eyes widened in shock. "No!" she objected, gestur-
ing wildly with her hands. "Yes, your skin is light, but there
is fire behind it. And your hair—" She reached out to
touch, but perhaps something showed in my face, for she
halted long before contact was made. "Is it your color?"

"My color?"

"Do you dye it?"

"Oh. No." Why would anyone dye their hair red?

"Oh." And she was disappointed. Her body practically
drooped. "So I cannot find that color."

I stared at her. Her hair was a glorious, deep black. "Your hair is beautiful!"

She shrugged. "It is common," she said dismissively. "Almost everyone has this color. Like your man."

I had thought, the previous day, that Atara had either been rude in her assessment of Karish or was showing the insensitivity of a trader trying to shove the price down by claiming there was no value in the product. Perhaps, though, it was a cultural characteristic. "Who are you?" If they could be blunt, so could I.

She laughed again. "I am Kahlia. Daughter of Atara."

Ah. A family trait, maybe. "Pleased to meet you." But wait. Atara was so dark, and Panol nearly so. And both had the slimmer frames of most of the other islanders I had seen.

But then, family members didn't really have to look alike. I supposed.

"So, you are not linking?"

What damn business was it of hers? Unless. "Why? Do you want him?"

She shook her head quickly. I was both relieved and annoyed. "There is no light behind his smiles."

Please. Not a whole tribe of people who spoke like Sources. "I don't understand."

"He smiles because he has to, not because he feels to."

Was he still doing that? I thought he was getting over that, a little. And why would he feel the need to do it here? These were complete strangers, with no foreknowledge of the Triple S or the Stallion or the Karish family. "He's certainly not smiling now."

"I will help you choose your clothing," Kahlia announced.

"Is that what this whole conversation has been about?"

"The clothes you wear now, I have never seen anything so ugly. You must have no eyes."

"These are travel clothes."

"So?"

"So, they are meant to be sturdy and comfortable, not beautiful."

"They can be both."

"Perhaps, but to make things beautiful takes time and effort."

"So?"

"So, it's time wasted on something that's made to be functional."

She rolled her eyes. "Beauty is never a waste of time. You have such strange ideas."

I longed to tell her the same thing.

"Your costume for dancing, you concede it must be beautiful?"

If I had to. "Yes."

"You will let me choose it?"

If I had to.

She would know best what would appeal to her own people. And I should be grateful that she was willing to invest so much effort in me. "Yes, thank you. That's very kind."

She pressed a small cloth bundle into my hand. "Give your man that. It will make him feel better."

I unwrapped the bundle and found small polished pebbles, light brown in color. "What do you do with them?"

"You eat them."

"They're medicine?"

"No. They're sweet." She winked at me and then skipped away to join someone farther up the line.

I climbed up into the wagon as quietly as possible, in case Karish was asleep. He raised his forearm off his eyes only long enough to see who I was. I couldn't blame him for his lethargy. It was even hotter in the wagon. "How are you feeling?" I got a grunt in response. "Kahlia gave me something for you to eat."

"Not interested."

"She said it would make you feel better."

"She said it was sweet." His mouth scrunched up in disgust.

"You heard her?"

"I'm not deaf," he snapped.

I put the small bundle down, near enough for him to reach if he should change his mind. "You weren't such an impossible patient when you were stabbed."

He bared his teeth to the canines. "So sorry I'm not entertaining you."

"Do you want me to get you something to drink?"

"Stop fussing, Lee."

I climbed down from the wagon, deciding not to talk to anyone else for a while. I seemed to be coming off for the worse in these conversations. But this was a resolution the others in the slowly moving troupe chose to ignore. Many in the troupe came back to ask questions they had no right to ask. They were entirely resistant to my hints to go away.

I gave up on trying to get anyone to call me Dunleavy. They merely gained amusement from the attempt. They wouldn't even settle for Lee. They liked the way Leavy sounded, and they refused to move from it.

Shortly before the softening of the air announced the imminent arrival of sunset, a halt was ordered. Everything was moved off the beaten track that served as a road. Many of the adults pulled out large-bladed knives and cut away undergrowth and small trees. The tents were erected, but along different lines than they had been at the outpost. Much smaller, with no ovcas, in order to squeeze into the smaller space.

Karish finally emerged from the wagon to put together our tent, because I hadn't the vaguest idea how to do it. Fin came by to show us how to prepare the ground and set up. He was a wonderfully patient man, and a good thing, too, because I was incompetent and Karish was barely hanging on to his temper. I came out of the trial with my fingers scraped and pinched and bruised, and I began to suspect that there was a reason why I never did anything with my hands.

As soon as the tent was set up, Karish unrolled a mat and put it directly on the ground. Then he stretched out on the mat and the forearm went back over the eyes.

"Have some water, Taro."

"Don't nag, Lee."

"You'll feel better if you drink something."

"The water's not cold."

What a child. "So?"

He didn't bother responding to that at all.

I unwrapped some cold rice. I didn't care for eating it that way. The only way to eat rice at all was in pudding. But I was starving and too tired to try preparing anything. Though the pace had been slow, I had been walking most of the day, and I wasn't used to it.

I watched the others preparing their food, fires and torches piercing the fading light. Some of the troupe members were practicing their acts, apparently unwearied by the travel of the day. I noticed Corla looking at us, and frowning. I kept my face free of impatience as I watched her make her way over to us.

I really didn't feel like talking to anyone.

"Young man!" she snapped at Karish. "Why is your mat on the earth?"

He sat up for her. "It's uncomfortable lying directly on the ground, ma'am."

"And why are you lying outside?" she demanded. "You want to lie down, you go inside. Come. Up. Get up."

It always amazed me that old people seemed to think they had the right to tell absolutely everyone else what to do. And if she was aware of Karish's clenching jaw, she gave no sign of it as she prodded him to his feet and ordered him to roll up the mat. Then she asked, "Where are your croppers?"

"Our what?"

Apparently two of the unrecognizable bundles we had received the night before were collapsible chairs of small wooden bars and cloth. We had been given only two, however, so Karish was stuck sitting on the ground while Corla and I sat in the croppers. I pitied Karish, who so obviously wanted to lie down in the tent, but he was afflicted with too stringent a set of social graces, and he wouldn't leave until Corla did.

Then she asked us for wine, chiding us for not offering it to her immediately. And we apparently had it. One of the water skins actually had wine. Very very pale and light, and a little sweet even for my tastes. "None for you," Corla said to Karish. "You are too red. Did the tree beads help?"

"Your pardon?" Karish asked.

"The tree beads. I had Kahlia bring them to you."

"Oh," I said. "The pale brown things I gave you. The little bundle."

"Ah." Karish turned on her a tired version of his usual smile. "My apologies, ma'am, but my stomach was a little uncertain at that time."

"So you didn't eat them? Where are they?"

Karish's face froze. He'd probably left them in the wagon.

Corla clicked her tongue in disapproval. "Go fetch them."

Karish opened his mouth to object.

"I didn't give them to you to have them thrown away."

Karish shut his mouth and rose to his feet.

"And you eat them," Corla shouted after him as he disappeared around a bend in the road.

Then she settled back in her chopper and gave me an intense look.

"You're going to read my fortune, aren't you?" I asked with resignation.

"I already have." She grinned. "Atara lets no one travel with us unless I see a clear reading."

"You haven't looked at my palm or my tea leaves. I see no crystal balls or cards."

"Are you going to pay me?"

"I'd rather not."

"Then don't demand a show. I don't need any of that, and you know it. You're a fool, not an idiot."

Zaire, what was with these people? "I see." But I didn't, not really. Atara had been using candles and a stone to get guidance from some invisible force to learn where the troupe should go next. Surely that sort of thing was on an equal footing to telling fortunes.

"Do you want to know why?"

"Why I'm not an idiot?"

"Why you are a fool."

Perhaps she had heard from the talkative Fin that Karish and I slept apart. Many would consider that foolish.

"You are letting your guilt crush you."

Now that was a shock. "I'm not feeling guilty about anything."

"You killed a man."

And all of a sudden, just like that, I couldn't breathe. I pressed a palm to my chest, trying to push air through my lungs. Oh my gods. How did she know? Where had she heard? Oh gods.

Actually, I'd killed two men. Creol, and a Reanist. But I thought she meant Creol. For some reason, killing the Reanist hadn't disturbed me nearly as much as killing Creol. I spent a brief moment wondering why.

She rubbed my shoulder, trying to reassure me. Or something. "Now, now," she said. "If you were not a good person, I would not have been able to see it. It is a shadow on your light."

Breathe, damn it.

"You are a creature of balance. You crave it. You cling to it, when you can. But you had to leave your balance, to kill this man, and you haven't been able to find it again."

I pulled in a breath. It hitched painfully in the middle, but at least I was getting in some air.

"And now you are afraid. You need to go so far the opposite way, yes? To restore your balance? But you are afraid to leave middle again. You will never find your balance if you are afraid to move."

"I don't understand," I confessed. And I couldn't believe I was listening to her with anything other than polite disinterest. But how had she known? No one but Karish and I knew I had killed Creol. How did she find out?

"What I said." Corla appeared impatient with my lack of comprehension. "If you do not move, you cannot find your balance. If you stand on one foot, you need to move, just a very little, to stay balanced. If you are rigid, you fall over. Correct?"

"Aye. But what does going the opposite mean?"

"Did I tell you to kill that man?"

I wasn't going to answer that, one way or the other. I wasn't going to confirm that I'd killed anyone. I didn't know what the hell was going on.

She didn't require an answer. Thank the gods. "So I can't tell you how to balance it, can I?"

Nice dodge, lady.

Karish reappeared around the bend, bundle in hand. "I have to beg your forgiveness, Corla," he said, and there was an ease to his voice I hadn't heard all day. "I ate one and it—" He halted, his gaze on me. "What happened?" And he narrowed his eyes at Corla. "What did you do?"

She smiled. "They're so pretty when they're fierce," she said to me.

I did not smile back. I wanted her to leave. I pressed my hands together to keep from hugging myself.

"This man she killed," Corla said. "He needed killing."

Karish stared at her.

"Ah. So you . . . encourage her guilt?"

He looked at me. I looked back at him and moved my head to one side just a fraction. No, I'd said nothing to her.

"She has a bright core," Corla went on. "If she did not, I would know nothing of her darkness. She needs to find her balance. You can help her, but you do not. You're afraid, cowering like a whipped dog. You stay outside the walls."

Gibberish. Would she please leave?

"You look outside too much," she said to Karish.

She'd found a new target. Hoo-ray.

"What?" He was confused. Imagine that.

"She tells the future," I explained, my voice nicely

sarcastic. "Only right now she seems more interested in picking apart the present."

Corla ignored me. "Always with you it is what others think," she scolded Karish. "Is not what you think important?"

He glowered at her, lips pressed into a thin line. "You don't know me," he reminded her.

"I know you put on a fine show," she said. "Always for other people. Why smile when you don't feel joy?"

"Diplomacy is such a harsh taskmistress, isn't she?"

"Pah! Diplomacy. Another word for lies."

"Don't you miss the color?"

This time she looked confused. Turn about and all. "What?"

"If all you see is black-and-white."

No, she did not like being the one on the receiving end of confusing statements. "You will never find your core if you always look outside," she said sharply. "If you do not find your core, you will always be empty. A false face is an empty face."

Karish pulled in a deep breath. "I have noticed among your people a tendency to be blunt." Oh, had he been a victim of it, too? "In the spirit of embracing the customs of my new home, I'm going to ask you to leave now."

That unexpected ending was almost enough to make me choke on my own saliva.

Corla, surprisingly enough, didn't find this offensive, if her cackling were any indication. "Not to worry, young man." She rose to her feet and tugged the hem of her short skirt infinitesimally lower. "You are less foolish than most. You will find your way."

"Your predictions for the future are less impressive than your perceptions of the present," I muttered, too shaken and annoyed to worry about courtesy.

The old woman sobered up. "All right, then," she said coolly. "You will be made an example of. Is that what you wanted to hear?"

I was struck speechless by her certainty, and the ominous jolt her words delivered upon me.

It had to be the darkness. And the torchlight. Torchlight always did things to my emotional state. And this whole crazy island. It was infecting me.

Karish scowled at his feet.

Corla nodded at us. "Fair eve, young ones." And she picked her way back to her own tent.

I waited until she had disappeared from our view before I cleared my throat. "It's trickery and sham. No one can see into the future." Or into one's mind, to see things they had no right seeing. Unfortunately, my voice didn't sound convincing to my own ears, and although what I said was the truth—of course it was—I was having a hard time believing it right then.

Of course I felt guilty about killing Creol. Who wouldn't feel guilty about committing murder and getting away with it? But it hadn't marked my entire life. The guilt was there, lurking at the back of my mind. Occasionally it flared to the front. But that was natural and healthy and right. It hadn't thrown my whole life off balance. It hadn't made me afraid to move.

Made an example of. That couldn't be good.

"Any of that wine left?" Karish asked, his voice rasping.

I handed him the skin, deciding not to remind him he wasn't in good shape for the consumption of alcohol. I just hoped he didn't drink it all. I had a feeling we'd both be needing it.

Then, all of a sudden, Karish announced, "There's an earthquake about to happen."

I clamped down on a spurt of excitement. "Oh," I said.

"It's a mild one, and"—he frowned—"quite a way off. I'm kind of surprised I can feel it at all."

"Oh," I said again.

"No reason not to channel it, though. Are you ready?"

"Of course." It would be nice, actually. It seemed like I

hadn't Shielded in ages. I felt Karish lower his protections and I erected my Shields around him.

Only nothing happened.

"Something wrong?"

He looked at me, appearing puzzled. "I think—I feel—someone else is channeling it."

"Someone on Flatwell?"

"I guess."

"But there are no Pairs on the Southern Islands." So I'd always been told.

"Not posted, but maybe there's a Pair like us here. You know, just visiting or traveling or something."

Or something. Perhaps banished here by a crazy monarch.

It struck me as strange, though, two Pairs to be somewhere where Pairs were neither assigned nor wanted.

"I have a bad feeling about this," Karish muttered.

"Lovely." So did I.

Chapter Seven

"You see, you need a costume that looks good, but won't hamper your movement."

The inside of Kahlia's tent was a mess. A single room, there were strips of cloth, strings of beads, and ropes of feathers draped over every piece of collapsible furniture. Some of the clothes were mine. At least, they were the clothes that had been given to me. I feared some of it might be absorbed into Kahlia's domestic mire. Not that I had developed any attachment to the garments, but they were almost all I had.

The chaos was hurting my head, but Kahlia seemed to have no trouble with it. Every time she needed something, she pulled it out without having to look for it. I found people like that eerie.

"Ma's right. Golds, coppers, maybe some light browns and oranges."

I thought they really were taking the flame symbolism too far.

"Tattoos would show up really—"

"I am not getting any tattoos."

She seemed surprised. As though what I said actually sounded odd. "Why not?"

"Marking my skin does not appeal to me."

"Why not?"

It was wonderful that these people were taking Karish and I on, but they were starting to irritate me. Did she really want me to tell her I thought permanently marking the skin was hideous and bizarre? "Why don't I like red wine? It isn't to my taste."

Kahlia didn't take offense. "Hm. Maybe a paste. Some kind of copper glitter. Not solid, but maybe curving lines along your arms and legs. And your face."

"I sweat when I dance," I told her bluntly. "Cosmetics will run."

"They're not cosmetics. Not like what the townies wear, anyway. We all sweat when we perform." She dug into a pile on the floor. "You don't wear anything on your feet when you dance, do you?"

"No."

She held out her hand, loops of small copper beads dangling from her fingers.

Two small hoops on one end, a mass of beads, a larger hoop on the other. I had no idea. I raised my eyebrows at her.

She put her foot through the large hoop and hooked the smaller hoops on her largest and second-smallest toes. And there it was, a beautiful delicate sandal with no sole. "This won't slip your steps, no?"

"I don't think so." The hoops might chafe a bit until I got used to them.

"And they'll catch the light well. Here's its mate."

And so it went. I wasn't sure why I was there, really, except for reference for size. Picking through what she had and what had been given to me, and without asking my opinion, she assembled an outfit that was exotic, daring, and looked utterly ridiculous on me.

"I am not wearing this."

She'd stuck to the color scheme. On my upper body I was wearing something little more substantial than my usual undergarment, a light brown halter that would offer my breasts adequate support for dancing but didn't do much to hide their shape. Kahlia spoke of having beads of a suitable color sewn onto it, but I couldn't have cared less because I was never going to be seen in public in it. Likewise the skirt—sort of—that rode low on the hips and consisted of wide flaps of light brown material that parted at the slightest movement. This was also to be beaded to be suitably flashy. Around my bared midriff Kahlia had clipped the lightest golden chain, just in case anyone was in danger of missing the fact that there was naked skin there.

There was no white braid telling everyone what I was. Kahlia was horrified with the idea of adding it. Maybe that was why I felt so naked.

Aye, that was it.

"The beading and the paste, and when your hair is done up proper, will make it all shine. The torch light will dance."

Was she not listening to me? "I am not wearing this."

"Of course you are." She looked me over, her eyes narrowed. "You won't carry it off if you don't stand proud."

"There is nothing wrong with my posture." True, it wasn't as rigid as Karish's could be, but then I'd had a normal childhood.

She rolled her eyes. "Not straight. Proud." And she pulled in a breath. Suddenly her breasts were much more prominent.

I raised an eyebrow. "My breasts are of what I am to be the most proud?" I asked dryly.

She grinned. "It is our asset most envied by men."

I imagined that depended on the man. And the breasts. "I lack your stature."

"It's not the size of them but how you display them that counts."

"I'm not displaying them at all. And this skirt." To demonstrate, I shifted a foot a hand span to the side. The cloth flaps fell away to reveal my leg up to the hip.

"A shorter solid skirt will ride up and leave you no modesty at all," Kahlia explained. "A longer solid skirt will fence your steps."

Unfortunately, she had a point. I took a few more experimental steps and hops. The cloth flaps always parted, and they threatened—or promised—a lot, but they never actually revealed anything other than leg. Still, "I'm not thin enough to carry off clothing like this."

She frowned. "Thin enough? You have a pleasing shape." She drew a fingertip from my ribs to my rather ample hips.

"I'm not slender like you." And she was gorgeous, not a scrap of extra flesh on her.

"That is one of the reasons Ma wants you. Because you look so different from the rest of us. And people who come to see you will then come to the rest of us. It is good for all of us."

Was she missing the point on purpose? "I look ridiculous in this, Kahlia. More important, I feel ridiculous. I'm not wearing this."

"This is not so different from what we wear. Do you think we look ridiculous?"

Just a little, to be honest, but, "You people seem able to make it work. You have a kind of flair that I lack."

"So you must learn flair."

"I don't think I can do that." Flair hadn't been part of my training.

"Leave behind the dead voice, for a start."

I frowned. "Dead voice?"

"Your voice never changes. No pitch to it."

"Of course it has pitch."

"Kai kai, a very very little. Most of your words all sound the same. Even when you ask questions. Your voice doesn't go up."

"I'm a Shield." Of course, that, by itself, was not a sufficient answer for these people. "We're trained to speak calmly, to maintain a moderate tone of voice."

"They should stop training you," she muttered.

"It is so we don't impose our emotional responses on others. It's part of our responsibilities to keep the environment calm. Because sometimes our Sources are very excitable."

"It's aggravating."

"My apologies." I made no effort to subdue the sarcasm ringing through my voice.

"Do you talk like that all the time?"

"I imagine so."

"I feel sorry for your lovers. Between your face and your eyes and your voice, I would have no idea what you were really feeling."

"My face?" What, there was something wrong with that, too?

"It's always blank. Everything about you is blank. Your voice, your eyes, your face. Your body, even, the way you move. So careful. It is discomforting."

This had been a really bad day. Why did these people think they could say whatever the hell they wanted to me? "A lot has happened to me today," I said. "And I'm not used to it. Perhaps we should delay this until tomorrow."

Kahlia caught my arm. "Maybe you're tired," she said. "Maybe you're angry with me. But I can't see it from your face."

"So?" She was really testing my patience. "My feelings are my business."

She whistled. "You don't want to be my friend?"

She was nearly as good as Karish in skipping from subject to subject with no thought to logic or how much it might hurt my head. And how was I supposed to answer that question? "I don't know yet."

She pouted. "You don't like me?"

Purported wise woman to petulant child in under a moment. "I don't know you yet."

"And you can't know me if I never show you how I feel about things, can you?"

Hell. Emotional people weren't supposed to have a good grasp on logic. "I was trained—"

"Your training doesn't matter here," she announced imperiously. "As a performer, you must love what you are doing, and you must show that love to the speccies. The dead voice and the dead eyes must go."

"Yes, ma'am." Did I really have a dead voice and dead eyes? I was supposed to appear calm, not emotionless. I mean, dead. That sounded awful.

"And walk proud."

"All right, all right." I was not walking around with my breasts thrust out. That just looked ridiculous.

"Come, then. They're waiting for us."

I followed her out of the tent. "Who?"

"Leverett, Sacey, Panol and Setter. You need to start working on your show."

Damn it, I was tired. And without knowing exactly how, I found myself in public with that ridiculous outfit. And people were staring. Not laughing, which was a relief, but definitely interested. No polite aversion of gazes here. People were as frank with their eyes as they were with their tongues.

I clenched my teeth. I refused to strut. I'd better not be blushing.

Kahlia led me a little farther up the road, out of sight of the tents. I was introduced to Sacey, a burly woman incongruous with the dainty wooden pipes she played. I eyed Panol and Setter. "Usually there need to be four stalkers." But then, there were usually four bars. I saw only two. That's all I had used at the trial the night before, but I had expected, for a proper performance, four bars.

"Well," Panol drawled, "the more of us you have, the more of us you have to pay."

"Ah," I said. I was disappointed to hear they expected to be paid, and angry with myself for being disappointed. Of course they needed to be paid if they were going to take time from their own performances. Though I hadn't heard that Panol and Setter did anything but handwork. "I'm not used to dancing with only two bars."

"That's what rehearsals are for." Kahlia patted me on the shoulder.

They once more expected me to dance directly on the ground. I couldn't keep that up. It would make a mess of my toes and ankles. "How do I go about getting benches made? Or one, at least." If I was dancing with only two bars, I supposed one bench might do. With some adjustments to the steps.

"Fin could probably make one," Panol said. "You'll have to wait until we get to Shade Valley, to get the right kind of wood. You'll have to pay for that, too."

I was caught between being irked at the reminder, and being irked at having to admit that I needed the reminder. "That'll be good." I looked at Sacey. "I've never danced to pipes before."

"Sounds like you've never done a lot of things, Leavy-kin," she retorted.

True enough.

The rehearsal was actually pleasant. We experimented with different music, different steps, different ways of moving. It was difficult to convince my body that this was not bench dancing as it knew it. Kahlia expected me to do more with my upper body and arms than just provide a counter balance. She wanted meaningless curving gestures, and more sway to my hips. At times, I wondered if she was just having me on for her own amusement, but no one else seemed to find what she was saying odd.

The drumming was different from what I expected while bench dancing. A more syncopated rhythm, pretty and stirring, but hard to dance to. It helped once Sacey started playing, too. The pipes added a plaintive, soulful air to the music that made it easier to engineer the twists and convolutions Kahlia seemed to feel were necessary.

But then I landed wrong and wrenched my ankle, and I

had to stop. Kahlia took me back to her tent, where she gave me a wrap and a green gel she told me to put on my ankle. When I asked her what I needed to pay for it, she was offended, which irritated me. She knew, by now, that I didn't have to pay for things in my own land. Obviously, I didn't know the etiquette concerning when to pay for things and when not to.

She forgave me when I begged sufficiently. Wasn't she gracious?

My fatigue, which I had forgotten during the rehearsal, flooded back to me on the way back to our tent. I couldn't wait to shut myself away from all the eyes. I couldn't wait to lie down and sleep and forget all this for a while.

Karish, hedonistic little rebel that he was, had once more laid his mat on the ground outside the tent so he could lie out in the open air and stare up at the night sky. He seemed contemplative. Not an adjective I would have applied to him, once upon a time.

Looking at Karish, I almost failed to notice the man who seemed to be examining the back of our tent. I didn't remember meeting him, but that didn't mean anything, as I didn't remember half the names or faces I had been introduced to so far. I was annoyed that he seemed intent on eavesdropping. "Can I help you with something?" I asked him.

Then I was embarrassed, because that had come out a lot more snappishly than I had intended.

He bowed, muttered something I couldn't understand, and backed away.

Fine. I didn't feel like company anyway.

Karish had bolted upright and he was staring at me, his eyes widened, his mouth dropped open.

Damn it. I'd actually forgotten what I was wearing. How was that possible? I was suddenly freezing, and that didn't make sense. It wasn't that cold and I was a Shield.

"You are not wearing that!" he sputtered.

I raised an eyebrow at him. "Kahlia seems to feel it is necessary."

He drew his knees up to his chest, looking very ill at ease. "You can't wear that, Lee. It's . . . indecent."

I agreed, but I couldn't tell him that. "I never knew you had such stringent morals, Taro."

"You've never walked around in anything like that before!" he retorted.

"It's not that different from what everyone else wears." And yes, I was aware of the hypocrisy.

"We are not them!"

I sighed. "Please, Taro." I'd already had this argument, only speaking his side. I'd lost. And I really didn't need reminding of how ridiculous I looked. "It's been such a long day."

He rested his forearms on his knees, pushing a hand through his hair. "Am I superficial?" he asked me.

Where did that come from? "Of course not."

He scowled. "Don't lie to me."

"I'm not." I sat down next to him on the mat, trying to find a posture that was both comfortable and unrevealing. I didn't know if there was any such thing.

"Then why do these people all tell me I live on the surface and speak without air and throw at me all sorts of other metaphors I'm not sure I understand?"

Ah. Now he knew how I felt. "I find these people extremely arrogant."

"That doesn't necessarily mean they don't know what they're talking about."

Well, true. Unfortunately. "I thought you were superficial, too, when I first met you. But it wasn't anything you did, really. I was expecting to find you superficial."

"They have no expectations. What's their excuse?"

"They don't know you, Taro."

"That doesn't stop them from disliking me a lot."

"I don't think that's it." Because how could they not like Karish? He was adorable. "I think they just believe in expressing themselves. Telling the truth as they see it." No matter how much it hurt.

He snorted. "I'll say."

I opened the small bundle that held the gel, rubbing it on my ankle. It left a pleasant tingle. "I don't have a dead voice, do I? And dead eyes?"

His scowl returned momentarily. "No!" he answered vehemently. But he ruined the effect when, after a pause, he added, "But I thought you did, or something like it, back in the bad old days."

"Oh." How awful. Dead eyes. Was that what people thought of me?

"It's just, I know you're all trained to stay calm, but I never met a Shield who . . . did it as thoroughly as you do. And sometimes you hide what you feel when it would be better to let it show. Though, after today, I have a better appreciation for discretion, believe me."

I wasn't sure what I thought of that answer. Kind of as if, yes, I had dead eyes, but he'd learned to appreciate it. Or something. So, what, he could enjoy my flaws?

"What's that you're doing?" He nodded at my ankle.

"I hurt my ankle a little. Kahlia gave me this. It feels nice." It kind of tingled, and it smelled like nothing I'd encountered before, fresh and light and pleasing.

"You shouldn't be dancing on the ground. Especially after walking all day."

"I don't think I have a choice. For the time being, anyway. Try this, though. Maybe it'll feel good on your burn."

He dipped his fingers into the gel, sniffing it. Then, before I could stop him, he caught my shin and pulled my injured ankle into his lap. He spread the gel over my skin.

Of course it made the pain slither right away. I couldn't be sure whether that was the gel working, or whether it was the result of our bond, which always seemed to ease our aches and pains. Handy, except it really only lasted as long as we stayed in physical contact.

It felt really, really good. Better than I was comfortable with, so I pulled on my foot.

He stopped me from removing my foot by holding my

leg just under the knee. And giving me a look that said he was not in the mood to be annoyed.

Neither was I. The ankle wasn't that bad.

But I left my foot in his lap. I watched him use careful long fingers to dip into the gel, which he slowly spread over the bone of my ankle. Then along the edge of my foot, under the arch, over the top, down to my toes. I pulled on my ankle again, and once more, he wouldn't release me.

"Karish . . ."

"What's the matter, Lee? Think this will make you lose your vaunted control?"

"Of course not." Prat.

Then he just looked at me, and grinned, the most evil look in his eye. And I knew he'd interpreted my last words as a challenge. Which I resented. If he wanted a challenge, he could go climb a mountain.

Chapter Eight

The first settlement on the itinerary was Shade Valley. I was expected to perform in Shade Valley. Forget that I had done nothing like this before, and hadn't had a chance to properly learn how to prostitute my talent for money. Whenever we stopped in a settlement of some kind, I would be expected to put on a show.

After the severe sunburn he'd gotten, it was the first day that Karish was able to walk, properly covered and wearing a hat. He moved stiffly, awkwardly, his clothes as loose as he could find. He was not a hat man. With his skin an angry red and peeling and his eyes squinting in the sun, he was not a thing of beauty.

I had to smile. Poor boy.

The presence of Shade Valley wasn't announced by a valley. Just more dense foliage that showed signs of a settlement. The undergrowth appeared to have been cut back, and the footpath widened into more of a road. We drew to a halt.

No one started unpacking their gear. That seemed unusual to me. Previously, as soon as we had stopped, everyone erupted into instantaneous activity to set up camp.

I turned to the man who had been walking behind us all day. Beril, the fire-eater, who was very tall and unpleasantly skinny. "Is there something amiss?" I asked him.

"We don't usually camp here," he said. "There are flat grounds on the night side of the main scoop. That's where we usually stop."

All I really understood from that explanation was that we were experiencing a break in routine. That was enough. A change in routine was never good.

Shortly thereafter, we were moving again. I remembered where we were, and why, and my anxiety returned. In a few short hours, I would be performing in front of people, trying to convince them to give me money for nothing more than the privilege of seeing me. I wasn't ready for it. I didn't know what I was doing. Standing *proud*. Trying to be alluring. That wasn't me. I was no performer. The very idea was ridiculous. I'd come off looking pathetic. Laughable.

The residents of Shade Valley had lined the street to watch us pass. And it didn't take long to realize their attention was not imbued with any element of welcome. In fact, there was outright hostility coming from some of them. Lovely. There was my audience.

Children pointed at Karish and me as we passed. So did a fair number of adults. Yes, yes, we knew we were freaks.

It was hearing the muttering of the others in the troupe that let me know this was not normal. We kept walking, and everywhere we went there were residents watching us. Some of them were holding out objects to us, and they looked like the tokens I'd seen on the tents of the troupe. They were not being offered to us, but seemed to be used to . . . ward us off?

We passed an area of empty flat ground and I assumed that was the camping ground Beril had spoken of. We didn't stop there. Shortly after, I realized we had left the village behind.

"All right, what happened?" I asked.

"I don't know," said Beril. "Word will come back to us."

And it did. It didn't take long. The word, oddly enough, was "curse."

"Ah," said Beril, as though that explained everything.

"A curse?" I had to ask. "Really?" Was he serious?

Beril moved up a little, so he was walking beside me. "Ma had a curse put on her a while back. Sometimes the stops don't want us staying because of it. Shade Valley always let us before, but they have a new Speaker. Last time we were there, he wasn't happy to see us. I guess he's talked enough of his folk around to his way of thinking."

Who could blame them? This was a curse, after all. Serious stuff. "What's the nature of this curse?"

"If Ma, or any of us while we're part of the troupe, stay in one place for more than four days, something bad will happen."

"Like what?"

"Usually someone dies."

I stared at him. Now he had my attention. "Someone has died?"

"Kai."

"Who died?" What kind of people had we hooked up with?

"We used to have a blade throwing act. Ciya would throw knives and stars and axes at her husband. She was really good."

All sorts of really bad jokes sprang to mind, but not off my tongue. Who would stand there and let someone else throw blades at them? It was just stupid.

"We went to Center Circle. The biggest city on the island. We were having a really good run, so we stayed longer than usual. A week. And then, during the act, Ciya's axe came apart after she threw it, and it cut Rennie's hand clean off."

"Good gods!" Karish muttered, and my stomach clenched.

"Rennie died from the shock. Ciya left us."

"That's awful." I was picturing it in my mind, what a

severed hand looked like. Thank you, Beril. "But there are any number of reasons for an accident like that. Fatigue. Distraction." Logic. The fact that if you do something dangerous again and again, the chances of being injured from it increase.

"We usually stay only one night in Parrot Range. It's a small place, not much money to be made. Last year a tsunami forced us to stay too long. Vala's little one got lost in it, and he drowned."

All right, two deaths would make a person pause and think. But that still didn't mean there were such things as curses.

"I don't care to go through the list, Leavy," he said solemnly. "But there are more."

They lived in a place with no Pairs. They had dangerous jobs. They were always on the road, never establishing any kinds of roots. Of course there were accidents, fatalities.

Beril shifted the straps of his pack on his bare shoulder. "May you never know rest. May darkness grip your heels. May you wander the lands in search of peace that will never come."

"That's a quote?"

He nodded. "I've heard it often enough."

"So, you mean, someone actually put a curse on her? Deliberately?" I'd thought he was saying the troupe merely had permanent bad luck. But someone actually said something like "I'm cursing you" and expected it to work?

These people were unbelievable. Captain Vo and her crew thinking our channeling was unlucky. Atara with her good omens and her trick for deciding directions. I supposed flipping a coin wouldn't work when one had more than two destinations to choose from. And then these people of Shade Valley who wouldn't let us stay because of a curse. A curse!

"It was her brother. Yesit. He thought he would get this troupe from their mother, Fiona, because *she* got it from his father, when his father skipped out. But he never worked with the troupe, scurrying around and coming back only when he ran out of coin. Ma was always right in there, working hard, and she was there when Fiona died. So she got it. A couple years later, Yesit shows up and demands the troupe, and Ma says no, and good thing, too, because Yesit would have ruined us. Yesit gets mad and curses Atara and the troupe and that's that."

"And you really believe the curse works?"

"He performed it over a red pentacle with ferret fat candles."

Oh, that clinched it then.

"How is the curse to be broken?" Because that was how it worked, wasn't it? For every curse there was a means of breaking it.

"Yesit said Ma would need to beg forgiveness from him, and give the troupe back to him."

"And she's never thought about doing it?" If she really believed in it, why not? It wasn't fair, but it was better than being surrounded by fatal accidents and thinking you were responsible for them.

"Of course not!" He seemed horrified by the suggestion. "She has done no wrong!"

"I see." I was impressed with myself. I was sure I sounded as though I believed this was a rational conversation. "And you don't mind traveling with her under these conditions?"

"I have no family," he said.

"Ah." I didn't dig, even though I didn't know why Beril's lack of family meant traveling with a woman he believed to be cursed was a viable option. Lack of family was never a good thing to ask questions about.

We walked for several more hours, and it was almost dark before we stopped. I was nearly ready to cry with relief, I'd been so incredibly bored. How could these people do it, walking all day every day their entire lives? What a colossal waste of time. Really.

Didn't the kids have to go to school? Did they even know how to read?

My relief was short-lived. Karish and I, after setting up our tent, had barely had time to scarf down a few cold rice balls when Kahlia was back and prodding me to my feet to practice. Because I was a collected and mature Shield, I didn't smack her.

But as I was being put through my paces, pounding my aching feet into the ground and putting more sway into my hips and more arch into my back just so I could change an athletic event into a sweaty erotic episode of ridicule, I was thinking that it was a good thing I didn't believe in curses. Because if I did, I'd be running screaming from my life. Yanked from the roster, sent on a ridiculous mission by an indifferent monarch, made to endure a horrible sea voyage, dumped into an ignorant society that didn't know we weren't supposed to need money, then lured into a superstitious and ostracized troupe. If there were gods up there, surely they were laughing.

Chapter Nine

Hardly Fare There was the next settlement along the road. Strangely enough, I was even more nervous upon entering it than I had been Shade Valley. Because, really, what were the chances that this village would be as superstitious as the last one? I was really going to have to perform that night.

As soon as we stopped, Karish took off to help unload the wagon. I had nothing to do. I stretched out on the ground in the shade cast by our tent, and earned some sounds of disapproval from the islanders. It was too hot to lie inside the tent, so they could just not look if they found it so disturbing. What was wrong with these people anyway, that they could prance around practically naked but found it immoral to lie on the ground?

I dribbled some water on my face. Rather than providing any relief, it seemed to make my skin sizzle.

Why did this place have to be so hot? I wondered whether any of these people had ever had a properly cold drink. If they knew what cold even felt like.

Snow. I missed snow.

But then I noticed someone standing over me. I didn't like it. I opened my eyes. It was Karish. "Back already?"

"You've been sleeping all this time?"

"I suppose so." I noticed the sunlight was much softer. "I'm a lazy wench." I sat up.

"You'll burn."

I hoped not. I didn't need yet another thing to feel irritated about.

He sat beside me on the ground. "You have to dance tonight," he said. "In front of other people, I mean."

"Aye." I preferred not to think about it until I absolutely had to.

"Are you nervous?"

"Aye."

He looked surprised. What, had he thought I wouldn't admit it? Or that I didn't even feel it? Of course I was nervous. Anyone would be nervous.

"It is important to you that I watch?"

Damn it. I had been trying to avoid thinking about that. When I was honest with myself, I admitted I really wanted him there. I didn't want to be out there, dancing, exposing myself in front of all those strangers, with no one there who knew who I really was. But there was still that part of me that dreaded him seeing me do this ridiculous thing, this dance. My pride cringed at it.

"You don't want me there?" Karish asked in a neutral voice.

"It's not like proper bench dancing, Taro," I said. "I feel so foolish when I do it." Not entirely true. I felt foolish before I started doing it, and after I stopped doing it. While I was doing it, I kind of forgot what I must look like to others. "I look so stupid. I'd rather not have you see me like that."

For a few moments, he just pressed his lips together and appeared to think about that. I didn't immediately recognize that he was trying to keep from smiling. "You're worried about looking foolish, what a shock," he snickered.

"Oh, shut up."

"It's only me, Lee. Is that the only reason you don't want me there?"

"Aye. And, because, bench dancing isn't your interest. If you don't think it's laughable, you'll probably find it boring."

"I never found bench dancing boring, Lee. Just sometimes the tournaments go on a little long. And it's not my choice for gambling."

"This isn't bench dancing. It's a horrible, ridiculous perversion of it." With costumes and cosmetics. And people throwing coins at me. If I was lucky.

"Lee," he said, sounding patient. I hated it when he sounded patient. "Do you want me there or not?"

I looked down at my clenched hands. "I want you there," I muttered.

"Fine," he said tonelessly. "Then I'll be there."

He couldn't have sounded more disinterested if he'd practiced.

Most of the others, after resting briefly and eating, left the camp to set up their performances by the street. The children went out seeking age mates. Karish left me to fetch and carry for anyone who needed it. I was forbidden by Kahlia to oversee the setup of my performance area, as I might be seen by a potential "speccy."

A large part of me was hoping someone would come back and tell me the residents of Hardly Fare There refused to be exposed to Atara's curse. Or that it was the wrong phase of the moon to have strangers within the town limits. Or that no one wanted to have to look at those hideous Northern freaks. Anything to get out of performing. Because I really really really didn't want to do it.

I briefly considered breaking my own leg. Except that it would hurt. And it would make traveling a nightmare.

I would have been happy going on as we were. Just walking from place to place, wearing borrowed clothes and eating donated food. Because really, how different was that from the usual life of a Shield?

Except that the food had run out. And if I didn't get any coins that night, there would be no food tomorrow. None. I just couldn't believe it. What if I was terrible? What if I got nothing? What would we do?

Well, I, for one, wasn't going to panic. At least, not until it actually happened.

Once the heat became a little less stifling, I gathered some water from the stream and washed the sweat from my skin. I went through my routine in my head. I thought about chewing my nails.

And then Kahlia came, bearing an armload of stuff. "Time to get ready," she announced cheerfully.

I looked up at the sun, past its zenith but still high in the sky. "I thought I wasn't supposed to start before dark."

She tsked, kicking off her sandals. "My, but you learn slow, Leavy-kin. It takes time to prepare. Shall we go in?"

I wasn't thrilled to be in the tent when the sun was still up. Even with the flaps up to let in fresh air, it was a stifling place, made worse by the lighting of candles.

"You really are spending a lot of time on this," I said. It could be interpreted as an expression of gratitude. It was really more of a question. She was always there.

"I am moved not only by pure spirit." She grinned. "If they love you, it flows over. More will come to see me and Corla and the others. You are strange and beautiful and word will carry before us to the next village and the one after that. If all is good people will hear of you in Center Circle long before we reach there, and everyone will want to see you and, also, us." She knelt on the mat and started laying things out, producing lines of bowls, tiny corked pots, and short sticks of various colors. "There is only one first night, and it must go right."

"No pressure," I muttered.

"Change into your costume."

"Yes, ma'am."

While I was changing into the ridiculous, scanty outfit I hadn't gone near since it had been assembled, my tormentor was mixing pastes and lining up small colored sticks. "Spirits!" she hissed. "You haven't sewn the beads on."

Oh. I looked down at the plain brown garments I was barely wearing and shrugged. "I don't know how to sew."

Her eyes widened in shock. "You can't sew!" She sounded scandalized.

"Of course not."

"What do you mean, of course not? What do you do when you lose a button?"

"I leave the shirt at the haberdashery and have them sew it on." Or, more likely, simply got a new shirt.

"Can't you do *anything*?"

Back in my own sane, comfortable world, I wouldn't have felt the need to glare at her. Roll my eyes, certainly, but not glare. Here, however—"I am a Shield." And that meant plenty, thank you very much.

She sniffed. "That's no use here."

Oh aye. Then why was someone out there channeling?

"It's too late to do anything about it now. Sit down."

I frowned, as I didn't care for her brusque tone, but I sat. "Did you play your games today?"

"You mean my shells?"

"Aye."

"Of course."

"Did you do well?"

"Well enough. It's always better on the second day."

So it wasn't a poor day's earning that had her in her little mood. I didn't know where else to safely prod, and I realized for all her constant presence and her brutal honesty, I really knew very little about her.

And that was because we always talked about me, when we were together. My past, my dancing, what was wrong with my personality. I should make more of an effort to turn things around, so there would be more discussion about her.

The problem was that it would be an effort. Just being around her took work. I felt like I had to be so careful about what I said, to spare myself the blasts of her honesty.

"I'm going to put this on your skin," she said then, holding out a small bowl of unpleasant-looking, opaque paste. "On your face, arms, shoulders and legs. It's to prevent your cosmetics from running."

"Ah," I said. Wasn't really looking forward to having that rubbed all over my skin. It looked vile.

She was quick but thorough as she spread the paste on my limbs. The paste turned out to be odorless and, while slightly greasy, not at all uncomfortable. In fact, it felt nice to have her spreading it on, her fingers light but slightly calloused, giving her touch a pleasant friction. It relaxed me.

"You'll have to sit still for this next part," she warned me, wiping her hands off with a cloth. She picked up one of the small sticks.

She was working near my eyes. Joy. But the end of the stick was soft, her grip on my chin was gentle and sure, and her use of the stick was confident and careful as she drew along my eyes. The other stick was for my lips, an odd dark brown color that I couldn't think would look attractive. But what the hell, she was engineering the whole look. I had to trust her. I supposed.

Then there was another bowl. Another paste, orangey, sort of, and it glittered. "Now this is going to be fun," Kahlia promised with a grin.

"What is it?"

"Your tattoos."

"No tattoos," I objected promptly.

"Only for a night, silly Shield."

She said the word strangely. Not quite derogatory. Not with any sort of respect. Almost like she was trying to tease but, not having any real idea what a Shield was, missing the mark.

She dipped her finger into the paste, then drew her index finger down my nose.

"Do we really need to be drawing attention to my nose?" I asked.

"Hush, you foolish child," she chided me in a low, gentle voice.

Next, just over my eyebrows, along the cheekbones, and over my jawline. She lightly tapped the tip of her pinky over my lips. She dipped into the bowl again and spread more of the cool mixture over my throat, along the jugular, and then following the line of my collarbones.

The paste was cool on my skin. The silence of the tent was soothing to my ears. I couldn't help relaxing a little. It was almost, almost, comfortable enough to make me drowsy.

The next step in the process was more artistic use of the paste, swirling it in coiling lines down my arms and legs, over my stomach and the back of my shoulders. This took a while.

"Are you nervous?" she asked.

For some reason, the question I had no difficulty with from Karish irritated me mightily coming from her. "I have been bench dancing most of my life," I informed her coolly. "I won't let you down." I hoped.

"You'll do better than that," she said, drying the paste on my skin by waving a fan over it. "You'll steal everyone's breath tonight. Everyone who sees you will fall in love with you. If they haven't already."

Something in her warm tones made me shiver.

I didn't want anyone to fall in love with me. That never ended well.

"Look," she said, fanning that last bit of paint. She moved a couple of candles around, then took one of my hands and drew my arm out.

It was a shock. Glittering flames seemed to writhe over my arms and legs. With an expression of pride, Kahlia handed me a mirror. Wide green eyes, dramatically curving lines surrounding them, stared back at me. My lips seemed full and the lines of glitter over my cheekbones, jawline, throat and collarbones gave them a strange emphasis they lacked in the everyday.

The whole image looked uncomfortably bizarre. Like a caricature of myself.

"Imagine meeting her as a stranger," Kahlia whispered. "For the first time, this is what you see."

And at her words, it was as though my perceptions just flipped over. A grotesque perversion of me became a stranger, a glorious exotic stranger of flair and drama. Wide-eyed and vibrant and absolutely stunning.

I couldn't believe that was me.

I was gorgeous.

I'd never been gorgeous before. It made me feel strange. Not in a bad way, though. "Gods, Kahlia." I reached up to touch a cheekbone.

"Ah ah. Wait 'til it dries." With a thumb and forefinger she caught my wrist and kept my hand from my face. She was beaming. "I'm only showing what there is, to those too blind to see on their own."

"No," I objected softly. "You've done magic, you have."

And her smile slipped away. "Have you water?"

"Uh." How was that for a sharp shift in subject? "You're thirsty?"

"No. I mean to wash after you perform. You won't want to sleep in this paint. And you won't feel like gathering water after you've shown." She began collecting up the items she had brought, tossing them into her bag. "I'll fetch some for you. Have you soap?"

Had I offended her in some way? How? Should I ask? "Of course, but you don't have to—"

"I'll be right back." She was out of the tent.

Feeling a little disoriented by her abrupt departure and having no idea what to do about it, I ended up staring at myself in the mirror.

I couldn't believe what I was seeing. I couldn't believe what I was seeing was me. I had always been plain, almost bland. If someone had shown up with a magic wand offering to make me beautiful I wouldn't have said no, but being plain had never disturbed me. It was what I was, and it had its advantages. But this face I was seeing in the mirror, it was almost otherworldly. It would certainly be hard to forget. How could mere paint do so much?

The tent flap was pushed aside. The dying dusk light flashed in. Karish stopped midentrance and stared at me. "What the—"

"It's for my performance," I said. A little proudly, I had to confess.

He didn't respond, just kept looking at me.

"You don't like it?" I was stunned. How could he not?

I was disappointed. A sharp ache blossomed in my chest, all out of nowhere.

He was so glorious. I had thought, for a brief moment, that for once I might be able to match him.

"It took great artistry to create the appearance," he said.

The hand holding the mirror dropped of its own volition. "Zaire, you're being diplomatic." Always a bad sign.

"You don't look like you anymore."

"That's the point."

"It shouldn't be. It's your skill that matters."

"Not here. Here it's about the show of it."

"That's the problem." He held up his hands before I could protest. Not that I was going to. I felt too deflated to want to say anything. "I know, I know. You don't really have a choice. You have to go through all this as part of the job. And I'm sorry about that."

I wrapped up the mirror. I wished I could wash all of the mess off my skin. I didn't dare. Kahlia would kill me.

"Can I come in?" Kahlia called from outside.

Karish scowled.

"Of course," I answered.

She squeezed in by Karish, who was unwilling to make much room for her. "Water for after." She hefted the bucket before placing it in a safe corner. "And I thought of this. You can wear it on the way to the bars." It was a plain hooded cloak, of rough brown material. "I know it's got no flash, but that's all to the good. People will be taken aback by the dazzling creature underneath." She grinned at Karish. "Isn't she beautiful?"

"I prefer her as she was," he said, reaching for my face.

She slapped his hand away.

He gaped at her, shocked.

"You'll blur the paint," she explained.

He glared at her.

She smirked back at him, an air of challenge about her stance.

"Are you sure people will even show up to see this?" I asked hastily, feeling a distraction was in order. "How will they even know I'm here?"

"We've been telling them," she said, sounding like she thought the question was stupid. "Leavy the Flame Dancer. Come and be entranced."

Oh lord. I hated that name already.

She saw my expression and giggled. She was too old to be giggling. "I'm going to go and help set up. I want to make sure it has the right flair. Come out as soon as it's completely dark. Just follow the road. You'll know it when you see it." She winked at Karish and ducked back out of the tent.

"I don't like her," he announced.

"Why not?" Yes, she could be too blunt, but there were worse things. "I don't know what I'd have done without her, to be honest."

He snorted.

I looked down at myself. And I saw myself through his eyes. The short skirt, the scanty top, the childish paint all over the limbs. I did look ridiculous. What was I thinking, being seen by people like this?

"I know you need the costume for the performance, Lee," he said in a soft voice. "I've seen the others. This is the way it's done. I just . . ." He shrugged. "You remind me of the Empress's court, with all that paint. It's all so fake."

I felt a spurt of irritation. I didn't need to be made to feel this way just before exposing myself in front of strangers.

"Cosmetics are no different from fashionable clothes," I pointed out. "You fuss over your clothes all the time."

"Ah, but I'm a useless peacock," he retorted. "Decoration is all I'm good for." He paused a moment. "Though not even that here, apparently."

I pressed my lips together to keep from speaking. I was not going to pander to his ego after he'd just finished shredding mine.

He pushed his hands through his hair, then shook his head. "Don't mind me, Lee. I'm being a brat." He offered up a weak, bent smile. "How are you feeling?"

Annoyed. Embarrassed. Nervous. Oddly cold. Very hungry. Slightly panicked.

I didn't want to talk about it. I shrugged.

The sun slid down behind the horizon too quickly, and the knot in my stomach spread to my chest and threatened to crawl into my limbs and freeze my muscles.

I pulled in a deep, deep breath. I was nervous. Yes, I was nervous. There was no point being nervous. Because what would happen if I did badly? Nothing life threatening, not for me or for anyone else. There would be jeering. People would leave in the middle of it. Hopefully there wouldn't be any flying vegetation. There was great possibility for humiliation, but nothing fatal. I could handle humiliation. I just needed a few years and a cave. Really, it was nothing to be afraid of.

Oh, and the fact that Karish and I would starve to death. Mustn't forget that.

"We should get going." I picked up Kahlia's cloak, draping it over my shoulders, assuming Kahlia wouldn't have given it to me if it were a danger to the paint.

"I imagine you should have this up," Karish suggested, standing before me and drawing the hood up over my head. "Heighten the suspense and all." He fussed with it a few moments, settling the folds to his satisfaction. "That'll do. Ready to go?"

No. "This is the stupidest thing I've ever done," I confessed.

"Oh no." He waved a hand in dismissal. "You've done much stupider things."

I glared at him.

He grinned, then leaned down for a quick peck on my lips. "You'll be brilliant, Lee. Don't worry."

I brushed the trace of glitter off his lips with my thumb and sighed. "All right. No use delaying anymore."

I breathed very carefully as we walked, trying to settle my stomach. Too much of a panic would render me unable to dance at all. We walked past the other tents, huddled close together in the small clearing we had cut out ourselves. And then by some sort of field that smelled unpleasantly damp, the foliage stripped out of the ground year after year by the residents, opening up the sky to our view. And then some small squat buildings of the same open, multipurpose styles we'd seen elsewhere.

We passed the jugglers throwing torches at each other, and Rinis, who was coiling and jumping in candlelight. Corla was reading palms to the gullible in a tiny and intimate circle of black felt. With so much to see, no one paid attention to us, and I really wished circumstances would keep it that way.

As Kahlia had assured me, the site of my humiliation was easy to find. We heard the music first, and light and playful sort of drumming with the odd pipe notes tossed in. Then we traversed a bend in the road and saw the scattering of torches, glinting off the skin of far too many spectators.

"Damn," I muttered.

I felt the lightest touch on my shoulder. "They'll love you, Lee," Karish said. "They won't be able to help it."

I didn't care about making anyone love me. I just wanted to avoid laughter.

I wondered if I should tell him Kahlia had said almost exactly the same thing.

"Must they have started the music so soon?" I griped. "They're attracting too many people." The crowd among the torches was much larger than those around the jugglers or Rinis.

"That's the point, isn't it? To get as many people here as possible?"

Don't talk to me of logic. "Shut up, Karish."

He chuckled, the bastard. "I don't think I've ever seen you so jittery, Lee."

I wasn't jittery. I was apprehensive. A whole different emotional state.

Kahlia, the wench, must have been looking out for me. "And now!" she called out, and the music stopped. "Your wait is over! Ladies and gentlemen, watch and admire, be entranced and bedazzled by the mistress of fire and air! Here she is! Leavy the Flame Dancer!" And Karish, with his usual sense of drama, slipped the cloak from me from behind. So all of a sudden, I was completely exposed.

People turned to follow the direction of Kahlia's pointed arm. They all stared. Some of them gasped. Was I that freakish looking? Was everything covered as it should be? Were they all thinking I was the most hideous idiot they'd ever seen? They parted, leaving a path for me to walk to the bars.

Hell. What a nightmare. What was I supposed to do? How was I supposed to get from here to there?

Well, it took a step. Forcing my head high and my shoulders back—I refused to thrust out my breasts—and keeping my gaze trained on Kahlia, I took a step, and then another.

And Leverett slid his fingertips over the drum, in time with each step. Everyone was silent, watching me in the dark as I took step after step, each footfall emphasized with a smattering from the drum.

Zaire, this was awful.

"Oh, I know what you are all thinking!" Kahlia shouted. "You have all seen bench dancers. Every sole-hole village has someone who can claim to dance. But as we all know, the fumbling of our poor dancers lacks the grace, the beauty, the pure Northern magic, of the dancers of the frosted lands."

The frosted lands. A rather poetic way to describe cities drowning in snow for half of every year.

"Our Leavy has been dancing since before she could walk."

Not quite that long.

"She has been touring the Northern continent, defeating all who come against her with her beauty and her power."

Actually, I lost more often than I won.

"And now, after years of pleading, we have lured her down among our people, to share her gift with us. You are the few privileged to see her first performance among us. Welcome her!"

They most obligingly applauded. I was finally free of the audience and stepped between the bars. I noticed Panol and Setter were looking particularly naked, wearing nothing more than scraps of red cloth about the waist that barely—barely—hid the genitals and buttocks. A light dusting of glitter had their dark muscles gleaming in the torchlight. I looked at Leverett, who was identically undressed. Sacey and Kahlia wore a few more straps, which seemed to almost cover their breasts, though I wouldn't have wanted to make any guarantees for modesty once they started moving.

Leverett rapped a roll off his drum, smart and sharp. A second roll echoed off the night sky, disappearing into the silence. At the third roll, Panol and Setter began moving the bars, low off the ground.

The idea was for me to begin with a short demonstration of almost real bench dancing. Or as real as it could get, with only two bars, no bench and no competitor. I was to show them all that I was a proper bench dancer, with all the skills required by the sport. And then, after, I was to get weird.

It wasn't at all the same as the real thing, of course. But it felt nice, something of a warm-up. Nice and easy swinging of the legs, working out the aches of the day. It was soothing, and it calmed my nerves a little.

The spectators, though, weren't terribly impressed. They applauded after Leverett and I came to a halt, but it was polite applause. I could tell. And that didn't feel wonderful. A few coins were tossed. Even I knew they were of the smallest currency. Pity money.

But before I could feel more than the first flare of disappointment and apprehension, Leverett started drumming again, a livelier beat. A few bars in and Sacey joined him with the pipes. Sprightly, exciting music, really more suited to ballroom dancing than bench, but I could move to it. The bars went up just a little higher and I leapt over them, letting the music guide me into throwing in those hip swings and arm gestures Kahlia seemed to find so important.

Thank the gods for the music. I could concentrate on it, follow it, let it move me. It shielded me from feeling too stupid about what I was doing. And when it sped up, thinking became even harder.

It stopped too abruptly, and for a moment I thought I was going to trip over the suddenly halted bars. But the applause was much louder, much more enthusiastic, so I supposed no one noticed. Many more coins were thrown, and I watched this, dazed. Apparently they liked what they saw, though I wasn't sure why. It wasn't proper dancing of any kind, really.

Karish and I would be able to eat. I wondered if it would be possible to buy food immediately after my performance.

Then Sacey handed the pipes over to Kahlia and picked up the sand singer. My stomach, which had settled, roiled up again. This was the one I was most afraid of. I sought Karish out in the crowd, suddenly afraid that he might have left. But he was there, and easy to spot in the crowd with his pale skin and clothing that covered him from throat to ankle. His eyes looked so black.

Which was a stupid thing to think. His eyes were always black.

The first sinuous note of the sand singer slithered through the air. It wrapped right around my heart and

squeezed. Everyone in the audience stilled once more. The
next note found me moving my arms in a long winding
sweep with no prodding from my brain, my spine bending
of its own accord, my body twisted by the long, reaching
note.

The pipes and drums joined in together and then I
just
stopped
thinking.

It wasn't as though I wasn't aware of what I was doing,
because, oh, I was. I could see the black night and even the
multitude of stars. I could smell the torches. The hard
ground stung and scraped my feet. But I didn't think about
anything. I couldn't. The music invaded every curve of my
body and every corner of my mind. Muscles working and
stretching, limbs curving and leaping, all of it driven by the
music with my brain having nothing to do with any of it. It
was hot and fast and hard and so so glorious.

But it wasn't enough. The music called me, I moved, but
it awakened a drive in me, and I was all alone up there. I
craved something more. Hair around my hands, skin beneath my tongue, a form to wrap my legs around, to arch
against. I moved, searching for it, but there was nothing but
earth and air, and the lack was almost painful.

And then, again, it all stopped. My muscles trembling,
breath burning through my throat, the sound of shouting
penetrated the fog in my brain. Something other than the
music seemed to have gotten control of my body and I
was dimly aware of being dragged somewhere, tripping
over the uneven ground. Noise was crowding into my
head and I couldn't make sense of anything. I couldn't
see.

And then I felt the right touch. Hands sliding over my
skin, exciting and claiming and possessive. I reached for
them, for that touch. It felt so good. I wanted to melt into it.

But instead I was tripping again, and walking, and the
shouting seemed to have fallen behind, though music still

seemed to be reverberating through my skull. I could still feel that particular touch, grasped too hard around my wrist, and I wanted more of it elsewhere. "Karish?"

There was no response.

Vaguely, I became aware that it was night, and we were on the road. Alone.

I yanked hard on his hand and he stumbled to a halt. I wrapped myself around him, tangling my legs with his, pressing against him as hard as I could and pulling his head down by his hair.

His mouth opened against mine and I ground against him when he pulled me up so I could wrap my legs around his waist. It wasn't close enough and my blood was racing so hard I thought I would explode and the music was just so loud. I shrieked as the world spun.

I shrieked again when something wet and icy cold slapped onto the overheated skin of my nearly bare back, a stick or something digging into my flesh. It hurt, it rattled the music in my head, and cleared some of the fog.

I was lying on the damp ground, arms and legs wrapped around Karish, and we were going to have sex right then and there if I didn't do something about it.

Did I want to do something about it?

His hips were settled into mine, grinding, his hot tongue trailing up my throat.

Sometimes I really hated—hated—the rules. Sometimes they seemed so stupid.

I deliberately jabbed myself on the stick, the spark of pain spiking through the lust rushing through me. "I'm sorry, Taro," I gasped. "We have to stop." Oh aye, that was convincing.

He kissed me, and ah gods, he was good at that.

Another jab of the stick, and the hand so conveniently buried in his hair grabbed a fistful and yanked. "Stop, Karish!" I said, sharpening my tones. "It's the music! It's just the music! Please!"

Karish froze. I pulled my arms from him, taking my

feet from the backs of his legs and settling them on the ground. He was shaking, and he had closed his eyes.

I loved the feel of his weight on me. I could still hear the music in my mind. My blood was still racing, my breath still flowing hard, and it was all I could do not to wrap around Karish again. I pressed into the stick again.

"I'm sorry," I whispered, humiliation slicing through the arousal. "I'm so sorry." That last performance was obviously a very bad idea. Wasn't going to be doing that again. Ever.

After another moment, Karish carefully raised himself off me. He stood and stepped back up onto the road. I sat up, hugging my knees to my chest. I closed my eyes and breathed.

Why the hell shouldn't we have sex, if we wanted? It was just a rule. Not even a rule. A custom. A guideline. Advice. General advice applied to everyone with no recognition of the differences in people. The most useless sort of advice there was.

"Go back to the tent, Taro," I told him, my voice shaking.

For several long moments he said nothing. He stood tensely, his face pinched, pushing his hands through his hair again and again. And then, in a strained voice, "I'm not leaving you here."

I closed my eyes. Disgusted with myself that he, even in these horrible circumstances, was showing such concern. "I won't be making such a fool of myself with anyone else." Though my blood was still singing.

I was surprised to see how far we'd gotten before deciding to take a tumble in the field. There were people on the way, though. I couldn't face them. " Please go back to the tent." Or wherever he wanted to go. I didn't care. I just wanted to go somewhere by myself, somewhere dark and quiet, and curl up into a ball.

"I wasn't taking advantage," he said in a broken voice.

"I know." I wasn't blaming him. That wasn't it at all. "I need to get my head straight."

I couldn't look at him anymore. I hugged my knees tighter and stared down at the ground and waited.

I heard him walk away.

I took a deep, deep breath.

Chapter Ten

The music was still there, of course, singing in my blood, trying to drive me on after Karish.

I really really wanted him. I had to admit it to myself. And I'd wanted him for a long time.

And why shouldn't I have him?

People were coming. Away from the light of the torches, I didn't glow so damned much, but once they passed me they couldn't help but see me sitting in the field. I wasn't far from the road. And the last thing I felt like doing was talking to anyone. Especially Kahlia. I thought I might just try to strangle her if I had to look at her. So I jumped to my feet and started walking, away from the road, away from both the houses and the tents. I had no idea where I was going. I didn't care.

My feet were on fire. It was good that my feet hurt. It helped drive away the music, helped me think.

What a horrible night. And it was all my fault. I should have expected it. I'd known what the music did to me. I could have foreseen the consequences if I'd just thought about it a little. So why had I done that to myself?

Why had I listened to Kahlia? She might have been well-meaning, sort of, but she didn't know anything about Shields. She had no idea what music could do to me. I did. I'd had warning. Rehearsals had been getting uncomfortable for me. True, not nearly as bad as the performance had been, but I'd suspected that losing control was a possibility. Yet I'd insisted on doing it. And on having Karish there to watch, and to take care of me when it was over. How could I have possibly not known what the result would be? I wasn't that stupid.

Damn the music. Go away go away go away.

I hated what it did to me. Made a fool out of me. Made me do stupid things I'd never choose to do on my own.

Which wasn't necessarily always a bad thing.

I pressed my hands to my head. Damn it, make it stop!

The glint of the glitter on my arms caught my eye. I stretched out my arms, looked down at my legs, and I could feel my lip curling in disgust. Stupid gaudy stuff. What was I thinking to appear in public looking like this? I rubbed at the paint, but it was firmly dried to my skin. The application of fingernails was a little more successful, though they left long red welts in their wake. That was all right. It all helped fight off the music.

Deep breath in, long breath out. Another in, so much air it made my lungs feel overfilled and uncomfortable, and out in one controlled flow. Don't think of it. Don't remember. Think of a map of High Scape. Home, sort of. The six quads. Each with its own hospital and Runner headquarters and markets. The streets that made no sense, the hideous architecture. The noise.

Not really home, though. I hadn't been there long enough for it to be home. Home was the Academy, still, with my small room and the classes from morning to midnight and all the calm serene people. No dangerous music. No royalty. No one expecting me to do things against my training and my nature.

I sighed.

No Karish, either. I would not have wanted to spend my life without knowing Karish.

I was going to start drawing blood soon. I stopped scratching at my arms. The paint wouldn't really come off without soap and water. The temporary thought of going to the stream was quashed by remembering that one of the Southerners' quirks concerned the use of water. All water was taken far from the source before being used for laundry, bathing, or cleaning dishes. Which was why Kahlia had brought water for washing to my tent.

I sighed. My tent. Our tent. I didn't want to go back to our tent.

The music and its effects were gone. That was something, at least, though that meant I had to stop procrastinating and think things through.

Why had I done that dance, knowing how I would react?

Because Kahlia was a force not to be denied. Not that I'd really tried.

I had had no idea how to go about this performing thing and had accepted the bad advice and reassurances of someone with no experience with Shields.

I hadn't wanted to think about how to go about it myself, because such a large part of me hated the fact that I had to perform at all.

I had underestimated how badly I would react.

No, I had underestimated the consequences of my reaction.

And I had wanted Karish to see me. That was the shameful truth. No one had ever thought me beautiful or alluring. And for the longest time that hadn't mattered, it really hadn't. But to hear it. To come to this place and have people tell me there was something about my plain, unmemorable appearance that was beautiful, that had been surprisingly gratifying. And I had wondered if Karish would have been able to see it, too.

If it hadn't been for serendipity and a well-placed stick,

I would have had sex with Karish right then and there. I had no doubt about it.

I really hated serendipity and the well-placed stick.

I could feel something new then. Anger. Genuine bubbling anger. And resentment. For if I hadn't been brought to myself, we would have had sex, and it would have been incredible, and it wouldn't have been my fault. Shields weren't held responsible for anything they did under the influence of music. I would have gotten exactly what I wanted and would have still been able to pride myself for being ever so sensible and disciplined. A slipup, of course, but under such trying circumstances, no one could find me at fault.

What a hypocritical, sanctimonious wench I was. And childish. And weak. And cowardly. Engineering the desired result while shielding myself from any responsibility. Disgusting.

And the thing I had to face was that it was the desired result.

I wanted him. I couldn't be completely sure whether, at that particular moment, it wasn't just a lingering effect of the music, but that didn't matter in the grand scheme, because music had nothing to do with my wanting him every other instant of every other day.

It had been months now. At least. My plan to keep my distance and regain my senses clearly wasn't working. And using Doran, that was horrible. I hadn't thought of him once, not since setting foot on Flatwell. That was appalling. When had I become such a bitch? Or had I always been a bitch, and just hadn't known it?

It was still a bad idea. When it all ended we'd be in a horribly awkward situation, trying to cobble together a working relationship out of whatever wreckage the emotional maelstrom left us in. But this may be a case where the only way out was through.

The camp was as silent as it ever got by the time I reached it. Our tent was dark and quiet, too. My heart seemed to triple its pace as I ducked under the flap. Partially because it was necessary, but mostly as a delay tactic, I poured out some of the water Kahlia had left me, moistening a cloth. The soap of these people was thinner than what I used at home, almost oily, and it didn't require hot water to be effective. It wasn't exactly soothing on the scrapes I'd left on my arms, but it seemed to wash off the glitter and the paint. And make my feet just a little less filthy. They were pretty beaten up with all my stomping around.

And then, once I was done and I had thrown out the water and wiped out the basin and could think of no other way to procrastinate, I cleared my throat. "Taro?"

Silence.

"I know you're still awake, Taro." I didn't know how I knew. Just a hunch or something. The bond at work.

A pause, and then a gruff "What?"

"Can I come in?"

Another pause, even longer. "Not a good idea."

"When has that ever stopped me?" I wasn't going to let him say no, anyway. Or he'd have to say it and make me believe it. I pushed aside the divider.

It was dark. Little light could seep into the tent. But I'd been working without light all this time. I could see Karish easily enough, lying flat on his back on top of his cot with no sheet and his hands laced behind his head. Naked.

My throat tightened, and I had to force a swallow. He was so beautiful.

"I warned you," he muttered.

"So?" My voice came out harsh and strangled. I swallowed again. "I've seen you naked before." Not much better, thready and weak. I sat down on the mat, squeezing in beside his hip. "I'm sorry about assaulting you earlier," I said, even as I fought down the urge to assault him again. I wanted to slide my palms over all that bare skin.

He grunted.

"I shouldn't have asked you to come watch me dance." He had told me, after all, that he thought me beautiful when

I danced. I had brushed that aside and made myself forget it, or at least I'd tried to, because how could he possibly feel that way? I always looked my worst when I danced, wearing loose clothes, my hair a tangled mess, sweaty and dirty.

"Do you blame me for not having control over myself?" he asked after a while.

"I kissed you, remember?"

"Because of the music," he muttered bitterly.

"Aye. But I don't usually need music," I confessed.

"What?"

"To want to kiss you." And that was possibly one of the most difficult things I've ever had to say.

I'd never had to talk about it before. I just kissed people, when I wanted to.

When had I convinced myself that I couldn't have what I wanted? That I shouldn't have what I wanted? Who would it hurt? Except me, in the long term, but that was a choice I had every right to make.

He made a sort of sound. I couldn't describe it. A sound of shock, with perhaps a touch of anger.

"Ever the diplomat," he hissed.

That came out of nowhere. "What?"

"Saying what I want to hear to smooth things over."

"When have I ever done that?"

"All the time."

What a ridiculous accusation. "You really believe I'll tell you I want you just because I think it's what you want to hear? Are you crazy?"

"What the hell am I supposed to think!" he snarled. "You try to claim you don't feel anything like I do, and that it's all wrong and stupid and *insensible*, and at the same time you're *looking* at me and your eyes are—"

Are what? My eyes were what? Not that I was going to ask. I was humiliated as I listened to him. "Do you believe I am playing a game with you?"

A short bark of a laugh. "No. I wish. I could do something with that."

I wanted to ask him what that meant, too. I held my mouth shut as he continued.

"You believed what you were saying. About it all being wrong. And I could just see you thinking it was wrong for the rest of our lives and once you think something, no one and nothing else can change your mind."

I was not that rigid. I was not. "Not wrong. Just—"

"Insensible."

Dangerous. For me. Because Karish would have his fling and move on and I'd have to be mature and decent about it. And I wasn't really sure I could be.

I touched the tip of my finger to the clear skin between his eyebrows, drawing my finger down along his nose. He tensed but didn't move away. "You might have noticed I'm not very good with people who aren't like me."

He had no answer for that. He couldn't very well deny it.

"Am I too late?"

"Too late for what?"

Oh, he was smarter than that. But I supposed he had the right to punish me a little. I hadn't been playing games with him, not intentionally, but I had been indecisive, speaking one way and, at times, acting another.

"To offer the invitation I'd extended earlier." I couldn't just say it. I couldn't be that blunt. I'd never thought myself so squeamish before. "Only this time I won't revoke it."

Karish pulled in a quick breath. "The music—"

"Is gone."

"Are you sure?"

"Yes."

"Then why the change?"

"I'm tired."

"Of what?"

Gods, this was hard. Why were we still talking? I told him I wanted him. I told him I wanted to do this. I told him the music had nothing to do with it. Why couldn't that be enough? Much more of this and I would lose my nerve. "Being sensible."

"So you'd be doing this convinced it's a bad idea?"

I shrugged. "Prove me wrong." He couldn't, of course. But the only way out was through.

He didn't smirk in triumph; he didn't look smug. But then, I wouldn't really have expected him to. Even though the challenge he'd set for himself hadn't turned out to be so much of a challenge, after all.

I kissed him, and this time, I didn't revoke my offer.

Chapter Eleven

"Good gods, woman, what did you do to your feet?"

I jerked awake and grimaced at the sunlight glaring into my eyes. Momentary disorientation cleared into irritation. The bastard had opened one of the tent flaps. "Why are you waking me up?" One of the few days, apparently, when Kahlia isn't compelled to drag me out of bed before dawn, and he chooses to do it for her?

Granted, not before dawn. But I'd been asleep. By definition, he was waking me too early.

"Did the dancing last night do this to your feet?"

I buried my head under the hard pillow. "I guess." It was too hot to stay under there. "No, I was walking around a bit, too."

"Lee! Look at this, damn it!"

I sighed and looked at him. He was kneeling at my feet. Naked, of course, which was one of his most flattering states. And I could finally look at that gorgeous lean form without appearing intrusive and inappropriately personal. I could, for a while, just think about how incredibly beautiful he was.

Or he would be, once the sunburn healed. The scratches must have really hurt, though he hadn't seemed to mind them at the time. I wasn't sure I would have noticed it if he had.

It had been a terrible mistake to sleep with him. Just as I thought it would be. He could claim all he wanted that he wasn't nearly as experienced as the rumors said. His skill said otherwise.

To pacify him, I looked at my feet. A bit bruised and raw, but nothing too bad. "You had me expecting great bloody gashes."

"You're not dancing until they're healed."

"I'm taking on challengers today."

"The hell you are."

I wasn't thrilled about the idea either. I wasn't in serious pain but I was sore. However, I wanted to make as much money as soon as possible. I wanted our debts paid off. "They don't hurt."

"Like that means anything. You could be gushing blood and you'd dismiss it as a scrape. Shield."

I snickered at him. "What a little mother you are." But it felt nice, how carefully he was cradling my foot. Which made me think of something. "Wait a moment. Let go of me." When he did, the soles of my feet started stinging. Really stinging. "Ah."

"Ha." He raised an eyebrow. "Hurts, eh?"

"I wouldn't go that far." But it wasn't comfortable.

"You can't dance today. I don't want you ruining your feet over this, doing permanent damage. Leave it for at least a day."

"Did I bring in any money last night?" I remembered some coins being tossed to the ground, vaguely, but I had no idea what happened to them.

His face fell. "I didn't collect it." And he started swearing at himself.

He was berating himself, harshly enough that I felt no need to add any criticism. I couldn't really blame him. I had been in no condition to think of it, either. But I suddenly remembered I was hungry, so hungry my stomach had curled into a hard, sharp knot. "Massage my feet again. I liked that."

"Yes, ma'am." He settled more comfortably on the mat, folding his legs, and carefully propped my feet on his shins. The stinging disappeared. So did the sharpest edge of the hunger. "Was last night about the music?" he asked in a quiet voice.

"I told you last night it wasn't."

He shrugged. "The music might have still been affecting you last night without you knowing it."

He was expecting morning-after regrets, was he? I was supposed to wake up, confused about where I was, slowly realize with dawning horror that I had made the most horrible mistake, and either tell him it hadn't happened or just freeze him out. Well, he was out of luck there. I'd made the decision to give this a try. I was still aware of the likelihood that this would, indeed, be the worst decision I had ever made, but once I picked a path of stupidity, I stuck with it. "It wasn't the music."

"Are you sure?"

"Yes." Not entirely. It could have been a bit about the music. I couldn't be sure. But I wasn't going to tell him that. He would jump to the worst conclusions, and possibly spend too much time brooding about how he had taken advantage of his insensible vulnerable Shield. A good nine-tenths of the decision had come straight from my own irrational mind, and he didn't need to know anything different.

But my Source wasn't stupid. "How can you be sure?" he demanded.

"I'm extremely talented."

He smiled slightly and appeared ready to let it go.

"Are you two awake?" a voice called from outside.

Karish rolled his eyes, hissing a little under his breath. "No!" he shouted.

"Can I come in?"

"No!"

I nudged him with one foot. "Taro."

"She is *always* here."

"So you should be used to her by now. She's been good to us." And we needed all the help we could get. I reached under the division between our cots and dragged out a wrap from the pile of clothes I'd been given. "Don't come out if you don't want to talk to her."

"Oh, I'm coming out," he muttered. "She's too lean." Whatever that meant. He reached for his trousers.

I slipped into the tiny public rectangle of our tent. "Sorry for the delay, Kahlia. Please come in." I shook one of the tea sacks to determine whether we had anything to offer her to drink. But of course we didn't. We'd used all the tea to ward off hunger.

She stepped into the tent. She was carrying some kind of pan—maybe for baking bread?—and thrust it into my hands.

It was about half-full of coins. Gray, brown and yellow. I took the pan and rustled the coins with an index finger. I looked at Kahlia again. "This is what we earned last night at our performance?"

"Yes," she said, and her smile seemed oddly proud.

Thank Zaire. We could eat. "Is this a pleasing amount?"

"It is highly good, especially for a virgin night."

"How much do I owe you and the others?"

"We've already taken our portions, and I have taken Ma's tax and given it to her."

"Thank you," I said, as polite as I could be in the face of such meddling, her going through my coins that way. "And thank you for collecting this for us. I forgot to last night."

"We noticed," she said and grinned, shooting a look at Karish.

And Karish, damn him, appeared almost smug.

"Are you ready to go?" Kahlia asked, although it was obvious to see that I was not. "We have to rehearse a little before the first of the challengers come."

"Lee isn't dancing today," said Karish. "Her feet are a mess from last night. She can't continue dancing on the bare ground. We're going to the mill and we're ordering a bench. She's not dancing again until she has one."

"She should not be seen in the markets without her costume. Part of her show is her glitter. No one will believe that if they see her trudging about buying eggs."

"You're not suggesting I spend the next two or so years hiding away from people when I'm not performing." She'd better not be. That was a guaranteed way to make me homicidal.

"Are you going to meet the challengers today or not?" she asked me.

"I am not. I'm not prepared to ruin my feet over this."

"I told everyone you'd be meeting challengers today."

"You'll have to tell them you were mistaken. Or that I'm throwing an artistic fit."

She shrugged. "They're your hides."

Yes, they were. "Thank you for bringing us the coins. I really appreciate it."

She shrugged again and left the tent without another word.

The next thing I knew, Karish's hand was wrapped around the back of my neck and I was being thoroughly kissed.

"What was that for?" I asked, breathlessly, once I could.

He just chuckled, gave me one more quick kiss, and then started pulling on some clothing. "I'm going to find us something to eat," he said. "I don't know about you, but I'm starving."

Karish traded a couple of coins for dried fish that was savory and flaky and the most wondrous substance to ever touch my tongue. The cold rice rolled in dried seaweed was also unusually tasty. I had clearly left all civilization back on the mainland, for I ate too much, too quickly and was rewarded with unpleasant stomach cramps.

After breakfast, we got a few directions and some recommendations and headed for the markets. I was oddly excited. I was going to spend money. I had coins, that I had earned, and I was going to use them to purchase goods. That excited me.

I was a sad, sad person.

We went to the mill first, and the miller told us she'd made dancing benches before. And thank Zaire for that, because I'd never considered the possibility of a miller not knowing how to build dancing benches. For a little extra, she could make sure the bench was ready for the next morning.

I hated handing over the coins without knowing whether I was paying a fair price. I had never paid much attention to the price of things, but even I knew that a meat meal should cost somewhere in the range of three coins rather than thirty. Dancing benches, I had no idea. I was probably the only Shield in history who'd ever had to buy a dancing bench.

I'd have to start paying attention to these things. Everything, not just benches. I was going to have to watch every coin.

An attitude not shared by Karish, apparently. "Duty's done, time for fun," he announced, eyes gleaming.

That didn't sound promising. "We can't go wild, Taro. We have to save every coin we can."

"That's a whole lot of money you earned last night, Lee. I'm still not totally pegged on the coins here, but I know that's a lot. More than even Kahlia was expecting."

"Aye, and I didn't hear her recommending a shopping spree." I was tired, and my feet were killing me.

He rolled his eyes. "Some clothes that are suitable for this climate. That's all I'm asking," he promised. "That and a good meal."

I could feel my eyebrows performing a little leap of enthusiasm at that. I couldn't help it. I was hungry again, and the thought of eating something other than cold rice and dried fish made my mouth flood with saliva.

Karish positively cackled. "Ha! Clothes first, though."

To his credit, he didn't go berserk trying to buy things, clothes of every possible shape and huge. We bought two pairs of trousers for him—he couldn't be convinced to buy skirts and the fact that I teased him about his lovely legs helped not at all—that were looser and of a finer material than his Northern garments. I got two skirts that fell well below the knee but flowed freely about my legs. Two shirts apiece and a pair of sandals each, all of it made to measure and before our very eyes. It was fascinating.

And then . . . food.

Not the kind of food I was used to, nor what I was craving. At the first mention of a tavern, I'd had visions of chunks of beef drowning in gravy, topping a mound of finely whipped potatoes. There was no beef available in this tiny little town on the wrong end of the planet, and the only potatoes I saw were tiny and an odd green color and not at all appetizing, though the other patrons were gobbling them up eagerly enough.

I ended up with an incredibly savory fish stew with a side dish of thin, almost flaky bread. The wine with it was oddly sharp, but palatable enough.

The dessert was awful.

And I never thought those words could ever go together in a sentence.

Weird bland colors, strange gushy consistencies, and a flavor I could only describe as watered down sugar. Too much sugar watered down. How could anyone do so well in the main course yet fail so spectacularly with the dessert?

A cultural thing, I supposed, as everyone else ate it with apparent enjoyment.

I didn't know if I could last two years without a proper dessert.

"We should do something," Karish announced when our half-eaten desserts had been taken away.

"Aren't we?"

"No. Something exotic, because we're in an exotic place. And," his grin widened, "something to celebrate."

I almost asked him if he always celebrated sleeping with someone for the first time, but I choked back that incredibly stupid question just in time. "It has to be something that doesn't cost any money."

His eyes narrowed. "You're not going to turn into a nag about this, are you?"

"We are going to pay them back."

"After we get back to Erstwhile."

"We shall pay whatever amount of the debt is still owing if we find the line before we pay off the debt, but in the meantime we will pay off as much as we can."

"We still have to live."

"Celebrating is a requirement for living?"

"Obviously, or people wouldn't always be doing it."

As arguments went, it was flawed. People didn't need to get drunk or paint their houses awful colors, but they did it all the time. However, I knew of a better method of getting my way. "My feet hurt."

He rolled his eyes, not the least bit fooled, but he picked up my hand and kissed the back of it, and the pain I really was feeling on the soles of my feet eased. "Subtle you ain't, Lee."

"And don't you forget it."

But we did walk a bit. My feet could bear it, and I really wasn't all that anxious to return to the suffocating heat of our tent. We wandered about the market, looking at wares, most of which I didn't recognize the use of. There were toys, and an awful lot of those tokens the others hung from their tents. For luck, a merchant told us. The jewelry was nice, delicate with a simplicity of line that made the thick heavy metal and flashy stones of Northern jewelry seem blunt and graceless.

They all tried to solicit our custom, which I had to admit was a novel experience for me. Most merchants had no interest in luring Shields or Sources into their shops.

It was then that I felt a light tugging at my belt. My hand shot out and grabbed the wrist of the person trying to steal my purse. "Hey!" was my intelligent accusation.

The owner of the wrist stared up at me. She was a child, perhaps around eleven, but she was only a couple of inches shorter than me. Her long black hair was matted and rough. She had the same black eyes as everyone around me, but her dirty skin was several shades lighter than the other islanders. She was far too skinny, her cheekbones sharp in her face, her wrist boney. My impression of her clothing was that it was too tight for her.

And she was trying to steal from me. I couldn't believe someone had tried to steal from me. I was a Shield, damn it. Irritation snapped down my spine.

She stared at me, stunned, then her foot shot out and hooked my knee. I let her go as my leg buckled, and she took off.

"Lee!" Taro caught my arm. "Are you all right?"

"She tried to steal our money!" I exclaimed.

"Did she get anything?"

"No, but . . ." Damn it, she'd tried to steal from me! No one had ever tried to steal from me.

Of course, on Flatwell that didn't mean anything. On Flatwell, there weren't regulars and Triple S members. There were only people. There were all sorts of ways being only a person was just unpleasant. I couldn't wait to go home.

All right, relax. You're shopping. Shopping was supposed to be fun. I swung my foot to ease the pain in my knee. Monstrous brat.

"Sir, madam!" crowed one merchant, and his accent instantly drew my attention. Very very light, it seemed to me, almost like he had arrived from somewhere else a long time ago and had taken on a bit of the accent, rather than someone who had had the accent and lost it. I looked at him closely. He appeared like everyone else, the same dark hair, eyes and skin, the same lean form.

"You are in the greatest luck, for I was to pack and move any moment."

I thought his voice might be good for the stage, it was so strong and strident. Not so good to listen to while standing right in front of the man. It felt like he was yelling at us. And there were no signs of packing up that I could perceive. "We're not interested, thank you," I said.

"Oh, but you can't fly this op without hearing!" he protested, leaping in front of us to halt our progress. "You're strangers here. You don't know of the healing waters and plants that are found only here."

Here where? On the island? In this village? "We have no need for healing," I told him, and Karish and I tried to ease around him.

Who would have thought such a slender man could be such a big obstacle? "Of course you need healing, madam. I can see you're in pain. I have an ointment—"

"*I* have an ointment."

"Not like mine."

"True. I know mine works. I have no such knowledge of yours."

He was undeterred. "Do you know the dangers of breaking your leg?" he demanded.

"Pain," I answered, then cursed myself. Why was I encouraging him?

"Blood clots!" he announced with twisted triumph.

"Oh." Never would have thought of that.

"A broken leg can cause blood clots. Blood clots can kill you."

"How?"

"They grow bigger and bigger in the leg until they stop all blood flow, and then you die."

"Oh." Nasty, if it were true.

"A daily dose of this"—the bottle he picked up that time was rose colored—"will prevent blood clots. No one else sells this. You should stock."

No one else sold it? So who made it? Someone who had probably never had a day of healer training in his life? "You expect us to buy and take medicine daily in case we break a leg which *may* cause blood clots that *might* kill us?" How stupid did he think we were?

"Prevention is the best medicine, madam."

"And using your head is the best form of prevention, you repulsive little fear monger."

He drew himself up stiffly. "There's no need to be slacking me."

"There's every need. Get out of our way."

This time he made no move to stop us as we strode around him.

Karish followed me, snickering. "Not your most diplomatic moment."

"He didn't deserve diplomacy. Imagine trying to create a fear of some unlikely ailment just to try to sell us something. How disgusting." And it must work, or he wouldn't do it. Was this the sort of thing the regulars had to put up with all the time?

No wonder merchants were despised. I hoped my family was nothing like that creature. If they were, I didn't want to know about it.

Chapter Twelve

The success of my first night was surpassed by my second, and equaled by my third. The arrival of the promised bench helped, mostly by sparing my feet. The other acts of the troupe also seemed to enjoy unusual popularity. Despite this, on the fourth day we moved on, due to the demands of the curse.

The following three weeks were hard. We hit a series of small settlements, spending at most two nights, and sometimes only one, in each, as they were too small to support multiple performances. I began to recognize certain people from the other villages. Merchants who wandered from place to place selling their wares. Storytellers. News carriers, which was a new profession to me. People who collected and sold gossip and information. An interesting conceit, especially as no one had the means of testing the accuracy of said news.

I saw the fear-mongering, medicine-selling creature a couple of times. I glared at him. He ignored me. I saw people buying his poison. Fools.

Karish's sunburn faded away and he took entertaining

care to make sure he didn't acquire another. I became a little more comfortable about performing and yes, parts of it were even fun. I still hated the costume, but I drew a great many spectators at every performance. Not all of them would pay with money, some instead contributing fruit or vegetables or dried meat. That was fine with us; it expanded our supplies.

Leverett and his lover, Sol, had an explosive argument that everyone found out about. I noticed a strange man lingering around the tents late one night, but no one else had seen him. And Rinis found out she was pregnant, to her very public disgust. It was not the sort of news a professional contortionist wanted. And I could sympathize with that. Zaire knew I would find a pregnancy highly inconvenient.

Karish and I adapted to the routine of things, walking and setting up and performing and collecting and taking down and moving on. The freakishness of my person was an even bigger draw than either Atara or Kahlia had predicted. Karish and I were clearing off our debt with greater speed than anticipated, and the overflow effect enjoyed by the other performers seemed to buy us their appreciation. Which was fine with me. It helped shore up the fragile sense of security I'd managed to construct.

This security had a downside. Once I was no longer so worried about the two of us being tossed out into the jungle to starve, I had plenty of time to wonder how the hell we were going to find these relatives of the Empress. We had ridiculously little to work with. The family name that had been assumed by the Empress's sister. The last known location of the family that had taken her in. A picture of the tattoo. That was all. And seeing as how we were supposed to be discreet about it all, not even speaking of it to anyone unless we were already pretty sure they had useful information, I didn't know where we were going to start.

Karish was no help. He said we'd figure out what to do when the time came. But how were we even going to recognize that time when it did come? We simply lacked adequate information.

Worrying about it didn't accomplish anything, of course, but I couldn't help it. We couldn't go home until we found these people. What if we never did? What if we were stuck on this island forever? It began to prey on my mind. It was the last thing I thought of before I fell asleep, it woke me up at night and niggled at me, it was the first thing I thought of when I woke up in the morning.

And because I'd begun thinking about it all the time, an idea came to me. I didn't think it was at all stupid. In fact, I was stupid for missing something that now seemed so obvious.

Then, one day, we woke up to rain. Heavy hard rain. I looked outside and I could see people tying down flaps and collecting children and animals. Fin came by to show us how to prepare. No one was panicking, but everyone was tense. I certainly didn't like the idea of bearing out a bad storm in shelter as flimsy as a tent. We'd weathered rain, of course, but nothing so strong as what I felt was coming this time.

Once we'd done everything we'd been told to do, everything we could to prepare, we sat in the dark, all lights out, and waited. And waited. And waited.

"Do you think Kahlia might be one of the line?" I asked at one point, driven by boredom to reveal one of the weird notions that had been plaguing me.

"What?"

"You know what I mean." I didn't want to be any more explicit. While I doubted anyone would be lurking outside our tent in this weather, it never hurt to be cautious.

"Kahlia?" he said.

"She doesn't look anything like Atara or Panol. And her eyes and skin are very light. She might have some Northern blood in her." Not that all Northerners were pale. Karish would know what I meant.

"Why would she be traveling about like this?"

"Why wouldn't she? Contact was lost decades ago."

"I haven't seen the mark," he said dubiously. "And she doesn't wear much."

"With all those tattoos, it might be covered up or obscured."

"That's true," he said.

And that was all he said, which I found frustrating. "So how are we going to figure it out?" I prodded him.

"Ask her."

"What? Ask her if she's the next—" I shut up. My desire to be sarcastic had almost overpowered my good sense.

"Ask her where she was born. Be as blunt as she is and find out where her father's at. And where she's from. You two spend a lot of time together. What do you talk about?"

"Um." I thought about it for a moment, then admitted, "Me."

He snickered.

It was true. My dancing. My costume. How strange I was. That was almost all we talked about.

"Time to be a little less self-centered, my dear," said Taro.

"Why am I the one who has to do it?" I demanded. "It's your task."

"You're the one she actually likes."

I sighed. That seemed somewhat true. But it didn't necessarily follow that she was prepared to reveal to me any potentially embarrassing secrets.

And the storm raged on. It was only rain. Not a hurricane or anything like it, which was what I had been fearing. But even rain could do damage, when it lasted three days. And three longer days I had never felt. Trapped in our tiny tent, it was too dangerous to light the lanterns. Sudden gusts of wind would find their way into the tent, making lighting lanterns in turn futile and hazardous. So it was too dark to do anything. It was too hot for sex, even if either of us were in the mood, which we weren't.

The only break in the tedium had been the occasional visits from other members of the troupe, checking up on us, and those visits that we returned. Oh, and that time one corner of our tent had been ripped up by the winds and we'd had to scramble to get everything pinned down again. That had been fun.

After three days, when Fin poked his head in, we were both grateful for the interruption, even knowing it was going to be brief.

Until, that is, he opened his mouth. "Get your kit together," he ordered. "We're moving out."

I stared at him.

"In this?" Karish demanded. "Are you insane?"

"You know of the curse," Fin said impatiently. "We're past time."

The curse? They wanted us to start slogging through that mess because of some stupid fear over a curse? "That's ridiculous."

Fin shrugged. "We're going. You want to stay, you stay alone. And we're taking the tent." And he disappeared.

I had my hand on a sandal, all ready to throw it at the memory of Fin's head, before my brain caught up and realized what I was about to do. I unclenched my fingers. Of all the stupid, superstitious, dangerous . . .

"Lee," Karish whispered. "Let's try it."

"Try what?" Staying behind on our own? Without a tent? Much as I would love to provide an example of sanity to these crazy people, I didn't think we would really survive the process.

"You try to fix the weather. So we don't have to walk out in this."

We had tried to fix the weather the summer before, when it had been so crazy in High Scape. I'd been able to affect the weather, but not control it. The results had been, at times, disastrous.

This again? "This is a completely different place and climate. I'll probably call up a blizzard instead."

"Just take a look. What could that hurt?"

Of course, looking never hurt anything. It was just that looking too often led to trying, and trying could hurt a whole hell of a lot. I really didn't want to be out there walking through a hail storm.

But I didn't want to be out there walking through the rain, either. It wasn't light, poetic rain. It was eyeball piercing rain that made it hard to breathe and churned up mud that ate your sandals.

Stupid curse. I couldn't believe these people would drag their children out into such dangerous weather over something so brainless. How could such a large group of people engage in identical insanity?

"All right." Maybe I could do something. Maybe a small island would be easier to manage than one small part of a huge continent. Aye, that made sense. Really. I could convince myself the forces were organized in discrete chunks rather than a whole continuous flow. If I thought about it hard enough. "We don't have much time, though." I didn't want to get left behind in that mess out there.

I felt Karish lower his internal shields, and I erected mine. It felt like it had been ages since we'd done this. I spent a moment wondering if I should worry about getting out of practice. Especially if, gods forbid, we did end up on this island for two years or more.

Karish was not channeling. He was merely allowing himself to become a conduit through which I could access the forces, something tradition claimed neither of us could do. Karish could channel the forces, allow them to flow through his body and direct them out again, out somewhere safe. That was what was needed to stop natural disasters. I couldn't do that. Manipulating the weather, the normal kind of weather like simple rain and fog and whatnot, required a much gentler touch, the finer adjustments of the smaller details. Karish seemed unable to perceive those smaller elements. Perhaps they were lost to him in the more powerful forces. I could feel them, though, and change their flow.

So, potentially, I could make adjustments to the weather. I had before. Only to date, I hadn't been very good at it. The results of past experiments had been unpredictable, and usually negative. It wasn't something I could really afford to practice. Besides, I didn't know if playing with the weather, ordinary weather, was really a good idea. Something told me that all weather everywhere might be connected somehow, and for all I knew, stopping the rain where I was could cause a flood—or a drought—somewhere up north or wherever.

But no one could tell me for sure, and someone was going to break a bone trying to sludge through all that mud and rain. I was certain of it. And besides, I was just going to take a look, to see if there was anything I could do. Really.

One thing I had learned from my previous experiments was that there was supposed to be a sort of constant base to the weather upon which all permutations were based. The base in High Scape had been a rich warm green. And as I looked through Karish at the curls and swirls moving imperceptibly around us, I easily found the green again.

Hm. To me that implied the rain was perfectly healthy and natural. And, of course, it was. There were no Reanists sacrificing aristocrats to nonexistent gods.

"Can you feel that?" Karish asked.

"Going to have to be more specific than that, Taro."

"The other Pair is trying to work on this, too."

I couldn't sense anything like that. "Are they accomplishing anything?"

"No. They're very weak. And . . . there is something strange about the way they feel."

"Strange how?"

"Very much in tune, more than I would have thought possible. Their minds work as one."

"Yet they are weak?"

"It feels so."

"Hm." Intriguing, but not something I was going to think about too much right then.

"How are you doing?"

I had found the base, but it would take time to study the other colors and movements in order to understand them well enough to even attempt any manipulation. "I can't do anything right now." And I felt unaccountably ashamed for my inability.

"Are you sure?"

"I'm sure. Everything's too different here." It was the wisest decision. I wouldn't even want to try it in High Scape, where I was more familiar with the courses of the weather. It would really be stupid to try it on Flatwell. Really. But the inability rankled. Karish always seemed to be able to do everything he put his hand to, and to do it well. It was irritating that I couldn't do the same.

Karish swore and raised his shields. "Trudging through that mess out there is going to be a nightmare. These people make me crazy."

"I'm worried about that other Pair knowing about manipulating the weather. The council must have told them." Though I didn't know how the Triple S council would know of the potential for manipulating the weather. We hadn't told them of it.

"They could have figured it out themselves, Lee," he snickered. "I know we're brilliant, but we're not necessarily the only ones who can discover things."

I supposed that was a possibility. "I hope they don't miscalculate their abilities and cause a catastrophe."

"Catastrophes, I can handle."

And then we had to get moving, packing up and soaking everything in the process because we didn't know what we were doing. Wet leather straps chafed against wet skin. I couldn't tie my hair tightly enough to keep it from whipping into my eyes and my mouth. Karish was threatening to have his head shaved. The mud sucked our feet deep into

the earth, and I almost wished I were wearing the same
scanty clothes as the others. Drenched and stuck to the
skin, they truly left nothing to the imagination, but they allowed greater freedom of movement and they were, I
guessed, less clutching and heavy then the trousers and
shirt I was wearing.

It was the nightmare we had anticipated, and worse.
Dark, the rain almost horizontal in the wind, stinging every
inch of exposed skin—there were advantages to my clothing after all—and painfully blinding. All hands were
needed to push the wagon through the mud, mind the animals, and make sure none of the children got themselves
lost. Karish pulled wagon duty while I held the small hands
of Ashti and Glynis. Not that it did either of them any good.
I lost my footing more often than they did, a few times
falling completely in the mud and coating myself with it.
Which was a nice shot at my bench-dancing self-esteem.

I didn't know how far they felt they had to go to defeat
the alleged effects of that ludicrous curse. Not terribly far,
for surely we weren't able to cover much ground in those
horrible conditions. As far as I could bear, though, because
I was sure I was going to drop long before everyone was allowed to stop moving.

And then we had to set up again, which was even harder
than pulling everything apart had been. Trying to erect a
tent in the driving rain had to be an exercise in futility, and
what was the point? Every single thing we owned was
soaked through. And even once we had the tent set up, we
couldn't dry anything. We couldn't light a fire or even a
lantern. All we could do was strip naked and lie on the wet
mat, not bothering with blankets as they were equally
drenched. Finally we weren't hot. We were freezing, right
to the bone, and we curled together in the pathetic hope of
producing some body heat.

Karish was shivering so hard I could hear his teeth chat-
tering. "If you get sick because of this, I'm going to kill
Atara." This was ridiculous.

"Man, I hate this place," Karish stammered out through his teeth.

I crushed a handful of his hair in my fist, trying to wring out some of the water. "Aye." I sighed. "So do I."

Chapter Thirteen

Another village, another performance. I was starting to get used to it all. Walk, set up camp, put on paint, dance, go to sleep. My mind seemed to lose track of what I was doing. Which, I knew, wasn't a good thing. I wasn't on Flatwell just to dance and earn money. I had a more important task to perform. But sometimes, in the drudgery of the constant walking and dancing and walking and dancing, I kind of forgot.

We had walked, stopped, and set up camp. We were in our third evening in a little town that smelled overwhelmingly of mint. I had put on my ridiculous costume and all the paint. Taro had escorted me to the dance site.

And someone in the audience caught my eye. A young girl, too skinny, barely clothed. It took me a moment to place her. The little thief, the one I had caught in the act of trying to take my purse. And there she was, one of the spectators, in the front, not a jot of shame to be perceived anywhere about her.

Kahlia had already announced me with her usual flair.

The spectators were waiting for me to step onto the bench. It would look other than elegant—an essential element for a creature with the ludicrous title of Flame Dancer—to face off against the little street urchin right then. But she had better not try to take any of our coins, because elegant or not, I'd grab her.

Piece one. The light piece that demonstrated yes, I was an actual bench dancer who could participate in the sport, while at the same time looking elegant and easy. Some mild polite applause, as usual, and a few coins. Piece two, the more technical piece, designed to show off the more difficult moves, at least those that were possible with only one bench and one pair of bars. Piece three, the "comedic" piece. Piece four, which showed off nothing that was from the original sport and was comprised entirely of "artistic" moves Kahlia had made up. That, of the four, garnered the most interest and the most coins.

Then, the grand finale, what Kahlia had taken to calling the snake dance. Because she thought snakes were sexy, which still took my brain to places I really didn't want it to go. It was still the most humiliating piece in the repertoire. Though I never felt that way at the time of performing it. Oh no. There was something about the sand singer that just eliminated every inhibition I had, and shortly after hearing its first raspy notes I threw myself into the curving arms and arched back with abandon.

Until I felt the piercing pain along the bottom of my left foot, stumbled over a bar with my right, and landed flat on my back, the air knocked completely out of me.

I can't breathe, I can't breathe, my foot is screaming, I can't breathe, don't panic.

Then I was being pushed upright. Someone was rubbing my back. Kahlia was murmuring soothing nonsense into my ear that accomplished nothing.

Where was Karish?

All right. Calm down. Breathe. Not too deep. Shallow.

Shallow. Don't panic when it doesn't come. It will come. Shallow. Breathe. Careful. Good girl. Well done.

What was all the shouting about?

I couldn't believe it. I'd let my foot get caught in the middle of an artificial bench dance performance. Obviously my skills were going to hell. I'd be completely useless by the time I got off this Zaire-neglected island. If in fact I ever did.

All right. I was breathing. Nice and slow and smooth.

I wondered if the people who'd already thrown coins would be taking them back after that spectacular finish.

"I can't say I think much of your man," Kahlia said. "Here you are, in the dirt with pain, and he's fussing over Panol."

"What's wrong with Panol?" Now that I could breathe, I could see. Panol was stretched out on the ground, clutching at his knee and holding his ankle off the ground. Leverett was at his head, holding him down by the shoulders, and Karish was lightly touching his upheld ankle.

"He was bitten by a vashi. A snake. That's why he fumbled the bars."

Oh. Snake. I shot a few glances about and could see nothing under the dense foliage.

"Don't worry. Sacey clubbed it. It's dead."

"Poisonous?"

"Very. Setter's gone to get the ahkar. It's medicine for such things. But it's already too late. The poison will have gone too far by the time Setter gets back."

Why had no one warned us of such snakes? There we were, wandering around in sandals, and there were lethal ankle biters slithering about. And why wasn't everyone carrying around their own supply of this ahkar for the purposes of instant application?

These people were making me crazy.

Karish was watching me, waiting for me to notice and return his gaze. Once I did, he raised his eyebrows.

I lowered my head slightly, a subtle half nod.

Karish's internal shields lowered. Mine rose. I waited as Karish sifted through the pulses and ebbs working through Panol, the pain in my own foot becoming forgotten. The tension in Panol's muscles eased.

Leverett noticed immediately. "No, Panol!" he cried, misunderstanding. "Not yet! Setter's coming! Panol!"

"Quiet, fool!" Taro snapped. I wasn't sure why.

"He's dying!"

"He's just relaxing."

Oy. Karish. You can do better than that.

Leverett shot Karish a withering glance, which he, in my opinion, fully deserved. "What would you know of such things, offlander?" he sneered.

The insult, if such it could be called, was a new one on me.

"We've got snakes up north."

We did, and from what I heard, it took hours for a person to die from a snake bite, if they ever did. How could these people feel Panol was in immediate danger?

Well, Southern snakes. What did I know?

Kahlia chose that moment to start prodding at my foot. But by that time, much of the pain had faded, so the touch tickled more than it hurt. It was a distraction, though, so I hissed at her and yanked my foot free and strove to keep my attention on Karish.

Was he accomplishing anything? I knew he was easing Panol's pain, but did that do anything in the long term, or was it merely making Panol feel better as he died?

See, this was why Karish's ability needed to be studied and quantified. But did he ever listen to me?

Setter, breathless and sweating in a way I hadn't witnessed on any of the islanders before, broke back through the crowd carrying a small green bag. He was opening it as he knelt beside Panol, swiftly unstopping a small vial and tipping its contents into Panol's mouth. Panol swallowed without prompting. Ripping open another bundle, Setter squeezed a small amount of gel onto Panol's ankle. "Rub that into the bite," he ordered tersely.

"It's too late," Kahlia murmured in a broken voice.

"Go to him," I ordered. "I'm fine."

She didn't move. She seemed frozen.

Karish rubbed the gel as instructed, continuing his unseen manipulations as he worked.

We waited.

I became aware that none of the spectators had left since my fall. They stood in a small cluster around us, silent, watchful.

"When will we know whether it's working?" I asked.

"It's too late to work," Kahlia said.

"If it weren't too late," I said sharply, "how would we know?"

She didn't answer, tears welling up in her eyes.

That was her brother. Why wasn't she hovering over him instead of me?

Karish dipped his fingers into the bundle Setter still held and rubbed the additional gel into the bite.

"Ah!" Leverett said with satisfaction. "His color is coming back!"

Everyone seemed to find that a particularly optimistic sign. Kahlia gave a pleased little gasp. I heard some soft applause.

Still, we waited.

Then Panol pulled in a deep breath. Leverett grinned.

Could endangerment and cure really work that quickly?

Everyone else seemed to think it could.

To me, Panol didn't look all that much better, but everyone around him appeared relieved. Taro carefully lowered Panol's foot to the ground. That meant to me that he thought either Panol was fine, or there was nothing more he could do. He shifted over to me, and glared at Kahlia.

Who glared right back. "What were you doing, meddling with him when she's hurt?"

"I could ask the same of you," he retorted. "He's your brother."

"I'm fine, Kahlia," I said, before the argument could take off. "Really. By far the lesser of the two injuries. Go check on him."

Another few moments of glowering, and she left. Karish knelt beside me. He didn't insult me by apologizing for going to Panol first. Without a word, he picked up my right foot, and the last lingering sting faded away. "No damage here," he said.

"No." I looked at Panol. Setter was wrapping a strip of cloth, dampened with something, around Panol's ankle. "Is he all right?"

Taro shrugged. "The yellow's gone."

I guessed that was a good sign.

I was fine. Embarrassed but fine. I leapt to my feet before Karish could offer to assist me.

The audience was still there. I hoped they didn't expect any more to the performance, because it was definitely over. I could go on, but Panol was done, and I didn't want anyone replacing him at such short notice. Instead of a pinched sole, I'd end up with a crushed ankle.

Leverett and Sol arrived back to the dancing ground with a stretcher—it kind of disturbed me that they had something like that on hand—and shifted Panol onto it. He looked awfully pale and still to me.

To my very great surprise, members of the audience threw coins as Panol was lifted and carried away. Not as much as we got for a full performance, but a generous amount, I thought, for an incomplete one. Sacey, Karish and I collected the coins, putting aside a larger portion than usual for Panol. I wondered when he'd be able to participate again. Perhaps we had to look into training a new stalker for the bars.

And when I was finally ready to go back to the tent, I found myself face-to-face with the thief, standing there looking at me, as bold as brass.

"What are you?" the thief demanded bluntly.

I had no idea what she meant by that question.

"Northerners," Karish said.

She looked at him with an expression that declared she thought him highly stupid. "Not all Northerners are like you." She was studying us, looking from him to me and back again. "What are you?"

"I don't understand the question," I said. And I wasn't in the mood to be talking to her. Little thief.

"You're not like everyone else," she said with blatant frustration, her black eyes glinting. "What are you?"

I was a Shield, but that wasn't what she meant. Her people didn't really know about Shields and Sources, and it wasn't as though it were something a regular could sense. That was why we had to wear the braids on our shoulders.

I touched my left shoulder. I missed my braid. It had solved so many problems.

"Aryne!" a loud, powerful voice shouted.

The slight figure before us jerked in surprise.

Looking up from her, I saw the figure of the fake medicine seller bearing down on us, red faced and furious.

The thief—Aryne—dashed away, darting through the remainder of the spectators and disappearing into the dense brush.

And suddenly, for some reason, I felt a great deal more sympathy for her.

"Get back here, before I—" I supposed he remembered he was in front of an audience, then, for he cut himself off. Then, scowling, he shouted, "You'd better be back before I am!" He turned and stomped away.

So that was the girl's father. No wonder she was a thief, with that as an example.

"We should head back to our tent," Karish said. "We've no doubt got an early start tomorrow."

Ah yes. The curse. Pushing us forever onward. Ours was not to reason why.

Chapter Fourteen

We did leave early the next morning, even though Panol was in no shape to be traveling. He was stretched out in the back of the wagon, as Taro had been when his sunburn was at its worst. The curse meant that we had to move on, no matter how ill anyone was. No exceptions for anyone, not even Atara's own son.

On the contrary, Panol's injury was declared to be a punishment for lingering too long, even though we hadn't been there for a full three days.

We walked all day with no incident, to settle down in the middle of nowhere when dusk fell. I went to practice with no prodding required from Kahlia. She had me well trained, she did. Karish met me on my way back to the tent, telling me Atara had summoned him.

"Oh," I said.

"So let's go."

"She didn't ask for me. Did she?"

"No, but when did that ever matter?"

Almost never. Karish did seem to enjoy dragging me

into his private affairs. "I need to wash up. I've been danc-ing."

"She lives with a troupe in what must be the hottest part of the world. She's used to sweat."

"Says the man who won't be seen by anyone unless his hair is perfect."

"I left that man in High Scape. Let's go see what she wants."

He took my hand and pulled me along, and I let him because I was curious. Atara rarely showed herself. She was always at the front of the troupe when we traveled, and she seemed to sequester herself while we were stopped. She never came to any of my performances. I imagined Kahlia told her anything she needed telling, and we delivered money on a regular basis so she had to know we were doing well. But I would have thought she'd be a little curious and want to see at least part of the act her-self.

"Do you have any idea what this is about?" I asked.

"None."

His tone was curt. And I didn't blame him. It was never a good thing to be summoned by authority figures. Good news was allowed to trickle down; bad news was delivered directly.

I was gripped with sudden panic. "You don't think she's going to dismiss us, do you?" She couldn't do that, could she? Leave us out there in the middle of nowhere? She had no reason to dismiss us. I'd been getting along with every-one fairly well, hadn't I?

She couldn't cut us off. We would be helpless without her. We didn't know how to get anywhere. Why the hell didn't we know how to get anywhere? Why hadn't I gotten a better map? Why had I just handed our lives over to these complete strangers and just trusted them to take care of us? Stupid. Careless. Irresponsible. Damn it. I was such a moron.

Karish looked back at me and frowned. I realized I was squeezing his hand. I loosened my grip.

Unlike the first time we were in Atara's tent, it was evening and all the flaps were tied up, letting in what breeze there was. It was therefore something less than stifling, despite the dozens of black candles she'd lit. I wondered how many tents she'd burned down with those candles.

Atara, her excessive jewelry glinting in the candlelight, hesitated when she saw me. She didn't object to my presence, though. She was seated at her table, and there were long lines of colored beads stretched from edge to edge. I didn't recognize the pattern, and I couldn't guess what it was supposed to mean. "I have been made to understand that I owe you my son's life," she said to Karish.

Good evening to you, too.

Karish stammered, as he always did in such situations. I still haven't figured out whether it was a genuine display of shock or part of an act to look as though he'd been taken by complete surprise. "I put the gel on. Setter had fetched it and told me what to do."

"Too late to be effective, Kahlia tells me."

"Obviously not. It worked."

"Panol has been bitten before."

Maybe Panol needed to invest in some boots. Speaking of . . . I glanced down at my bare ankles. My pale skin was practically glowing. It probably acted as some kind of beacon to the snakes.

"What he felt before was not what he felt with you yesterday," Atara continued. "He says he felt you do something."

"I put the gel on him," Taro said, sounding puzzled.

That, of course, was entirely an act.

"You have healing magic," Atara declared. "Why do you hide this?"

That's what I wanted to know.

"There is no such thing as healing magic," said Taro.

She cocked her head at him. "Who told you that?"

Karish opened his mouth to answer, and then shut it without responding. He frowned.

I couldn't blame him. I would be similarly dumb. I couldn't remember a single person ever telling me there was no such thing as magic. It wasn't necessary. It was just something I'd always known. Because it was obvious. Of course there was no such thing as magic.

Taro wasn't prepared to make that kind of argument, apparently. Instead he said, "Whether such magic exists or not, I don't have it."

"What about this thing you say you do when the earth moves. Is that not magic?"

"No."

She frowned. "Then what is it?"

"It's an ability I have, to kind of reach in and guide the power of an event out. With my mind." He looked back at me for help.

I shrugged. What did I know of channeling? I wasn't a Source.

"Can anyone learn to do this?"

"No. You have to be born with the ability."

"Just like magic," she said with a triumphant smirk, and she moved a red bead into a line of white beads.

"No, just like anything."

"People can learn many things and not have inborn talent."

"You can't do anything without inborn talent." She was looking mutinous. He sighed. "Can you sing?"

She appeared startled by the question. "Somewhat."

"Were you trained to learn?"

"No."

"I can't sing. And no amount of teaching will enable me to sing. I have absolutely no talent for it, and I can't hear the difference between notes. But I don't think people who can sing have some magical ability. They just have an ability I lack."

Atara was not as impressed with the analogy as I was. "Can you explain how you can do this interference with storms?"

Not storms. Typhoons, maybe. Tsunami. Big difference.

"Can you explain how people sing?" Karish retorted, obviously not expecting an answer.

"People draw breath and push it through their throats and shape their mouths to release the air with different notes."

"There must be more than that, because I do the same, and I have been reliably informed that I can't sing."

By who? I'd never managed to get him to sing. I'd even tried to get him drunk for that very purpose. And I'd seen him drunk, but it hadn't been enough to get him to open his mouth for anything other than speaking.

Atara's jawline firmed in that way that said she was gritting her teeth.

Atara, unlike most of the other members of the troupe, had actual furniture. Tables with legs that didn't fold. Dressers an arm length in width and waist high. A full-length mirror. She opened a drawer in one of the dressers and took out a palm-sized black box. She opened the box, curling her fingertips into the contents.

She blew the contents, a fine, silvery powder, into Karish's face.

Taro sputtered and sneezed. I gasped uselessly and clutched at his arm.

Atara grabbed up the nearest candle and sort of waved it around Karish.

Please don't set my Source on fire.

The flame of the candle flared up oddly, here and there. No doubt in reaction to the powder hanging in the air.

"It is there," Atara announced solemnly.

I avoided rolling my eyes. Barely. Charlatan.

"We had a healer for many years. She died."

A victim of the supposed curse?

"Will you take her place?"

"I am not a healer," Karish snapped, his temper finally showing through.

"We gave her coin. We'll give you coin, too."

He scowled. "What are you suggesting? You want me to lie to your people? You want me to claim to be something I'm not and take money from them, all the while endangering their lives because of my ignorance? I thought honesty was so important to you."

Atara's eyes narrowed. "You speak so little of yourselves," she said flatly. "The city you come from, these tasks you perform, this is all you tell us, and little enough of those. Nothing of your families, your raising. All we learn is nothing more than the answers of what we ask. When you are not working, you hide yourselves away. In your tents, or wandering apart."

What, she was the only one allowed to take time for herself?

"How am I to know what to make of you? Whether you are speaking true or for your own convenience?"

Karish had clearly had enough. Through my hand on his arm, I felt tension solidify his muscles. "Don't you think I'd want to do this, if I could?" he demanded with frustration. "I'm useless. And I can't learn anything that will serve anyone else. I have no skill with my hands. I have no talent for performance. I don't know how to do anything your average regular can't do for himself, and better." He let loose a sharp snicker. "I don't even have a face anyone wants to look at."

I scowled at Atara. Her stupid, brutal insistence. Her nosy, judgmental arrogance. Making Taro feel this way, feel useless.

He wasn't useless. I needed him. He kept me sane. I would have snapped and murdered everyone long before this, if it weren't for him. And if he were slightly less useful on the island than he was at home, that was only because the island was full of idiots.

"Do you think I don't know I'm here only on sufferance?" Karish continued. "That I'm tolerated only because I belong to Lee? That you'd happily leave me in any village—or a ditch—and go on your happy way with the Flame Dancer?"

I glared at him. Like I'd ever consider going on without him.

It appeared Atara felt equally insulted. "We do not," she interrupted coolly, "value people like trinkets. We do not feel them animals to perform for us, or serve us, or to be discarded."

I was happy to hear it, but I thought Taro could be forgiven for thinking otherwise.

"I would love to be able to do something more than fetch and carry. I would love to bring in enough coin that Lee doesn't feel paying off our list of debt is her sole responsibility. But I will not lie and swindle people for money. I will not."

Atara stared at him for a long, tense moment. Then, something in her air, something almost imperceptible in her posture, seemed to relax. "You cannot do this?" she asked.

And this time it seemed an honest question, rather than a challenge.

So Taro relaxed a little, too. "I cannot," he said. "I am sorry."

Don't apologize to her.

"It is, indeed, unfortunate. We need a healer."

Don't you dare try to make him feel guilty.

"I have been on the Northern continent," she said. "When I was a younger woman, before my mother died. She thought it important for me to see a broader world. At some time, I would like Kahlia to do the same." With her fingertips, she moved a number of beads around with a light touch and no apparent design in mind. "The air was so dry. It made my skin peel, and I felt always thirsty. And dirty. As though dust were clinging to my skin, and no amount of washing could rid me of it. The food was so heavy and thick, it seemed to layer the bottom of my stomach for days. It became so cold in winter, I felt as though my very bones had turned to ice, and I would never be warm again. My fingers and wrists and ankles hurt." She held her hands before her, bending her fingers as though testing them for pain. Then she shrugged, putting the black box back in its drawer. "They called my prognostication witchcraft. Some would offer money to me, to do it on their behalf, as though I would sell my gift, like Corla."

I kept my eyebrows from rising up, but only just. So it was all right to have someone selling their gifts for the benefit of the troupe, but Atara was too good to do it herself?

"Others, though, they drove me out of town. They thought I was evil." She smiled at that, strangely enough. Then she looked at Karish. "I had forgotten how difficult such things could be."

Taro tilted his head in his approximation of a bow. "I can imagine."

He was completely relaxed. I had anticipated an evening of trying to get him out of whatever mood this conversation was putting him in, and probably failing, but it was unnecessary. His arm beneath my hand was loose and fluid. The tension had drained out of the air. He was so changeable.

Atara seemed pretty relaxed, too, so I thought I'd dare a question. "This trip up north you took, was it before Kahlia was born?"

"Kai."

"How long before she was born?"

Atara raised an eyebrow. "Her father was a Northern man. I would not recommend traveling while pregnant."

I was stunned that she answered the questions so easily. And she didn't even hint that I had no business to be asking those questions. These people were so strange.

I guessed that meant Kahlia wasn't one of the line after all. Which was too bad. It would have been so handy to have our problem so easily solved.

We went back to our tent. I flipped aside the entrance flap and stepped inside, ready to shut out the rest of the world.

Only the thief was sitting in there, waiting for us.

Chapter Fifteen

She was just sitting there on the mat, cross-legged, her hands resting limply on her knees. A small, leather bag lay on the mat beside her. Her relaxed air suggested she hadn't been caught in the act of stealing. Indeed, I wouldn't have even suspected her of it, from her posture, if I didn't know what she was.

Aye, she didn't look startled, or guilty. But a thief obviously didn't feel guilty about stealing, and if she had any experience at it, she'd know how to prevent reaction to surprises.

She looked like she'd been waiting for us. Certainly, she made no move to run.

"Empty your bag," I ordered.

She rolled her dark eyes and sighed hugely, but she didn't utter a word of protest. She jerked on the laces of the bag and upended the contents on the floor. A shirt, a skirt, a bracelet, a needle and some thread. That was all the bag held, and none of it looked familiar.

"Stand up."

"Why?"

"Because I told you to."

I heard a faint sound from my side. Like Taro was trying to hold back a snort. I didn't look at him. Neither did the girl.

She did indulge in another eye roll, though. She stood, shaking her long dark hair off her shoulder.

She didn't smell too wonderful, and she had horrible posture. She'd better hope her spine didn't grow into that shape once she was an adult. She'd be gorgeous if she were clean. She had the wide eyes, the lovely cheekbones, and her mouth would probably be pretty if it weren't being held in a scowl.

She was as scantily clad as any other islander I'd seen, the fabric of her clothes faded and in some places worn almost indecently thin. I couldn't see anywhere that she could be hiding anything, and I wasn't about to search her with anything other than my eyes. "What do you want?"

"You're a cool one," she muttered.

No. I was just in a bad mood. "Speak."

"What are you?" she asked.

"Northerner."

"Not that!" she snapped with impatience. "I know that. But you're not like regular Northerners."

Not like regular . . . Surely she didn't mean that. Why would she even think to ask about that? "I'm a Shield."

"What's a Shield?"

Zaire. Where to start? I looked at Taro, and he just shrugged back. Revenge for my refusal to help him with defining a Source earlier with Atara. "I work with a Source." I nodded at Taro. "When there's an earthquake, a Source can"—here was the hard part—"use his mind to redirect it." I looked at Taro again. He shrugged again. I supposed that meant my definition was good enough. "I protect him while he does it."

She sneered at Taro. "You need protecting?"

He cocked an eyebrow at her. "All Sources need Shielding when they channel, little one."

The "little one" could have been an expression of affection. He used it because he knew it would tick her off.

And it did. She thrust out her flat chest, eyes flaring. "I don't need no Shielding when I link," she declared.

I stared at her. "You channel?" I asked.

" 'F's that's what you call it."

"And you don't work with a Shield?"

"Don't work with no one."

It was supposed to be impossible for a Source to channel without a Shield and live. That was the reason Shields existed, after all. The reason we spent years in academies, the reason why we were Chosen by Sources and bonded to them for the rest of our lives. I'd known a Source who almost committed suicide by channeling without a Shield, surviving only because he changed his mind at the last moment. According to everything everyone knew and learned, Sources needed Shields to operate. And that was that.

But Taro could heal without a Shield. He'd done it before he met me, though not since we had been bonded. He claimed he couldn't. I thought he was just afraid to. Or was trying to spare my feelings. I'd often wondered if he could channel without me and survive, if he would just dare to try.

Someone had been channeling. Taro had felt it.

"Who trained you?" I asked.

She snickered. "Nobody."

"Perhaps that's why you're so bad at it," Taro said coolly.

"I'm not bad at it!"

"You're very weak. You can't channel much. You'd never handle the events up north."

"You can go stick yourself!" she retorted.

For shame, Taro. Tormenting an eleven-year-old. Or whatever she was.

I crossed my arms. "What do you want?"

For the first time, the little creature looked uncertain. "Take me with you."

One shock after another. "Your pardon?"

"You heard me."

"You want to join the troupe?"

"No. North."

"Why?"

"Because I want to. Been on this island all my life. Wanna get off."

"We're not going home for at least a couple of years."

She bit her lower lip, glancing about as she thought. Then she said, "I can wait."

"Why?"

"I'm your kind, right? Or"—she looked at Taro without much enthusiasm—"his kind."

What an odd sentiment. "There's more to it than that."

She raised her chin proudly. "I can make you coin."

"I could not be less interested in the proceeds of theft."

"Huh?" she said, looking confused. Then she worked it out. "I can do other things. I don't have ta steal."

I didn't really want to know what other means of gaining funds she used.

Really, Lee. Do you have to always assume the worst? Kids worked for money all the time, had all sorts of ways. Just because I didn't know what they were didn't mean they didn't exist.

Money had nothing to do with anything.

"What about your father?" I asked her.

"Got no father."

"The medicine man . . ."

"Is not my father."

"He's your guardian, though?"

She shrugged. "Not really."

"What does that mean?"

"I lived with him."

"He takes care of you?"

She snickered.

"Does he have the right to tell you what to do?"

"He's no kin of mine."

Damn it. She knew what I was asking, even if I didn't know the proper words for asking. "Does he feed you?"

"When he feels like it."

"How long have you lived with him?"

"Forever."

Good enough. "So he's going to come after you when he finds you gone."

"Don't see why. Always snarking about me being more trouble than I'm worth. Says I eat more than I bring in."

And she hadn't been eating much.

So this was the situation. This child, a thief, wanted us to take her from her guardian. Or whatever he was. We would have this child, a thief, with us for the next however long we were on the island, feeding her, housing her, and making sure she didn't rip off the entire troupe and anyone else we met. Then, we were taking her to the Northern continent and . . . what . . . dropping her off? Fare thee well. Nice to know you.

In theory, members of the Triple S were to take to the academies any Sources or Shields they discovered among the general population, but that wasn't why we were on Flatwell. And I had no doubt that the Empress's explicit orders trumped vague ongoing duties imposed by the Triple S.

She was staring at me, an unnatural intensity in her eyes. She was too young to have such weight in her gaze. And she had the uncomfortable ability, it appeared, to know what I was thinking. "I'll do whatever you want," she said. "You gotta take me. I'm your kind."

And how had she known that? How had she known what we were?

Had she felt Taro? The way he had felt her?

That didn't explain me, though. She'd come to me, asked me what I was first. If she didn't know what a Shield was, she wouldn't have thought to go to anyone other than Taro himself.

She could be lying about the whole thing. Someone she knew could be the Source, working with a Shield as all

Sources did. Maybe they had mentioned to her that they had felt Taro working, and she had spotted some kind of opportunity. But what?

To get away from the medicine man? Could that be all?

Zaire. Why was this sort of thing always happening to us?

"I don't need much space," she said, desperation tingeing her words. "I can curl up anywhere. Always do. Can scrape up my own food. Really. Just need . . ."

What did she need? Really? If she didn't need space, if she could do for herself, what did she need us for?

For someone to be with. Because she was a child, and small as this island was, it was still a big place to be alone.

Hell.

"Lee?" Taro said, touching my arm. "A word?"

Aye, that was a good idea. I looked at the girl—Aryne. That was the name the medicine man had screamed out, wasn't it? "You move so much as a hair's breadth, I'll know you've stolen something."

"Lee!" Karish chided.

Lee, what? "She's a thief."

"Am not!" she objected hotly.

"I caught you trying to steal my purse! What do you think that makes you?"

"Really bad at it," she muttered.

"Don't move," I ordered, and I followed Karish out of the tent.

Finding a place to talk was a bit of a challenge. Not only did we have to be far enough away from our tent not to be overheard, we had to be far enough away from everyone else as well. Not that I could really hope no one had noticed the little creature sneaking into our tent.

"What are we going to do?" Taro asked.

"That was my question."

"We can't leave her here."

"Why not?"

"Lee!"

"Really. We don't have the means for rescuing people."

"She's a Source. Or something. She should be going to one of the academies. She is prepared to run away. She's latched on to us, and if we don't take her, she'll latch on to someone else. At least if we take her, we'll know she's not being taken advantage of."

"It'll be a nightmare. You know that, don't you? For all we know, she's just looking for a means to rob this whole troupe blind." And after my recent scare about being exiled from the troupe, I really didn't want to take any chances. "She claims to be a Source who doesn't need a Shield. How can we know she's telling the truth? There aren't even supposed to be any Sources—or Shields—on the Southern Islands."

"We can check that part of her story, at least."

"How?"

Taro raised an eyebrow at me.

I raised mine back as I clued in. "You can't be serious. You're going to cause an event just to test her?"

"Aye."

Aye? *Aye?* "Where's the man who found the very idea of creating an event an unnatural and perverse use of his talent?"

"It does no harm."

"We don't know that."

"It'll be just the slightest tremor. To see how she reacts."

"So what if she is a Source? Or what if she's not?"

"Let's just find out, shall we?"

What was he saying? If she were a Source, we'd take her, but if she weren't, we'd leave her behind? If we were going to take her, shouldn't we take her regardless?

If we took her, and she wasn't a Source, we would be stuck with her until she chose to leave. It could be years. And I had no intention of inheriting children who were half-grown with no fear of me trained into them.

If she was a Source, we really had a duty to get her to an academy. She could do all sorts of damage to herself if she was left to run wild. Regardless of how well, sort of, she had survived to date.

Oh, I didn't know what to do.

"I still don't think this is an appropriate use of your skills."

"Token protest is noted. Ready?"

"Of course."

His shields went down. A moment later, I felt the lightest of forces flow through him. I didn't feel anything physically, though, no shift in temperature or in earth. If I weren't Shielding him, I wouldn't have known anything was going on.

"She's not catching it," he said. "I'm going to step it up a little."

The flow of forces became a little heavier. I could feel the barest tremor through the soles of my feet. But again, if I hadn't been Shielding, I probably wouldn't have noticed.

"Still nothing," he said.

"Hm."

"Just a little more," he muttered, and the tremors grew hard enough to be easily felt before I could make any objection. "There she is."

"She's channeling?"

"Aye."

I felt a spurt of panic. I couldn't help it. "She doesn't have a Shield."

He caught my wrist before I could dash back to the tent. "She says she doesn't need one."

"Children lie a lot."

"She's doing fine."

"You can't feel what's going on inside her."

"No, but she's not dead yet, is she?"

"We just started."

"She's fine. Leave it. She'll pull out if she gets into trouble."

"She can't pull out once she's engaged." Her instincts wouldn't let her. He knew that. What was he doing?

He growled in annoyance, but the tremors faded, then, and halted.

I was still annoyed. "We could have killed her."

"Calm down. I was right there, taking over when she was overwhelmed."

"So she was overwhelmed?"

"Aye, but not for the lack of a Shield. She's just not very strong."

"She couldn't channel that herself?" That had been so minor. Probably no one had even noticed it.

On the other hand, she'd done it without a Shield. That was amazing enough.

He shook his head. "Maybe she could have if I'd let it go longer, let her build up to it. But something that mild, it should have taken only a few moments."

So she could channel alone, but she was bad at it. Would she do better with a Shield? Would she do better with training?

Damn. This meant we had to take her, didn't it?

"Think we should sleep on it?" Taro asked.

"Is there really a point?"

He offered me a bent smile. "Not really."

Damn.

What the hell were we going to do with her for the next two years?

We looked at each other, realizing together that we had just let ourselves in for a horrific, gargantuan task we had no idea whether we were up to performing.

"All right. So." He pulled in a deep breath and let it out. "All right," he said again. "Let's go tell her."

We returned to the tent. The girl didn't appear to have moved, not even to pick up the items she had dropped from her bag onto the mat. She was coated in sweat, however, and when she looked at us, her eyes were tired.

"Well?" she asked.

"Sit down," I said.

She melted into a sitting position on the mat, a strangely

fluid and appealing motion. She rested her head on her hand and looked up at us.

"We are prepared to take you with us, under certain conditions."

"I can get you coin," she said.

"We're not interested in that. More importantly, you are not interested in that."

"Oh."

"I mean it. You steal a single item—"

She rolled her eyes.

"—and I will beat you within a breath of death."

She shrugged and grinned, and at this first nonsullen expression, I saw how truly beautiful she was. Why did I have to put myself in the company of such people? "I been beat before."

Sad as that was, I wasn't going to let it sidetrack me. "Then I will find something that will torment you and dig right in. And I will find it. I'm smart."

"Kai, kai. I figured."

"I mean it. Not a single, solitary thing. We won't bail you out. There will be no second chances. If we so much as suspect you of lifting anything, we will ditch you, whether we are in the middle of a city or the middle of nowhere. Understood?"

"Understood," she echoed, mimicking my accent right down to the final over-articulated "*d*." Cheeky brat.

"And that's not all."

" 'Course not."

"We are taking you only on the understanding that once we hit the Northern continent, you are going straight to the Source Academy."

"The what?"

"Where Taro went to school. Where all Sources go to school."

"I'm not going to any school!" she protested, her lower lip protruding in a pout.

"That's the only way we're taking you."

"Then you can go to hell!"

"Fine." I gestured at the entrance flap. "You can leave now."

She bit that lower lip and stared at me.

"I think this might be my job," said Taro.

"Convincing her to go?"

"More like explaining to her what the Academy is like, and why it's in her best interest to go."

"Like I can believe you," she muttered. "You'll say anything, won't you?"

"I've got no reason to lie," he told her. "I really don't care whether you go or stay. In fact, it's much easier on both of us if you just disappear."

She glared at him.

He was spectacularly unmoved.

He looked up at me. "You might want to talk to Atara."

"Why?"

"I imagine we need her permission to take on someone new."

Oh. Right. I'd forgotten about that.

So I was the one who got to convince Atara that we should introduce a thief to the troupe. "Thank you so very much."

He smiled before blowing a kiss at me. The prat.

"Tell her I've got good doings for her," Aryne said.

"What does that mean?" I asked.

"That snake that bit that man, it wasn't natural."

"Wasn't natural how?" For Zaire's sake, could she not just spit out the whole story instead of doling it out in tiny morsels?

"It was put there. By some man. He had it in a bag, and he released it on the ground."

"And no one saw him do this?"

"Everyone was watching you," Taro said.

"He wasn't with the other speccies," Aryne added. "He was hiding in the trees. He threw something on the ground, but I couldn't see what. Then he threw out the snake. He left before it even bit the other fellow."

"You saw this and you didn't think to warn anyone?" Taro demanded.

"Snake struck too fast. No time. No one'd believe me, anyway."

Of all the—What kind of prank was that, setting a poisonous snake among a crowd? Thought it was funny, did he, risking the lives of performers and their audience? Sometimes people infuriated me.

I went to Atara's tent and sought entrance.

She granted it most regally.

"Good evening, Dunleavy," she said, surprising me by using my proper name. I'd practically forgotten what it sounded like. "Why do you look for me?"

She was still seated at her table, but the beads were gone, replaced by a black piece of parchment. She had a fistful of what looked like purple sand, and she was carefully sprinkling it over the parchment, lining it next to a long sinuous shape of light blue sand. There was a silver glint to the sand, and against the black parchment it looked stunning. "May I ask what you are doing?"

"Sand painting," she said. "It is one of our arts. People like to buy them."

I hadn't noticed her selling such things. "It is beautiful."

"It also speaks of the future," she said.

"Does it?" I was careful to keep the disbelief out of my voice, and that, I was finding easier and easier. These were their beliefs. I didn't agree with them, but they did no harm. "How?"

"I think about a person, and their future, and the colors come. The colors speak of the paths the person's life will take. Not small details, such as whether someone will fall in love, or be wealthy. The larger paths. Will someone be happy? Healthy? Will they shape the lives of others?"

"I see." What a wonderful thing for an artist, to find so much inspiration in so many places.

"What do you think of this person's future, Dunleavy?"

Atara brushed off the last of the blue, and dug her hand into a jar of dark red.

"I have no skill in such things."

"Try. There is no harm in trying. Except, of course, appearing incorrect. And you do so hate to appear incorrect."

Wench.

She trailed the dark red across the two streaks of lighter color. The red, while pretty in itself, was harsh against the other colors. Violent, almost, and painful. And the lighter colors below the red suddenly seemed pale, while above the red they seemed vibrant. How could that be, when they were the same colors?

"From what I see here, if I had to guess . . ." This was stupid. I knew nothing of such things. "I would say the person is coming up against some kind of change, or shock. And it will hurt. A lot. But afterward, I don't know, it seems their life will be the better for it."

"You are not incorrect." She smiled. "Though you are not complete, either. Still, for a nonbeliever, a remarkable job. Now, can you guess who this is for?"

"Me?" Because why else the abject lesson?

She tsked. "So you are not perfect after all."

And I was embarrassed by my self-absorption. It appeared that not everyone else was as fascinated with me as I was.

"No, this is your thief."

I hated when people did things like that. Knew things before I told them.

"She is facing a very difficult task," she said. "Be gentle with her."

"You don't object to her joining the troupe?"

"I do not."

A part of me was almost hoping she would, so we could cut the girl loose with no responsibility. But things never turned out so simply. "Thank you."

Atara nodded, choosing a dark, heavy blue to trace immediately beside the red. It emphasized the differences in the lighter purples and blues even more dramatically, giving the appearance of brutally cutting them in half.

"She mentioned seeing someone set the snake on Panol."

Atara looked up at me swiftly, her eyes narrowed. "Do you believe her?"

"I have no reason not to. She has no reason to tell me such a story if it isn't true." No more reason than a person would have to toss a snake among people in the first place.

"Did she know him?"

"She didn't say, but I think she would have if she did."

Atara looked grim, but not shocked.

"Has this sort of thing happened before?"

Atara shrugged. "Players are not welcome by everyone."

"So they try to kill you?"

"Not usually."

Not usually. Wonderful. But that was all Atara was prepared to say, and there was nothing I could do about any of it anyway.

I left Atara, feeling unsettled.

I was always unsettled. I hated this island.

I lingered away from the tent, to give Taro plenty of time to convince Aryne she had to go to the Academy. And she did have to go. I had been told stories of people, Sources and Shields, who had managed to grow up outside the academies. They were old stories, and Aryne seemed to be doing all right, but I had no way of knowing whether Aryne could stay sane if she progressed into adulthood without the direction of the Academy.

Besides, whatever the failings of the Triple S, Aryne would always have enough to eat and a roof over her head.

Unless some crazy Empress sent her off on a fool's errand in the middle of nowhere.

Eventually, I went back to our tent to find the girl gobbling down rice and fish, prepared for her by Taro, who was watching her lack of eating manners with an aristocratic curl to his lip.

"Well?" I said to Aryne.

"I'll go to your blasted school," she said through a mouthful of food.

I reached down, put a fingertip under her chin, and closed her mouth.

She was lying.

But she couldn't complain when we dragged her to the Academy whether she liked it or not. After all, she'd been warned.

Chapter Sixteen

Kabis, I had learned, was the word for the entrance flap of the tent. Each piece of a tent had its own name. And if the same piece of fabric made up the eastern wall—or skevin—of one tent, but was later used as part of the ceiling for another, its name was changed to sheder.

I was learning this from Aryne. Having a Southerner living in our tent was quite the education.

It had been a week since she had joined us, and a tense week at that. For all sorts of reasons. Panol had arranged for another length of fabric to enable Aryne to have a "room" of her own. There was little space, and days when we were stuck inside due to rain were tortuously slow. And, of course, there was absolutely no privacy. After Aryne had walked in on no less than three conversations pertaining to the Empress's descendants, we decided we couldn't speak of them at all.

The lack of privacy had other ramifications. There was no way I was having sex with nothing more than a thin piece of fabric between us and the girl. Taro wasn't too keen on it, either. During my less mature moments, I railed at the inherent unfairness of life. I had only a short period of time when I would hold Taro's attention. It was being squandered due to the presence of the girl.

Plus, I was waiting for her to steal something. I knew she was going to, sooner or later. A person couldn't change a lifetime habit just like that. She, of course, claimed she hadn't been trying to steal from me that day at the market, she had only fallen against me accidentally. She had never stolen anything in her entire life. I, of course, didn't believe this revision of history, but I wasn't prepared to call her a liar. Not out loud. All I could do was wait. Wait for her to do something stupid, and figure out how I was going to handle it when she did.

How to handle it. How to handle her. Aryne was baffling. Although she was quick with an objection or a cutting remark, she was reticent about her personal information. She claimed to have no last name. She claimed both her parents were dead, though she didn't know how they died, or even what their names were. She didn't know where she had been born. She had been following the medicine man—whose name was Leslie Border—around the island all her life.

The medicine man suddenly disappeared, it seemed, for we no longer saw him at the villages at which we stopped. I had feared he would come after us, but Aryne claimed his traditional route branched west as we went east and that was one of the reasons she had chosen the time she had to come to us.

Apparently, she had been planning to chase after us from the moment she had first encountered us. She claimed that at the market, she had noticed something different about us and had been determined to find out what it was.

She was a driven little thing, for a child.

She was skilled as well, for one so young. She had spent her life cleaning and repairing clothes, valuable talents for a troupe such as Atara's. This was the source of the coin she had claimed when convincing us to take her with us, not the more nefarious routes my mind had leapt to.

She also knew how to whip together medicines that

looked good, felt effective, and accomplished nothing. She claimed they did no harm. I'd forbidden her to make them and had so far caught her selling them to Rinis twice. No one else would back me up on the snake oil ban, and Aryne purchased the ingredients with her own funds—acquired through the sales. I had to give up on it.

She had settled in too easily, with too little disruption to everyone else. Something had to snap. It was inevitable. Waiting for it, however, was enough to make me snap.

She did not appear to be a typical Source. Well, obviously she wasn't, in that she didn't need a Shield, but it was more than that. I witnessed no emotional extremes in her. She didn't display any weird tricks with speech. She did, however, stumble too close to the fire and was a little slower about getting away from it than I liked. There was no noticeable expression of pain, either, as I spread on the burn the gel I got from Kahlia.

We, Taro and I, were stunned by her reaction to music. One morning, after a performance, a shaken Taro briefly described having to drag an extremely amorous adolescent back to the tent. He refused to tell me of the other difficulties he had experienced, and teasing him about it had earned me nothing more than a very curt dismissal. He banned Aryne from attending any more of my performances. As he threatened to leave her tied up in the tent if she didn't comply, that was a ban that stuck.

I didn't know what to think of our newly discovered Source displaying clearly Shield traits.

She had taken to following me around, all day, every day. I couldn't say I cared for it. "Run off. I have to go to the challenges."

"Can I come watch?"

"No."

"Why not? There's no proper music. Just the drums."

"I don't want to be distracted." And I didn't want her stealing from such easy targets whom she'd likely never see again.

"I should learn how to do this, if I'm going to be going to that school of yours."

"You won't be going to my school. You'll be going to the Source Academy, and they don't dance the benches. Not much, anyway."

"Then I want to go to the Shield school. I want to do the dancing."

"You're not a Shield."

"Aye, I am."

I looked at her curiously. "You're a Source."

"I'm a Shield, too."

"You can't be both."

"Why not?"

"Because it's impossible." I made an effort never to use that word. It was too uncompromising. But of course she wasn't both Source and Shield. That was just . . . impossible.

"I feel music like you do."

"Not like I do." No one, it seemed, felt it like I did. "Most people are sensitive to music to some extent. Regulars, Sources and Shields."

"Not like me." She grinned.

"It's nothing to be proud of."

"I want to go to the Shield school instead."

"Let's say you were both Source and Shield, and could choose which school to go to. You'd want to go to the Source Academy. You'd want to be a Source."

"Why?"

"Because—"

And I froze. Because . . . why?

I could say that Sources were rarer, and were more desperately needed, and that would be true. But that wouldn't be the reason why I said what I said.

I said what I said because I thought it was easier to be a Source. Because I thought Sources were treated better by everyone else. Because Sources didn't seem to worry so much about things, about whether they did their tasks properly. No one really expected them to memorize the maps and read the reports and do anything, really, but channel forces. Whereas Shields had to do so much more than Shield.

I liked being a Shield. I was too proud of it, and of how seriously I took it.

But my automatic reaction to the possibility of being able to choose whether to be a Source or a Shield, was to suggest the choice be a Source.

Was that what I really felt? Really?

I didn't want to think about it. I had enough to think about as it was. Shelve that.

"Because why?" Aryne prodded.

"Because there are fewer Sources, and we need more of them." There was a sharpness to my voice that Aryne didn't deserve. "You'll be going to the Source Academy. You don't need to learn how to dance."

"Dunleavy," she whined.

"This is not the proper way to be learning anyway. I'll show you at a better time. Go find something to wash."

She scowled and stomped off with a sullen look.

Well done, Lee.

Zaire, I was always in a bad mood.

Once the challenges were over, I hunted up Taro. He had been helping Leverett grease his drums and was in the process of scraping the clinging stuff off his hands. "I need to talk to you," I said to him.

He nicked a towel from Leverett's pile, and followed me as I looked for a place where we could possibly speak without arousing anyone's attention or being overheard. "Something wrong?" he asked after we'd crashed through a stretch of undergrowth to get away from the camp.

"We're getting close," I said.

"Close to what?"

"Golden Fields." He still looked blank. "Golden Fields. The whole reason for this whole thing. From what Atara says, we'll get there in a little over a week."

His mouth opened on a silent "oh." Then he closed it to a thin line. "We're going to have to start thinking now, aren't we?"

"Unfortunately."

"It may take us more than a week to . . . figure out what we want to figure out."

"Aye."

"I won't be able to work while we're looking. And you won't be able to practice or perform."

"Aye."

"Are we leaving the troupe, then?"

I didn't like that idea. First, we still owed them a pile of money. Second, we still had to make our way from Golden Fields back to the harbor to catch a ship to the mainland. "We told Atara we were looking for family in Golden Fields. This won't come as a surprise to her. We could ask her to be excused for a while, tell her we'll catch up again after we've made our investigation."

"What do we do with them if we find them?" he asked.

"Huh?"

"The line. What if there are dozens of them? The tent can get only so big."

I stared at him. "Hell. I never thought of that."

"How are we supposed to manage all of them?"

"Maybe they won't all want to go."

"Aren't we supposed to bring them all?"

"She didn't say." The Empress had said very little. For something that was so important—and it had damned well better be important if she sent us out there—she had given us precious little information. I would have hoped the ruler of our world would have been better at giving directions.

"So, what do we do?"

"Not panic until we know what all the problems are."

He scowled. "I am not panicking."

"I'm more worried about actually finding them, rather than their number." I still had no idea how to begin, once we were there.

"I told you. We go there. We ask what happened to the Bryant family. We move from there."

Right. Who cared about discretion?

But what I thought in sarcasm was probably actually true. I doubted word of anything we did on the island would follow us back to the mainland.

"So we have to tackle Atara." Again. I hated having to account to her for everything. "Rather, you should."

"Me?"

"Aye. You know. Lay on the Stallion charm."

He glared at me. "The people here are immune to my charm."

"Only because you haven't really used it. And that's dangerous. If you don't keep it in use it'll fade away altogether."

"Will you stop?"

We found Atara in her tent, as usual. It seemed the woman never left it unless we were trudging somewhere. This time she was reading, however, instead of doing something discomforting. She had lit only two candles. Black, as usual.

"Good afternoon, Atara," said Taro. "You are looking particularly elegant, today."

She raised an eyebrow at him. "What do you need?"

Huh. She could at least pretend to be charmed.

"I believe Dunleavy spoke to you about Golden Fields?"

Atara closed her book and set it aside. "We were discussing when we would arrive there."

"You may recall that when we first met, we told you we were looking for someone in Golden Fields."

"Did you?"

Yes, we did.

"We need to be free to look for them."

"What do you mean, free?"

"Free from our obligations to the troupe for the time it takes to find these people."

"So you want to be able to benefit from our protection without having to contribute to it."

"Well—"

"Yes," I said.

Karish looked at me, which transferred responsibility for this conversation over to me. Prat. Though I supposed that was my fault for opening my mouth in the first place.

"This is the reason we came to the island in the first place."

"And if you find this person you're looking for, you'll leave Flatwell."

A statement, not a question. "We have every intention of paying off the debt we owe you," I promised her.

"That wasn't what I asked."

Damn it, she wasn't supposed to notice that. "Maybe not the words, but that's the meaning."

"So what is your meaning?"

"That the debt will be repaid."

"You seem to forget," Atara drawled, "the reason I allowed you to join our troupe was because you were to be good omens. It is not merely a matter of the debt."

Oh for the love of—She felt we hadn't performed adequately as good omens? How did you measure something like that?

My performance was bringing additional coin to everyone, not just me. Taro saved her son's life. What the hell more did she want?

Well, here was an idea. "Good omens can't lift your curse," I told her.

Her eyes narrowed. "Kahlia has been speaking to you."

Was she serious? Everyone had been speaking to me. "We'll leave as much as we can behind as security. We need the tent, obviously, the cookware and our clothes. Anything else we can, we'll leave behind."

"That's not enough."

"There is nothing else."

"You could leave Shintaro."

My mouth dropped open. "What?"

"You value him."

"Not as security!" Besides, finding these people was his task. I was the one who was only along for the ride.

She crossed her arms. "Then I see no way that this can be done."

"I can. Taro and I pick up and leave right now and do what we have to do, and your troupe be damned." Please don't make us do that.

"You'd have to leave everything. What you have paid for would have to be left as payment for what you still owe."

"Understood."

She wasn't expecting that. "You would be leaving with nothing more than the clothes you came with."

"Fine." Not fine. Terrifying. But the whole reason we'd come to this Zaire-neglected island was to look for the Empress's descendants. I wasn't going to be controlled by this woman to the point that we couldn't even do what we'd come to do. We'd be on this damned island forever.

We'd manage. We'd figure out some way to manage. We'd already learned a lot about how to get on with these people. Maybe I could figure out some way to perform on my own, or challenge people to bench dancing in proper competition. Without having to worry about sparing feelings or fetching and carrying, Taro could get into some gambling and turn whatever I made into more. And Aryne—I'd forgotten about Aryne—maybe she could scrape together some coins with her laundering and tailoring.

We'd figure out a way. We'd have to.

"Fine," Atara said back.

"All right. Let's go get our stuff, Taro."

"No!" she cried. Then she sighed. "Stupid child. Stubborn."

"You have no idea how stubborn," I warned her. Just for effect. Secretly, I was extremely relieved.

"What do you propose?"

"What I said. We'll leave whatever we can behind as security. You give us clear directions where you're going to be. We'll catch up with you as soon as we're finished in Golden Fields." I felt so bad about this. I was lying so very much.

"How long do you think it would be?"

"I have no idea." I looked at Taro, who shrugged. "We really can't afford to take too long. We don't have the money. Maybe a couple of weeks?" Taro shrugged again.

"That wouldn't be too burdensome," said Atara.

And if we couldn't find any of these descendants, we might as well just join the troupe forever. How could we go back with failure?

I was not going to think that way.

"I will perform while the troupe's in Golden Fields, of course. We'd just remain behind after you leave, and catch up after."

She still didn't like the idea, and she drew out her decision, to make us worry. But she had already given her answer away, and when she finally nodded it came as no surprise.

So that was settled. Now we just had to worry about finding these people.

Chapter Seventeen

I wasn't a light sleeper, and I'd been getting accustomed to the various noises one heard during the night while sleeping in a tent surrounded by other tents. So I wasn't sure why I woke in the middle of that night. But I did wake, unusually alert, and I listened.

I heard a rustling in our own tent.

I rolled under the "wall" and clamped onto Aryne's legs. She fell with a thud and a curse, trying to kick me off, but I held on to both feet. "Taro!"

"What the—?" he muttered.

"She's trying to steal from us!"

"I am not!" she hissed. "Let me go!"

"Stay still!"

"Bog off!"

"Check her bag, Taro."

"Wait a moment."

I held the squirming child to the mat while Taro fumbled about. He lit one of the lanterns and yanked Aryne's bag from her clutches, despite her fluid and colorful objections.

He upended the bag and rifled through the contents. "Nothing of ours here."

"Told you!"

I released Aryne and she began shoving the articles back into her bag. "Doesn't mean you haven't got anything of anyone else's in there."

"I didn't take anything! I'm not a thief."

"Then why are you sneaking out into the middle of the night like one?"

"I'm tired of being your dogsbody. Work harder here than I did with Border."

The twinge of guilt those words inspired was totally inappropriate. "You mean because we don't let you run around lifting from people like he did?"

"Go to hell!"

All right, so maybe that was a little harsh. "That still doesn't explain why you're leaving in the middle of the night."

She hugged the bag close to her. "Figured you'd try to stop me."

"If you could slip away from Border as easily as you did, you couldn't feel you'd have any problem getting away from us."

She pouted mulishly.

"What's going on?"

"Nothin'."

"If you're going to leave, why don't you wait until morning?"

She picked at a ragged thread on her bag. "Why're you going to Golden Fields?"

"The troupe is going to Golden Fields."

She glared at me. "You and him are leaving the troupe to stay in Golden Fields. I heard you."

Eavesdropping. Lovely. "We're looking for people."

"To buy?"

It was my turn to stare. "To buy? As in buy people?"

She sneered. "That's where the slave pens are. Everyone knows."

"Everyone knows? Who's everyone? I've never heard of such a thing." Slave pens? Was she serious? I'd never heard of any slaves in the Southern Islands, not at any time before coming to Flatwell, not at any time since. "I've never seen anyone who could be a slave."

"You ever asked?"

"Of course not." Why would I even think to?

"There you are."

"What's she saying?" Taro asked.

He had pulled a shirt on over his head. His hair was wild and his eyes widened with the shock of being pulled out of a deep sleep in the middle of the night.

He was stunning.

"That there are slaves on the island. That they sell them in Golden Fields."

"I've never heard anything like that," he said.

"Why would you?" Aryne demanded scornfully. "You're offlanders."

"Why would they bother hiding it?"

She clearly didn't have a response to that.

"I don't care what you didn't hear," she snarled. "I'm not going to Golden Fields."

"What difference does it make to you, one way or the other?"

"None of your mind."

"Well, the troupe is going to Golden Fields. If you're basing your decision on wrong information . . ."

"I'm not. You are. And you've got something planned for Golden Fields. I heard you."

Damn it. We'd been so careful. "We're just looking for people there. Family. Not to buy anyone. And it has nothing to do with you."

"I'm not going."

"Why not?"

"Told you. None of your mind."

Irritating little brat. But she appeared frightened in a way I hadn't seen in her before. There was something significant going on there.

"Are you afraid of someone who's there?" Taro asked.

She tightened her grip on her bag before she said, "No."

She was lying. "Who's there?" I asked her.

"No one!"

"There is something there that you're afraid of. You can tell me now or you can tell me hours from now after I've done nothing but nag you about it."

She made a run for it, but I grabbed her arm before she could take so much as a step.

"Let me go!"

Taro wrapped his arms around her waist and sat her down. "Be civilized," he ordered her.

"Bog off!"

"Calm down," I said, and I snatched the bag back from her. I figured she wouldn't leave us without it.

"Eh!" she objected.

"Calm down. Be still. Tell us what is going on. And if I'm satisfied, you get your bag—with everything you own in the world in it—back."

She made a grab for it and Taro restrained her.

"Talk, or you don't get this back." I felt like such an awful bully. But I didn't know what else to do, and the options weren't good. Trying to drag her to Golden Fields against her will, letting her take off, letting her remain behind and then rejoin us. All would cause ridiculous complications.

She started swearing, and I didn't understand half of what she said. And then, finally, she said, "I'm a slave, right!"

Taro was shocked into letting her go, and she got moving. She didn't leave, though. She just squeezed into the opposite corner of the tiny room.

"You are not a slave," I said.

"What do you know?" she quite rightfully demanded.

"There are no slaves!"

"Like you would know."

"So you are saying you are Border's slave?"

"Nah. Not really. He didn't buy me. He stole me."

"That's what he told you?"

She rolled her eyes. "He says he 'rescued' me. I figure he says that so I'll feel obliged to him my whole life. I figure he stole me, though. That's why we never go to Golden Fields. He's dragged me all over this damn island, but we don't go anywhere near Golden Fields. I figure whoever he stole me from might come after him or something."

"Has anyone been after you that you know of?"

"Nah. But if we go there, it'll be pushing it." She made another grab for her bag, no doubt feeling I was relaxing my vigilance. I proved her wrong by yanking it away from her reach.

"I don't know what they do down here," I said, "but up north we don't have slaves."

"Ain't up north, now, are you?"

"That doesn't matter. I didn't leave my personality back on the boat."

"That's a subject for debate," Taro muttered.

I shot him a glance. What was that about?

"Are you going to give me my bag?"

"Are you going to take off as soon as we close our eyes?"

"My right, ain't it?"

"Not when we let you join us with the understanding you'd be going north with us and going to school."

"What do you care?"

"We don't know what it'll do to you if you keep developing outside of the academic environment. We hear nasty stories about Sources and Shields who don't go to school."

"Like what?" she demanded skeptically.

"Like going crazy." That was a gross simplification of what happened, but since I was no expert, that was what I was prepared to go with.

"Still no mind of yours."

"You're a child. We can't just let you wander around

loose. Especially if you are, as you claim, a slave. Someone else might snatch you up. Someone who'll work you much harder, and much differently, than we would."

She made a rude noise. I wasn't sure which part of my response she found difficult to believe; that I was concerned about her welfare, or that there may be guardians worse than us out there.

Perhaps she would be better able to accept a self-serving reason. "I'm not prepared to let you go when you do so well keeping my costumes in order, and when you bring in as much money as you do."

Taro shot me a look of amazement, but made no comment. Fortunately, Aryne was looking at me, not him, and didn't notice.

She didn't bring in much. I suspected she was keeping most of the money she made, which was fine with me. I wasn't about to live off the proceeds of a child. I took what she gave me because I had a feeling Aryne was more comfortable dealing with people with mercenary motives. If I took her on out of the goodness of my heart, she'd no doubt be wasting a lot of time being suspicious and waiting for the other shoe to drop. As long as she believed that all she had to do to keep me happy was throw a few coins my way, she would be easier to manage.

That was the theory I was working with, anyway.

I was putting aside all the money she gave me. The intention was to give it back to her once we had deposited her at the Source Academy. Of course, she wouldn't need it then. But I wasn't sure what else to do with it.

"You'll get a lot more for me if you sell me," she said.

"What can I say to convince you we have no intention of selling you?"

She thought about it a moment. "You could tell me about these people you're looking for."

Well, that had been predictable, hadn't it? To anyone whose brains were actually working.

What to say? It had to be convincing. So it would be

good if there were no lies involved. I wasn't really that good at lying.

And I really shouldn't be disappointed about that, even though it made life more difficult at times.

"We've been hired by someone wealthy to find members of her family," said Taro. Bless him. "She doesn't like the person who's due to inherit. So she asked us to find lateral descendants, to see if she thinks they'll manage her money better."

"What does she care, if she's dead?" Aryne demanded.

"Things like that are very important to Northerners," Taro told her. "Some people spend their whole lives scheming to get inheritances, others molding their heirs so that they'll treat the money properly after the first holder is dead. Wars start over it."

And he would know.

Aryne studied him, her natural inclination to distrust him in conflict with the fact that everything he had said was the absolute truth. Some significant omissions there, but that was the bare bones fact of our task. Why hadn't I thought of that?

"We were told Golden Fields was the last place any of these people lived. We're going there to ask questions and see if we can find out what happened to them."

"Slavers, were they?"

"Not to my knowledge, no. Not to the knowledge of the woman who hired us, either."

"What are you going to do with these people you find?"

"Take them back north, to meet her. If she likes them, and they like her, she might choose them to carry on after her."

Aryne smirked. "Her heir won't like that, eh?"

"I don't imagine," I said. But that, fortunately, was not our problem. He didn't even know we were down there, or it would be. "That's all we're doing, and the reason we're here. That's the only reason for us to go to Golden Fields. You're just a"—burden that had dropped into our laps— "new duty that popped out of the blue."

"Huh?"

"We have an obligation as members of the Triple S to report anyone we find who may be a Source or a Shield, and to bring them to the Academy if we can."

"Huh."

"So what's your decision?" I asked.

"I still don't want to go to Golden Fields," she said, but not with that same mulish air. It was fear at work, not stubbornness.

"You could be sick the whole time," I suggested.

"Eh?"

"Once we arrive at Golden Fields, you could develop a mysterious illness. No one will expect you to go out of the tent, and no one will want to get near you. You can recover once it's time to go. No one in Golden Fields will even know you're with us, never mind that you're a slave." Or whatever she was. I was going to have to look into that. "I won't have you taking off while we're there, though. You either come with us, or you leave and go your own way, and that's the end of our arrangement. That's the deal."

She scowled.

I was either going to watch out for her, or I wasn't. None of this do and don't stuff. Because all I would do while she was away from us was worry, and I'd always be wondering whether she was going to pop up again somewhere. I had far too much occupying my brain as it was, without having to add something new and totally useless.

"All right," she muttered. "Bag?"

I gave it back to her. "Bed," I ordered in response.

She huffed and snarled and made a big production out of yanking free her blanket and returning to her tiny section of the tent.

Taro and I exchanged a long look but said nothing. There was no point. Everything would be overheard by the girl, who had apparently overheard too much already.

I didn't sleep at all that night. I was listening for noise of her leaving. And there was none. I almost resented her the next morning, finding her there. All that worry for nothing.

Still, I wanted to make sure I had nothing to worry about. I went to Kahlia's tent. "Are there slaves on this island?"

She blinked in surprise. "Slaves?"

"Aye."

"Of course not." Then she scowled. "So little you think of us. Primitive Southerners, is that it?"

"That's not it," I said quickly, before she could work her way into a rant. "Someone mentioned it as though it were fact, and it surprised me, so I thought I would come ask. So sorry for disturbing you."

She grabbed my arm as I prepared to leave. "Are you ready to practice?"

I had to love her. Insult with one hand and the expectation of compliance with the other.

But it was time to practice. And with all that we had been asking from Atara lately, it was in our own interest to be as amenable to everyone as possible.

"Aye, aye, just give me a moment to tie up my hair."

So, no slaves in Golden Fields. As I suspected. But I would have sworn that Aryne had been telling the truth. Not that I was any expert at sniffing out lies, but something of her story had struck me as being sincere.

So, she was telling me a story.

Or, someone had told her one.

Chapter Eighteen

Another village, a tiny one, with a scanty collection of houses and little in the way of money. Not really worth stopping for, Beril was heard to mutter.

Apparently, Atara agreed with him. We performed our first night and throughout the next day, but the order came through to pack up the morning after that. Which was too bad. I'd been hoping to make it to the market to buy some new sandals.

Taro and I were in the process of rolling up our tent when we noticed the disturbance. Some shouting.

Aryne, tying up her bundle, cocked her head, then ran, disappearing into the undergrowth and trees.

"Aryne!" Taro hissed at her, to no effect.

"I know she's here!" I heard, and the voice sounded familiar. I couldn't place it, though, until I saw the man himself, Panol and Leverett on his heels.

"You!" he shouted at Taro, as soon as he saw him. "Where is she?"

Taro wrinkled his brow in that perfect, "I'm too dim to understand what you're talking about" expression. "Who?"

"Who!" Border echoed with disgust, shaking Panol's hand off his arm. "Aryne. I know she's with you!"

Taro held on to his expression of confusion. "You know Aryne?"

That made him angrier. Of course, it was supposed to. "She's mine!"

"Your what?" I asked him in my mildest tone.

My interjection seemed to make him more aware of himself, what he was saying, and that he had an audience. He took a breath. "My responsibility," he said in a milder tone. "She went missing in Black Tooth. I've been frantic."

"My apologies," Taro lied sweetly. "We were unaware she had any family. We had noticed her in various settlements, and we have hired her occasionally for odd errands. But that was the extent of our connection. We haven't seen her for the past few stops."

Border wasn't believing a word of it. "I saw her last night. She would never come this way on her own."

Because he had convinced her she was a slave, and that Golden Fields was where slaves were bought and sold. Or so she claimed. I couldn't ask him that, though. That would ruin the lie about not knowing there was a connection between the two of them.

Taro shrugged. "There's nothing I can say about that."

"I know she's traveling with you." He looked about at the audience we'd collected, searching for the truth in the faces of the spectators.

All he found were blank expressions. No one was saying anything.

Of course, that was probably confirmation enough, in his eyes.

We had to get rid of him. We didn't need yet another complication, in the shape of this creature following us all over the island and giving us a hard time. "What would we want with her?" I asked him. "She is no kin of ours." I still wasn't sure why being without family was so much worse for these people than ours, and was surprised to learn that it was one of the few things the islanders didn't like to talk about. Still, I could use information when I had no clue what it meant, if I had to.

"Aye, but—" He looked around at our audience once more.

"She is not here," Taro said. "We are packing up to leave. If the child were traveling with us, she would be here to pack up, too. She is not. And you will find none of her possessions with us. You can look, if you like." He waved an elegant hand over the mess that represented our belongings.

Border scowled, and he spent several moments looking at the jumble. I wondered if he was going to dare going through it with his hands, and then I wondered whether I would let him. On the one hand, it would help convince him Aryne wasn't with us. On the other, well, it was just too obnoxious for him to think to go pawing through our stuff.

But, apparently, he was prepared to leave it with a visual inspection. "Next time I see her, I'm taking her back," he threatened.

I shrugged as though I couldn't care less. "It has nothing to do with us."

He grumbled under his breath, then called out to everyone. "I'll be giving a reward—coins—to anyone who can tell me anything about the girl. Aryne is her name. More to anyone who finds her and brings her to me."

That sent me a little jolt of panic. I was sure that would be enough to get one of the members of the troupe to talk. None of them had any reason to be loyal to us, or to Aryne.

None of them said a word. In fact, sensing that the best part of the show was over, they all turned away and returned to their own preparations for leaving.

Scowling, Border stomped away.

Taro and I exchanged a look and resumed rolling up the tent.

Aryne didn't return to us before the troupe was ready to leave. I didn't know what to do. I wasn't prepared to wait behind for her, or leave the troupe to go looking for her. We needed the troupe, while the girl was only a duty and a burden. And I was annoyed with her for not returning promptly.

I was also afraid that Border had managed to find her after all.

But there were only so many duties I could juggle. First on the list, unfortunately, was going to Golden Fields and finding out what happened with the descendants of the Empress. Next, though far inferior in importance, was the duty to the troupe. The girl was even further down the list of priorities, and if she wasn't prepared to act in her own best interests, there wasn't really much we could do with her.

So Taro and I moved on with the troupe. And through the hours we spent trudging in the humid sunlight, I was worrying about Aryne. Wondering if Border had caught her. If she had been bitten by one of those nasty snakes and was now rolling around in agony. If she had fallen into some kind of hole or something, hoping someone was going back to look for her.

I almost turned around. Several times. Not physically, of course. Physically, I just kept putting one foot in front of the other, following the others, keeping my head down to protect my eyes from the sun's glare. But in my mind, I was telling myself to turn around, and then telling myself not to be ridiculous.

And I was ranting at her, silently. Stupid girl. Why did she have to pick us? Why did she have to notice us? She could have run away with anyone. And if she had to pick us, why couldn't she be sensible about it, and stay with us?

My brain spent the whole day whirling with all these questions and conflicting influences. I was not fit company for anyone. And by the time we had finished walking for the night, and Taro and I had settled down with our little meal by our little fire, I was in a state to take Aryne's head off when she appeared out of the darkness and joined us.

"Where the hell have you been?" Taro demanded, bless him. I feared I might have been far less temperate if I had asked the question.

"Around." She shrugged, tossing her sack aside and sitting on the ground. "Any food for me?"

"Where, around?" Taro asked.

"Following off the trail." She reached for the bowl of rice.

Taro snatched it out of her grasp. "And what was the purpose of that?"

"Border was here."

"And we convinced him you weren't."

"Doubt he believed you. He'll come looking again."

"You said he wouldn't come looking at all," I reminded her, having regained control of my tongue.

"Guess I was wrong, eh?" she answered with no apparent concern. "He's come once, he'll come again. You gonna feed me or what?"

Taro rolled his eyes and thrust the bowl into her hands. She used her fingers to grab out a small ball of rice and shoved it into her mouth.

I, for one, would not be looking for any seconds that night.

"You can't go running off like that," said Taro.

"If I stayed, Border would have seen me," she retorted through her mouthful of food.

Which was true, but not quite what Taro meant. "Hiding was fine," I said. "It's the staying away all day that was the problem. I had no idea what happened to you."

"What did you care?" she demanded.

"I was afraid he'd taken you back. Or that you were hurt."

"Couldn't have been too afraid," she said matter-of-factly. "You kept on going."

Oh, she was brilliant at inspiring guilt, she was. "We had to keep going. The troupe was moving on. We couldn't afford to be left behind."

She shrugged. She didn't look hurt or upset by the notion that we hadn't gone looking for her. Merely stating a fact.

Which kind of made it worse.

"We do not have the ability to delay to look for you should you go missing," I said. "That is simply the way of things. Which is why you shouldn't go off on your own. There's nothing we can do about it if something happens to you and you don't show up."

She snorted through her current mouthful of food, and a couple of grains of rice went flying. "I can take care of myself," she mumbled. "Have my whole life."

"Which is no doubt why I can count your ribs." But it was a weak response, and I knew it. So did she. "Hiding is fine. But as soon as the danger has passed, come back."

"He'll be hanging around waiting for that."

"That's a risk we'll have to take. It's better than you traveling off the road for hours where anything could happen to you without us knowing about it. Can you see the logic of that?"

She stared at me as though she thought I'd lost my mind. What? What had I said that was so strange?

She swallowed, and snickered. "Sure," she said.

Sure? What did that mean? "We're in agreement?"

"Kai."

"Good."

It was anticlimactic, as triumphs went. I had the feeling I was missing something important.

People were so confusing sometimes. I hated that.

Chapter Nineteen

Sunset Shores was a beautiful village near the water. It was full of the wealthy of Flatwell, who lived in beautiful homes of bamboo, built on elaborate networks of platforms right on the shore. The platforms prevented the homes from being flooded when the tide came in. When the tide was out, hundreds of little crabs skittered about the damp sand, and the troupe's children ran out to catch them.

Only the servants came by to watch the performances, and the takings were slim. Where the real money came from was when those same servants returned with notes from their employers, invitations for the players to perform in their homes. I was told one could make more money from a single private performance than from half a dozen villages.

Kahlia, Beril and Rinis all received such invitations. So did I. Taro did his lord of the manor act and forbade me to go. Because I couldn't encourage such behavior in him, I raised an eyebrow at him and told him where to go. We had a glorious argument over it, which I let him win. Because I didn't want to go. The idea of performing in the private home of a stranger made me uncomfortable.

Kahlia called me an idiot, and Taro a heavy-browed perkrit. I was happy that I at least understood my insult.

We stayed for three days. The morning of the fourth day, we started packing up to go. And that was when they came. Two young men, slim and bronzed, bearing short swords and square shields, jogging in unnatural unison. Panol was trotting along beside them, apparently trying to ask them questions, which they were ignoring.

Young men wearing identical gear, moving in unison. Stank of some form of law enforcement. Lovely.

Each man wore thin bands of silver metal on their left bicep, in differing numbers. The one with the most arm-bands looked me over, and then Kahlia. "You were at the home of Taroon of Karvart last night?" he asked.

"Yes," she answered without hesitation.

"What is your name?"

"Kahlia of Atara."

The man next to him pulled from a small pouch at his waist a metal triangle. He struck it once, and after the light "ting" stopped, the first man announced, "Kahlia of Atara, you have been by Merchant Taroon of Karvart accused of the theft of a wind idol, made from onyx and gold, perpetrated on Third Middle Night of the Slope Month. You are given four days to craft your plea for the Accounting. Do not leave the boundaries of Sunset Shore. Should you leave the boundaries of Sunset Shore, all residents shall be given leave to hunt and execute you." The triangle was struck again and then stashed back in its pouch.

Hell. Justice in its brutal, simplest form. Cheaper than prisons, too, I imagined.

I looked at Kahlia. She looked stunned. "I did no such thing."

"You will have your opportunity to prove so in four days."

"We can't wait four days," Panol protested. "The Accounting must be earlier. We could be ready by tomorrow."

"Custom demands four days."

"I can't stay here for four days," said Kahlia. "The four days is for the protection of the accused. I waive it."

"You don't have the right," the Sunset Shores version of a Runner informed her, his abrupt change in tone and language suggesting a certain boredom with the whole affair. "Too easy to claim you were pressured into waiving after, if the Accounting doesn't go your way. Four days. Be here at sunrise." He pressed a small piece of parchment into her hand. "Sun bright to you," he said, a mockery of the usual morning greeting. Then the two men turned on their heels and walked away.

"Did you do this?" Panol demanded of Kahlia.

For a moment, Kahlia stared at him, her eyes narrowed. Then she swung at him, slapping him so heavily across the cheek that his head was whipped to one side. Before he'd even straightened his stance, wiping blood from his lip, she was striding back to her tent.

But a thought had come to me, one that had me jogging back to my own tent. I whipped aside the front flap, and Aryne looked up at me. "Empty your bag," I ordered.

"Why?"

"Because I told you to."

She glared at me. "No."

Impudent little brat. I reached for her bag myself, but she was quicker in snatching it up. She clutched it to her stomach. "It's mine! Don't touch it!"

That sounded suspicious to me. "What's yours?"

"The bag!"

"Taroon of Karvart was robbed last night."

"So?"

"So empty your bag."

"You think I lifted something?" she demanded, outraged.

"Obviously."

She went rigid for a moment. Then she shoved the bag at me. I caught it by instinct, unable to react as she dashed out of the tent.

There was no gold and onyx idol in her bag. Or anywhere else in the tent.

All right. So maybe I shouldn't have so quickly assumed she had stolen it. She had, to my knowledge, not lifted anything since joining us.

But she had tried to steal my purse. How could she expect me to forget that?

On the other hand, if she was trying to straighten out, which was theoretically possible, I shouldn't be constantly throwing her past indiscretions in her face. She might come to believe that if everyone thought she was going to be nothing but a thief, then she might as well be nothing but a thief. I didn't want to be responsible for that kind of outcome.

I thought it was safe to assume the troupe wouldn't be going anywhere for a while, so I hunted Aryne down. I found her a good half hour walk down the stream, sitting on the bank with her knees curled up to her chest, hurling stones into the swiftly moving water.

"Go away," she said as soon as I was in earshot.

"I'm sorry," I said.

"Good. Go away."

I sat beside her. "It was very wrong for me to jump to conclusions like that, and you have every right to be angry with me."

"Thanks very much," she sneered.

"But you did try to steal from me once—"

"I did not!"

"—and the fact that you won't even admit it and explain it and apologize for it makes me think you don't think you

did anything wrong. That's why I have difficulty believing
you won't do it again."

She rested her chin on her knees and stared into the
water.

I watched the water, too. And waited.

"I was trying to get away from Border," she said finally.
"I needed coin. I couldn't get it any other way. Not without
him knowing and taking it from me."

"You've been with that man all your life, aye?"

"Aye."

"What made you decide to leave him now?"

"Started saying how I was getting all grown-up. I knew
what that meant."

I frowned. "What did it mean?"

She just looked at me, as though it were obvious.

And then I thought it might be, but I was hoping not,
and for my own peace of mind I had to have it cleared up.
"What did it mean?"

She rolled her eyes. "He'd start whoring me out. Or
using me himself."

"Surely not." It was just too vile. I mean, yes, I knew
such things happened. But to hear this child speak of them
so nonchalantly, it couldn't be true.

"He said I had to be grateful to him, for protecting me
from the slavers."

"Why me? Why did you try to steal from me?"

"You're the Flame Dancer, eh? I'd heard of you.
Thought you'd have piles of money, and it wouldn't hurt
you to lose a bit."

I raised an eyebrow. "I trust you now understand that
isn't the case?"

She shrugged. She still didn't appear terribly repentant.
"You get more coin than I'll see my whole life."

Hm. I supposed all things were relative.

"I'm not stupid. I know you'll toss me if I steal from
anyone here. And I'm pretty sure you'd catch me if I tried

anything." She slanted a look at me. "It's 'cause you're a Shield, eh?"

"What's because I'm a Shield?"

"You notice things."

I cocked my head to one side, thinking about it. "I suppose I notice some things more than others. But then there are other things I don't notice very well at all. That's part of being a Shield, too."

"I'm going to be a Shield," Aryne announced. "Not a Source."

Not this again. "You are a Source," I said. "You just have Shield tendencies."

"Could be a Shield with Source tendencies."

"Have you ever Shielded anyone?"

"No."

"There you go."

"Never met a Source, have I? Maybe I could do your man next time he, what do you call it? Channels."

No way in hell. All other issues aside, it appeared she was a person without much talent, and certainly little skill. I was not trusting my Source to an inferior Shield, all for the sake of experimentation. "No," I said, and deciding that sounded just a little too blunt, I added, "It is my task to Shield him. I will not pass it to another unless I am unable."

Zaire. Stupid way to put it. Here was to hoping she wouldn't decide to try disabling me in order to get her chance to experiment.

"You are a Source, Aryne. There is no way around it. Why would that displease you?"

She hugged her knees again. "You give all the orders, don't you? I'd rather give them than take them."

"I don't give them."

"Kai, you do. I see you. It was up to you whether I came with you or not. You make all the decisions."

What a remarkable interpretation of events. "Neither

one of us is in charge of the other." Though, if I were totally honest, I'd admit that perhaps Taro thought I did order
him around. "And there is no one way that Pairs function.
It depends on the people involved. Don't model yourself
after us. It's too limiting, and it's not appropriate. Especially for someone like you."

"What does that mean?" she objected, her lower lip
pushing out in a pout.

That she wasn't as talented as Taro, and she probably
wouldn't get a Shield as talented as me. But there was no
need to tell her that. "That you are unique. Because you are
a Source with Shield tendencies. And because you have
grown so much outside of the academies, and can channel
unprotected. I have no doubt your future will be equally
unique. I feel you'll have to forge your own way."

"Oh," she said, apparently appeased.

"Do you accept my apology?"

"Do you accept mine?" she shot back.

Little demon. "Aye." She is not a thief, she is not a thief,
she is not a thief. Get that through your head and make sure
it sticks.

"Then so do I."

"Then let's head back. Kahlia's been accused of stealing from Taroon, and I imagine the whole troupe will be
involved in dealing with it."

"Do you think she did it?" Aryne asked as we rose to her
feet, a bitter tone in her voice.

"No."

"Why not?"

"She's not an idiot."

The whole troupe was collected around Atara's tent, all
talking at once. The flaps of the tent had been rolled up and
strapped to the supports, so the interior was revealed to
everyone. Only Kahlia and Panol were within the tent itself, however. Kahlia was speaking, her gestures agitated
and quick, but I couldn't hear anything she said with all the
babbling.

I went to stand next to Taro. "Where were you?" he asked.

"We were talking." I nodded at Aryne. "Have any decisions been made?"

"No. They're all in a panic because they have to stay here for another four days."

It was amazing, the way the curse seemed to rule everyone's lives. And in the current situation, the solution was very simple. Send everyone on ahead, so that only Kahlia and Atara risked the alleged curse. Though that would probably appear very cold to everyone else, so I wasn't prepared to suggest it. And as there really was no curse, it didn't much matter one way or the other.

Panol started clapping his hands to get everyone's attention, and the troupe members fell silent. "We need to talk to Setter and Leverett. Everyone else go away."

"Whistle for it, Panol!" Rinis shouted. "This is about us, too!"

"It is, and the earliest we straighten this, the sooner we can fly. All right? So go away!" And to make his point, Panol started yanking on the ties that had the walls of the tent settling back down.

Many muttered and walked away. Others lingered, probably hoping to eavesdrop through the tent walls. Aryne, who didn't appear interested, wandered off.

"This isn't good," said Beril. "Something's going to happen."

I said nothing. No point in trying to talk him out of it. Four days of nothing happening would be better proof.

"Some things are worse than being stringless," he said, and then he strode away.

"I haven't heard that one before," I commented to Taro. "Stringless?"

He shrugged.

"Well, at least it's a pleasant place to stop." A little cooler, as we were so close to the water.

"Kai, but how long will it stay that way?" said Taro.

"They feel a little like the regulars did last year, before the weather returned to normal. All jittery. Like when they were all getting ready for a reason to tear down a building. I don't like it."

Great. Nice to know Beril's paranoia was contagious.

Chapter Twenty

The rest of the day was spent searching the camp for the idol. The search took longer than I thought it needed to, because the whole troupe was involved. Every single tent, including Kahlia's and Atara's, was dismantled, the possessions stretched out on the ground to be picked through. Only one tent was searched at a time, a handful doing the dismantling while everyone else watched, and no one was permitted to take a hand in the dismantling of their own tent. It seemed to take forever.

And, of course, nothing was found.

Kahlia wasted a day she should have spent preparing her argument. Though I didn't know what she could say. The charge lacked the details to demonstrate that Kahlia hadn't been in the building when the idol was stolen, or that she wouldn't have access to the area where it had been kept.

Kahlia found nothing odd about the scanty details. It was considered normal on the island. Then, the speech presented to the Accounting Clerks would be believed, as it wouldn't be crafted to accommodate the nature of the crime.

That didn't mean she wasn't tense. She was. I'd never seen her features so stiff. Nor her patience so short.

But then, she wasn't the only one.

"What is wrong with these people?" Aryne asked, as we sat under our ovcas and waited for the sun to go down.

"They're worried about Kahlia," I said. Aryne snorted, as if such a level of concern for another was so foreign as to be incredible. "And they think they're cursed."

Her eyes widened in alarm. "They're cursed?"

Oh, Zaire, not another one. "So they think. They think by staying in the same place for as long as they have, one of them is going to die."

"Krick!" She leapt to her feet, looking panicked. "You never told me!"

Wonderful. I didn't need this. "Because it's none of your business."

"None of my business!" she shrieked. "I'm getting—"

"Sit down!" I found myself barking.

I was stunned when she dropped back into her cropper. From the look on her face, she was rather surprised herself.

"You will not add to these people's fears."

"They're right to be afraid, ain't they?"

"You don't have to be."

"Why not?" she demanded suspiciously.

"You weren't among them when the curse was made." That sounded reasonable, didn't it? As reasonable as talking about a curse could sound. "So it doesn't apply to you."

I wasn't going to try to convince her there were no such things as curses. She'd probably grown up believing in them. And wouldn't she be having a lovely time of it at the Academy, with beliefs like that?

She studied me skeptically. "Huh," she said.

So I hadn't won her over. I'd calmed her down and shut her up. That had been the only goal.

Too bad I couldn't do the same for everyone else. The very air about the camp felt awful, everyone snapping at each other, stiff with fear.

It didn't help that none of us had anything to do. I wasn't sure whether the residents of Sunset Shores had been forbidden to see us, or if the members of the troupe were afraid of the risks inherent in their acts, but there were no performances. Nor were there any practices, which were nearly as dangerous. And we weren't permitted to go to the market.

Nothing to do but sit and think.

And worry. Because what if Kahlia was found guilty?

I didn't believe for a moment that she had stolen the idol. I couldn't imagine someone so brutally honest, not to mention proud, lowering herself to theft. Especially when it wasn't necessary for her survival. But what if this Accounting found differently? They would kill her.

I'd asked to go to the Accounting. I was told it was not permitted, for it was none of my affair. Which was true, and even I knew that claiming I might be able to help would be just too arrogant. I hadn't been with Kahlia when she'd gone to the merchant's house. I had no gift for advocacy.

But what if Kahlia went to the Accounting, and never came back?

Yes, she was an aggravating person. She was also a good person. Generous with her time and her care. And I would miss her.

And I hated the fact that someone could die over stealing a useless little idol. It was such a stupid waste. I just wanted to storm into this merchant's fancy home and smack him.

The fourth day came. Kahlia left, with only Panol in attendance. Atara stayed behind, which seemed to me a little cold.

Taro and I were sitting in our croppers in front of our

tent, sipping wine and trying not to think about what might be going on, when Sirok, Rinis's partner, came running up, sweating and agitated. "Please come," he gasped out. "Something's wrong with Rinis." Then he dashed away again.

We ran to Rinis's tent, finding a crowd already collected around it. From inside I could hear Rinis screaming. "What's happened?"

"Something's wrong with the baby," said Leverett.

Well, I'd gathered that much.

"I can't heal!" Karish said urgently.

"Please!" Sirok said. "They won't let me fetch the village healer!"

Taro looked to me.

I didn't know what to say. I did think he could heal, to an extent. But I didn't know whether he could help Rinis, whatever her ailment was.

Taro swallowed. "I can't heal her, Sirok. Truly, I can't. But I can—I can ease her pain. A little."

Sirok just nodded and ducked into the tent.

Taro gave me a pleading look. So I followed, though I didn't wish to, and it wasn't necessary. I didn't need to see him to Shield him, especially from such a short distance.

The interior of the tent held the heavy, suffocating scent of blood, ill concealed by incense. It was too hot, the many candles adding to the discomfort. I could see Rinis lying on the mat, shining with sweat and clutching at Corla, who knelt beside her. "Make it stop," she whimpered. "Please make it stop."

Corla looked up at our entrance.

"Shintaro's going to heal you," Sirok announced.

"Stop saying that!" Taro snapped. Then he took a deep breath, kneeling on the other side of Rinis. "Rinis?"

She just whimpered, her hands clutched into fists into the blankets beneath her.

There was blood trailing down her legs.

I had never been around a pregnant woman in need of medical attention. It was a terrifying experience.

"Rinis." Taro put a palm to her forehead, smoothing back her sweat-soaked hair. "I'm going to make you feel a little better, all right?"

"Make it stop," she pleaded.

"I can't do that, Rinis. I can only ease the pain a little."

I Shielded him as he worked, though the nature of his work was beyond my perception. More delicate than when he channeled, I was unable to feel what he did.

I was able to see the effects, however. The gradual loosening of Rinis's muscles. The easing of her breathing.

"Thank the wind," Sirok murmured to himself. "Thank the wind."

I was thinking he was precipitous in his relief.

Then again, maybe Taro had healed her. He had done so many other amazing things.

In moments, Rinis's eyes closed, and Sirok gasped. "Is she—?"

"She's sleeping," Taro said quietly. "She needs a healer."

"They won't let us to the healer!"

Taro looked up at Sirok hesitantly. "I—I don't know what's wrong with her, Sirok."

"You will heal her."

"I can't."

"You will heal her!" he insisted.

What could Taro say in the face of that?

Brilliant man, he thought of something. "She would be more comfortable with a change of sheets and some fresh water."

Sirok nodded briskly and left the tent.

"Does she have something to wear that's less confining?" Taro asked Corla.

"She's soiled everything," Corla said. "I'll fetch something from my tent."

"Thank you. A clean mat, too, if you can."

Corla left, and Taro looked at me. He tilted his head toward the entrance flap. I didn't like the idea of leaving Rinis alone, but evidently he didn't want to risk her hearing what he had to say. So we left the tent, moving a good distance away from Rinis and everyone else. "The child," he said in a low voice. "It has no force."

"What does that mean?"

"It's dead."

I gaped at him. "Are you sure?"

"Aye."

"Hell." What did that mean? Could a woman give birth to a dead baby? I had no idea. And what if one couldn't? What were we supposed to do then? "Are you going to tell them?"

"How? How will I explain how I know?"

He had a point. I looked back at the tent Rinis was in, and frowned as I saw it shake. "Something's going on."

He strode back to the tent, ducked in, and nearly shoved me aside as he ducked out again. "Stranger!" he shouted, running around to the back of the tent. I followed him, seeing him take a leap at the man running from the back of Rinis's tent.

The man went down under Taro's weight, but was quickly able to twist around and shove Taro off. Then he punched Taro in the face.

Not the face!

Next thing I knew, I was flying at the stranger, and I landed against him with a stomach wrenching crunch. Then a dizzying whirl, and I found myself lying on the ground with a fist heading toward my own face.

The man was shoved off me, and I crawled backward from the melee. I looked for Taro, and saw him sprawled on the ground with a hand pressed to his nose, blood leaking through his fingers.

Our savior was Beril, and Sacey and Fin were piling on top of a man who looked vaguely familiar. "Yesit!" Beril shouted. "What are you doing here?"

Taro sat up, still holding his nose. "He was in Rinis's

tent," he said. Then he looked at me. "It's just bleeding, not broken," he assured me. "Go check on Rinis."

Sirok and Corla were back. Sirok was hovering over Rinis, hysterically demanding if she was all right. Rinis was choking and coughing and unable to answer in anything better than gibberish.

Corla looked up at me. "She said Yesit was here," she told me. "He tried to strangle her."

And my brain finally caught up and reminded me that Yesit was Atara's brother.

And that I'd seen him before. He was the stranger I'd seen wandering around our tent one night. I'd forgotten all about him. I went back outside.

The whole troupe had by this time been attracted by the noise, including Aryne. "That's the one with the snake," she told me.

"The snake."

"What bit Panol."

"Oh." It was starting to make sense to me. Yesit cast the curse on the troupe. Then he followed them around—or perhaps merely arranged to be in the same place at the same time at certain points in their journey—and sabotaged acts to make the curse appear real.

He had nearly killed Panol and Rinis. He had apparently succeeded in actually killing other members of the troupe. All over possession of a circus that seemed to make just enough to keep moving on. It was really quite insane. And it was really quite convenient that he had been discovered in this location. He could be turned over to the island Runners who had arrested Kahlia. And everyone would realize there was no real curse and be able to settle into more normal lives.

Atara, apparently, hadn't gotten that far in her thinking. She stood over Yesit, who was being held on his back by Fin and Beril. "Yesit," she drawled. "You have back."

You have back. You have spine? You have nerve to be coming back here?

"Nothing wrong with visiting my friends," he snarled back.

Oh. He was going to try to deny everything. Interesting choice.

"And killing them?" Atara demanded coolly.

"Of course not!"

"You were strangling Rinis," Taro accused him, his voice muffled as he continued to attempt to staunch the blood flowing from his nose.

"What weight is the word of an offlander?" Yesit sneered.

"I saw you throw the snake what bit Panol," Aryne piped up.

"Whose life the offlander then saved," Atara added.

"And I saw you a while ago," I said. "Lurking around the tents."

"That's three blows, Yesit," said Atara.

"Given by offlanders," Yesit sneered.

"I'm not an offlander!" Aryne objected.

"They have been our omens," Atara said. "They have brought us good fortune. You have brought us ill. Whose word do you believe holds more weight?"

Yesit's expression slid from belligerence to pleading. "I am your brother."

"I am your sister. That didn't prevent you from killing members of my troupe."

"It should have been my troupe."

"Then you confess to killing them?"

His eyes widened. "No!"

Too late. I thought amoral liars were supposed to be better at it than this.

"How do you find?" Atara called out.

"Murderer!" was the almost unanimous decision from everyone who stood around us.

"The curse is real!" Yesit insisted. "I've come around only to watch it work. But there is a curse, and the only way to revoke it is for me to forgive you. For you to ask my forgiveness." He gave a triumphant smirk.

Atara's eyes narrowed, and her lips thinned.

She wasn't actually considering letting him go, and begging his forgiveness, was she? He'd tried to kill Panol and Rinis. He'd practically admitted to killing others.

There was no curse. Just the belief in one. Don't let a murderer escape justice over fear of a curse that wasn't real.

"I am forced to wonder if you have been here every time your curse struck," Atara said. "You have not been so very clever. Others have seen you at times, and we have been fools not to think you might have been more directly responsible for our misfortune than a curse. But in the end, it does not matter. Our people have died, by your hand or by your curse."

"All you have to do is ask my forgiveness and it will end," Yesit said, with a bit more desperation.

"I have only your word on that," Atara told him. "Your word has no power."

Excellent. So she didn't let superstition completely rule her reason. Because, really, if she turned him over to the authorities, the accidents would stop.

"Sacey, fetch Leavy's dancing bars," Atara ordered, and Sacey ran off.

"Sol, my knife." Sol nodded, and he was gone, too.

"No!" Yesit's face had paled. "Atara, don't do this. I beg of you. I meant no real harm. No one was supposed to die. Just be hurt and frightened. So you would give the troupe back to me. It was supposed to be mine. You know that."

Atara didn't respond. She just watched him, her expression cool.

"Shouldn't someone go for those guards?" I asked Leverett. "The ones who arrested Kahlia?"

He appeared surprised by the question. "They have nothing to do with this."

"Are they not the law enforcement here?"

"For the people of Sunset Shores. Not for the likes of us."

"So what's going to happen to Yesit?"

"Execution."

I stared at Leverett. "You're going to kill him?"

"It is Atara's right."

In what perverse version of justice? "You can't do that!"

"Why not?"

"He hasn't had a trial! An Accounting!"

"We don't do Accountings."

"Who is we?"

Leverett was clearly getting annoyed with my series of questions. "The troupe."

"So, what, you have your own laws?"

Leverett shrugged.

I couldn't believe what I was hearing. They were just going to kill him, right then and there. No weighing of evidence. No chance for him to defend himself. I looked at the others, and none of them seemed to find the plan objectionable. Some were cutting away the underbrush and stomping it into a flatter surface. Preparing the killing space. Sirok and Corla helped Rinis walk out to watch the death of her would-be killer. Rinis, pasty and sweaty and barely able to keep her eyes open, probably wasn't even aware of what was going on.

My bars were brought. Yesit's arms were stretched wide, and his hands tied to one bar. The same was done with his feet. "No!" I protested. "You can't do this. There has to be a better way."

Leverett sneered. "And you would teach it to us, offlander?"

"There is a proper way to do things. To make sure he is actually guilty of the crimes you think he committed."

"He's already confessed."

"Not really."

"This is our way, offlander. If you don't like it, go home."

It wasn't a matter of me not liking it. It was just wrong. I opened my mouth to say so, but felt Taro's hand on my arm. He tugged on it.

"Let's go," he said.

"Taro!"

"You want to watch?"

"Of course not, but we have to stop this."

"We can't, and we shouldn't."

"We shouldn't? Taro!"

He yanked me away with more force. "We don't have the right to interfere."

"This is more important than what we have a right to do! This is a man's life!"

"This is their land, Lee. Their rules. We do not have the right or the knowledge to be telling them how to handle their own affairs. Just because we don't like something doesn't mean we can be telling them to change. We don't belong here, and we won't be living here long. We have to stay out of it."

He was right. I hated it when that happened. I felt there was something I should be doing, but what would happen if we did stop it? Yesit would not be punished at all. He would be able to continue to injure or kill others. True, the troupe now knew to look for him, but he'd already demonstrated an ability for sabotage without anyone suspecting. It wasn't impossible that he would be able to continue.

I understood all that. But I couldn't help cringing at the visions in my head. The manner in which they knew how to prepare the killing space, with no discussion. They had done this before. And that disturbed me more than anything else.

I should be watching. If I wasn't prepared to stop it, I should watch. I wasn't sure why. It just seemed less cowardly.

And then I heard Yesit screaming. I didn't rush back to see what was being done to him. I just couldn't.

The next time I danced, there would be bloodstains on the bars.

Chapter Twenty-one

Rinis went into labor that evening and died early the next morning. Taro eased her pain, which was all he was able to do, something neither Sirok nor Corla seemed able to accept. They kept asking him what to do, and kept shooting glances of disbelief at him when he said he didn't know. And when she died, well, Sirok definitely seemed to blame him, and it was all I could do not to hit him. The ungrateful bastard.

Karish walked out without a word.

I found Taro by the stream, scrubbing at the blood staining his hands and forearms. His shirt would have to go. The blood could probably be soaked out of it, but I wouldn't imagine Karish wanting to wear it again. I wouldn't.

If anyone saw him washing right from the stream, they'd have his head. I wasn't telling. "You did the right thing," I said, to announce my presence. And because it was true. "And you did a hell of a lot more than anyone else here could."

The skin on his arms was reddened with his scrubbing. "I'm not a healer," he muttered. "Never been a healer. I'm sick of people expecting me to do things I've never been trained to do."

He was thinking of last summer, I supposed, when the regulars of High Scape expected him to stop the blizzards from devastating their crops. Or maybe he was thinking of being sent out by the Empress to look for her exiled relatives.

Hell, maybe it went as far back as having to create an event to get away from Creol. Though he seemed to be getting more comfortable with that sort of thing as time went by. And I would have to worry about that later.

I sat down beside him, but not so close that I crowded him. "You're going to need soap to get it out from under your nails," I told him.

He sighed and shook out his hands, sitting back from the stream. He held his hands out, away from his trousers, to let them dry. I didn't know why he bothered. His trousers had blood on them, too, and were almost soaked from his attempt to scrape every speck of blood from his skin.

His hands had gotten rough. He had never, since I'd known him, had the milky soft hands of most of the aristocrats I had met. Still, his hands had always appeared clean and almost untouched, the nails rounded and buffed. Now, his hands were browner than I'd ever seen them, a scar down the back of his left hand where he'd ripped the skin unloading the wagon one night, and two of his nails had been torn off during the trials of changing a wheel.

He still refused to don the skirts the men of Flatwell wore. His shirts and trousers were of a much lighter material than he wore in High Scape, but they were still heavy enough to keep him permanently flushed in the high temperatures of the island. And one day, his hair seemed to push him over some sort of line, because during the midday rest, he took a knife to it and cut it short. He insisted on doing it himself, and the result was a weird mess that wouldn't stay flat because of the curl in it. It stayed out of his face without needing to be tied, though, and I supposed that was the point.

He was still gorgeous, of course. The darker skin went

nicely with his black eyes. I was sure there were people who would spend a fortune trying to imitate the attractive mess of his hair. He still had the finely drawn features that so thoroughly trapped a person's gaze. And though he moved more slowly than he used to, due to the heat and the heaviness of the air, he still had that surety of step and that grace I so envied.

It was just that a person might not look at him long enough to see that he was gorgeous, what with the terrible loose-fitting clothes and the cracked hands. And it kind of concerned me that Karish was willing to let himself be seen looking so ragged. I would have never said he was shallow or vain—well, I wouldn't mean it—but he had always cared about his appearance. His argument was that once one was out in public, one had a responsibility to present a clean and neat appearance. It was a way to demonstrate respect for oneself and others. I didn't quite agree with him, but I could sort of see the logic of his opinion.

I wasn't sure why he had decided to put all that aside. Perhaps it was just a lot more difficult for him to keep up his customary look, his clothes being unsuitable for the climate. It was possible that he had come to agree with my opinion concerning everyday apparel, that comfort was more important than appearance, and easier to manage while traveling. I hoped it wasn't a matter of him thinking there was no point in caring, since everyone on the island was blind and thought he was plain.

I had to get him off that damned island.

I eased over closer to him, wrapping my hands around his arm and resting my chin on his shoulder. I felt him relax. "You have had a very hard night," I said. "We'll go back to the tent so you can sleep, and when you get up you will have red wine and island chicken and those slimy green vegetables you like so much."

"We don't have any of that," he reminded me.

"Aye, but there must be someone in the troupe I can buy them from."

His eyebrows rose in surprise. Kai, kai, I was a tightfisted wench who nagged him over every unnecessary coin he wanted to spend. But this was necessary. He'd had a hellish night, held responsible for the health of a woman who ended up dying. If getting a break from cold fish, rice and water would give him some pleasure, I was all for it. "Let's go before someone starts screaming at us for using the stream."

We headed back toward the tents, trying to find a path and keeping an eye out for snakes. When we reached the camp, we found almost the entire troupe standing outside Rinis's tent, arguing over whether she'd died as a result of Yesit's curse, and whether it meant they should leave the troupe. I didn't know which I found more shocking, the fact that they thought Yesit's curse might still have power over them, or the fact so many spoke of leaving Atara. I'd thought they'd had more loyalty than that.

We didn't even slow down. I knew I was exhausted, and I just couldn't handle another confrontation of any kind. Still, I was curious about what I was hearing. "I don't understand," I whispered to Karish once we'd entered our tent.

"Don't understand what?" Aryne piped up.

My annoyance at once more forgetting Aryne's existence made me want to tell her it was none of her affair. But that wasn't true. If the troupe suddenly shattered, it put all of us at risk. "Why they think the curse is still"—I was too tired to think of a suitable word—"in effect. The man who cast it is dead."

"The only person who can break a curse is the one who cast it," Aryne said. "If he didn't lift it, and now he's dead, it'll go on forever."

"He admitted he actually made sure the accidents happened," I reminded her. "He followed the troupe and sabotaged their acts. You saw him do it, with the snake."

"Maybe he helped the curse along, but he still cast it, and 'cause he's dead, now it can never be lifted."

Why would these people cling to the curse? They had the perfect opportunity to release themselves from a belief that crippled them. Instead, they found reasons to hang on. It didn't make sense.

Taro was looking through our bags, searching for something he apparently couldn't find. He seemed a little disoriented.

"Go to bed, Taro," I told him.

Aryne chuckled. "Take to mat," she corrected, because, of course, no one on this damned island slept in actual beds.

Taro was tired enough not to react to the orders except to obey them. I wanted to give Karish what privacy and space I could. From the bags, I pulled out towels, stretching them out on the grass under the ovcas of our tent, using one of the bags filled with clothing as a pillow. If anyone had a problem with me sleeping on the ground, they didn't wake me up to let me know. Too busy arguing over whether to ditch the troupe.

After sleeping a couple of hours, I asked around the camp for something good for supper. I was able to buy skins of red wine and three island chickens, but no slimy green vegetables. For the hell of it, I inquired about chocolate, but, of course, no one had any of that. I did get my hands on some nice sharp cheese, and sweet juicy yellow fruit that I knew Taro liked.

The sun was setting when Karish woke up. When he shuffled out of the tent, he had changed his clothes and scrubbed his fingernails. "They back yet?" he asked.

"No."

"Everyone still here?"

"You expected people to actually leave?"

"If they're so afraid of this curse."

"Hm." I doubted they would leave Atara immediately. They all wanted to get out of Sunset Shores as soon as possible.

That evening, the members of the troupe held a funeral for Rinis. Although Taro, Aryne and I had no real wish to attend, I was surprised to be told that we weren't welcome, as we hadn't known Rinis for a full year. Something about only those who had witnessed a significant portion of a person's life were permitted to witness their return to the ground.

What these people chose to reveal and what they chose to keep private continued to baffle me.

When I woke the next morning, Kahlia and Panol had returned. Kahlia had been absolved of the theft. Apparently, one of Taroon's servants had taken the idol. He had been at the Accounting, and had been surprised to be found guilty when a member of a troupe was there to be blamed.

Taro and I barely had time to take down the tent before we were moving again.

Chapter Twenty-two

We walked into Golden Fields. Very different from anywhere else on the island, it looked like farmland of the sort
I was used to, wide dry fields of golden something or other.
Not wheat. Not any kind of grain I'd ever seen before. The
dense foliage that had darkened most of our days had
thinned out considerably, allowing for wider roads and
larger buildings.

Aryne was cowering in the covered wagon. She called it
resting, having allegedly twisted her ankle that morning.
I'd suggested the wagon as a way to make her feel better,
until she was really convinced that there were no slaves
and, more importantly, that she wasn't one. I also liked
keeping her out of sight of Border, should he choose to
make another appearance. She objected to the idea when I
mentioned it, but within the hour announced she had
wrenched her ankle and shouldn't be walking on it.

It was just slightly cooler that day. No, not cool. More
like an absence of that extra ounce of drenching, suffocating moisture in the air that made the sweat run on the

skin. I hoped it was the beginning of a change of season, and not just an aberrant dip in temperature meant to torment us.

Taro seemed a little more at ease, too. He smiled more quickly. He joked with Beril. He frequently touched my hand or my shoulder, or tucked my hair behind my ear. I realized he hadn't been touching people like he used to. Or flirting like he used to.

We walked through the village. We stopped somewhere just beyond the general settlement limits and stood. And waited. I thought nothing of it until I heard the whispers and saw the frowns.

"What now?" I asked Beril.

"Wait for it," he said.

And not long later, I heard the words. The Glassing Fair had set up where Atara's troupe usually camped.

And Beril swore.

"What?" I asked him.

"There's another troupe here."

Aye, I got that part. "And?"

His expression told me he thought I was being stupid. "Not enough coin for us both."

"Oh," I said. "So now what?"

"Ma's call."

So we might stay to perform, or we might move on. Or, rather, the troupe would move on. Taro, Aryne and I would remain in Golden Fields.

Panic squeezed my chest. Oh my gods. Taro and I would be left on our own. For the first time since our second day on the island. With all these crazy people who expected us to pay for things.

I hadn't felt anything like this when I'd left the Academy, knowing I'd be taking on the big wide world with a complete stranger. Why was I overreacting now?

Well, I wouldn't be able to perform without the others. There would be no more money coming in. I suffered the inappropriate urge to pull out my purse and start counting coins.

All right. Calm down.

"Lee?"

I looked up at Taro.

"You all right?"

"Of course."

"You got tense all of a sudden."

"I'm always tense."

He raised an eyebrow at that.

I noticed a stranger lingering around the wagon, fingering its colorful cloth. "Excuse me for a moment," I said to Taro, and I strode up the line to the wagon. "Kiyo," I said to the stranger.

Who noticeably started, and then seemed to shy away, eyes down. "I meant no harm," she said.

"No, no. I have a question."

She stilled, but her gaze stayed down.

I had to give it to her; I did look ridiculous. Only she was the only native of the island who seemed to think so, so I wasn't used to it. "Do you have slaves here?" I asked her.

She looked at me, then. And she looked horrified. "What?"

"Slaves. I was told there were slaves in Golden Fields."

Horror turned to outrage. "You were lied to," she snarled, lip curling. "A filthy lie. And you have a filthy mind, to think it might be true."

Take it down a peg, woman. I'm obviously a foreigner. "So there're no slaves on the island."

Her eyes narrowed. "You looking to buy?" And her tone suggested I'd better not be.

"No. I'm just making sure I don't have to worry."

"Ah," the woman said, unappeased. "Because you are such a beauty we would fracture our laws to have you." She tossed her head and strutted away.

I'd caused enormous offense and perhaps destroyed any chance of me, or possibly anyone else in the troupe, earning any money in Golden Fields, but I'd achieved what I'd set out to accomplish. I moved to the back of the wagon and pulled up the drop.

Aryne was kneeling in the wagon, and her head flew up as the light poured in, her eyes blinking. I could see her trembling, the muscles in her limbs quivering with tension. Her lips clenched in a grim line, her eyes boring into me.

I had engineered the conversation for this purpose. Knowing it had worked, I had no idea what to say.

Aryne stood and made to descend from the wagon.

"No," I told her. "Stay here."

"Why?" she demanded. "I'm not a slave."

The joy she should have felt in that knowledge was absent, her voice flat. "Border might see you and try to take you."

"He doesn't come here," she insisted.

"Because he didn't want to bring you here. That doesn't mean he won't come here looking for you."

"I don't care." And she climbed out of the wagon before I could stop her. "I hope he does. I'm gonna kill him."

"You will not!"

She glared at me and stomped away.

"Aryne! Come back here!"

Who was I kidding? That only worked when I surprised her.

"Be back here before we leave!"

Zaire, when had I turned into a nag?

Atara's call was that we needed to spend the night to rest and get some supplies. There was no place for us to camp, nor to perform, however. So we had to split up and spend coin to spend the night in bunkers. The troupe would meet again on the outskirts of town the next morning and move on. Aryne hadn't returned when this decision was made, and I fretted about it.

"She'll find us when she's ready to," said Taro, pulling on my hand.

"The medicine man might find her first."

"She was with him only as long as she wanted to be. Then she left him."

"So?"

"So she's a force unto herself. You won't be able to find her. Neither will he."

I knew he was right. I knew that if we went out looking for her, we wouldn't find her, and the sensible thing really was to stay in one place and let her find us. Still, it felt irresponsible to do nothing. Not to mention callous. She was upset.

Taro assumed an expression of shock. "You're not turning into a mother, are you?"

Prat. "I'm going to slap you."

He grinned. "Later." And he winked.

There was the usual dispute as we bickered over which bunker—cheap or extravagant—we should stay at. I won only because his choice was fully booked. I did, however, allow myself to hire an extra room for Aryne.

And as soon as our door was closed, Taro had me back against it, kissing me with a hunger I had to admit to myself was flattering. I couldn't help giggling through it. Because no one had ever been so eager to kiss me before.

"Heartless woman," he muttered.

I laughed.

"We have been too long in the company of other people," he muttered, pulling the hem of my shirt out of my skirt. "Enough to drive me mad. Just think, when we're finally back home, all those long hours at the Stall, all to ourselves."

That probably wouldn't happen. Taro was sure to have tired of me before we were back at the mainland. But all I said was, "Aha, the real reason they don't want Shields and Sources bedding down together." And really, with the level of distraction it created, who could blame them?

When I woke the next morning, I could hear voices in the next room. Taro, who was doing most of the talking.

Aryne, speaking the odd word here and there, in such a low voice it was hard to hear at all.

I shouldn't have let her come back on her own. I should have gone looking for her. It didn't matter that I wouldn't have found her. It was the principle of the thing.

But the selfish part of me wanted to take advantage of nights like the night before, while they were available to me. And the time to overcome that selfish part of me was the night before, when it would have done some good, not the morning after.

I dressed and stepped out into the corridor, knocking on Aryne's door.

There was silence on the other side of the door, until I heard Taro say, "Are you going to tell her to come in or what?"

"Her room, ain't it? She paid for it."

I rolled my eyes and pushed the door open.

Taro was dressed and shaved and sitting on the floor by the door. Aryne was still lying on her mattress, dressed in the clothes she'd been wearing the day before. "Are you all right?" I asked her.

She shrugged, her expression shuttered. " 'Course."

"Must you lie to me?" I sighed. "Of course you're upset about what you've learned. I'd have to be an idiot not to know that."

"Why'd you ask, then?"

Patience, please, patience.

And once I'd thought no one would test me as much as Taro always had.

"She's going to start her deep breathing, now," Taro told Aryne with a wink.

"Heh?"

"It's what Shields do, when there's a chance their vaunted calm might suffer from the slightest imperfection."

Git.

Aryne took a deep breath.

I wasn't going to try to pry information about her feelings out of her. Her feelings were her own, and she would share them with those she wished.

And I supposed she wished to share them with Taro. At least, she had been talking to him before I had come in. "Have you had breakfast?"

She shook her head.

"I'll see to it. But I'd like you to hang about your room for today." It might have been the whole horse and barn door thing, with her running around the night before, but I wanted to cut down on any opportunities for Border to snatch her.

The bunker's cook was assembling the traditional Flatwell breakfast of bright fruit and dense bread. I collected it from him and brought it up to Aryne's room, where she and Taro still sat. And I had the feeling I had interrupted them again.

For some reason, that saddened me.

I left them to it. I had an unpleasant duty to perform. I might as well get it over with. I had to remind Atara that we needed to stop at Golden Fields. I headed out to the designated meeting place.

There was a group of people already collected there. But I noticed a lack of the usual possessions, the rolled mats and the animals, and the wagon appeared half-empty.

"—gratitude?" Atara was hissing back at Leverett.

"How long are we to be grateful?" he demanded. "All our lives? Might not be too long, way things fall around here."

"You think the Glass Fair will do so well by you?"

Oh lords. A mutiny.

"There's less chance of us dying. That means a lot."

"You've had a good run, Atara," Beril told her, sounding reasonable. "But you can't expect people to live under your curse for the rest of their lives. It's happened too many times."

"There is no curse! That was proven. It was all Yesit."

"Yesit didn't cause Velly to drown in Red Heights."

"That was a storm."

"A storm that came after we'd lingered in Red Heights for four days," said Leverett. "The curse can't be broken, and I'm not living under it anymore."

Gods, how could these people do this to themselves? A few words spoken over candles. That was all it had been. Just words, people.

Atara looked furious, and was glorious in her fury. I imagined I could see light dancing about her head and shoulders.

I had to admit to myself that I was disappointed by what I was witnessing. I'd thought they were like a kind of family.

Then again, I'd seen enough to know that family could wield the sharpest weapons.

"If honor cannot keep you," said Atara, "I will not waste throat."

Leverett hesitated at that. Sol grabbed his arm and pulled him away, back toward the village.

I felt uncomfortable as I remained in place, watching the others leave. I was even more uncomfortable when Atara noticed my presence.

"We need to search for our family," I reminded her, speaking first, as it appeared Atara wasn't going to speak at all. "It's the reason we came to Flatwell. You know this."

She stared at me for a long, uncomfortable moment. I worried that she was going to object, to claim that we'd never made the agreement that we had.

"You still are in my debt," she said.

"And we will repay it."

"However, many to whom you owe debt have slithered to the Glass Fair."

"I see." I hadn't been aware that our debt was shared by the others. I had to admire Atara for admitting it. She could have claimed the whole debt was hers, and I wouldn't have been the wiser.

"You have been good omens."

I liked to think so. We were good everything.

"I will release you from any further obligation."

That was it? I would have expected more of a fight out of her.

But perhaps, with the loss of her troupe, all of the fight had been leaked out of her.

"Get your man and bring him to me. I will release you from your bonds."

Huh. Wasn't sure what that meant. Except we could take leave of the troupe without making anyone think we would be coming back in two weeks, which was a huge relief.

As she requested, I found Taro, and we went to Atara's tent. She had set up a small table and three croppers in the open air. She had a black candle burning on the table, three goblets, and a knife.

And what the hell was the knife for?

I really hoped it wasn't the same knife that had been used to kill Yesit.

"Please sit," she said. And when we had done so, she took one of our hands in each of hers. "Friends have come and friends have parted," she said. "May good fortune lighten their heels." Then she let go of our hands, and picked up her goblet.

So we picked up ours. She sipped, so did we. Really sweet wine. I liked it. Taro probably hated it.

And after we had set our goblets down, Atara picked up the knife. That was just a little alarming. She put the blade to her left palm, and lightly drew it across her skin, leaving no mark. She took my left hand, and drew the knife across the palm, again, leaving no mark. No blood. She did the same with Taro.

Then she picked up her goblet again, lifting it in a toast to us. "May good fortune lighten your steps."

That was it?

Atara smiled. "I know you have little patience for such things."

I was so tired of being transparent to absolutely everyone I met.

Chapter Twenty-three

Those who had chosen to stay with Atara's troupe left Golden Fields that morning. The Glass Fair remained behind, and we learned they planned to stay for one more night. We didn't want to look for the Bryants until the Glass Fair, and the remainder of those who knew us, left.

The oddest thing happened to me when I received word that Atara's troupe was definitely gone. My stomach suddenly tied into a knot, my heart picked up its pace, and my throat seemed to tighten. It was almost as though I were descending into some kind of panic. All because Taro and I were now cut off from our only means of making money, in a place that didn't care that we were a Pair. How uncharacteristic of me.

"We're moving into another bunker," Taro announced.

"This one not fine enough for you?"

"The owner here knows we're from the troupe," Taro said.

"So?"

"So we want to be somewhere where no one knows we're from the troupe."

Really, my control over my temper was shockingly thin.
There I was, getting so aggravated because Taro was deliberately drawing out this conversation for the sake of dramatic effect. That was Taro. Why was it annoying me so
much? "Why?"

And he grinned. "I'm going to play some cards."

He was going to gamble.

It made sense. Take what we had and turn it into more.
Simple. I'd even suggested he do so.

But at that time, we knew more money would be coming
in. If he lost it, it wouldn't have been too calamitous. We
had the ability to replace any lost coin. In our new circumstances, all we had to get us through the search for the Empress's family and then get us back to the harbor was what
was in my purse, everything that I'd managed to horde
from my performances. Once the money was gone, it was
gone, and there would be nothing to replace it.

Taro was a good gambler. I'd seen, once, the pile of slips
from those who had lost to him, who had owed him money.

But it wasn't called gambling for nothing. And it had
been a while since he'd played cards.

Taro was losing his grin, and a frown was imminent. He
was starting to realize why I was hesitating.

"Sounds like an excellent idea," I said. Because there
was nothing else I could say, really.

So let's just wind up that panic one more notch.

We moved into another bunker, chosen for being the
greatest distance from the original one. And that evening
Taro went out hunting for a card game. I tried not to be nervous about the fact that he was playing a *game* with our
money. I wanted to be not nervous in private, but Aryne
had invited herself into our room and was sitting on the
floor, mending one of her flimsy little skirts.

"He's going to get blanked," Aryne commented without
looking up from her work.

"He's going to get what?"

"With wine."

Oh.

"And he'll lose all your coin."

"No, he won't," I snapped.

"Then he'll come home angry and slam us."

"He definitely won't be doing that." That, I could be sure of.

Aryne snorted. "All men do."

There were questions there that should be asked. I just didn't know if I should be the one asking them. "I wouldn't know about all men."

"All the men I've met."

"I've seen Taro drunk. He gets silly, not violent."

"Huh."

I really didn't want to talk about Taro getting drunk while he was gambling with our money. "Have you ever heard of the Bryants?" Didn't hurt to ask.

"What are the Bryants?"

"A family."

"A family of what?"

"Farmers. That's their name. Bryant."

"Never heard of a name like that," she said.

"Bryant?"

"Kai. Or the Bryants."

Oh, I was an idiot. For I had never heard anyone on Flatwell using family names as we did at home. It was always personal name of personal name. Kahlia of Atara. Zenna of Panol. So either the Empress had gotten the name wrong or . . . or . . . the Empress had gotten the name wrong, damn it.

Just one more straw on this stack of idiocy.

How were we supposed to find these people when we didn't even know their name?

All right. Calm down. Aryne's grandmother had been brought to Golden Fields by someone acting as a governess. Golden Fields wasn't so very big. Surely people would have been aware of the arrival of a Northern fosterling. And surely some of such people would still be alive?

Taro arrived not too late that evening, with a grin and a lightness to his step that I hadn't seen in a good long time.

So he hadn't lost. Thank Zaire. "Have fun?"

"It's fascinating that a place so different from home in so many ways could have the same card games," he said.

I really wanted to rip his purse from him and count the coins in it. It didn't look any heavier—or lighter—than it had earlier. "Really? They do?"

"Well, not all card games, but apparently everyone in the world plays slider."

Really didn't care. "So you had a good time?"

His grin got even wider. "Kai."

Aryne chuckled.

"And you didn't lose?"

Then, he hesitated. "No."

And the panic was back. "That wasn't entirely convincing."

"I did at first. It's been a while. But I recouped."

"So you won?"

"No. I drew even. I left once I was back to where I'd started."

Not bad news, but not good news, either. "I see."

"I'll do better next time."

Perhaps, but I wasn't sure that my nails could survive "next time."

The next morning, we hid out in our bunker until we were sure the Glass Fair had left. Then it was time to begin our sure-to-be-futile hunt. But before Taro and I left, I said to Aryne, "I expect you to stay in your room until we get back."

"Do ya, now?"

"Yes, I do. It's for your own safety."

"Thought you were so sure I wasn't a slave."

"I am. But the whole point for the slave story was to keep you out of Golden Fields. We don't know why Border thought that was necessary." Though I suspected it was to keep Aryne away from the rest of her family, to keep her from being recognized.

"Can take care of myself."

Aye, that was why she'd latched on to us, complete strangers that we were. "I'll buy you an entire fee-sish while I'm out." Fee-sish was a bright pink, sweet, juicy fruit encased in a hard prickly shell. I suspected it was a favorite of Aryne's from the way she tried to snatch any that appeared on a plate in her vicinity, though she had never said as much to me. "If I come back and feel no suspicion that you've left the room, the whole fruit is yours."

Aryne's eyebrows rose.

Yes, I was aware of the wiggle room I'd left her in that statement. I would have to give her the fruit if she managed to leave the room and return without my suspecting she had ever left in the first place.

But then, I'd given myself breathing room, too. All I had to do was suspect. I didn't have to prove anything.

I was able to outwit an eleven-year-old. Occasionally. I was proud of myself.

"Do we have an agreement?" I asked.

"Kai."

"Good."

So we left the bunker, and I had no real faith that she'd actually stay in her room. I just hoped her lust for the fruit might make her careful if she did go out.

"Where to first?" Taro asked.

"The record keeper." Every settlement I'd ever been in or heard of had someone dedicated to keeping the history of that settlement. A place as small as Golden Fields would have at least a chance of recording the arrival of two Northerners in a time when Northerners never went to the Southern Islands.

At least it was a place to start.

Chapter Twenty-four

I was turning into a cynic. Which was possibly nothing more than a euphemism for whiner. But I couldn't help feeling skeptical about our chances for success upon hearing that Golden Fields's record keeper was called a story holder.

Then we found the little bamboo hut in which the story holder worked. And, of course, lived. I was afraid my skepticism was justified, especially once we learned, during our initial conversation with the man, that he didn't use anything as simple and as sensible as paper, or parchment, or even stone, for the recording of historical events. Oh, no. He kept it all locked away in his mind.

He looked to be in his forties, and I could detect nothing in his braids, his leather skirt, or his tattoos which signified his position, which was usually one of some respect in most settlements. He sat in a cropper. An apprentice sat at his feet, listening to everything he said. That was the traditional manner of instructing an apprentice, I was told.

Oh, no. No chance of inaccuracies creeping in over the years. I believed it. Really.

Nothing to do but plunge in. "Do you have any stories about a farming family, one of the members called Bryant or something like it? They would have taken in a fosterling from the North, perhaps sixty years ago?"

No chance in hell.

The man sat and thought about this. At a gesture, his apprentice handed him a thin square slate and a small sack, the size of his palm. He shook what looked like ordinary white sand onto the black surface, and with his index finger he drew nonsense designs into the white sand.

It looked pretty.

"Ah, yes," he said.

Ah, sure. Ritual and superstition.

"White lines and fire," he said.

Kai, that made sense.

"Three years into the Speaking of Relan of Dalia," he continued. "The farmers of brown rye on the northeast concession had visitors from the North."

I opened my mouth to ask when exactly three years into the Speaking of Relan was, but was kicked by the apprentice before I could speak. She ignored my glare with the insulting ease of her people.

"A child, named Ara, and her mother, Laura of Secord."

Oh my gods. He got that from white sand on slate?

"Nine years into the Speaking of Relan of Dalia, Laura of Secord married Apol of Ranter, and within the year they left the farmers and left Golden Fields, leaving Ara behind. There is no further record of Laura. Ara of Laura was apprenticed to the dye maker at age seven. She was very plain, and was old before she bore her daughter, Nevress, and died in childbirth. Nevress . . ." The story holder hesitated there, dribbling more sand from the bag onto the slate. He added, "Nevress of Ara had no family and no letters. She bartered herself, and lifted. Shortly after giving birth to a daughter, she was hanged, for thieving."

I repressed a shudder. Hanging as a form of execution. How brutal. I'd prefer to be stabbed.

Taro cleared his throat. "What was the daughter's name?"

The story holder stared at the slate, added some more sand, and then shook his head. "That is not known. She was left at the circle. They have not added her sand here."

I wasn't going to ask what that meant. I didn't really care. Except for, "The circle? What does that mean?"

The apprentice piped up then. "Where the stringless are left."

"The stringless?"

"Kinless."

"Orphans," I said.

"Kai," said the record keeper.

"Does it say when this child was left?"

The holder shrugged. "It is unclear. Nevress died less than twenty years ago."

Damn it. No one was going to remember anything from twenty years before. "Where is this circle?"

The apprentice gave us directions. She also held out her hand and cleared her throat when we started to leave without paying.

I had honestly forgotten about it, but really, did we have to pay for *everything*? For less than a quarter of an hour of a person's time? And what happened if we learned the story keeper was wrong? Could we return and get our money back?

The circle was an actual circle. A single-story structure of bamboo and wood, constructed into a circle around a circle of bare, sandy land. Through one of the wide windows I could see very young children playing with balls and hoops and the other useless things children played with. They were concentrated in the center of the circle. Around the perimeter, older children were sitting in croppers hunched over a variety of tools, most of which I couldn't recognize. Adults wandered about, watching them, sometimes stopping to give instruction.

I wondered whether they were learning, or working. I hoped for the former, couldn't do anything about the latter.

We were waiting for the person a child had told us was called the Watcher, the person in charge of the circle. I was expecting to meet someone matronly, a settled woman of wisdom and years who would remember every child placed in her care with affection and clarity.

What we got was some twenty something lad of broad shoulders and a scandalously short skirt, and wouldn't you know it, he was the first person on the whole damned island to look at Taro with any interest. I could tell by the way his eyes barely hesitated on me before taking just a little too long to travel over my Source's form.

It was the ache in my jaw that alerted me to the fact that I was clenching my teeth.

"I am Zilran of Zonfar," he said with a smile, revealing those ridiculously straight teeth all the islanders seemed to have. "I am Watcher here."

"I am Dunleavy Mallorough, and this is Shintaro Karish."

Zilran was polite enough, looking at me as I spoke, but he kept glancing at Taro.

I wanted to glance at Taro myself, to see how he was reacting to this attention. I wouldn't let myself. Because I really didn't want to see how he was reacting to this attention, which he had been used to before we came to Flatwell, but had to have been starving for ever since.

"We are looking for some family we think may have some connection to the circle," I said. "A child was left here. Her mother, I understand, was called Nevress of Ara."

Zilran frowned as he thought about it. "That doesn't sound familiar."

"The child would be twenty years old, or less. I don't know when it might have lived here, but the story holder seems to feel it was placed here after Nevress died."

"I have been here only two years," he said. He poked his head out the nearest window. "Saya!" he shouted out. "Please join us! She has been here over thirty years," he told us.

Finally, someone old enough to be of use.

And then, Zilran turned his full attention on my Source. "You are from the North?"

Obviously.

Taro smiled back at him, and I looked out the window. "We are from High Scape," I heard him say. "Have you heard of it?"

"No, but it must be an exciting place."

And there was that tone. Playful, not flirtatious, yet an invitation that could be easily rejected without causing offense.

Taro was supposed to ask why this gorgeous young fellow assumed High Scape must be an exciting place. And Zilran would then say, because someone as—pick the adjective—as Taro could only come from an exciting place. And they would take it from there.

Taro said, "It is disturbed by a great many natural events. But we have seven Pairs in total, so we are able to keep it calm."

I looked at Zilran then, wondering what he was going to do with that.

From the expression on his face, he was wondering the same.

The woman I presumed was Saya walked in, and this was the lady I had been expecting. A heavily lined face, dark hair graying, her shoulders stooped with age.

She still wore the scanty clothes and tattoos everyone else wore, though.

"Watcher?" she said, and though her tone was respectful, something about her stance, her gaze, made me feel she didn't like him.

I wouldn't like him, either. Not just because he was trying to flirt with my Source, but he seemed awfully young for his position. I wouldn't like to be told what to do by someone a third my age.

"We are looking for a child who was placed here within the last twenty years," I said, and I felt really stupid asking the question. How the hell would she remember? "The mother was named Nevress of Ara, and she was hanged as a thief. The mother would have had some Northern blood." Well, so would the child, but it might have been more evident in the mother.

"Brought in during the last twenty years," the older woman clarified, just to make sure I was really feeling stupid.

"Kai," I admitted.

"Come with me," Saya said, moving down a hall without waiting to be dismissed by Zilran. I wondered if that offended him. I hurriedly thanked the Watcher and Taro and I followed Saya. She led us along the curve of the building and then down a rickety set of stairs that took us down to a dank dark room below ground. She had us wait at the entrance while she lit a series of candles that lined the long walls of the room.

The room was filled with stones. Truly. Black stones, flat and rounded, polished and each about the size of my palm. They'd had holes bored into them and had been strung onto some kind of slim rope. The strings of stones were hung from the ceiling and were left to dangle over the floor. A single touch had the stones clattering against each other. Perhaps out in the open air the sound would have been pretty, but down in the dark it was disquieting.

"Every child who enters our circle has a stone," Saya said, and her voice seemed to echo in the room. "We mark on the stone all the circumstances of the child's life. Origins,

why they came to be here, age, name and when and why
they left. If the child was here within the last twenty years,
then we may restrict our search to this portion of the
room." She gestured at a couple dozen strings, each with
several dozen stones. Not an insurmountable amount, but
more than I liked. There had to be a better way to do this.

"The child may have had a tattoo," I said. Then again, it
might not. It didn't make sense for the tradition to have
been carried down that far. Would Nevress have had it
done? Would she have known the significance of it? It
would seem hard to believe, that she would willingly take
the life of a criminal without crying out that she was de-
scended from royalty.

Then again, if the child didn't have the tattoo, we
wouldn't be able to recognize it anyway, and that part of
the family would be truly lost.

"That is not unusual," Saya said.

"Putting tattoos on very young children?" I asked in
surprise.

"Kai."

"I haven't seen any tattoos on children."

"I don't know of the children you know," said Saya.
"But many people have their children marked at birth, so
that their family is known should the child be lost. The
mark is not usually made in a place commonly bared to
view."

"Why not?" What would the point of it be, then, to keep
it in a private place?

"Some marks are well known. Their families are
wealthy or strong. Children can be the prey of those who
seek power. You steal a family's child and seek advantage
in exchange for return."

"I have been all over this island and I haven't heard of
anything like this," I objected.

"You are an offlander." Saya shrugged. "Why would
you know this?"

Suddenly, I felt that I hadn't learned anything about these people, in all the time I'd been on Flatwell. And that was sad.

Saya picked out a stone and had Taro and I peer at it. It was a *v* shape with a horizontal bar through it. She told us it was the symbol for a female parent who had been hanged, and it was the only symbol she bothered to show us. When we found it on a stone, we were to call her, and she would interpret the rest of the symbols.

There really wasn't enough light to be doing such work, even though what light there was really seemed to bounce off the polished stones and reflect about the room. Fortunately, the symbols were deeply etched into the stones, and it didn't take long for my fingers to become accustomed to the shapes of the grooves. But I really had to concentrate on what I was doing. If I let my thoughts wander, my fingers would glide over the surface of the stones without really feeling anything.

It took hours. A distressingly large number of the orphans had had mothers who had been hanged. But only one had a mother whose name had been Nevress. Apparently, it wasn't that common a name on Flatwell, thank Zaire. I'd already started imagining what it might be like to try to track down multiple possibilities.

"A girl," Saya announced. "Brought here in the second year of Avol of Rikin. Around ten years ago," she translated. "But the name of the child is not written."

"What does that mean?" Taro asked.

"That she had no known name when she was left here, perhaps," said Saya. "Or that it was forgotten by the time the stone was carved."

"But if the child lived here—" said Taro.

"She was not here long," Saya interrupted. "She went missing shortly after she was brought here. And she was never found."

This was just ridiculous. We'd come all this way and

gone through hell just to reach a dead end? "I understand you were working here when these events would have taken place."

"Kai."

"Do you remember this child?"

"No."

Frustrating wench. "How can you not?"

"Many children go fly and then are caught again. I have no time to linger over events ten years by."

I couldn't decide whether I found that appallingly cold or just good common sense.

"Are there any other such circles for stringless children?" Taro asked her.

"Not on Flatwell."

Damn it, this was ridiculous. This couldn't be the end of things. But that seemed to be all the useful information that was available at the circle. So we took our leave, with no appointment to meet up later between Zilran and Taro that I could determine.

"We don't know for sure that Ara had no other children," I said once we were out in the open again.

"The story holder told us she died having Nevress. He would have told us if there were others."

"We don't know for sure."

"And where else are we going to check?"

"The Bryants."

"You mean the farmers of brown rye," he said in a tone of flat annoyance.

"That can't possibly be where she got the name." Please, let that not be how she got the name.

We headed to where the story holder's apprentice had told us the Bryants lived, but there was nothing there. No crops, no buildings, no people. And the nearest neighbors couldn't figure out who we were talking about.

I didn't know what the next step was going to be, but we'd burned enough of the day away. I was tired and hungry and frustrated. So we went back to the bunker to arrange for something to eat, and of course Aryne wasn't there, the aggravating little brat. Seriously, I was going to kill that kid.

Chapter Twenty-five

Aryne didn't return before Taro and I went to bed. I assumed she was avoiding a confrontation, hoping we wouldn't yell at her if she snuck in while we were asleep. She would have been wrong. I was well able to hold on to anger through a night's sleep. Though I hadn't noticed in her any serious reaction to our yelling, anyway.

Then I woke up the next morning and learned that Aryne still hadn't returned. I was furious.

"Be reasonable, Lee," said Taro as he tucked into a breakfast of fish and rice that I was too angry to eat. "She's believed her whole life that she's a slave, and that Golden Fields was something to fear above everything else. It's not surprising that stewing in a room alone for hours on end might prove to be too much for her."

"So she goes out into the open where she can be caught?" I demanded. "That doesn't make sense."

"Children often don't, I'm told."

"No, she caught a faster ride up north." And I should have been relieved about it. She really was a complication we didn't need.

"Then why did she leave all of her stuff?"

My cup of tea—a poor substitute for coffee, really—halted on its way to my mouth. "She did?"

"Kai."

I set the tea cup back on the table. "Then where the hell is she?"

I didn't know what to think. Maybe she liked being out all night. In the Academy, there had been those who seemed to think being out when they were supposed to be in bed was thrilling all on its own. Yet I hadn't known Aryne to do anything simply for the pleasure of it.

Which was sad, now that I thought about it.

"We'll have to go look for her," I said. I didn't know what was going on with her, but I'd felt awful about not looking for her the last time she'd gone missing, and I wasn't going to repeat that mistake. This time I was going to find her. And shake her.

Zaire, I was getting violent in my thoughts.

I shouldn't think so ill of her. She'd had a horrible life. And Taro was right. She'd believed her whole life that Golden Fields was a place to be feared. She couldn't be expected to just put that fear aside, no matter what facts had been presented to her. She was just a child. And a Source. Feelings would always rule her.

I just couldn't understand why the medicine man would tell her such a tale. What could possibly be the point of it? Had he stolen the child from her family, like what Saya had been speaking about? If he had, wouldn't he have returned her by now, and gotten whatever ransom or power he'd been looking for?

Or perhaps it had nothing to do with Aryne at all. Perhaps he had his own reasons for fearing Golden Fields.

Would he have disregarded his reasons, whatever they were, to come looking for her?

Oh, tell me he hadn't grabbed her.

But she would know better than to stay away so long. As far as she knew, we'd just leave her. We still had another task to perform. She had no way to know we'd reached a dead end.

Hell, there we were again, looking for someone. We were no good at this. Why were we always ending up with this sort of task?

But at least we had a place to start. If it weren't for the medicine man, I wouldn't know where to begin looking. And if the medicine man had nothing to do with Aryne's disappearance, well, we were all in a knot, because I didn't know what our next step would be.

We headed to the market. I didn't expect him to actually be there, especially if he were responsible for Aryne's disappearance, but other traveling merchants might know him, and might notice him if he had been in Golden Fields at all. But those merchants who did know of him said they hadn't seen him.

There was a traveling medicine man there. He refused to talk to us unless we bought something, which led me, for one, to believe he had something useful to say. So we bought a small bottle of something useless, and he told us he hadn't seen Border. Border never came to Golden Fields. The parasite.

I was all for dashing the useless potion to the ground right then, but Taro thought the bottle was pretty and wanted to keep it.

"The livery," said Taro.

"What about it?"

"If he was here, and he didn't stop in the market, which he wouldn't under these circumstances, than he had to leave his gear—what did he have, anyway?"

I searched my memory. "A kind of stall, but it had wheels. So it could be dragged."

"By a horse?"

"I don't think I've seen a horse on this island. People seem to use mules or some kind of steerlike animal."

"All right, he'd have to leave that somewhere while he was looking for Aryne. And that's probably the livery, because he wouldn't know anyone who lives here if he's avoided this place for so many years."

That made sense, so we got directions to the two liveries in Golden Fields. The first one we went to had had no one leaving a stall like Border's during the past few days. The second one was on the outskirts of the settlement, and had held such a stall.

The first piece of positive news. I almost went into shock.

"He left yesterday afternoon," the livery woman told us.

"Did he have a young girl with him?" Karish asked her.

"Kai," the woman answered.

For some reason, it felt like my heart was pounding right in my throat. "What did she say?" Because she had to have been saying something.

"She was asleep. Or ill. He was carrying her."

My gods. Why hadn't I heard about this from any of the market people? "Who did you report this to?"

The woman stared down at me, jaws working as she chewed on the end of some kind of wheatlike stalk. "No one."

"A man comes here alone and leaves with an unconscious child and you don't tell anyone?"

"Told lots of people. Don't think that's what you meant, though."

No, that wasn't what I meant. I couldn't believe a man could carry away a child who clearly didn't belong to him without anyone doing anything about it. Maybe that was what he'd done the first time, too. Though, clearly, he didn't need to avoid Golden Fields because of it. "He didn't happen to say where he was going, did he?" I asked without much hope.

"He went that way," was the response we got, as the woman pointed to the only road out of town.

And he'd left the day before, damn it. "Do you have any horses?" I asked her.

She snickered. "No."

Some livery. But it didn't matter, really. We didn't have enough money to buy a horse. But how else could we catch up with Border? He'd have to know we would figure out that he had taken Aryne, and there was only one road out. He would be driving his animal hard, and probably taking some weird turns.

We ran back to the bunker to get our gear and pack up Aryne's. We spared some time to buy some travel rations. And then we headed back out at a brisk walk, speeding up to a jog when we had the energy, slowing right down to almost a stroll when the midday heat hit.

As predicted, Border left the road. Or so we assumed. There were other wheel tracks, though not many, and when they turned off it was to follow a path to a house or some other useful location. When a set of ruts turned off the road into untouched grass with no particular destination in sight, we took the chance that those wheels belonged to Border.

We could be going in the wrong direction. We were assuming that Border was being really stupid, or that he thought we were really stupid and wouldn't have the first clue how to follow him. And we didn't, not really. We were lucky that we weren't buried in the forested part of the island, which I thought would make following a person impossible, or that there had been no rain to wash away wagon tracks. And that we'd thought to look for wagon tracks at all was probably due only to the fact that we'd been traveling with the troupe and noticing the deep impressions their wagon left in the ground.

Walking off the road was harder work, and it was harder to see the wagon ruts. At times, the tracks made sharp turns to the right and left, for no reason I could discern. I couldn't imagine what Border's destination was.

Night came and we had to stop. Even with a lantern, it was too dangerous to keep going when we weren't even on the road, and we couldn't see the wagon tracks at all. It was damned frustrating. I had no idea whether Border would need to stop so soon, or for so long, with an animal to draw his wagon.

We rose early the next morning and got moving. We kept to the same pace we'd held the day before. We didn't talk much, and I was glad of it. I was oddly anxious, and I hated knowing that we could be completely wasting our time. Certainly, we could still see the tracks of the wheels, but what if they were the wrong wheels? The temptation to go back to the road was so strong, and it took so much effort not to suggest it.

I was not made for this kind of work.

And what did he want with the girl? Why was she so important to him that he'd come all the way to Golden Fields just to get her?

I supposed that all depended on why he'd taken her in the first place, when she was younger. I had no answers for that, either. I couldn't imagine why anyone would steal a child, especially when one had no desire to love and raise them properly. All right, Saya had given me a reason for that, for stealing children. But not for keeping them. Children were nothing but work and expense, when you didn't love them.

Not that his reason for taking her mattered at all. He clearly hadn't been treating her properly. She clearly didn't want to stay with him. And she had a much better life waiting for her at the Source Academy.

The day passed without our catching up to Border. Or to anyone else. When the light of day began to fail again, my anxiety grew tighter and more intense. I worried that the longer it took us to find Aryne, the less likely it would be that we ever would.

Then again, did it matter? I had no idea where else to look for the Empress's relatives, and I didn't like the idea of going back home without finding them. A part of me thought we might as well spend the rest of our lives wandering this damned island looking for Aryne.

And then, it started raining.

And Karish started swearing.

I always enjoyed listening to Karish swear. He was so good at it.

We kept going. We had to go as far as we could, before the rain washed the wheel ruts away. And then, once that happened, I didn't know what the hell we were going to do. Keep going in the same direction, and hope that Border didn't change his?

Night came. Karish didn't suggest we stop. Instead, he lit the lantern, and we pressed on. Maybe he could see the tracks better than I could. Maybe he had an instinct or a hunch, and if he did, I wasn't going to interfere. I followed him.

Our first hint that we'd found our quarry was the beautiful lilt of Aryne loudly swearing.

Followed by the sharp crack of someone being slapped. Aryne was silenced.

I wanted to rush forward with a roar of anger. How uncharacteristic of me.

In a few more steps, we could see the faint outline of a tent, glowing from within. Taro blew out the lantern. He and I quietly divested ourselves of our packs, leaving them on the ground. I kept the money with me, though, just in case we found ourselves in circumstances where we had to leave everything behind.

We crept up quietly, the glow of the tent the only source of light. Because we were moving so slowly, it didn't hurt at all when I walked right into the wagon. The steer, still hitched to the wagon, didn't stir. It was asleep, I imagined.

I wondered how fast a steer could travel. Not nearly as fast as a horse, I supposed. Thank Zaire the islanders didn't seem to use horses. We would have been completely out of luck if Border had had a horse.

"Not being drugged again," I heard Aryne mutter.

"Don't need to drug you again, do I?" Border's hateful booming voice chortled. "Just need to keep you tied right and tight until you remember your place. But if you're not going to eat it's not my nevermind. More for me, and you've gotten fat."

We stepped up closer to the tent. It wasn't a big tent, though it seemed constructed on the same lines as every other tent I'd seen on Flatwell. Tall enough to stand in. From their voices, though, both of the occupants were low to the ground.

"Leavy and Taro have loads more money than you," Aryne said, and it seemed an attempt to taunt him. Why would she do that? "They always had lots of food."

"Probably why they left you behind. You ate too much."

"Didn't leave me behind. And they'll come find me, too."

For some reason, it pleased me that she thought so.

Border laughed. "You're so stupid," he said. "Why would anyone but me give two nuts about a useless, string-less little wench like you?"

"'Cause I'm a Source. They think I have to go to one of their schools."

"Sure, when you fall into their laps. But they're not going to go out of their way to find you. There are millions of Sources up there, properly raised. Who aren't thieves. Believe me, they're relieved to be rid of you. And even if they weren't, even if they weren't like every other lazy, overindulged Pair in existence, they would have no idea how to find you."

"Sure they would. They're smart."

Border laughed again. "They're smart," he echoed mockingly. "It's a Pair. None of them know anything."

"Like you would know," Aryne said.

"Kai, I would know. I'm from up there. I lived in the coldest city you could ever imagine, and her right whorish Majesty just loved Sources. We had a new Pair every other year, every single one of them as stupid as pigs. All they know how to do is channel. And that Pair must be dumber than most, to be sent to a place like this. So give up your ridiculous little dreams of rescue, bitch. It ain't gonna happen. And don't try running away again, neither. I'll take you up north when I'm ready."

Border was a Northerner? But he'd looked like every
other islander I'd ever met. And he planned to take her
north? Had she known that when she'd come to us?

"I'm not going to whore for you, Border."

"Damn well better not. I see any man sniffing around
you and I'll kill him and break every bone in your face.
You'll be untouched when I take you north or there'll be
hell to pay. By you."

I was relieved to hear that Border never used Aryne as a
prostitute, and never planned to, but really, what was his
game?

There was no more conversation from inside the tent.
That seemed to be all that we were going to learn for the
moment.

Karish ducked and reached into the tent. I heard a yip
from Aryne and when Karish reappeared he was dragging
Aryne with him. It was a hard job. Her hands and ankles
were bound.

Border, predictably, objected to that with a slew of vit-
riol. Karish literally dumped Aryne into my arms, and I
dragged her away as Border came charging out of the tent
and barreling into Karish, bearing him down to the ground
with a painful sounding thud.

"Stop wiggling!" I snapped at Aryne as I lowered her to
the ground. My objective was to untie her, but the ropes
were thin and tight and already slick with rain. There was
no getting them undone without the use of a knife, which I
was currently not carrying.

I couldn't imagine why, when I left my packs on the
ground, I didn't think a knife might come in handy.

Border got his knees up under him and started punching
Karish in the face and upper torso. Having learned a little
something from when we were in a similar situation, I left
Aryne and jumped up behind Border, clawing my hands
and sinking them into his face.

Border's hands rose up to mine and I pulled hard, trying
not to think about what parts of the man's face my fingers

might be sticking into. He fell backward and Karish scrambled away. Border twisted and suddenly I felt a huge mass shoved into my stomach, forcing all the air out of me. The pain was incredible.

The next strike went to my face, landing over my mouth and nose. My head snapped back and my vision blacked out. I landed on the ground hard, the impact stinging along my side.

I have no idea what happened next. I tried to pull myself away while curling in at the same time, trying to protect a stomach that was burning with pain. I still couldn't breathe, but no further blows fell on me. That was good, right?

I couldn't hear anything. My ears were ringing.

I probably would have shrieked when I felt a hand grip my wrist, if I'd had the air to do it. An instant later, the pain faded almost to nothing, and I relaxed. Taro.

His shields dropped. With no warning, damn him. He had to stop doing that. I hastily erected mine around him, and felt him channel.

Only the channeling wasn't the natural sort. It didn't feel like the forces of the world rushing through him and threatening to burst him open like an overripe fruit. Instead, it was like he was pulling the forces to him, luring them in and redirecting them. That meant he wasn't actually channeling a natural disaster. He was doing something else.

I didn't know what. It was all I could do to keep breathing and guard Taro. I wasn't being struck, and it seemed like Taro wasn't being struck. That was about all I could hope for at the moment.

I didn't really become aware of the vibrations and the rumblings until they abruptly stopped. It took me a while, though, to really hear what was going on.

Namely, Border swearing and yelling to be released, panic threaded through his voice. A few moments later, I blinked rain out of my eyes and saw what had happened.

Border was upright, sort of, but he was buried up to his

waist, sunk right into the ground. And I realized what the channeling had been about.

Karish had involuntarily spent time with an insane Source who could do much more than channel forces. He could create natural disasters, and manipulate earth to such a degree that he could actually control how and where it moved. Karish had had ample opportunity to observe him and figure out how to do it himself.

This was the first time I'd seen him do something so precise. It seemed that he was getting better at this skill as time went on. Which made sense. The more he did it, the better he got.

Except the first time was supposed to have been the only time.

"What the hell was that?" Aryne demanded.

Taro released my wrist. Pain flooded back to my stomach and my face, but it wasn't as intense as it had been before. I climbed to my feet, a little unsteadily, and felt my way back to the bags Karish and I had left behind. I needed a knife to cut Aryne loose.

"Get me out of this or I'll kill you!" Border shouted.

I rolled my eyes. Knife in hand, I went back to Aryne and started sawing on the rope.

"Get me out!" Border ordered. "Right now!"

Karish went into the tent.

"I was ordered here by the Empress," Border declared, and suddenly his islander accent was almost gone. "I am part of her personal guard. If you interfere with my mission, you'll both be hanged."

That made me stare at him. He was sent by the Empress?

Oh. Suddenly, things made a lot more sense.

I looked at Aryne. "It's really important that you tell me the truth right now," I said. "How long have you lived with this man?"

"All my life," she said, and the absence of any kind of slang in her words or derision in her tone made me think she was telling the truth.

Hell. She was the heir. Or Border thought she was. And if he'd seen her as a baby, he would have seen her with the mark.

"We were sent to find her, too," I told him. "Because she's a Source. She needs to go to the Source Academy. And we won't take ten years to bring her back."

"I'm on a mission from the Empress!"

I sniffed, hoping the sound would denote disbelief.

Taro came out of the tent holding a rag and, I could see as he got closer, several small jars. He knelt beside Aryne. "Tell me which one smells like what he used on you, Aryne." He quickly opened the jars and waved them under her nose.

At the third jar she gagged and jerked her head back. "That's the one."

Taro dumped a bunch of the contents on the rag.

"Are you stupid?" the medicine man demanded. "I'm here under orders of the Empress."

I had a feeling he really was. But so were we. And I suspected he was the reason we'd been sent and gone through all sorts of hell, because he'd felt like playing games and kept the child for years.

I found it interesting that with all his shouting, Border didn't mention why he had been sent to find Aryne. He clearly didn't want her to know.

Well, neither did we.

Border shook his head in an attempt to avoid the rag Taro held. Taro grabbed a fist of the man's hair, keeping Border's head still while mashing the cloth over his face. Border grabbed at his hands, and when he couldn't move them began striking out at random. He landed a few good shots to Karish's torso, but Karish held on grimly, and it wasn't long before Border's movements became slower and weaker. And when all movement stopped, Karish held the cloth over his face a little longer.

"You'll kill him if you give him too much," Aryne warned him. "'Course, that might be what you're after."

"No, we don't want him dead. We just don't want him able to follow us for a while."

Having freed Aryne's hands, I went to work on her ankles. The ropes were tough, and the knife I had wasn't designed for such work. "What did he mean about being sent by the Empress to find me?" she demanded.

"I'm not sure," I lied. "I have to think about it."

"What does someone like that want with me?"

"Quiet. Let me do this and let me think."

Karish was emptying the tent of everything he thought useful. He did the same with the wagon. I relit our lantern and took a good look at Aryne. She had a swollen lip and a blackened eye. Her wrists and ankles had been ripped bloody by the ropes. "See if you can find something soothing for broken skin," I called out to Taro.

"You don't look so good, either," Aryne said. "Your face is bleeding."

I carefully touched my mouth. My fingers came away colored with blood that was quickly washed away by the rain.

"You'll look a treat tomorrow," said Aryne.

Great.

I packed whatever Taro was stealing into bags, which he slung over the steer. He unhitched the steer from the wagon. I guessed that meant we were taking it with us. I felt not the slightest prick of remorse about stealing from that man. He deserved it.

Taro stuck a spade in the ground, close enough to Border that he could reach it if he stretched. He plunked Aryne on the steer and we headed off blindly, in the rain and in the dark, just to get a little bit of distance between us and Border.

We didn't go far. We just couldn't. Aryne was falling asleep on the steer and almost slipped off a few times. We weren't on a road, so we were in danger of walking into a crevice or something. I hated the idea of stopping so close to Border, but it was too dangerous to go on. We propped up a tent and tried to weigh the steer down by burying its reins in the ground and dumping everything we'd stolen from Border on top of them. After a brief argument, it was agreed that Taro would stay awake for a few hours to act as sentry, and then he'd wake me and sleep while I stood watch.

The argument of who would stand watch first was merely for form's sake on my part. I was exhausted. All the new ideas attempting to penetrate my brain were no match for the heavy fog already in residence. As soon as my head was on the hard islander pillow, I was asleep.

Chapter Twenty-six

I was roused far too early for my liking, and it was still dark. Taro shoved a mug of cold tea into my hands and muttered something to the effect that everything was quiet before crawling into my blankets on my mat and collapsing. I then had to yank myself out of the blankets without spilling anything. Quite the accomplishment.

I sat out in front of the tent. I felt useless and stupid. The night was completely black, and we didn't dare alert any unfriendlies of our presence by lighting a lantern. It was raining and not silent enough. I had no weapon and no skill to use one. If I was anything more than useless out there, it wasn't by much.

I really hoped Border wasn't awake yet. If he came after us right then I could easily be overcome without even getting a word out. But then, he didn't just have to wake up. He had to dig himself out, a dangerous task at night. And then he'd have to decide whether to leave the wagon behind or try dragging it with him. And if he did look for us at night, he would need a lantern, and I would see him long before he saw us. So, all right, I could provide a useful warning.

And hey, it had stopped raining.

I was hungry, but my stomach still felt a little tender from the scuffle with Border.

Really, all the brawls I was sucked into were just shocking. Shields weren't supposed to fight. My professors would be appalled. So would my mother.

All right, Border claimed to have been sent by the Empress to look for Aryne. I had taken him for an islander, but once he dropped the accent he had sounded pretty much like any other Northerner I'd ever heard. And why in the world would he claim to be a member of her personal guard on a mission if it weren't true? There were so many other things he could have said that would have made so much more sense.

If he spoke the truth, if he had truly been one of the Empress's trusted personal guards, sent on this mission and never returning, it might be some explanation as to why she had been so unorthodox in her next choice. But then, why didn't he go home, if he'd found the heir?

Unless Aryne wasn't the heir. Perhaps his luck had been as bad as ours, and he'd feared returning in failure. Maybe he preferred Flatwell to his life up north. I would imagine being in the military involved a lot of hard work and a lot of stupid rules. He'd have a lot more leisure as a traveling medicine man on Flatwell.

But no, he'd spoken of taking Aryne up north when he was ready. Why would he do that if she weren't the heir? But if she were the heir, why would he go to the effort of taking care of her himself instead of sending her back home? Either way, it didn't make sense.

The rest of the night passed with no appearances from Border or anyone else. Karish began stirring as the forelight of the sun began creeping up in the east. He dragged himself out of the tent, looking a sorry sight. His black hair was sleep mussed and not in an attractive way. He had slept in his clothes. His left eye was puffy and bruising.

My poor boy.

He gasped when he saw me, lifting a finger to my face but withdrawing before contact could be made. "Shall I go back and kill him?"

"Don't be silly." There were far better reasons for killing Border than my banged-up face.

He looked back into the tent, then looked at me, raising his eyebrows in inquiry.

I shrugged in response. I had no idea what to think of Aryne.

"We should start getting ready to go," he said.

I agreed. "Aryne," I called into the tent. "Time to get up."

Her answer was a groan.

"I'll dig out something to eat," I said.

"And I'll load up the cowlike thing."

Steer, I thought.

I pulled out some cold rice and clumsily wrapped it in dried seaweed. It was fare I was getting really sick of, but it was filling and portable. "I mean it, Aryne. You have to get up. We don't want to give Border a chance to catch up."

She grumbled and crawled out of the tent, looking as much a mess as Karish. I shoved one of the rice balls into her hands and rooted around for something to put on her chafed wrists. They looked even worse in the light of day.

"So what he said about the Empress sending him to look for me," Aryne mumbled around a mouthful of rice. "That true?"

"Swallow, then speak," I chided as I rubbed some cool green gel on Aryne's ankles. "I have no idea whether it's true or not."

She narrowed her eyes at me. "Kai, you do."

"Never met the man before coming here."

"Doesn't mean you don't know what he was talking about."

I was really tempted to tell her to just be quiet. I was surprised by the impulse. This was all about her. Of course she

had the right to know what was going on. Why did I think I
could tell her to shut up? Was it because she was a child?

On the other hand, I, too, was under orders from the Empress. I looked at Taro, to see if he was listening. I wanted to
make sure he knew exactly what I was saying to her, in case
she talked to him about it, too. He looked up at me briefly.
"The woman who sent us wasn't looking for a member of
her own family, but a member of someone else's," I said.

"Who was this woman?" Aryne demanded.

"The Empress."

Aryne barked in laughter.

I shrugged. "There's no real need for you to believe me.
Especially since you're a Source."

"What does she want with me?"

"She didn't tell us."

"So all that stuff about finding some heir . . ."

"We made that up."

"You lied," she accused me.

"That is another way to put it," I agreed blandly.

"So am I this person you're supposed ta be looking for?"

"I don't know." But I might as well embrace the opportunity. "We've been told that a lot of people on this island
are tattooed with the mark of their family. Do you have a
mark like that?"

Her eyes widened in shock. "He said it was a slave
mark!" she exclaimed.

"Border?"

"The bastard."

It really couldn't be this easy. "What does it look like?"

Her answer was to flip up her skirt with no thought to
modesty. "Aryne!" Karish blurted out, holding his hands
over his eyes.

And there it was. The same tattoo the Empress had shown
me. Much darker lines, thicker and more crudely done, and
the gut-wrenching image of some kind of blade digging into
the tender flesh of an infant made an unwelcome appearance

into my brain. But that was definitely the same kind of flower. "Please put your skirt back down, Aryne."

"That the mark you were looking for?"

I hesitated before answering. If I said no, I'd have to come up with a reason why we were leaving the island without the person we were looking for, which I had no doubt Aryne would see as another lie. I certainly wasn't able to think of a decent excuse right then. And we were leaving the island. I wasn't wandering around it any longer than I had to, just to attempt to convince Aryne that she wasn't anything special. "Kai," I said.

Taro frowned, but he didn't jump in.

Aryne stared at me. "I'm a heiress!" she crowed.

"Don't be ridiculous, kid," I said with as much of a sneer as I could muster. "I have no idea why they want you, but you can bet if you were someone important, they wouldn't have sent the likes of us to find you. Do you really think they'd have an heiress subjected to the kind of travel we've been doing?"

Hell. She was a princess. And we were subjecting her to bad food and harsh conditions. Taro and I were going to be in so much trouble.

It was too, too bizarre. Aryne was a descendant of the Empress. And both a Source and a Shield. How could one person be so many extraordinary things?

What was that going to mean? Which role was she going to play? Technically, a Source had to go to the Source Academy, regardless of title. Even if she didn't act as a Source once she'd bonded, she needed the training and protection the Source Academy would give her. But if she became the chosen heir of the Empress, would the rules be bent for her? Had that ever happened before? While in history there had been members of the royal family who'd had talent, they had never been any of the ruling members.

It was too early to worry about that.

A part of me was hugely relieved. I'd really had no idea how we were going to go about finding these people. Now we had at least one person to bring back with us. We hadn't failed.

But she was a princess. Did this mean I had to watch what I said for the months it would take us to get back home? She could decide to cut my head off because she didn't like what we'd had her eat for breakfast.

I'd worry about it all when we got off the island.

We packed up the tent, piled the bags and Aryne on the steer, and got moving. That was when we realized we had no idea where we were. We'd gotten totally turned around while following Border. On Aryne's advice, we kept an eye out for a stream and followed it once we found one.

I was worried about Border finding us again. The steer was so damned slow, and the medicine man would know his way around much better than Karish and I. There were two of us against him, to fight him off, but he, I assumed, would be trained to fight. And if he killed one of us, the Pair bond would kill the other. We were very vulnerable. And he, being a Northerner, would know that.

We followed the stream for two days with no sign of Border or anyone else. They were a hard two days. I kept imagining I could hear someone following us, and that was a good way to go insane. Taro and I slept the nights in shifts, and during the day we didn't stop unless we absolutely had to.

On the third day we finally, finally reached a settlement. We traded the damned steer and just about everything else of Border's for a handful of coins. The tiny settlement was called Silk Purse, and we learned that in following Border we'd been traveling in the opposite direction from where we now wanted to go, which was Promise Harbor. I couldn't raise the energy to be annoyed. That was just the kind of luck we were having.

We rented a single room in a bunker for a night so we could dry out everything that was still damp from the rain and eat some hot food. I took the first watch that night, standing by the door just outside the room, bored out of my mind while still managing to jump at every unexpected noise.

All I could do was think. Sometimes I got so tired of thinking. But so much had gone on that hadn't made sense, and I hadn't been able to talk about it to anyone. Talking was the best way to void one's mind of unwanted thoughts. So when Taro slipped out of the room to relieve me, I asked him in a whisper, "Is she asleep?"

He nodded.

"Are you sure?"

He shrugged.

Good enough. "What do you think Border was playing at, keeping her all those years?"

"I can't be sure," he whispered back. "But I'm thinking he came here and realized she was cut off from everyone who might know who she really is. He thinks if he takes her back immediately, all he gets is a slap on the back and a job well done. If he raises her, makes her loyal to him, he has a future"—he hesitated—"you know, in his debt. Who knows what kind of power and wealth that could bring him, in time?"

Seemed a pretty long-term plan with an uncertain outcome to me, but lots of people did things that made no sense. "He might have tried a better job at garnering her loyalty."

"Probably felt saving her from slavery was all he really needed to do."

Zaire. What a bastard.

This poor girl. A third generation victim of politics she knew nothing about. And it wasn't going to end, either. We were going to deliver her to the Empress and then Aryne was going to become some kind of pawn between the Empress and the Crown Prince. And neither of them were going to be thinking about her, at all, or her best interests. She was going to be completely on her own.

I slipped into the room. Karish had left the lantern on, the flame turned low, and I could see the girl sprawled on the mat by the wall farthest from the door. She had kicked off all the sheets, and her sleeping gown was bunched up under her armpits. It'd be delivering her into a life of material ease. I couldn't say with any confidence that it was going to be a life that was any better.

Chapter Twenty-seven

I learned a great many things on the way from Silk Purse to Promise Harbor.

One was that three people moved much faster than thirty. I wouldn't have thought so, because human legs could only travel so fast, and the troupe had never given the impression of dallying. But Aryne looked at me like I was some kind of idiot, and told me the wagon hampered movement more than anything, and thirty could travel only as fast as the slowest individual, which, for the troupe, had included children.

Two, Taro could gamble. He really could. I'd seen evidence of it, but before I could never quite believe it, because I could beat him, and if I could beat him, surely everyone else could. But he was the one who enabled us to eat and find shelter during our hard hike through the jungle. He took small portions from our stash, and played cards every night, and sometimes he lost, but usually he won something.

Three, children needed a scary amount of food. And it was really difficult for me not to say anything when the food disappeared into Aryne's mouth. I was not about to let her go hungry; she'd obviously been underfed most of her life. But it was hard, and there were times when Taro and I didn't eat, to make sure she did.

Four, being hungry made me irritable. And kind of irrational. I'd get angry at the most stupid things, like the laces of my sandals becoming untied while I was walking down the street.

When we finally reached the harbor, I was almost ready to kiss the dirt in relief. It had been hard to believe we would ever get there. I'd really been expecting something to stop us, certain we were going to die on that Zaire-neglected island.

I had little experience with harbors. Just the one on the mainland, from which Taro and I had left. This one was smaller, quieter, less overwhelming. Less of an appalling assault on the senses, especially one's sense of smell. I was delighted to be there, because it meant soon we'd be on our way home. I tried to restrain my excitement, because Taro was stiff with the apprehension of a poor sea traveler, and Aryne was silent in apparent terror.

Crews were loading supplies for their boats. One appeared to be largely Northern, so I approached the person of that crew who appeared to be doing nothing more than watching the others work. I figured she was in charge. I asked where the boat was going, then showed her the clothes I would be wearing on the boat—with the white braid—and the pass I'd managed to hang on to from the Empress. She warned me that the ship, the Wave Crusher, wasn't really suitable for passengers, but I ignored the stomachs of my companions and assured her we didn't care. Her boat was going to the right place. Her name was Ellen Furt, and I was inclined to kiss her feet simply for existing.

I was elated. We were going home. Finally.

"How much money have we got left?" Taro asked.

"Why? What do you need?"

"Nothing." He grinned. "But you've arranged for passage, yes?"

"Aye."

"And we're leaving?"

"In a few hours."

"For a place where we don't need money."

"Ah." I was starting to get the point. "I don't want to spend the last of the coin."

He rolled his eyes. "Lee . . ."

"Call me paranoid all you like, I'm not going to spend everything we have just because it's our last day. We don't know what might happen. We might somehow be prevented from getting to the boat. The boat itself might sink. The crew might turn unscrupulous once we're on board. Who knows? I'm holding on to what money we've got left." It wasn't like we had that much, anyway.

"Fine," he muttered, the word ending in a growl. "Mother."

"I am nothing like your mother," I snapped out.

"Thank Zaire."

"And where the hell is Aryne?" She'd been right there a moment ago.

"Damn. I told her not to disappear."

I scanned the crowd around us, but all I could see were a lot of backs. Damn it.

"She knows when to be—Hey!" And suddenly, Taro darted off.

I hurried to follow him. "What?" I demanded.

"Border!"

I swore under my breath. "He's got her?"

"I don't know. I can only see him. Hurry!"

It was a nightmare, trying to run through a crowd of people who were carrying bags and dragging boxes. I ended up colliding with more than a couple, and ignoring the curses that were sent my way. Leavy the Flame Dancer, indeed.

And then Taro just kind of bellowed—a sound I'd never heard from him before—and charged ahead. The next time

I could see anything relevant, he and the medicine man were on the ground, Taro struggling to dislodge the medicine man from his chest.

Aryne was nowhere in sight.

I shoved my way to them in time to hear Border shout, "Get me the port master! This man is a thief!" He saw me, then, and he pointed as he shouted again, "She is, too! They work together!" And I found my arms gripped by a multitude of hands.

Hell. Wasn't this a total nightmare? I'd really thought that the fact that we hadn't seen Border in all this time meant we were free of him. How did he reach Promise Harbor before us, anyway?

"I can't be a thief, you idiot!" Taro snapped, managing to sound like an affronted aristocrat even while lying in the dirt. "I'm a Source. And she's a Shield."

Nice try, Karish, but I would wager that half the people surrounding us didn't really know what Sources and Shields were, or what it meant to be one. And aye, we'd stolen Border's stuff. I hadn't felt bad about it at the time. I did right then, though.

Border snorted. "Oh, kai. Believing your own myths, now, are you? Despite what the stories say, I know Sources and Shields are as deviant and as villainous as the next person. Someone get the port master. I want these two arrested."

"I don't believe the gentleman claimed that he and his Shield weren't deviant or villainous," a new voice called out. Not an islander, by the accent, and while it took a moment of wriggling for me to get a good view of her, I could see it was the woman who had booked our passage on the Wave Crusher. "He said they couldn't be thieves."

"Same thing," Border sneered.

"Not at all. Sources and Shields are legally incapable of theft, as everything they need is to be provided to them upon request. It is required by law."

"What law?" one of the men holding my left arm demanded.

For a second, I wondered if it would help at all if I told these people I was Leavy the Flame Dancer.

Then I nearly died of shame.

"The law of the Empress," Furt answered.

There was a lot of laughter at that, and not the kind of laughter that sounded pleasant to the ear. "The Empress doesn't rule here!" a woman called out with a chuckle.

"True enough," Furt drawled. "She doesn't send her tax collectors here. She doesn't demand that you house her soldiers. She probably doesn't care if you engage in behaviors that in other people would be deemed treasonous. If fact, you're left completely free to go about your business, without giving the slightest thought to the Empress. As she doesn't give the slightest thought to you. It's almost as though she has forgotten you exist at all."

There was a bit of a silence in reaction to that. I would have been offended by the suggestion that I was so insignificant, if I were an islander. The silence was broken by a young man claiming, "Never ways what the Empress knows or thinks or remembers. She's got no rights here."

That, I thought, was really overstating the case.

"Only because she chooses not to exercise them," said Furt. "If she does remember you all are down here, breaking laws, engaging in trade without paying for it, she might decide it's time to start enforcing her rights. With swords and bows. And she has more soldiers just guarding her palace than you have people on this whole island."

Was that true?

"Now, I'm under order from the Empress to give these people passage," Furt continued. "Do you have any idea what kind of mess you all are going to create for yourselves if I have to go to the Empress and tell her I couldn't follow orders because you lot decided to hang a Source and a Shield, something the law strictly forbids, for theft, a crime Sources and Shields are literally incapable of committing? Even when regulars refuse to provide them with the goods they need which is, in itself, a crime?"

That sparked off a lot of muttering. I was impressed, myself. I had no idea sailors were so smart.

"Who knows what kind of people she'll send down here, poking into everything, trying to understand why the Empress's most treasured subjects were shown such an appalling lack of respect? And who knows what sorts of things those people will learn while they're down here?"

I couldn't quite understand what the man to my right was saying, his accent was so thick. It sounded like swearing, though, and he released my arm.

"Believe me, I don't want things down here to change, either. I don't want to have to pay the kinds of duties and licenses and harbor taxes and inspection fees I have to pay just about everywhere else. It means I can sell my goods here at lower prices than I'd usually be able to. It means I can sell your goods at a lower price up north, which makes them more popular and eventually results in more coin in your coffers."

There was a lot more swearing, and I found myself completely free of restraint.

"Don't listen to her!" Border shouted. "She's an off-lander!"

"So are you," another islander shouted back. Border had assumed his islander accent, but I guessed that only fooled us.

"What do you claim they stole?" Furt asked.

"My steer!"

Furt looked around. "I see no steer here."

There were herds of steer about. She just meant that none of them appeared to be under our control.

Border almost wriggled in his frustration. "They sold it, you stupid bitch!"

Now that, I thought, had been a spectacularly stupid move. Surely Furt had shipmates who'd jump in to defend her honor.

No one did, but then, she didn't appear to need it. "It is

illegal to give a Source or a Shield money in exchange for goods. Who are you accusing of this crime?"

I could almost feel the anger switching to Border's direction. But I wondered if that was true. Why would it be illegal to give a member of the Triple S money in exchange for goods? And did that mean everyone on the island had been breaking the law when they'd been giving me money for dancing? Had Taro been breaking the law when he gambled?

Border could feel the shift in the mood, too. This time, when Taro shoved at his shoulder, he stood up. So did Taro, slapping dust from his clothes and glaring at the medicine man.

"What else are you claiming they stole?" Furt asked.

Border's eyes narrowed before he said, "Nothing."

"Nothing? You claimed they stole nothing?"

"That's not what I said."

"You were lying? You caused all this trouble for nothing? What do you think you're doing?"

And Border began to sputter.

"Are you telling me you just came here to cause trouble and get people arrested? Are you trying to distract the port master? Is there something going on that you want to keep everyone's attention directed away from?"

"Will you just shut up a moment, you—"

"Do you have some friends breaking into a hold or something?"

"Of course not!"

"That's enough," an islander said. He was an older man, and the way every sort stopped and looked at him, he appeared to be someone of authority. "Del, Eppit, take him to the port master. He can explain himself to him." And two burly young fellows grabbed Border by the arms.

He was shocked, and I didn't blame him. "Have you people all lost your minds? Let me go!" But no one was listening to him. The two men carted him off, the older man following, and everyone else went back to work.

I looked at Furt. "You're a genius," I told her.

She just glared at me. Clearly she was just delighted with me.

"Thank you," I said.

"Don't bother," she snapped back. "If you weren't already on the books as passengers, I would have let you hang. Your sort have no business in this part of the world, fouling up a perfectly good arrangement for everyone involved."

Uh, all right.

"Now get back on the ship before you cause me any more problems."

"I'd love to," I said. "But we're missing one of our party."

Furt rolled her eyes. "Don't expect me to be catching your sling again. I have no problem telling anyone who asks that you booked passage and then didn't bother showing up. Sources are known for being unreliable."

"Unlike sailors," Taro muttered.

"Let's just go look for Aryne," I suggested, hoping to avoid another argument.

There was no sign of Aryne, of course. And as the time to embark approached, I became less concerned and more angry, promising myself I could wring her neck when I found her. "If that girl makes us miss the boat," I muttered, feeling fortunate that at least I didn't let Taro convince me to spend the rest of our coins. We might end up needing them, if we had to spend another night here.

We'd better not have to spend another night here.

"Relax," said Taro. "She'll find us."

"We don't know that."

"Of course we do."

I glared at him. He was just too sure of himself. The lowered shoulders, the easy smile.

Oh. That was right. This was what he was supposed to be like. What he'd been like before we came to this curse of an island.

We wasted more time looking for Aryne. Of course we didn't find her. And everyone else was getting on the boat, while we hung back on the deck and ignored the dark looks and warning comments from the ship's crew.

And then Aryne appeared by my side. "Are we going or what?" she asked, giving me an unconvincing innocent look when I glared at her.

I slapped her up the back of the head.

She returned my glare as she rubbed the afflicted area. "Don't need to get all maternal."

"Get on the boat," I snapped at her.

"It's a ship," said Taro.

I gritted my teeth, and told myself the island was entirely to blame for my poor humor.

Chapter Twenty-eight

I loved home. I loved the dry air. I loved the dull shade of blue of the sky, the dull shade of green of the grass. I loved the fact that I could see for miles, with only the occasional tree. When I got off that damned boat, I was tempted to skip or dance or do something equally childish. Because I was home.

Not in High Scape. We hadn't reached High Scape yet, and I couldn't be sure when we'd get there. I just meant the mainland. The Northern continent. Anywhere, really, that wasn't Flatwell.

Taro had once more been seasick the entire way. And so had Aryne. I was beginning to wonder if it was a Source trait. And while Taro made for an ill-tempered patient, Aryne was a rather frightening one. She had curled up in her bunk and hadn't made a sound. She had seemed surprised every time I tried to bring her water or offer her the most insignificant comfort or consideration. She didn't expect to be looked after, and it gave me strange and sad ideas of what she had been taught to anticipate from people.

Not that she would ever talk about it. Every time I tried to ask what life with Border had been like, she just closed down, her eyes going almost blank and her lips thinning into a hard line, like I was going to try to physically pry the words out of her.

It was really none of my business. And it wasn't like there was anything I could do to make it better. The life she'd had with Border was in the past; there was no going back and fixing it. So there was no point in disturbing her by trying to make her talk about it in the present.

Besides, she had enough going on to discomfort her. As grateful as she was to get off the boat, she didn't seem to regain her vigor on land. As we journeyed toward Erst- while, I could tell that Aryne wasn't happy with the strangeness—to her—of the mainland. Her skin became dry and cracked. She preferred sleeping on the floor to sleeping in a bed. She wasn't thrilled with the food. She never turned it away, of course, and she ate all that she was given. But there was a sort of grim acceptance about her, none of the joy she had sometimes shown while eating the fruit and meat on the island. And some of the food seemed to make her ill.

She watched us a great deal, Taro and I. I wasn't sure why, because I didn't notice her examining us like that on the island. There was a strange feel to her speculation, and it made me uncomfortable.

We were incredibly careless with her, in the beginning. It wasn't until we walked into the first merc shop, to ac- quire better, more suitable clothing, that we realized just how careless we were being. Aryne, whether she liked it or not, could not go striding around in the scanty clothing she was used to wearing. I wouldn't be caught dead in what I had left, not on the mainland. And Taro, well, he'd been wearing the same clothes for more than a couple of weeks and it was making him a little mental. And the merc, happy—or at least resigned—to provide Taro and I with new garments, balked at granting Aryne anything free of charge. Which was when we told him Aryne was a Source, on her way to the Academy.

Which was when we realized we had in our company an unbonded Source, and we were just letting her walk around free, with no thought at all to the possibility of a spontaneous bonding. The damage we could have unwittingly done to her horrified me.

Yes, yes, she had not been guarded on Flatwell. But Sources and Shields were practically nonexistent on the islands, and I was pretty sure the only reason she had the talent was due to her Northern blood. On the Northern continent, she might encounter an undiscovered Shield, and then both of them might have been sucked into some kind of obsessive bond that would have been disastrous for both of them.

That was when we commissioned a carriage, which made us so popular with the livery owner who had to provide it—and the horses—to us.

Neither Taro nor I had ever driven a carriage. That was embarrassing. And incredibly hard on the arms.

And keeping Aryne in the carriage, that was a treat. Because she didn't believe our explanation, and she hated being in the carriage for any length of time. The movement of it sickened her. Taro threatened to tie her into it if she didn't stay, and she claimed to be able to get out of any binds we put her into. Then went on to prove it. All in all, it was due to sheer luck that she didn't spontaneously bond with someone.

I was relieved when we finally reached Erstwhile. Because it meant we were done. This stupid, unsuitable task placed on our shoulders by an unreasonable monarch was over. We'd found a member of her collateral family and dragged her back. Now all we had to do was place Aryne in the Empress's care, and we could go home.

We went to the Imperial boarding house. That was Taro's idea, and for once I didn't dispute it. Aryne had never been in any such place, and I thought it would be interesting for her to sleep in such fine surroundings. A good introduction to her future. And perhaps a way to keep her in her room for more than half a moment.

I ordered a single room for all three of us. I wasn't going to slip the leash on Aryne until she was safe in imperial hands. Besides, it saved me from deciding whether I should reserve one or two rooms for Taro and I.

I was waiting for the time when he started to let me know our extracurricular association was at an end. It had already lasted months longer than I'd expected, and my only explanation for it was that we were still in relatively unfamiliar territory. But that would be changing. In Erstwhile, there were people he was used to dealing with, people who knew who and what he was. And I knew his dowdy little Shield was not going to hold his attention for much longer.

I was not going to let his waning interest ruin our working relationship, or our friendship. It wasn't his fault. He was the way he was, and there was nothing wrong with what he was. It wasn't his fault, either, that I was the way I was. We were just very different people, in what we needed from our lovers, and I'd known that going in. It was hard for me, but that wasn't his fault, either. So there would be no moods, no clinging, no blame. When the time came, it would be a graceful exit.

I could do graceful. I could. And any other, less noble reactions, well, they'd be worked out in private.

Still, I wished he'd get to it. The waiting was hard to bear.

At breakfast the next day, we received the summons from Her Majesty, for our immediate attendance. And I started to get nervous, because if she wasn't pleased, we were . . . well, we were in trouble.

Aryne was nervous, too. I could see it in the stiffness of her posture, hear it in her glacial silence. I wasn't sure why she should be nervous. I hoped she didn't know what this visit might mean for her.

We went in a carriage, and during the ride we put a blindfold on Aryne, which she just loved. And we were received at the front gate. There was none of the roundabout secrecy of our last meeting. We were taken into the palace proper, and brought into a waiting room. We didn't have to wait long. We never really did, for the Empress. Another reason why I liked her better than her son.

A footman led us through another maze of corridors and knocked on a door. When the door was opened by the maid from within, I stepped behind Taro, and he wrapped Aryne's arm in his and led her into the room. I followed a few steps behind.

The Empress was in a large parlor, sitting on a settee with another woman, some kind of lady in waiting, seated beside her.

I wondered if I was ever going to see her husband. I wondered if the Consort Prince even existed anymore. I risked a few fanciful imaginings of him being locked away in a dungeon somewhere.

"Source Shintaro Karish, Shield Dunleavy Mallorough, and . . . Aryne, Your Majesty," said the maid.

Taro bowed, and I curtsied. Aryne stood still as a statue. "Curtsy," I heard Taro whisper.

She tried, I had to give her that. But if it weren't for Taro, she would have fallen on her face.

I winced. I should have taught her how to curtsy. I hadn't even thought of that. What else had I not thought of?

Maybe her clothes. She wasn't, thank Zaire, in the scanty costume of Flatwell. She found the weather of the mainland too cold for that. But she certainly wasn't dressed as a princess, either. Or anything like what I would insist on wearing before the Empress.

And then the Empress's eyes were on me. "Why, Shield Mallorough," she drawled. "I don't think I've ever witnessed such a pronounced expression on your face before."

What in the world did that mean?

"There is something different about your appearance," she continued.

"I am still a little dark from my stay on Flatwell," I said.

"That's not it," she said. But then she was looking at Taro and Aryne again, and I didn't have to speak anymore. "Why are her eyes covered? Is she blind?"

Her Majesty's tone suggested Aryne had better not be.

"Aryne is a Source, Your Majesty," Taro said. "No one knew what she was, when we found her. But she is a Source, and we have covered her eyes to prevent any possibility of spontaneous bonding."

"Do you feel I might be a Shield, Source Karish?"

"It is unlikely, Your Majesty."

"Shields and Sources are discovered long before they reach adulthood, are they not?"

"Usually, Your Majesty. But here is Aryne. I was eleven before my family realized I was a Source."

But that was because his family was comprised of cretins.

"Still, neither of you were adults at the age of discovery. We are all adults here. Remove her blindfold, so that I may see her eyes. We will take the risk."

Taro removed the blindfold, because there was nothing else he could do.

The Empress stared at Aryne. "Was she the only one you found?"

"Yes, Your Majesty."

The Empress studied Aryne for several long uncomfortable moments. "Who taught you to stand that way? Source Karish, what have you been doing with the girl?"

"What's wrong with the way I stand?" Aryne demanded.

Well, the slouch, for one thing.

"At least she is comely," the Empress muttered, and that seemed to knock some of the wind out of Aryne. "Shield, take the girl away. I need to speak with your Source."

The order really grated on me, and apparently that

showed up on my face, too, because her gaze hardened as she watched me. I tried to gain control over my expression as I curtsied lower than was my custom, and I put my hand on Aryne's shoulder and applied pressure until she realized she was to curtsy, too. I also kept her from turning around and putting her back to the Empress as we stepped back toward the door, where the maid let us out.

"She thinks high of herself, don't—"

I clapped one hand on her mouth, the other on the back of her head, and hissed "Quiet!" into her ear as she tried to back away. I felt her mouth open under my palm. "You will not bite me," I warned her in the hardest voice I could drag up.

One tense moment, and then I felt her mouth close.

"You will not speak ill of the Empress in her own home, understood?" I wasn't going to let her create enemies for herself when she didn't even understand the significance of the danger.

A pause, and then she nodded. I lowered my hand and she asked, "What would she do to me?"

"Anything she felt like." Not true, in the strictest sense. The days when monarchs could rule without a single thought to law were long gone. Still, no one would be quick to question the Empress on anything she chose to do to a strange orphan from the Southern Islands.

Realizing that Taro still had her blindfold, I pulled a handkerchief out from my sleeve.

"Ah, not—" she whined.

I was tired of forcing the issue. "All right, I really don't care. You can risk bonding with some undiscovered Shield and falling madly in love with him or her—"

"Madly in love?" she echoed, her lip curling with disgust. "You never told me that."

"What did you think we meant when we said you'd become unhealthily obsessed with a Shield you had spontaneously bonded with?"

"Not that."

Not that I thought the two were identical, or that falling madly in love was the only direction an unhealthy bond could take, but hey, whatever worked. She turned around and let me tie the handkerchief on her with no more fuss.

She stayed silent as we were led back through the palace to the exit and the carriage that had brought us. I was wondering why this meeting was held in the palace, while the first had been out in the seclusion of the pasture. I'd assumed the first location had been due to a paranoid concern with being overheard. Why wasn't privacy important this time?

Perhaps the fact of our success had changed the Empress's priorities.

Aryne said nothing during the carriage ride, too, which was a little puzzling. I would have never called her talkative, but she usually had a comment to make whenever something struck her as strange or stupid.

But back in our room at the boarding house, the handkerchief came off and the mouth opened. "So that's your all powerful ruler, is it?" she asked.

"Kai."

"Doesn't look like much."

"Appearances can be deceiving." I doubted anyone looking at Aryne would contemplate for an instant that she was the future Empress.

The future Empress. Zaire. I needed to sit down.

"Are you sure you don't know what this woman wants with me?"

"One does not ask the Empress to explain herself."

"So why did she send you?"

"She sent Taro. He has gained her favor and her trust. I was just expected to go along." I went to the side bar, looking for something to drink. All there was, was wine. I had an inexplicable craving for tea.

"You don't seem the sort to just go along when you don't know all the answers."

"You don't know me very well."

She ground her teeth. "So that's why you picked me up? Because I was a member of this family you were looking for?"

There was an element of hurt in her anger. I had no idea what the source of this sudden shift in mood might be. "We allowed you to join us when you followed us," I reminded her, "because we realized you were a Source. We had no idea, at the time, that you were of interest to the Empress."

"And that's it, right? Because I was useful to you?"

I snorted at that. "Useful? Are you sane? In no possible incarnation are you useful to us."

I realized the words were a little harsh as soon as they were out of my mouth. The slight widening of Aryne's eyes before they narrowed confirmed the opinion. I sighed. "Sit down." Instead, she crossed her arms and glared. "Fine. You stand. I'll sit down." And I did. But I knew I shouldn't be doing this. This should be Taro's job. He'd be able to make Aryne feel good about this.

"We were sent by the Empress to find members of a family who were important to her," I said. "We came across you. We realized you were a Source, and we realized we had to take you with us. As you wished," I reminded her. "It wasn't until later that we realized you were a member of this family the Empress was looking for."

"So what's going to happen now? Am I going to be a Source or not?"

"I don't know. That will be up to the Empress."

"The hell it will be!" Aryne snarled.

I raised my eyebrows to suggest she should go on.

"I didn't come here to have someone else telling me what to do!"

"You'd be told what to do at the Source Academy if you went there."

"But you and Taro would be there."

I frowned. "We don't live there. Whatever gave you that idea?"

"You said everybody went to the Academy!" she accused me.

"Yes, for a while. Then they leave to work out in the world. Taro and I live in High Scape. That's where we work."

"You never told me any of that!"

"I never thought of that. I never knew you'd made that assumption."

"So you're just going to cut me loose? To this Empress or to the school?"

Oh lords. I really never imagined that this might be an issue. "I'm sorry, Aryne. I never realized you thought to stay with us."

She scowled and said nothing.

"Surely you can see you can't stay with us."

" 'Course not. I'm not stupid."

"Oh, Aryne. I'm sorry. I never thought you'd be expect-ing that." She had never said or hinted that she thought she was going to stay with us indefinitely. And I was sure we'd told her the Academy was in Shidonee's Gap and we were posted in High Scape.

"Wasn't expecting nothing," she denied.

"You can't stay with us. You really need to go to the Academy."

" 'Course."

"Why would you even want to stay with us?"

She shrugged. "No reason."

Aye, I'd blown it. I didn't know what else to say. All I could do was wait for Taro to come back and hopefully fix it.

Fortunately, he didn't take long. But he didn't enter the room with his usual flair, and that was never a good sign. He looked at us solemnly. "Someone die in here?"

"Aryne is finding the state of ignorance a difficult one to bear," I said.

"Ah," said Taro. "I can sympathize." He grabbed one of his travel packs from the wardrobe near the door. "Her Majesty wants us to stay at the palace."

I groaned. "All of us?" I had expected Aryne to be
moved to the palace, and Taro and I to be sent on our way.
There was no reason for us to remain in Erstwhile at all.
Unless, damn it, the Empress was taking this opportunity
to keep Taro with her indefinitely, as he would no longer be
weakened, according to her, by the lack of his Shield.

"All of us."

"Is that bad?" Aryne asked.

"Not really," I told her. "I just feel like I'm being
watched all the time while I'm there. And you will have to
be blindfolded the whole time."

Aryne scowled.

"The Empress has given us her word that no one under
the age of sixteen will be in Aryne's presence," said Taro.

"A difficult thing to guarantee, I think." There were
dozens of servants younger than that working in the palace.

He shrugged. "She wants us over there."

And that was that.

Chapter Twenty-nine

I didn't want to move into the palace. Not that there weren't wonderful things about living there. Exquisitely comfortable rooms, embarrassingly solicitous service, every possible food provided on a whim.

But I hated feeling watched all the time, and I knew, within the palace walls, that I definitely was. Not for myself, but because I was the partner of Taro. Part of me worried that the Empress had some grand plan in mind for Taro, one that wouldn't benefit him or anyone else who mattered to me. Part of me just found the whole thing irksome, the courtiers with their stupid little word games. And part of me felt that restlessness that came from not being able to do my job because someone else had decided there was something more important they needed me, or my Source, to do.

There was nothing more important than what Taro and I were born and bonded to do.

Worst of all, moving into the palace meant I had to get a whole slew of dresses, because Zaire forfend I be seen in the same thing twice.

I was tempted to show up in one of my Flatwell costumes. To attend to the Empress. Wouldn't that raise eyebrows?

She expected us to move that night, which of course we did. We were shown into adjoining apartments, Taro and I expected to share while Aryne had a smaller suite off to one side. Taro and I argued about whether Aryne should stay in our suite—I wanting to keep an eye on her, he claiming I didn't have the skills for being parental and I shouldn't waste my time, the prat. Aryne, of course, was firmly on Taro's side. So she stayed in her separate suite, crowing with triumph as she jumped from settee to settee in the large sitting room. She was either being prepared for her future, or spoiled for it.

But it did give us some privacy. It was the first time I'd been alone with Taro all day. "So what did she say?" I demanded.

"Who?"

Who did he think? "The Empress."

"About what?"

I opened my mouth to say something sarcastic, and snapped it shut while I looked at him. He stared straight back at me, eyes neither narrowed in irritation nor widened in feigned innocence. "You can't tell me."

"There's nothing to tell."

"It's all right, Taro." Well, not really. I hated the fact that the Empress was telling him things he couldn't tell me. But that she was, wasn't his fault. She was the one who'd pushed me into this mess and then refused to tell me what was going on.

"There's nothing to tell," he insisted. "She was disappointed that we found only one, and she wanted a little more detail about Aryne's circumstances. She did tell me who Border was."

"Who?"

"What he said he was. One of her personal guard. One of her most trusted. Except his name is Henry Thatcher, not Border. She sent him out to check on the family. Only he left and she never heard from him again."

"And she didn't send someone else after him then?"

"Apparently not."

"Why not?"

"Maybe she suspected he was up to no good. Maybe she didn't want to tell anyone else the secret."

Maybe she hadn't really cared overmuch. She'd felt, perhaps, that she had to do something for the sake of honor or family or whatever, and when that didn't seem to work out, she could say to herself she'd done her best and forget all about it.

Only something had caused her to change her mind and send us out.

Did she really think Prince Gifford was going to be that bad a ruler? Sure, I wasn't all that impressed with him, but he hadn't struck me as being feebleminded or grossly cruel. So what was so wrong with him that she felt it necessary to bring in a collateral heir?

I couldn't imagine, but it didn't have anything to do with me. "What about us?" I asked. "Why does she want us here?"

"She said it was for Aryne's sake, to allow her to have someone familiar about in these new surroundings."

"Do you believe her?"

"I see no reason why she would lie about it."

"That is true, I suppose."

"For now, she doesn't want Aryne to know why she's here," Taro said.

"That's obvious, but why not? I mean, I can understand why she doesn't want Aryne to know what her intentions for her future might be, but why not let her know she's one of the family?"

He shrugged.

I really got the feeling there were things he wasn't telling me. However, if the Empress had taken him into her confidence and sworn him to secrecy, I certainly wasn't going to give him a hard time over it.

All right. Time for a distraction. "So, did any of the—?"
And I cut myself off.

"What?" Taro asked.

I had been about to ask if any of the gorgeous courtiers
had caught his eye.

I was expecting him to fall into old patterns. So I was
falling into old patterns. Only it wasn't appropriate for me
to go first.

Why wasn't it appropriate for me to go first? It was going
to happen anyway. Why shouldn't I make the first move?

Because I didn't want it to happen at all, and I didn't
want to hurry it along. "What?" I asked back.

"What were you going to say?"

"I don't remember."

He narrowed his eyes at me. "Hm," was all he said, indicating that he didn't believe me. Then he grinned. "Did
you see how big the bed is?"

"I didn't really think about it."

"Ah, my young friend, all the things I have to teach you.
And so much room to play!"

I couldn't help smiling at that.

We were expected to eat a late evening meal with the
Empress. In her bedchamber, of all places. The Empress
was already in bed, dressed in a nightgown. A short table
had been brought into her spacious bedchamber, set for
three, so that we might all face the Empress while we ate.

A bizarre setup. Something about it struck me as rude,
though I couldn't quite put my finger on why.

The food on offer was incredible. Sugared spice bread,
thick slices of ham, herbal eggs, and fruit. Not the kind of
fruit one would find on Flatwell. This stuff, I had to admit,
seemed rather common and bland.

"Tell me, Aryne," the Empress said, after we had all
greeted each other and had filled our plates, "what is your
family name?"

"You mean like Leavy's name is Mallorough?" Aryne
said through a mouthful of bread.

The distaste didn't show in the Empress's expression. "Yes."

"Islander's don't do that." Aryne swallowed. "I should use my mother's name, but I don't know it."

"Here, you need a family name," said the Empress.

Aryne looked up at me. "Can I use yours?"

I choked on my mouthful of ham.

The Empress chuckled. "You can't use a family name unless you have been adopted into that family, child," she said. "And our Shield here doesn't have the authority to adopt you into her family."

"She's a woman grown," Aryne objected, with no acknowledgment that she was contradicting the Empress.

"Shields can't adopt."

"Why not?"

"It's a long explanation, Aryne," I told her quietly. Though, really, not so long. Shields didn't pay for goods or services, and neither did their children, until their children were old enough to work. No one wanted Shields and Sources to be able to invite others in for the free ride. "I'll tell you later." I really just wanted the girl to shut up. I'd told her to answer the Empress's questions and nothing more.

Of course, when had she ever listened to me?

"Don't worry about it, child," said the Empress. "Everyone here has a family name. Arrangements will be made for you."

Aryne scowled. I hoped she didn't come out with some declaration that she could choose her own family name, thank you very much.

She didn't.

"What do you know of Erstwhile, Aryne?"

Aryne looked blank, for a moment. "It's where you live," she said, in a rather pathetic start. "You have a court. Laws are made here."

"Do you find the law interesting?"

I had to shoot the Empress a look, there. Really, "the

law" was an abstract concept to someone of Aryne's circumstances.

Now Aryne looked irritated. "No, ma'am. It's too easy to bend. Pounds on those who can't stand up for themselves."

"Really?" The Empress raised an eyebrow. "Can you give me an example?"

"Riding around a village a while back, there was this old man sleeping under a bridge. Could tell he had nothing. His clothes were dirty. He was dirty. And he was skinny. And he was just sleeping there. Wasn't hurtin' no one. But then these two—what are they? Runners?—woke him up and pulled him away, and they were arresting him! Just for sleeping under the bridge."

"It's against the law to sleep under bridges," said the Empress. "And the law applies to everyone. Were a nobleman sleeping under the bridge, the Runners would have done the exact same thing."

Aye, sure. Somehow, I doubted it.

"But a nobleman wouldn't need to sleep under a bridge, would he? He'd have a house to sleep at."

"An interesting theory," the Empress said coolly. "Perhaps if you had a better understanding of how the law works, you would not dismiss it so casually."

Aryne shrugged and stuffed another piece of bread into her mouth. I thought about squeezing her arm or kicking her ankle, but she probably would have no clue why I was doing it.

"We have an extensive library here. Perhaps you would enjoy reading some of the treatises on law."

Was she crazy? What child Aryne's age would want to read something like that? What person of any age would want to read something like that?

Aryne scrunched her nose up. "Don't like reading," she mumbled.

"Can you read?" the Empress asked.

"Some."

"Have you been in school?"

Aryne laughed shortly. "No."

"Would you be interested in going to school?"

"These two say I have to."

"Really?"

"Because Aryne's a Source, Your Majesty," Karish said hastily. "I thought that the Source Academy might be an option."

"Ah, yes. Indeed."

And then the examination of Aryne was over, and she was free to eat as enthusiastically as she wished. The Empress spent the rest of the meal speaking to Taro, asking him what he thought of Flatwell and to describe his experiences there.

He gave a highly edited account of our journey. He spoke of working as a laborer for the troupe, ignoring the Empress's chuckle. He didn't mention what I did, for which I was grateful, and the Empress didn't ask.

There was a bitterness in his voice at times, which he made no effort to hide. That surprised me. He was usually so careful with royalty. It surprised the Empress, too, who frowned at such times. He affected not to notice.

All in all, a very uncomfortable meal, and I wasn't sure I understood the point of it. I was thrilled when it was over. We headed back to our suites, and I was wondering what we were supposed to do next. I wondered when Taro and I would be told to pack up and leave. We'd done our job. Why weren't we allowed to go home?

Chapter Thirty

I had to admit, there were worse places to wake up than in one of the huge, soft beds reserved for the honored guests of Her Imperial Majesty, with clean, sweet-smelling sheets. The room was over decorated, the walls filled with portraits, the drapes on the windows overwhelming the whole wall, but in compensation there was a low fire chasing away the last of the chill of the morning, and the glorious golden scent of coffee tickling my nose. I stretched, feeling the slippery sheets slide against my skin, and my foot brushed against something solid.

I turned to my side. Taro was still in bed and still asleep, which was unusual. During our whole acquaintance he was always up and out before me. Then again, we'd never shared such comfortable accommodations. Maybe he'd sleep as late as I did if he found the beds more comfortable. Something to think about.

I left the bed and poured myself a cup of coffee, marveling that someone had been able to slip into the room, light the fire and set up a tray of coffee and sweet pastry without waking either of us. I curled up in a wingback chair, sideways with my feet tucked under me, and looked at Taro.

He looked boneless, lying on his back, one hand dangling over the side of the bed. The poor man had been through hell, and he'd borne it better than I would have. I really didn't think I could have been so graceful if so many people had worked so hard to try to convince me I was useless.

Everything was going to change now that our task was completed. Once we were sent from the palace and relieved of our responsibility to Aryne, Taro would be free to be himself. And I would resume my proper role as Taro's Shield and friend. And nothing else. That was the natural way of things.

Yes, it would hurt, but I would just have to bear it.

I was on my second cup of coffee by the time Taro stirred and stretched. His nose wrinkled, and that was so cute. "Coffee," he muttered thickly. "Don't suppose there's any tea around."

And now that he had mentioned it, I was surprised that the Empress forgot her favorite's preferred beverage. Granted, I would hope that our ruler would have more important things to think about than what her pet Source liked to drink in the morning, but it still seemed strange to me.

Aryne walked through the adjoining door from her suite. "What's this about then?" she demanded, holding up a folded piece of paper.

"For Zaire's sake, knock, Aryne," I said with exasperation.

"Who's Zaire?" was her response as she shoved the paper into my free hand.

I sighed and shook the paper open, slowly interpreting the ridiculously ornate script. "She's been invited to a brunch tomorrow," I told Taro. "Hosted by a Lady Elspeth Shoji."

"Who the hell is that?" Aryne demanded.

"Daughter of the minister of justice," Taro answered, rubbing his face.

"What she want with me?"

"Maybe the Empress asked her to make you feel comfortable here," Taro suggested.

"Why would your Empress care about something like that?"

"I don't know."

Taro was sounding grumpy. Perhaps because he wasn't comfortable getting out of bed while Aryne was in the room. I found that hilarious.

"How old is this Lady Shoji?" I asked.

"Ah, around nineteen, I think."

So a safe age, or as safe as the Empress was willing to make it. I hoped the other guests at this brunch would be of a similar age, though that would make it more uncomfortable for Aryne.

The Empress had clearly made it known to everyone that Aryne was there, and that she was important.

"But she doesn't live on the palace grounds," Taro said.

"This says the brunch is being held in the Blue Room." Which I assumed was in the palace. I don't think I'd ever been to it.

"No one's expecting me to go, are they?" Aryne grabbed one of the pastries and tore into it, crumbs flying everywhere.

"You have to go," said Taro.

"Do not!"

"When the Empress orders you to do something, you do it."

"This isn't the Empress, this is Lady whatever."

"Who's never met you. This is the work of the Empress." Or the girl's father, trying to curry favor.

"I'm not going."

"Aryne, there's a lesson you have to learn, and you might as well learn it right now. When the Empress wants you to do something, you do it, or she'll make your life hell."

"Sounds like Border," Aryne muttered.

"Then he was good practice," I said.

Most of the rest of the day was spent trying to make sure

Aryne didn't try to escape from—or kill—the various people who arrived to begin making her presentable for the brunch. They were modifying a gown for her, a flowing fall of yellow the color of which I didn't care for, but which emphasized the darkness of her hair, eyes and skin. Her hair was cut, possibly for the first time in her life, so it fell evenly to just below her shoulders. Her nails were cut and her hands and feet soaked in an oiled water that softened her skin.

She looked stunning, but she didn't look like herself. I found it disturbing. Of course, her appearance was only the first and most superficial of a whole slew of changes that were going to be made to her. I imagined that if I were to meet her in five years or so, I would find her a completely different person. Which was too bad. I liked her as she was.

The next day, Taro and I took advantage of Aryne's attendance at the brunch to enjoy the huge decadent bed. Sharing a room with the child for the past few months had meant keeping our hands to ourselves, and I had to admit there were times when I resented it. That morning, to touch Taro wherever I wanted without having to worry about anyone overhearing or walking in on us was a real luxury.

Taro had extremely sensitive feet. I hadn't known that before.

We enjoyed hot scented water in the huge bathtub, and then a sumptuous meal brought on trays right to the room. It was lovely. Nowhere to be, no expectations, a few hours of pure relaxation. I could handle a little more of that with no regrets.

The door slammed in the suite next to ours. It appeared that Aryne was back. I heard a lot of thuds and bangs that sounded like more than Aryne's usual careless noise. With a frown, Taro crossed the room and knocked on the door to her suite. "Aryne?" he called. "Can we come in?"

She didn't say anything in response, but the banging about continued.

He opened the door anyway. "Why didn't you answer?" I heard him say.

"Don't need to" was the sullen reply. "You come in anyway."

"I wouldn't if you said not to."

A snort. "Oh, kai."

I followed Taro into her suite. Her hair had been curled and pinned up, and right then she seemed to be doing her best to pull it all right out of her head. "I'm not going to another one of those things," she said.

"What happened?" Taro asked.

"They're all shiny, flat people," she sniffed.

Taro was baffled, which I found ironic. "What does that mean?" he asked.

"That they're shiny," she repeated in a mocking tone. "And that they're flat." She yanked another tie out of her hair and took a few more strands with it.

"Give over, let me do it. Taro, fetch my brush."

He glared at the order but did what he was told.

"Sit down, Aryne. I'll get this stuff out of your hair." Aryne sat on a settee, and I angled her a bit so I could sit behind her and work on the pins in her hair. "What happened?"

"Doesn't matter."

"Of course it does, if it upsets you."

"It's passing, and talking sets no course."

"Of course it does," I repeated, hoping I was interpreting the context correctly.

"Why?" she sneered. "You gonna yell at 'em? Tell 'em to treat the poor little slave girl nice?"

"You're not a slave," I snapped.

Taro came in and tossed me my brush before taking a seat in the settee opposite ours, where he could see Aryne. "What happened?"

I took out the last of the pins and carefully pulled my brush through Aryne's thick black hair. I had to be careful, using short strokes at first to work out whatever firming agent they'd put in.

Aryne shrugged. "Nothing, really. Just not my kind of people."

"You weren't the first to go, were you?" Taro asked. Nothing but rigid silence came from Aryne, and Taro sighed. "Aryne."

"Think they'll hang me?" Aryne asked sarcastically.

"That's not the point."

"So what's the point? Why do I have to do all this? Where's this woman I'm supposed to be related to?"

"We haven't been given that information," said Taro.

Aryne twisted around to look at me. "Leavy?"

"Stay still," I said, turning her back around. "We can't tell you what we don't know." Lie lie lie lie lie. "You have to learn how to get on with people."

"I get along fine."

"Not according to Erstwhile standards."

"Erstwhile standards can go hang."

"Today was difficult," said Taro.

"Huh," was Aryne's response.

"Wouldn't you like such things to become less difficult? Because I promise you, you can't avoid them. There'll be people like that at the Source Academy, too."

"Thought I wasn't going to the Source Academy," said Aryne.

"I imagine you will, for a period of time. At least until you find your Shield."

"So what's all this in aid of, then?"

"Because you'll be coming back once you find your Shield."

"Maybe I won't. Maybe I'll just go wherever I want."

"Sources don't go wherever they want," I told her. I was finally able to use longer strokes with the brush.

"Why not?"

"Sources and Shields belong to the Triple S. We go where they tell us."

Aryne swore. "You do what the Triple S tells you. You do what the Empress tells you. Got no minds of your own, is that it?"

I had no answer for that.

"Mistake to come here," she said. "Shoulda stayed on Flatwell."

I wasn't going to say anything to that, either. I didn't agree with her, but I could see why she felt that way. I'd been pretty miserable on Flatwell, and I'd known it was only temporary. It would have been so much harder to go as a child, all by myself.

I wouldn't trade places with Aryne for the world.

Chapter Thirty-one

We ended up staying in Erstwhile longer by far than I'd expected. Close to a month. That was no hardship, really. After nearly a year of continual travel, the Empress's principal palace was a wonderful place to recuperate. I had a long, luxurious bath every single day. Sometimes twice. I ate what was surely the most luscious food ever concocted. And I slept. I slept a lot.

I had been a guest of Her Imperial Majesty before, and I found the palace an interesting place. The council met in the east wing, so all sorts of titleholders and their aids were always coming and going. So were people coming to plead some business before the council. Members of the Imperial Guard wandered around, apparently doing nothing. There were a slew of fascinating arguments to overhear, and no one seemed to care they had an audience.

People remembered Taro from his earlier stay in Erstwhile. They greeted him in the palace corridors and invited him to their social occasions. Taro and I went to one or two, briefly, to visit those people who were less obnoxious than the rest, or for something to do. And I watched Taro, waiting for the change to come.

I figured he had gotten out of the habit of flirting so much while we were on Flatwell, because such behavior would not be reciprocated there. He had become oddly formal with people, almost cool, and during our travels to Erstwhile, he had held on to that formality. I could see it surprised those who had met him before. As time went by, however, I saw some of the old mannerisms coming back, and it almost relieved me. I didn't like what Flatwell had done to him, and I was happy it had not resulted in a permanent change.

He didn't once spend the night somewhere else. In fact, he rarely left my side at all. It was confusing, and at times a little trying. Sometimes I craved solitude.

Aryne was invited to private interviews with the Empress, something I found nerve-racking and Aryne found annoying. She said the Empress asked her all sorts of prying questions about Flatwell, questions she didn't think she should have to answer. She did, though. At least, she claimed she did, and I had to trust her on that, because neither Taro nor I were allowed to attend these interviews.

More pieces of paper with times and dates with Aryne's name on them were delivered to her suite. Her poor showing at Lady Shoji's brunch didn't stop the offspring of other courtiers from including her on their guest lists. She really hated going to those events, and I didn't blame her. She was out of place in so many different ways, age and appearance and education and background. And it seemed to me that as time went by, her enunciation, eating habits, and general manners deteriorated. She may not have been able to avoid the gatherings, but she apparently had no problem making sure no one else enjoyed themselves any better than she did.

While I didn't blame her for the way she was reacting, her behavior wasn't going to help her in the long run. She was smart. Her manners made her look like a thug. That wasn't good. But I didn't tell her that. Every time I came near to suggesting she might do something a little differently, she reminded me that I wasn't her mother.

And really, who was I to tell anyone else how to behave? Sometimes I did the stupidest things.

After a few weeks of aimless relaxation, I was ready to go home. I wanted to be a proper Shield again. I kind of missed having a routine, a place where I was expected to be, and a job to do. The job I was trained to do.

And finally, after almost a month, Taro and I were summoned again. We were instructed, specifically, not to go bring Aryne with us. And I knew this was it. The Empress was going to thank us for finding her new heir and send us home.

I was right.

I was also wrong.

"Aryne will not be of use to us," the Empress announced.

I would not gape at her. I would not. But . . . damn. I gaped at Taro instead.

He was clenching his teeth. "I'm afraid I do not understand, Your Majesty."

"Aryne is not suitable as a future ruler."

I cringed at her plain speaking. There were no servants in the room—the Empress's attempt to keep things private—but anyone could be listening at doors or hidden passages or all the other little hiding spaces I assumed a palace had. It seemed to me that the Empress was no longer concerned about keeping Aryne's family link a secret. Perhaps because she wasn't going to use her.

"I see," said Taro.

Did he? Because I damn well didn't.

"She is a decent enough girl," the Empress said, but with reluctance. She didn't really believe it. "But she lacks the qualities of a ruler."

What? Initiative? Strength? Common sense that I was finding far too uncommon?

"She knows nothing of our ways."

Of course not. She wasn't from here.

"She's entirely uneducated."

So? Tutor her.

"And I doubt her ability to interact with those who would be her peers."

Was this woman serious? She plucked this girl out of her life from another part of the world, and then expected her to be exactly like any other child of the aristocracy? Hadn't that been the point of finding her? Didn't she want her because she was different from her own son, raised in Erstwhile as the heir of the Empress?

And she'd better not be telling us she'd put us through months of hell for no reason. We did not humiliate ourselves and go without chocolate and coffee, and strut around in glitter and get told that we had flat voices and plain faces, all for nothing. Because if we did, I thought I'd have excellent reason to give up all pretensions of being a calm, collected Shield and smack someone up the back of her royal head.

"I do, of course, expect you both never to mention what Aryne is to anyone," Her Majesty said, giving us what was supposed to be a steely look.

I was just too furious to take it seriously. I couldn't believe it. I just couldn't. How dare she rip us from our lives and throw us somewhere dangerous, all on a whim? I didn't care who the hell she thought she was. That was irresponsible and cruel and just wrong. "Your Majesty," I said, and then I halted. There was so much I wanted to say, and nothing that I should.

"Yes, Shield Mallorough?" the Empress responded coolly.

I opened my mouth, and all that came out was, "Your Majesty."

I could practically feel Taro screaming at me to shut up inside his head.

The hell with it. I was going to ask. I was sick of always

taking gentle steps. "Why did you send us to look for her if you weren't going to welcome her into your family?"

Was it just me, or were my words really echoing in the room?

"Did you honestly believe everyone you found on Flatwell would be housed here and made a part of Our family?"

Kai. And that was not a stupid assumption to have made. "Yes, Your Majesty."

She seemed surprised. "Really?"

Oh my gods, yes. Yes. All right? "Yes, Your Majesty."

She tapped her lower lip with the tip of her finger. "Do you not understand why it might be necessary for me to know if any of the collateral line survived, and what kind of people they might be?"

Yes, I'd already thought that through. Family feeling, which was unlikely. She didn't like her son as the next ruler, which was entirely likely.

Oh, and she was reputed to be very ill. Maybe she was worried about some kind of battle over the throne when she died. I hadn't considered that before. It seemed to me to be the most unlikely of the reasons. The mark wasn't the sign of the heir, but the sign of the royal family in general. The heir would need something more. And no one was going to support some stranger from the Southern Islands against the Crown Prince. It would be suicide. "Yes."

"Do you not understand how a collateral line, developing outside this influence of Our court, picking up who knows what kinds of ideas and values at the forsaken ends of the world, would threaten the very stability of Our rule?"

Oh, so it was the most unlikely of reasons. Sort of. We had been sent to hunt, not to search. I had to swallow before I could speak. "So you—so Your Majesty had no intention of considering anyone we found as a potential heir?"

"That was always a possibility. But you will agree that royalty are not like Our subjects. There is bred into Us resistance to influence that is essential in any true ruler, which the child clearly lacks."

She was accusing Aryne of lacking resistance to influence? Was she serious? The girl was doing handsprings to show how different she was from everyone else in the palace.

Or maybe that was the point. Perhaps she saw through Aryne's behavior, saw it as a reaction to influence that, as a descendant of royalty, Aryne should be above.

"Now, you performed your task admirably, Shield Mallorough. The child clearly has no idea who she really is. Which means she presents no threat to Us."

What would have happened to her if the Empress decided she was a threat? What had this woman turned us into?

"It is fortunate that she turned out to be a Source. That arranges everything nicely."

Aye, it did. Because with all its flaws, the Triple S would treat her better than the royal court.

I didn't know what to do with myself. I wanted to scream or hit someone or, ooh, smash that spectacularly ugly vase by the window. I had never felt so misused in all my life.

I took a deep breath and let it out, slowly.

"We believe it is now time for you to return to your charge," said the Empress.

She knew I was furious. She didn't care. Why would she? I was no one for her to worry about.

What were we going to tell Aryne? She was supposed to be a member of a family that was looking for her? Were we supposed to tell her she wasn't good enough?

"Of course, Your Majesty," Taro said with a bow.

I didn't trust myself to speak. I really didn't. Instead, I just curtsied, and hoped she took that for assent.

"We thank you for the assistance you have provided Us," the Empress said formally. "You have the gratitude of the Crown."

Great. That and an empty sack was worth an empty sack.

And we were done. No longer of any use to Her Majesty,

we were no longer of any interest to her, and she had other things to do. We backed out of the room before I had a chance to kill her.

I felt Taro's hand low on my back, and when the door closed before us he whispered into my ear, "Not until we reach our room."

How chaotic had the world gotten, that my Source was telling me to calm down?

You could hear Aryne's shriek of joy throughout the palace, I was sure, when we told her we were leaving. She didn't ask any questions. She didn't seem to care that she wasn't going to find out about this family to which she was supposed to belong. She just started packing.

Chapter Thirty-two

We left two days later, in a carriage in an attempt to keep Aryne safe. Which meant, of course, that the journey was around two weeks longer than when we rode. I wondered why I found sitting in the carriage all day just as tiring as sitting in a saddle.

Aryne grew quieter as time went on. Taro noticed and asked her what was wrong, to which he received a snapped "nothing." So I didn't bother asking her. I thought I knew what was wrong, anyway. She was thinking about joining this school she knew so little about, and the fact that she was going to be stuck there for years, with no idea whether she would hate it or not.

There was something to be said for sending the children to school when they were too young to know enough to be scared.

As we approached our destination, Aryne's eyes widened at the sight of the high stone walls that surrounded the Source Academy. "Hey now, what's this?" she demanded, and I could feel her anxiety vibrating off her.

"Nothing to be alarmed about," I told her. "It's to prevent spontaneous bonding."

"It's a nick!" she exclaimed, and it took both Taro and I to keep her from scrambling out of the carriage.

"Taro grew up here," I told her.

"He never did!"

"I did," Taro said. "This is not a prison. Wait until you see the inside."

"The hell I am!" And she started screaming.

The two middle-aged Sources who were pushing open the heavy oak doors looked at us in shock. They didn't impede our progress through the gate, however, and I pulled back the blind over the carriage window and said, "Look, Aryne."

"Let me out!" she shrieked, still struggling.

"Look!" I ordered her.

She stilled, and glared at me with lips pressed together. Then she looked out the window.

The Source Academy really wasn't a prison, and those who ran it weren't stupid enough to think no one in a school full of children wouldn't try to sneak out to see the outside world, just because they were told not to. Therefore, the grounds were meant to be as enticing as possible, with the immediate surroundings outside the wall made plain and empty for contrast. The Shield Academy was designed along the same lines, and I had heard rumors of those who had managed to get out, only to be caught or even voluntarily return shortly thereafter, unimpressed with what waited for them beyond the walls.

So the grounds were beautiful, and a rival for any palace luxury. Acres of lush grass and pools meant for wading in. Pitches for a variety of athletics, trees with treehouses, some built by the faculty and some by the children themselves. Somewhere in the back there would be stables and a corral. But probably what did most to ease Aryne's concerns were the students themselves. All ages, dressed in the red garments meant to identify them as Source students who needed to be returned to the Academy immediately, if seen outside its walls. They were playing as children free of labor and responsibility did, with laughter and teasing and a dizzying amount of running around.

"It's a school, Aryne," Taro told her, releasing her as she settled down. "The only reason for the walls is to protect the students from spontaneous bonding. The exact same reason we've inflicted that blindfold on you and this carriage on everyone."

"So how long will I have to stay here, then?" Aryne asked, sounding calmer.

"Depends how quickly you learn."

"Learn what?"

"How to channel."

"Already know that."

"Not well," he said. "There are other things you have to learn. Reading and writing and figuring. History and civics. Manners." He gave her a sharp look.

"What?" she demanded.

"What we tried to get you to do in Erstwhile, they'll be trying to get you to do here. I wish them luck."

"Bloody hell." She crossed her arms and sank lower on her seat.

She had picked that expression up from Taro. I found that cute.

The carriage drew up before the front entrance of the Academy, a three-story building made of light gray stone, with a lot of huge windows. Lots of light in an attempt to keep the emotional inhabitants in a positive frame of mind. I knew—because the Shield Academy was built along the same lines—that the center of the room was a large hall, three stories high, used for dining and performances and meetings of the school populace. Three wings branched out from it, one for classes, one for recreation, and one for personal rooms.

A group of students sat on the stairs before the wooden double doors, and a girl of about sixteen years rose from the group. The others halted their chatting immediately, and stared at the carriage. It was kind of eerie.

"Source Karish," the girl said as we stepped out of the carriage. "Shield Mallorough. I am Youko Timber. It is a very great honor to meet you both."

The students were really staring at us. What, did we have dirt on our faces?

"Pleased to meet you, Student Timber," I answered. "This is Aryne—" I halted, because we still hadn't solved the problem of Aryne's lack of family name.

"Malkar," she supplied smoothly, and it took me a moment to realize she had combined the first syllables of Taro's name and my own. Which was flattering, but didn't result in the prettiest name I had ever heard.

Timber nodded at her. "Pleased to meet you, Aryne. I have been requested to escort you to Headmistress Tausen's office. Please come this way."

There was something inspiring about walking through the halls of a Triple S academy. Protected by the Pairs that worked there, they were never torn down by events as other buildings inevitably were, and so they were among the oldest structures in the world. Centuries of students had walked those halls, and if I were of the sentimental sort, I might imagine hearing their voices and seeing them run.

The Headmistress's office would, I thought, be the envy of any aristocrat. It was huge, the solid dark cherry desk in front of a window that spanned nearly the entire wall, the remaining walls filled from ceiling to floor with shelves, packed with texts and scrolls. There was more than enough room for the three round tables scattered about the room, and the settees arranged in clusters for the purposes of conversation.

I imagined there was enough room for all the teachers to meet comfortably.

The woman seated at the desk was a little younger than I'd expect a Headmistress to be, perhaps in her late thirties. Her hair was dark and cropped to chin length, her eyes angular and blue. She was a woman of lanky frame and sharp corners. She struck me as someone who would be interesting to know.

A young pretty blond girl, a student of about Aryne's age, I guessed, was sitting in one of the settees. She rose as we entered.

The Headmistress stood. "I am Source Lilia Tausen." She gestured at the girl. "This is Jossen Van."

"Headmistress Tausen, this is Source Shintaro Karish, Aryne Malkar, and I am Shield Mallorough."

"You did not mention her family name in your report," the Headmistress said to me.

"She only recently chose it."

The Headmistress appeared surprised. "You have no family?" she asked Aryne.

No, that wasn't tactless.

Aryne raised her head up. "No," she announced.

"And you chose the name Malkar?"

"It doesn't belong to anyone else, does it?"

"It's not a name I've heard before."

"So there you go."

The Headmistress smiled. "I see," she murmured. I had the feeling she had already gotten a good grasp on Aryne's character. "Please, everyone, have a seat." She picked up my report from the top of her desk. "Aryne, you are from Flatwell."

"Kai."

The Headmistress glanced quizzically at her for that. "I assume that means yes?"

"Yes." Aryne didn't quite snap at her, but it was a near thing.

"You have lived there all your life?"

"Yes."

"You have received no training in performing as a Source?"

"No."

The Headmistress glanced at me before asking, "And you are able to channel without a Shield?"

Aryne tossed her head proudly. "Kai," she said. "Done it all my life, with no training."

"But not well."

Aryne scowled.

"You're in a unique situation, my girl. Someone of your age, having spent her whole life outside of the Academy, channeling without a Shield and without killing herself." The Headmistress pursed her lips. "I'm not sure what I'm going to do with you."

Aryne snorted. "You and everybody else."

Another wry smile from the Headmistress. "We're going to need to put you through a few tests—nothing painful, I promise you—to determine where you need to be placed in the classes. Are those the whole of your possessions?" She gestured at the two bags Taro had carried in for Aryne.

"Kai."

"I'll have them taken to your room. But I'm sure you're hungry right now, and wishing for a bath. Jossen will see you settled."

The blond girl nodded and rose to her feet.

Aryne stiffened and looked at Taro and I.

"But first," the Headmistress said smoothly, rising to her feet, "I would like to speak to you in private, Jossen. Come with me."

Jossen looked confused, but she nodded again and followed the Headmistress out of the office. The door was closed behind them.

Aryne was trying not to look as though she were scared out of her mind. Poor girl. Plucked out of the only life she'd ever known. Her choice, true, but now she was being left among a bunch of strangers who had, in her opinion, no reason to care what happened to her.

"You are safe here," I told her. "Really."

"Write to us," Taro added. "We'd like to know how you get on. And we'll visit you."

"Really?"

"As often as we can," I cautioned her. "As you know, our time isn't always under our control."

Aryne's face went blank, and she nodded.

"And no, that's not an attempt to make a promise without keeping it. I just want you to know it won't be once a month."

"I know that," she said scornfully.

"Good."

Taro ruffled her hair. "You're smart," he told her. "You'll do well here."

If she didn't lose patience and sneak away. I had no trouble believing she would be the first to escape, if she truly wanted to.

Taro hugged her, and she stiffened in shock. I wondered if it was the first time she'd ever been hugged before. Which meant I had to hug her, too. "We mean it," I said. "Please write." Once she learned how.

She nodded again. "I'm not stupid, you know."

"Of course not. I never thought you were." In fact, I had a suspicion she was more than commonly smart.

"All right, then."

"Why did you feel the need to point that out?"

Her lips curled into a small smile. "Think it's better for everyone if I don't tell you."

I had no idea what she was talking about, but as I suspected any further questions on the matter would give me a similar answer, I kept my mouth shut.

We left her in the office, and were escorted back to the front door. She would be fine, I knew she would be, but I worried about her nonetheless.

It took Taro and I a few hours to make arrangements for trading in the carriage and horses for a couple of horses we could ride, and to repack our gear. There wasn't much of the day left when we headed out, but neither one of us wanted to delay starting for home.

Home. We were going home.

Taro started laughing.

I looked at him with concern. "You all right?"

"Everyone's crazy, you know that?"

"Uh, sure."

"What are we going to do?"

What could we do? "Keep on keeping on."

He wrapped his hand around the back of my neck and nearly pulled me out of my saddle as he kissed me. "You'll keep me sane, won't you, Lee?"

"I make no promises," I said dryly.

I really, really wished he wouldn't speak as though I was going to be in charge of his sanity for any length of time. He was going to move on soon, by the time we reached High Scape at the very latest. I needed to be prepared for that. This was a situation when I really needed us both to be realistic.

But then, I wasn't saying anything to contradict him, was I?

THE ULTIMATE IN FANTASY!

From magical tales of distant worlds to stories of those with abilities beyond the ordinary, Ace and Roc have everything you need to stretch your imagination to its limits.

Marion Zimmer Bradley/Diana L. Paxson

Guy Gavriel Kay

Dennis L. McKiernan

Patricia A. McKillip

Robin McKinley

Sharon Shinn

Katherine Kurtz

Barb and J. C. Hendee

Elizabeth Bear

T. A. Barron

Brian Jacques

Robert Asprin

penguin.com

M12G1107